Mary Poser

By Angel A

Angel's Leap Pty Ltd

First published in 2017
by Angel's Leap Pty Ltd,
admin@angelsleap.com
www.angelsleap.com

ISBN: 978-0-9876222-2-8 (pbk)
ISBN: 978-0-9876222-0-4 (epub)

Cover design by Loraine Kiely
Edited by Lori Draft

Growing up in the Bible belt, I can attest that there are people like Mrs. Poser: the critical mama, sassy Southern Baptist 'bless-your-heart' walking stereotype...

And there are people like Mary: the dutiful one; "perfect" daughter. Also member of the 'bless your heart' club. She is her mother's daughter, at least, she tries, and pretends to be. We all know what happens when we try to fit into the boxes someone created for us.

When Simha Das, an Indian film director, begins to take Mary out of these boxes that she obediently put herself in, she starts to question and examine family loyalty, expectations, happiness, love, and faith.

This book was a blend in Southern hospitality that I'm familiar with, and a culture, and religion that I was not. I appreciate Angel A taking the time to reflect the differences between Hindu and Christianity. And bridging the gap of two seemingly different - and yet with some commonality - in a romantic love story wasn't lost on me.

Leila Tualla (Reviewer)

Mary Poser is a wonderful insightful book about trying so hard to please everyone. Mary is the perfect minister 's daughter, perfect friend, perfect girlfriend.....why isn't she perfectly happy. When a Bollywood filmmaker comes to her town of Nashville it shakes her life up makes her look at her life and everything around her in new ways. I read this book in exchange for a review and was cheering for Mary the whole time. I hope we will see more from author Angel A. I want to read Mary's siblings' stories too!

Eileen Pepel (Reviewer)

This was the first book I have read by this author and I was surprised at how much I enjoyed it. This was more than just another romance book with a love triangle. It delved deep into friendships, family, bigotry, religion, and multi-cultural beliefs.

... Angel A. did a remarkable job explaining customs and beliefs in the Indian culture. I was fascinated reading every time Simha explained his culture to Mary. Very descriptive and the characters were very well developed...

Scherry Jenkins (Reviewer)

Mary Poser is a cleverly crafted, delightful, and entertaining read.

Mary was from a strict Baptist home, and according to her mother, it was a sin to fall in love with a Hindu practicing man. The problem was, though, that Mary had fallen for Simha, an Indian film producer from the moment she had met him. Mary was a people pleaser to the extreme, so to keep peace, she knew that she'd have to deny herself the pleasure of Simha's company. But, Mary couldn't resist Simha's charms, and the guilt of being with him almost did her in. Mary didn't know whether she should choose her family and give up her happiness or choose happiness and give up the peaceful relationship she had with her family.

I thoroughly enjoyed this book. This novel is well-written with quirky characters, witty dialogue, and funny situations. The book touched on many serious subjects, such as racism, homosexuality, self-harm, self-acceptance, and love. In the end, as Mary discovered, there is only love.

Peg Glover (Reviewer)

Mary Poser by Angel A was the most interesting novel I have read in awhile. The culture and religious content made me even more curious. The entire story was entertaining.

... Mary Poser has what I call the real life syndrome. Struggles are just a part of life. Mary is at a crossroads...and when she finally finds the courage to make a decision it will be beautiful.

... Angel A created a realistic plot that readers can easily relate to...and feel connected to the characters. Overall, this story was a great read.

Danielle Urban (Reviewer)

This is one of the best books that I have ever read.

... Join Mary Poser as she finds her way through life and when tragedy almost strikes, she uses her Nashville, Southern roots and butterflies to get her through. With love and hometown life struggles, follow her as she keeps her head above water and comes into her metamorphosis.

Jennifer Durham (Bookseller)

This is a beautifully written book, with cultures clashing throughout. The book follows the path highlighting how it can all come together. It is a beautiful love story, with a great family storyline. There were many books that could lead from this one as some characters were only touched upon but would have had great stories to tell!

Along with the highs there are some sad lows for many of the characters. Set in the country music city sprinkled with a dash of Indian culture, this book is a great read.

Laura Jay (Reviewer)

This was a culturally diverse novel which I loved! There is also a nice juxtaposition between Hinduism and southern Baptist Christianity. This book touches on social issues such as bigotry, racism, homosexuality, and inter-racial relationships to name a few. There is practically no stone left unturned...

...What I can say is that this novel is entertaining and will undoubtedly appeal to a wide reader audience.

Amy Mathew (Reviewer)

...the novel succeeds, offering some hot erotic scenes, some surprises, a good metaphor in the uncrossable bridge, and a heroine who grows in understanding herself and her spirituality.

Kirkus Review

With crisp dialogue capturing the connections and clashes between cultures both within and outside of American boundaries, Mary Poser is a winning story of a girl who seeks to redefine what she wants in life outside of the society that she's long operated in, and is an engaging tale of cultural conflict and conundrums. All this is spiced with live and realistic characters whose lives, thoughts, and dreams convey an immediacy and life that encourages readers to not only care about them, but to become immersed in their quiet desperations and romantic entanglements.

Readers who relish multicultural stories, Southern roots, coming of age tales, and a powerful female protagonist who figures out how she can gain real happiness will find Mary Poser a completely engrossing read: vivid and hard to put down.

D. Donovan, Senior Reviewer, Midwest Book Review

Acknowledgements

I have known and loved Mary, my mariposa, for 6 years now. Together, we embarked on a revealing journey to explore the human conditions of pride, social expectation, intolerance, cultural clashes, spiritual awakening and self-harm. She offered me the perspective of a young woman who was bound to the traditions of her family and culture, plagued by high-functioning anxiety and motivated by love. I am pleased to share her perspective and experiences here with you.

There are a number of people I would like to thank who have contributed in helping MARY POSER find her wings:

Steve Alberts, Tommy Barnes, Jim Bartoo, Ben Bradford, Lynn Bryant, Jeremy Curtis, Susannah Devereux, Lori Draft, Benj Heard, Natalie Howard, Christy Hunniford, Kevin Hunter, Helen Jolly, Loraine Kiely, Rebecca Lines, Jack Lines, Michael Lopez, Adam Mackey, Zanah Martin, Ashley Miers, Sarah Murphree, Sheyla Paz, Seemi Rizvi, Ric Sandler, Keatyn Swift, Michealle Vanderpool, John Michael Weatherley, Sheila Wells, Kyler Wilson & Jack Young.

Angel A

Poser: (*noun*) A person who strives for social approval by mastering stereotypical behavior.

Your task is not to seek for love, but merely to seek and find all the barriers within yourself that you have built against it.

🌿 Rumi

Prologue

I'm confused. I haven't missed church on Sunday since I was six. And that day, it was only because my dumb kid brother cast a fishhook through my ear, and I ended up in the hospital in the company of a doctor and a pair of pliers. I've jumped through every hoop my family, my friends, and even my boss have told me to jump through. Everyone tells me I'm so cookie cutter perfect, I'm starting to think I was born in a cake tin. I've always got a smile on my face no matter how fake it feels. If I dressed any more 'country,' they'd stand me on the Nashville turnoff to wave to folks as they drove into town. I studied my butt off and completed both my degrees in sociology and theology with honors. I actually only wanted to study sociology, but I figured I'd make both Mama and God proud by adding religion to my list of interests. They elected me as valedictorian at Vanderbilt and, notwithstanding my morbid fear of public speaking, I did my best to make the university proud of me too. Despite all these efforts, my long-term boyfriend who seemed more in love with his guitar than me, dumped me with the usual, "it's not you, it's me" speech. My life has turned out to be a twenty-three-year-old version of what I've been doing all my life—desperately trying to make everyone else happy. I'd scream if I weren't so busy being the poster girl for "sweet and accommodating."

So why am I not happy? If there's a recipe for happiness, then God, my family, and the rest of the world have been holding back the secret ingredient. I put in four years' hard labor with Mr. Right despite his distracted behavior. Mama and Daddy were so proud of his emerging singing career. I felt like such a failure to them for not holding his attention long enough for him to put a ring on my finger. Despite this, they still label me as their "good girl." Bless their hearts. I'm just not as good as I'd be if I were married. No one ever tells me I'm a source of disappointment. But I sure feel like it sometimes. Am I the only one who's struggling to keep it together?

*This is love: to fly toward a secret, to cause a hundred
veils to fall each moment.
First, let go of life.
Finally, take a step out, but not with your feet.*

Rumi

Chapter One

I burst into my bedroom naked and dripping wet from the
shower. I'm not in the habit of scooting around my apartment in my
birthday suit, but I was running awfully late. Charlie looked up at
me from his bed with mild curiosity. He's quite accustomed to seeing
me rushing about frantically. The fact that I was naked didn't seem
to have any impact on his interest. He was probably only looking for
clues that he was going to be included in something.

My clothes were laid out on my bed in order of demand. I
grabbed my underwear from the corner of the bed closest to the
bathroom and slipped them on. Scooping up my bra, I shot my
arms through the straps and joined the clips behind my back
with lightning speed. I was usually running late and had devised
a system to accommodate. Tonight was a big night, and although
I was positive no one was going to see my underwear other
than Charlie, I'd chosen my favorite Victoria's Secret black lace
matching set to at least feel alluring and sexy.

I glanced back at Charlie, who had lost interest and turned his
head away to sleep some more. Not a great confidence booster,
but I was used to males brilliantly destroying my self-worth with
a dismissive gesture. I think it's conditioned me into being a little

paranoid about my nudity and the vulnerability of dressing in front of a male. What if he chose to reach for a TV remote to watch something more interesting? I'd be devastated. So I usually avoid the circumstance to save myself the humiliation.

Anyway, I couldn't be angry with Charlie for not commenting on or applauding my black-laced sensuality. He's a dog, and a perfectly adorable one at that. He's a pound mutt that I was told was likely a mix of labrador, terrier, and poodle. It was a rough guess as his curly coat is a random assortment of brown, gray, and tan. He has beautiful brown eyes that are only half visible under his thick bushy eyebrows.

I reached for my 'big night out' red dress with long sleeves that I'd carefully pressed earlier that was also laid out on the bed. I sometimes like to wear long-sleeved dresses because I've got some unsightly scars on my arms that I'd rather cover up. I quickly stepped in through the unzipped back. I wanted to keep the knee-length skirt of the dress off the ground so as not to crease it, so I lifted my other leg high to enter the dress. That didn't work. I hopped around the bedroom with one leg in the dress and one leg out before ungracefully tangling myself up in the material. I lost balance and landed on my butt right in front of Charlie's bed. So much for not creasing my dress. At least I hadn't torn it. Charlie was up and out of his bed in a flash. I had probably scared him awake. He started licking my face, his tail wagging wildly. He eagerly took my prostrate position as an opportunity to climb up and over me for a cuddle. I couldn't push him off. I didn't want to either. There's something wonderful about a dog's exuberant affection and unconditional love that beats any compliment a man could ever give about my red dress. I resigned myself to wriggling into the dress on the floor while Charlie pinned me down with his wet nose and paws.

Maybe Charlie's role in life was to remind me that I shouldn't be so eager for compliments. If I spent less time worrying about and preparing myself for public display, I could enjoy more time playing and rolling around the floor with my dog.

Who was I kidding? I looked across at my bedside clock radio. The LED display read 6:30 pm.

"Oh Lordy, I'm so late!"

Frankie Ballard was singing "Helluva Life" on the radio, an anthem to hard times, simple pleasures, and being a little lost. "I hear ya, Frankie," I remarked as I looked again at the time on the clock, quietly hoping I'd misread it. I hadn't. I rolled my torso out from under Charlie's weight and stood up. It's an escape technique I'd developed from the many occasions Charlie had enjoyed climbing all over me.

"I'm sorry, Charlie," I said apologetically. "I know this means we won't have our evenin' walk tonight. But I promised Chloe I'd come support her Yap promotion, and it's all the way across the river in Green Hills." I stopped for a moment. I'd forgotten what I was doing because I'd been too busy explaining myself to my dog.

"Shoes! I need shoes!" I scrambled to my closet and hunted through sandals, boots, sneakers, and pumps before I found my black high-heeled Christian Louboutin knock-offs. I pulled them out of the closet and resumed giving excuses to Charlie, "Then Chloe and Alice will probably want to go for drinks afterward, maybe even to a club, which means we could end up downtown, and—"

I grabbed my black clutch purse from the dresser. Shoes dangling from my left hand, car keys in my right hand, I hightailed it out the front door, shouting a final promise to Charlie that I would be back.

Five seconds later, I was back in my apartment, searching desperately for my emergency makeup bag. "Get it together, girl..." I muttered. I finally found it in a corner of my kitchen counter, buried under an avalanche of mail, bills, and invitations to save my soul by attending the Joseph Trinity Revival Meetings on Sundays. All of which tumbled out of my mail tray as I grabbed the makeup bag. I shouted, "I'll be back!" to Charlie and ran out of the apartment *again*. After a quick dash back to make sure the door was locked, I finally made it into my car. It's a blue Mazda hatchback I bought used last year.

I looked through the darkening evening for stray children, pets, bicycles, and other cars, threw my car into reverse, and backed out of my parking space. I'm always impatient waiting for a gap in traffic, so I gunned my car into a small opening. That got me an angry honk from the driver behind. I scooted on down the road for a couple of blocks with Miranda Lambert blasting from my radio about rage and grief her mama couldn't understand. That's a song my mama should listen to.

I live in East Nashville, which I like because it's so green. There are trees everywhere. I'm also just a short drive from Shelby Park, where the dog park that Charlie loves is located. Shelby Avenue is my main drag. I use it to get everywhere, especially over the Cumberland River to go downtown or to visit my Aunt Sara.

I began to put on my foundation, using red lights to do my eyeshadow and mascara. I know it's not the brightest thing to do, but I was in a hurry. I've had to put my makeup on in my car so many times I've got it down to a fine art. I need to use only one hand for my lipstick and rouge, so I'm able to weave in and out of traffic while applying it. If I can gain a few seconds here and there, I can make up a little for being so late *again*. Chloe was sure to be mad as a hornet because tonight was all about supporting her and her promotional stand at the event for Yap—the social network of the future! She insisted it was going to leave Facebook and Twitter for dust. She'd arranged VIP tickets for Alice and me, and I knew she was depending on us and probably already rehearsing her chiding remarks for my tardiness. I estimated it was a fifteen to twenty-minute drive from my apartment, depending on traffic.

Luke Bryan was rocking out "That's My Kind of Night," bless his hunky draws, as I started across the Cumberland River on the Korean War Veterans Memorial Bridge. We call it the Gateway Bridge—I guess because it's the gateway to all the downtown action. Downtown has the Schermerhorn Symphony Center, the Country Music Hall of Fame, and Broadway, of course, where all the honky-tonk bars shake, rattle, and roll until the wee hours of the morning. I balanced my nail polish bottle in the nearest corner of the box lid sitting beside me on the shotgun seat. The box was stacked with get well cards, another job I was late to deliver on. At least the stacked box held up my nail polish for now. I started brushing red nail polish onto my fingernails as I passed under the sweeping silvery-white arches of the Gateway Bridge.

"Shoot!" I'd forgotten to call my friend and coworker Hannah. What is wrong with me? Well, I'll just have to call her tomorrow night while I'm baking the pecan pies I promised Mama for the church social on Saturday. Hannah had just broken up with Henry, her boyfriend of three years, because he wouldn't pop the question. She just had to cut her losses and leave, even if he did have killer abs and a taut butt, which is what had caught her attention in the first place.

I wondered if Mama knew that Hannah and Henry had split up? If she did, that's all she'd be talking to me about at the church social, until she started talking about my ex, and that just killed me. I didn't like thinking about him, let alone talking about him. And I really didn't want to listen to my mama go on and on about what a fool I was to leave such a talented and handsome and nice young man. How was I supposed to tell her that the nice young man made it real clear that I wasn't good enough for him?

The next step would be to stop her from throwing me at every eligible guy she met when I didn't want to love, let alone trust, another man for as long as I lived. How could I tell her I'd locked my heart in a steel chest? It was safe and cozy in there, and that's where I wanted to keep it.

Mama married right out of high school when she was eighteen, and then she had me right on schedule a year later. She thinks I should have done the same. Now, all she can see are the horrors of me being a wrinkly old spinster all alone in the world. She worries that I'll have no one to cook for and no one but some cats to talk to. When I finally go to bed, I'm sure she thinks I cry into my pillow all night long over the waste I made of my life because I let a nice young man slip through my fingers. That's why I hope my mama doesn't know about Hannah and Henry.

Mama loves me, and she means well. It's just that she considers getting my brother and sister and me to the altar to be one of her main duties in life, and Mama takes her duties very, very seriously. When you're a pastor's wife, you have to be a shining example to the congregation, the community, and God...and the Bible is pretty clear about the importance of getting married.

I passed the "nekkid" statue at the end of Music Row, a statue of nine young men and women that celebrates music and life—and nakedness, I guess. It's pretty racy for a culture that's proud of its conservative values, according to Mama anyway. I began to breathe again because I now had a straight shot to Green Hills.

The Green Hills Regal Cinema is catty-corner to the upscale mall across from the parking garage. Thank God! was all I could think as I finally pulled into the cinema's parking structure. I was just about to gun it onto the ramp that would take me to the second level when I saw a big shiny black pickup pulling out of a space on the ground level. A miracle! Thank God again. I darted into it, set the brake, opened the car door, and slid on my high heels. How did I look? Imagine Mae West, a curvaceous dame with long waves of lush blonde hair and a bust you could set a dinner plate on. That's what I like to imagine anyway. Sure, I'm blonde, and my hair is long and can hold a curl or two for a couple of hours, but God had clearly run out of the ample-bosomed molds when he was designing me. I'm told my butt is worth a second glance, though. It should be. I work on it enough at the gym! But I think my legs are my feature. So killer heels are always a high priority in my wardrobe.

I hit the ground running. I dashed past the pedestrians in the parking lot and shuffled through the folks mingling outside the cinema on my way to the red carpet—a real red carpet!—and ended up outside a big white tent with security guards limiting entry to only those with official passes.

I stopped. I had no choice by the look the security guy gave me. I opened my purse and pulled out the plastic encased name card Chloe had got for me—"Nashville Film Festival - SPONSOR Mary Poser"—and slid its cord over my neck so that the card hung down over my chest. The security guy relaxed his staunch posture and kindly stepped away for me to enter. I took a deep breath, squared my shoulders, and walked further into the tent annex. I had made it, I was alive, and now I didn't have to do anything except give Chloe my moral support. No responsibilities for the next hour or two. Another miracle! I didn't have to think about Mama or Daddy or the church or my ex or no marriage prospects or work or Charlie or anything. I just had to focus on having fun.

Smiling happily, I walked deep into the noisy crowd of people. A musician was strumming out familiar country and western music on his guitar near the tent entrance. With his style and his voice with a distinctly Latino accent, he could have passed for John Wayne and Elvis Presley's Latino love child. He wore cowboy boots and a hat, and his shirt was covered in swirls of brightly colored sequins. I had to scoot around him as I looked for my friends Chloe and Alice. The tent annex has the bar, so the place was packed with the typical Nashville crowd with a mix of casual artsy-looking types to those, like me, who were dolled up for a big event.

You'd think in the capital of country and western music there'd be a lot of bling. But there isn't. This isn't Manhattan or LA, thank God again. This is Nashville, where folks are more relaxed in their attire and those with money prefer to flaunt their wealth with their land and homes.

I blended easily into the crowd as I continued looking for Chloe and Alice. I saw the mayor and his wife, a couple of Metropolitan Council members and their wives, some local TV personalities, and a couple of up-and-coming Hollywood stars who always seem shorter in real life than on the movie screen. But I couldn't see my friends.

So I worked my way into the much bigger main tent, which has the food and a special corner at the far end for Very Important People. *Oh lordy!* I gasped to myself. I was being tasered by a pair of gorgeous dark brown eyes. Goosebumps sprung up all over my skin as if it were Christmas morning.

Until you've found the fire inside yourself, you won't reach the spring of life.

❧ *Rumi*

Chapter Two

My heart was battering my ribs. The most gorgeous man I'd ever seen in my life was staring at me. His dark brown eyes widened as they met my gaze. Why was he looking at me?

I had to look away. I know what happens when I don't pay attention to where I'm going. I was likely to trip over something or bump into someone's drink. What a great first impression that would make. I had only looked at him briefly, but his image was burned into my retinas. He was likely in his late twenties or early thirties. He was tall, about six feet, with slightly curly black hair that fell past the collar of his white shirt. There was something wildly exotic about him. He definitely wasn't from these parts. He stood out like a Ferrari at a rodeo. He had a beautiful oblong face, a broad forehead, and an archer's-bow mouth with a full lower lip that seemed to burn my mouth from twenty feet away. He had a long, muscular throat and a lean, powerful body draped in a black suit that flowed like liquid silk over his body. His white shirt was partly unbuttoned, so I could see a bit of his well-defined brown chest. How on earth I remembered all that in just a glance is beyond me. It was like every cell in my body recognized and responded to him, but he was completely new to me at the same time.

I stopped breathing. An unfamiliar fear iced my lungs because of this electric connection I'd never felt before and the sudden urge I had to spend the rest of my life just standing there, basking in his hot gaze.

"There you are!" Chloe announced, pulling me into a hug that dragged me out of my intoxicating daydream. "Late again, but at least you're here."

I stared at Chloe, trying to bring myself back into my head, into the tent, and into this crowd of people who had all momentarily disappeared for me. Chloe's my best friend. She's about my height, pretty, with lovely ebony skin and a shapely silhouette—all blessings of her African heritage. When in public, with the way she talks and the way she walks, Chloe is the most perfect Southern belle I've ever known. But behind the scenes, she's got a sassy attitude that can be quite confrontational sometimes. I secretly wished I had even half her self-confidence. Tonight, she was on show with perfect raven hair and perfect makeup, all presented perfectly in an emerald green sheath cocktail dress.

Standing beside her was our friend Alice, a pretty and always cheerful brunette Maori girl from the north island of New Zealand. Alice has beautiful mocha skin and a very pretty Polynesian look about her. She radiates a tomboy cheerfulness that's always fun but sometimes a little rambunctious for some. She was wearing a black A-line dress with a V-neck and three-quarter sleeves. Her ever-present greenstone tiki was dangling between her enviably full breasts. I've never been able to convince Mama that Alice's pendant wasn't a symbol for a foreign devil-worshiping cult.

"Hi, bro," Alice greeted me in her usual casual manner, accompanied by her warm and welcoming smile. I never knew exactly how to respond to being called "bro." I had to constantly remind myself that "bro" is the same as "buddy" here in the US.

My head cleared. Late. I was late again. "Hey, y'all. I'm so sorry! I should've called and warned you I was running behind. I just didn't have time. I had to work late unexpectedly, and then traffic was terrible. I wanted to get you a gift, Chloe, so you'd have a special memento of your first gig as the official coordinator for Yap, and I wanted to get a present for you too, Alice. It took forever to find what I wanted, and then when I finally got home, I started to wrap them but couldn't find the tape, so I had to go to my neighbor Olivia's apartment to get some. She was havin' a problem with her cat because it was coughing up furballs, and she's seventy-eight and easily flustered—Olivia, I mean, not the cat—so I helped her pour some oil down the cat's throat to bring up the rest of the furballs. Then I left without the tape and had to go back for it. I finally got your presents wrapped, but then I forgot to bring them because I was rushing to get here. They're on my kitchen table. I'll bring them to our lunch tomorrow, I promise. I drove here just as fast as I could and... Well, I'm sorry."

Alice stared at me, amazed. "How do you do that without breathing, bro?"

"Practice," said Chloe with a frown. "You're forgiven, Mary, as always. Let's get you a drink. What'll you have? Champagne?"

"Sure." It's always an obligation to drink with Chloe. I'm not that keen for alcohol, but heaven forbid I ever order a juice or pop. So I just order whatever makes her happy for me to drink.

Chloe smiled broadly at me, knowing full well I was fixing to make her happy. "What about you Alice, champagne?"

"Beer. Thanks, bro."

Chloe winked at us. "I'll be right back."

While we waited, Alice told me about her latest part-time job. She now worked in the box office of the Grand Ole Opry. I barely heard her because I was looking for the man with the

up in time for the drinks."

"You know," said Rob, "we should make a documentary about this. The interesting interactions and experiences of a couple of filmmakers attending a film festival. It would be a huge hit...at least at film festivals."

Alice looked puzzled. "What did you say your name is?"

"Simha."

Alice grinned. "What a crazy-ass name."

Chloe and I both glared at her, but it had no impact. It never does. Whatever Alice thinks, she says.

"Ask him what it means," said Rob with a grin.

"I'll bite," said Alice. "What does it mean?"

"Simha is the Sanskrit word for lion," said the beautiful man in his beautiful voice.

"Sanskrit?" said Chloe.

"It's an ancient language of India."

"You're a lion?" said Alice. "Well spank me, that's so cool!"

Simha grinned, and I suddenly felt like I could feel myself being physically pulled across the table into his warm smile. "Thank you," he said. "I think so, too."

"So," said Rob with a flirtatious smile at Alice, "what's a gorgeous Kiwi like yourself doing in Nashville?"

"Just following the road signs, bro."

"To where?"

"Wherever they take me."

"What made you stop in Nashville?"

Alice shrugged. "I don't know, bro. This is where I'm meant to be right now." She pressed her fist to her heart. "I just feel it."

"Tell me," Chloe jumped in because Chloe hates not being the center of attention, "what kind of films do you make, Rob?"

"He makes Modernist New Wave musicals," Simha joked.

"I wouldn't know where to begin with that," Rob retorted.

"I, ladies, make film noir thrillers."

Alice turned to me. "Are they still speaking English?"

While Rob was explaining his film genre, Simha Das turned slightly and looked right at me.

I forgot how to breathe.

He seemed to shimmer in an aura of masculinity, sensuality, and sophistication. If he'd said he was from a different planet, I wouldn't have questioned it. I couldn't look away.

"So, Simha, what kind of films do you make?" Chloe demanded eagerly.

He turned back to her, breaking the spell he'd been weaving. "I prefer to work with music and dance and spirit-based stories," he replied. He looked up and nodded to someone behind me. I couldn't help but follow his gaze. I noticed Chloe and Alice were just as captivated by his every gesture.

A shaggy-haired, artsy-looking guy wearing a hat, a bit shorter than Rob and probably in his mid-thirties, staggered toward us with an eager smile. He had clearly interpreted Simha's nod as an invitation. He worked his way up to us through the crowd with a distinct lack of poise and balance. He was clearly drunk.

Simha politely introduced him to everyone as Virgil, a producer from LA, and, darn it, he casually latched onto me! Just when there were enough men to go around, I got stuck with an intoxicated producer named Virgil, who quickly made it clear that I was so lucky to meet him. He started asking me what films I'd seen at the festival and, particularly, if I'd seen his "amazing" movie, *Orion's Belt Buckle*. When I explained I hadn't seen any of the films, he started to tell me, scene by scene, the plot of his movie. Now, in the South, we're trained to be sweet and accommodating under all circumstances. It's called Southern comfort. It's an attitude, not a drink. This was one of those times where I had to paint on the sweetest smile I could muster and ride out the conversational storm as he excitedly slurred his way through a speech about his work and anecdotes about himself with the assumed possibility of impressing me into his hotel bed.

Drunks always make me uncomfortable. I don't know whether it's the loud and imposing behavior or the lack of a filter in their rambling that does it. I'd come across my fair share in the years I followed my ex and my brother and their trio The Nashbros in and out of Nashville's bars in my loyal attempt to support their music career. All I could think of behind my accommodating smile was how on earth was I going to get out of this?

"Virgil," said Simha, taking his arm and turning him away from me, "have you met Alice? I bet you can't guess where her accent is from."

"Start talkin', angel face," Virgil said, happily throwing an arm over Alice's shoulder. I felt sorry for Alice, but I was happy for the escape. We could call it sharing the load.

I was feeling a mixture of relief and gratitude, and then Simha touched me. He took my elbow and fried every synapse in my brain as he pulled me a couple of steps away from the other four.

"Have you lived in Nashville all your life?" he asked in his low, caressing voice.

Had I lived in Nashville all my life? I couldn't remember.

The festival guitarist began to sing a rocking Latino cover of "Sweet Caroline."

"Um…" I said brightly, my mind a complete blank as I looked at everyone and everything except Simha, desperate for something, anything, to say on any subject.

A lift in the music jump-started my brain. "Yes," I replied gratefully. "Both sides of my family have lived here for a few generations."

"Really?" Simha said. "So this town is your—"

The singer began singing the chorus of "Sweet Caroline". A

familiar cue popped into my head from the lyrics of the song.

I turned automatically with Chloe, Alice, and every other local in the tent to sing loudly, "Dum-dum-dum!" It's a regular Nashville thing. I turned back to Simha. "Sorry! You were saying?"

"I was wondering if you also work for Yap?" Simha asked politely.

The party singer continued to offer us cues in the song that were an ode to good times—good times we were all having right then.

Chloe pulled at my elbow enthusiastically. The crowd responded to the singer again. Chloe, Alice, and I had our own version of the reply to sing. "So good! So fine! All mine!"

I returned my attention to Simha. "No, that's Chloe's thing. I'm just here to support her."

"What do you do?"

The singer beckoned us to respond again.

"Dum-dum-dum," I sang along with the crowd, including a lot of the foreigners who were catching on. I looked back to Simha to find him smiling warmly at me.

"Is there more?" he asked.

"No, that's it. Until the next chorus."

We just stood there in the crowded, noisy tent, grinning at each other like teenagers.

"I like it here," he said without taking his eyes off me. Was he talking about Nashville? The festival? Being with me? I really wanted to ask him to be more specific, but it just didn't seem polite. So I diverted to small talk. Sigh.

"So, uh, what have you managed to see so far, besides the film festival, I mean?"

"Well, Rob and I went to the Country Music Hall of Fame and Museum. We also took the backstage tour of the Grand

Ole Opry. The people have been great. Southern hospitality is very appealing."

"We take hospitality and good manners very seriously. My mama always says, never offend 'cause you never know who's gonna give you your last drink of water."

Simha laughed warmly.

The song's chorus was back again already, but I didn't want to ignore Simha's conversation again.

"Dum-dum-dum," Simha sang with a broad smile.

The singer continued to prompt the crowd as he strummed his guitar.

"So good! So fine! All mine!" Simha sang along with me as we leaned in toward each other. His eyes never left mine as he sang the lines. I wondered if he could ever mean what he was saying.

The singer finished the final line of the chorus.

"Dum-dum-dum." We sang along with all the exuberance of children who were happy to act foolishly together. I didn't want the moment to ever end.

"What a great shot for the documentary!" Rob said. He pushed his iPhone forward, using it as a video camera to film Simha with me. "This will be great. Showing a more sensitive side of the tyrannical director."

"Rob," Simha said, a hint of warning in his voice, "do you have to do that?"

"I'm a filmmaker. It's in my blood."

Simha gave me an apologetic smile, and I gave him a reassuring one, and we could have just stood there awkwardly smiling at each other, but Rob had other ideas.

"I want to go to a bar! Simha, we need to experience more of this city while we can. Who's in?" he said. Alice threw her hand up with her usual instant enthusiasm.

"I'm game," she said happily. Alice and I looked to Chloe. For some reason, she usually had the final say on what we did or didn't do.

"Let's go," said Chloe, eagerly disengaging herself from Virgil, who had moved across to her after falling flat with Alice.

"It could be fun," I said a little tentatively because I couldn't read Simha's expression. Did he want to go or not? "How about Tiny's? It's less than ten minutes away."

"I love Tiny's!" said Alice.

"Then let's go," Rob said with a grin, hooking her arm through his.

I looked at Simha. "I guess we're goin' to Tiny's. Do you, um, want to go in my car?"

"That'd be great," he said with a warm smile that sprung my heart back up to full throttle against my chest.

I took a steadying breath. "Great!"

We followed Chloe, Alice, and Rob out of the main tent, then the tent annex, and into the cold night air.

"We'll take my car," Chloe announced. She makes good money. She's got a newish Camry.

"I'm going with Mary," Simha announced.

Chloe raised her eyebrows at that, and Alice grinned. From behind us, Virgil said, "I call shotgun, Chloe."

We all turned to the LA producer. Was he still with us? I guess so because he proceeded to follow us out of the tent.

"Great!" Chloe said with a forced smile.

"You're all set then," I said with an equally determined smile. "We'll meet you there."

We crossed the road to the parking structure. Chloe and company turned left, and I turned right with Simha.

"My car isn't very big, and it sure isn't fancy," I warned him.

"As long as it fits the two of us, that's all we need," Simha said.

The two of us. Oh lordy. I realized in that crystalline moment that I was alone with him. He was a stranger. And yet he wasn't a stranger.

I opened the passenger door for him, hurriedly shifted the box lid full of get well cards to the back seat, and then darted around to the driver's side.

"You drive a manual transmission?" Simha said with surprise as I fastened my seatbelt.

"Anyone who can't drive a stick-shift in the South should just hang their head in shame."

I turned the engine over, and Kenny Chesney blasted out of the car radio. I hurriedly turned it off.

"Do you only listen to country music?" Simha asked.

"Of course not! I also listen to western music and classic country," I joked with a smile.

He chuckled, which distracted me. I nearly backed into Chloe's car.

Alice was leaning out of the rear passenger window, her arms spread wide as the car sped past. "Woohoo! Look, bro, I'm flying!" Her voice echoed up and down the garage. Chloe dragged her back into the car. "How come she gets a lion?" was the last thing we heard as they drove off.

"Don't mind Alice," I said as I felt my face flush with embarrassment. "She's from New Zealand."

Love is the bridge between you and everything.

❧ Rumi

Chapter Three

We were heading down Hillsboro Pike, and I hadn't realized until just that moment how incredibly small my car is. But I was achingly aware of it now because sitting beside me in the dark was Simha Das. I was breathing in his subtle masculine scent that was my new favorite cologne, and I could sense his long, muscular legs stretched out so near mine. His shoulders were dangerously close to brushing against mine. I seriously needed to get a grip of my senses as they were threatening to drive me to distraction, and I *was* driving.

I was so fixated on not getting us killed as the car scooted on down the road that I didn't have a single intelligent thought in my head. I couldn't think of a thing to say. Blessedly, just when I thought the silence stretching between us was going to make him think he was sitting next to a mannequin with driving skills, he saved us.

"I've never known such a young town with so many churches," Simha said, looking out the passenger window.

"Young? Nashville? I think it's over 200 years old!"

"Comparatively young," he said with a smile.

Oh, right. I'm such a dolt! He comes from a country that's

thousands of years old. "We have lots of churches," I said, steering wide of a battered pickup truck that was lazy in keeping a straight line, "because we take religion very seriously in the South, at least on Sundays, and during music award acceptance speeches."

Without looking at him, I could feel his smile. It was a nice feeling.

"Is it important to you?" Simha asked, turning his body to face me.

"Well, I was raised on it. My Daddy is a Baptist pastor."

"You're a minister's daughter?" he said with interest. "Then you must be the eldest."

"How'd you figure that?" He's psychic too? If he can read minds, I'm in a pickle.

"I just imagined that if you were the youngest, you'd be more of a rebel. Maybe a Goth or a New Ager," he added.

I laughed. "That's Erin's job. My sister. She's the youngest. She's our little rebel. But don't give her any ideas. Mama'd flip if Erin went that hard at breakin' the mold."

"Any other siblings?"

"A brother. Toby. He's a year younger than me."

"So I take it you're the sensible one. The responsible one."

"Yeah, I guess so. That's what's expected of me anyway." If only I could admit to where I failed so miserably in that regard. "Is it the same for you?"

"Even worse," he continued. "I'm an only child. In my culture, that makes me the golden child. I'm expected to be as perfect as how my parents dream a golden child should be."

We laughed together. Okay, so he gets pressure from his folks too. I relaxed a little more. I wondered if he'd ever found an escape like I had. But that'd be the last question I'd ask. He doesn't need to know everything.

I turned onto Magnolia Boulevard, which divides into Sixteenth and Seventeenth Avenues. "This is a real famous part of town," I said, playing the tour guide. "We call it Music Row because it's lined with wall-to-wall record labels and music publishing companies. That one," I pointed to a large white house on our left, "that's Big Machine Records. They represent some big names. Do you know Taylor Swift, Tim McGraw, The Band Perry, or Rascal Flatts?"

"Are they Bollywood singers?" he asked with a cheeky grin. I couldn't tell whether he knew them or not from that reply, and again, I didn't want to ask. I had no idea where our worlds held common ground.

"Absolutely," I said with a grin. "That's Curb Records on the right. They're still releasin' records by some of the classic country artists like Bob Wills, Dottie West, Buck Owens, and the Bellamy Brothers. All of whom I'm sure are huge in Bollywood." He smiled broadly at this. I'd maybe have to find out if he actually knew any of these names another time.

"You realize I have no idea who most of those people are." He *was* reading my mind. And with that, he also put his world on the map for me—a long way away from mine.

"That's okay. I'll introduce you slowly to the best music in the world so you're not too overwhelmed."

Simha chuckled as I started into the "nekkid" statue roundabout. "That statue is marvelous," he said. "Can you go around again?"

"Sure," I said, beginning to circle all the way around. I was surprised that in the time it had taken me to go to the film festival and meet Simha, someone had dressed the statue figures in grass skirts and floral leis. They looked like a Hawaiian beach crew. There was even a surfboard tucked under the arm of one of the figures. I laughed. "That's a cute makeover. They're goin' to be hard pressed to find a wave around these parts, though. Music, we have. A beach, we don't."

"I love this town," Simha said. "I like your voice. I think *your* accent is quite sexy."

I didn't see that one coming. I blushed and laughed at the same time. I felt I needed a warning, like "compliment approaching."

"I talk just like everyone else who's from around here. To be honest, I think your accent is sexy." It's amazing how much confidence a compliment brings out in a girl. I thought I'd pry a little. "So do you take your wedding ring off for traveling, or are you more of a girl in every port kinda guy?"

"If you must know, I was recently engaged," he replied, his mood shifting. Maybe I had been too direct?

"Was?" I was committed now. Was this going to be a can of worms moment?

"My parents are quite traditional, and they had arranged for me to marry an Indian girl, the daughter of one of their friends. I conformed until I found my fiancée in bed with her lover. Apparently, I was to be her token husband to keep her family happy."

Darn it, I'd had no idea I was sticking my finger in a fresh wound. "What did your parents say?"

"They were angry with me for embarrassing them, and the other parents were angry because I refused their arrangements. I didn't tell them why I had refused. It wasn't exactly a golden child moment."

"I'm sorry." I really was. I wanted to slap his ex and give his parents a good talking to.

"Don't be. It's a blessing to have escaped before it was too late."

"And now?"

"They're likely busy arranging another girl for me to marry to make them happy. But enough of me and my little dramas. Why is the prettiest girl in Nashville not with her beau?"

Now who was on a fishing expedition? I appreciated the second compliment. I could get used to this. "Well, I just came out of a long relationship with a dud. Nothin' arranged, but it may as well have been. Mama sure thought the sun shone out of his heinie. It's simple with her—he has to be Southern, he has to be Christian, and it helps a *lot* if he plays the guitar. He sure fit the bill, accordin' to her anyway. I always thought he had someone else. I just never knew who… Anyway, it just fizzled out."

"So no foreigners?" he asked.

I had nowhere to go. Honesty was the best policy, I hoped.

"Hell no! With one exception, mind you—if I'd marry Jesus himself, if you know what I mean. Assuming he's not from these parts."

"So what if Jesus was reincarnated as, say, a Hindu from India."

I laughed so hard I almost wet myself. "Oh lordy, don't go there! Mama'd have a conniption fit—and that's just for mentioning the word reincarnation."

Simha laughed. He was no stranger to prejudice by the sounds of it. He seemed so much more comfortable with the idea than I was. I wondered what his secret was. I could do with a strong dose of level-headedness.

Tiny's is on Broadway, squeezed in between the Ernest Tubb Record Shop and The Wheel Cigar Bar. I pointed out the other bars to Simha like Legends, Tootsie's, and The Stage across the street. They were all heaving with people singing along and shakin' their thing to an assortment of honky-tonk and country classics as we crawled down Broadway looking for a parking space. Of course, there weren't any.

I had to turn onto Fourth Avenue, and I quickly found what I was looking for. I set the parking brake, and we began walking back up to Broadway. I liked walking with him. I wanted to see if we walked well together. It's not a strict science, but you can tell if you walk well with someone. So far, so good.

Tiny's is red on the outside and red on the inside. It has big plate-glass windows on either side of its inset doorway. On the other side of the windows, there are two red leather booths, big enough to seat six skinny people each, and they're always full. I'd been to the bar many a time, and I had never once sat at those prized window tables.

Tiny's broad wooden bar and beer taps run three-quarters of the way down the wall on the left. Behind the bar is a four-row-deep collection of liquor. Most space is devoted, of course, to different brands of American bourbon and whiskey. Ruling the bar is Tiny himself, a goliath of a man with two missing front teeth, an encyclopedic knowledge of country and western music, and a booming voice that shouts, "Howdy, folks!" to everyone who walks in.

He made Simha jump with his exuberant greeting, and that made me laugh.

A stage took up the entire back third of the joint. Tiny booked only the best of the local singers and bands, so you were always sure of having good music. Minuscule round tables with wooden chairs and a couple of somewhat larger tables filled up the floor between the bar, the stage, and the right wall. Chloe, Alice, Rob, and Virgil had managed to get one of the larger tables and already had two pitchers of beer on the table and a glass of champagne for Chloe, of course. They'd saved a tiny table beside them for us.

"Hey, y'all," I said to them, sitting down. Rob and Alice looked up and smiled and then went back to telling each other their life stories. Virgil was leering happily at Chloe, who was trying to appear engrossed by the female trio playing a rousing cover of Dolly Parton's "Packin' It Up"—a song that cheers getting off work to party with your man.

A twenty-something blonde waitress in skintight jeans and a sleeveless blue shirt walked up to our table, turned her back on me, and looked right at Simha. "What'll you have, darlin'?"

Thanks for ignoring me, darlin'.

He looked at me. "Mary?"

I wanted to say, "Yes, I'm with him," but that would have been smug, so I said, "Cranberry juice will be fine." Hopefully Chloe wouldn't notice.

Simha asked for a double of Glenfiddich for himself.

"Sure thing, darlin'," the waitress said with her best smile.

"Hold on a minute." Chloe was suddenly between us. "I thought you liked explorin' the cities you visit."

"I do," Simha said.

"Then why are you orderin' Scotch whiskey? You're in Tennessee! We have the best bourbon and whiskey anywhere."

He thought a moment then nodded. "What do you recommend?"

"Prichard's double-barrel bourbon. Straight up."

"Okay then." Simha nodded to the waitress.

Chloe was in her element. "I always take Tennessee whiskey like a favorite lover, straight up."

Oh Lordy! "Chloe! You're burnin' my ears with talk like that." I blushed on her behalf.

"All the best country love songs say real Southern gals drink whiskey straight up," she defended.

I looked to Simha for a cue. Do I fight this battle or let it slide? His relaxed smile made it clear. Let it go.

"What about you Mary? Same?" I assumed she meant did I want the same drink and not my opinion on how I prefer to take a lover.

"Sure." Another battle I wasn't about to enter. I had been looking forward to that cranberry juice. Let it go.

"Okay," the waitress said, walking away.

"You won't regret it," Chloe said to Simha with a smile. "Pritchard's is a small distillery, but they've got a way with bourbon that will make you forget you ever heard of the Scots."

That made him smile. He looked around the bar, at the red walls covered with pictures of country and western singers going back to the 1930s, at the other customers, the band, and Tiny shouting "Howdy folks!" to some locals who had just walked in.

"This is bloody marvelous," he said.

Chloe moved back to Virgil. His inebriated charm was starting to work on her, it seemed. I smiled at this. Everyone was happy, and I was enjoying an evening with a fine, upstanding gentleman who still seemed surprisingly interested in me. "Did you show one of your movies at the film festival?"

"No, my submission wasn't accepted."

"You're kiddin'!"

He shook his head. "I'm afraid that's the rule, not the exception. An independent filmmaker has to be resigned to being turned down more times than he's accepted. I'll try again. I came this year because both Rob and my producer insisted this was an important networking opportunity, a chance to get my name and projects in front of people who can help me get my movies into festivals and cinemas."

"Any luck?"

He smiled. "It's too soon to say...but I'm hopeful."

"You'll get where you want to go. I know it. Do you mind?" I asked, pulling my smartphone out of my purse. "I'd like to take your picture so someday I can prove to my family and friends that I knew you when you were still a struggling director and not a world-famous filmmaker."

He laughed. "By all means." He pulled me in close for the photo. His sheer magnetism wrapped itself around my heart and squeezed. *Keep breathing* was all I could say to myself. Such a simple function on any other day.

I took our picture together. "Thanks," I said, putting the phone away.

Fortunately, our waitress turned up just then with our drinks, so I was able to pull myself back together and take a sip of bourbon to help calm me down some. I looked guiltily at the other table, but my friends were engrossed in their own drinks, conversation, and the music. They weren't missing me at all. I turned happily back to Simha, who was taking a sip of his drink.

"So what do you think of Prichard's?" I queried. Were we winning him over?

He considered the dark liquid in his glass. "Plenty of oak, vanilla, and fire. It's…okay."

"Whatever…"

He laughed. "Okay, you're right. It's fantastic." He took another sip and set his glass down on the table next to mine.

His hand rested on the table…beside mine.

I became transfixed by his long, slender fingers. They seemed to glow, and I realized it was because of the ring on his index finger—heavy, intricately carved silver with an almost translucent gemstone. Silence was stretching between us, and a blush heated my face.

"That's a beautiful ring," I said hurriedly. "What is that gemstone?"

"It's a moonstone. Moonstones aren't valuable in and of themselves, but this ring is valuable to me. It represents love, personal power, and healing. It's like tying a ribbon around my finger to remind myself of these values."

I needed to order twenty of those rings. One for each finger and toe. "That's nice" was the best I could get out in the moment. I took another sip of bourbon. He talked of love, power, and healing, and all I had to say in reply was "nice"?

"So what do you do when you're not gracing the red carpet looking so glamorously beautiful?" he asked. This guy was never more than ten feet away from a compliment. Such a shame I was about to blow it.

"It's the furthest thing from glamorous," I warned. "I'm a social worker. I work for a government-funded organization that provides housin' services to the newly disabled when they leave a hospital or rehabilitation clinic. They're in such a vulnerable place, so desperate to return to life as usual and knowin' that can never be. We try to make the transition easier on them by puttin' in ramps, handrails, walk-in bathtubs, that sort of thing so they can be safe and independent in their own homes. If their homes just don't work, like a two-story house for someone who's been paralyzed in a car accident, then we help them find new housin'. I'm the one who reviews a client's needs. I send field workers out to review and report on housin' issues. I create the budget for the work, and then I assign work to the right contractors. If a client needs new housin', I'm the one who finds it. Like I said, it's not glamorous, but I love it."

"They who give have all things. It's a Hindu proverb," he said with an earnest tone. "You do vital work, Mary."

I shrugged to hide my flush of pleasure. "I like bein' of service to others and makin' our community function better for everyone. You make movies that speak to the heart. You're providin' a vital community service, too, I guess."

"You have a kind and generous heart. It shows through what you focus on."

I just stared at him, tongue-tied. What can a girl say to something like that? I would have loved to have given him an earful of how this heart has been trapped, torn, cut, and crushed. Maybe being too generous with it was the problem?

He stared at me a moment with those dark brown eyes, shadowed now, and I just wanted to sink into the floor. He took a sip of bourbon, watching the band for a minute. Then he turned back to me, his features controlled. "And are you relieved you're no longer with your ex?"

"I don't know," I said honestly. I felt safe revealing myself to a man I'd only known a few hours. I had absolute faith that he wouldn't laugh at me or judge me. "He was the only boy I ever really dated. I built my whole future around him, and I just can't seem to quite let it go yet."

"It's very hard, painful even, to let go of a long-standing and cherished dream."

"Yeah," I said, smiling at him. "That sounds like a country and western song."

He chuckled. "There is a good deal of truth in your music. I think breaking your heart allows it to open to the good fortune of finally finding the love of your life."

Maybe I should have stopped drinking if we were going down this road. "But what if you don't? Find the love of your life, I mean."

"Then I guess your heart wasn't ready for that kind of openness, vulnerability, and growth."

The band completed their set and took a break, which distracted me enough that I caught sight of the clock on the far side of the bar.

"Oh no! Charlie!"

"Who's Charlie?" Simha asked. "Should I be jealous?"

"Absolutely," I said. "Charlie is the love of my life."

"Then I *am* jealous," he said with a playful smile.

I laughed, much too pleased that Simha *was* a little jealous.

"No! Charlie is the ugliest, sweetest, most loving mutt in Tennessee."

Simha stared at me a moment then suddenly laughed. He had worked it out.

I grinned at him. "Charlie was on death row in the local animal shelter. One look into his eyes, and I just had to rescue him. I just had to, even though I've never owned a dog in my life, and I'm so glad I did. Now I have someone who's eager to start every day, makes sure I get plenty of exercise, and is always there to greet me ecstatically when I come home. He's just the biggest blessin' in my life."

"As you are in his," Simha said.

"And he's also a bit of a worry," I rushed on. "I've only had him a month, and if I stay away too long, he gets anxious and starts actin' out. Last week, he chewed up one of my throw pillows. When I got home, I found white fluff all over my apartment. Today was such a rush, and he didn't get his evenin' walk, so I'm kind of worried about what he might be doin' to my apartment now."

Simha stood up and held out his hand to me. "Well then, come on. Let's go rescue your throw pillows."

I have become a rose petal & you are like the wind for me.
Take me for a ride!

🌿 *Rumi*

Chapter Four

I stood up in the noisy, crowded bar. I was dizzy. Was it the alcohol that Chloe was insisting I drink or Simha's bold suggestion? I hadn't drunk *that* much. "You want to come with me?"

"Sure. I want to meet Charlie."

"But my apartment's so far out of your way."

"I can take a taxi back to my hotel after I've met Charlie, and you can show me more of what the city has to offer on the way. Come on," Simha said with a smile as he took my hand. "Charlie awaits."

Happiness pushed away all the confusion. My hand felt so good in his. "Okay," I said with a silly grin.

I turned to my friends in time to see Chloe removing Virgil's hand from her thigh. "I've gotta check on Charlie," I said, "and Simha wants to meet him, so we're headin' out."

Chloe looked like she wanted nothing more than to head out too—as far away from Virgil as she could get. "Okay," she said. "We'll talk tomorrow. It was great meeting you, Simha."

"It was lovely meeting you, Chloe," Simha said, "and you, too, Alice."

"You're leaving?" Alice said, looking up from her conversation with Rob. "Then plant one on me, handsome!" She stood up and gave him one of her enthusiastic, bone-crushing hugs.

He laughed and kissed her cheek. "A pleasure. I'll catch up with you tomorrow, Rob, before my flight."

"Fine," Rob said distractedly as he pulled Alice back down beside him.

"See ya, bro," Alice said, waving to me.

"Bye, y'all," I said, starting to leave, Simha's hand still holding mine.

Virgil looked at everyone blankly. "Who's Charlie?" I was sure Chloe would delight in explaining the details to him.

I waved goodbye to Tiny, who hollered "Y'all come back now, y'hear?" and we walked out into the street that was now crowded with tourists and the like, all eager for a big night on Broadway.

"This is a remarkable street," Simha said as we began walking toward Fourth. "I'm so glad I got to see it. There's no mistaking the cultural identity of the town. There's more country music going on in this strip than you could find in an entire city anywhere else. Thanks for bringing me here."

"That's the Southern comfort, darlin'. It's who we are."

He took a step closer to me. All I could do was stare up into his dark eyes and try to fend off the overwhelming urge to merge into his tall, lean body and stay there.

"So is this Southern comfort? Are you just being hospitable with me?" he said. "From the moment you walked into the party tonight, I couldn't take my eyes off you. I still can't. I don't want to." He lowered his head to me as I reached up for him.

A blaring car horn blast jerked us apart. "Hey, chocolate-dipper! Get yourself a white man!" shouted a leather-clad redneck. He was leaning out the passenger window of a battered Chevy Impala crowded with stupid white boys who roared with laughter before the car burned rubber down the street.

I grabbed Simha's arm and looked anxiously up at him. "Pay them no never mind. They're just know-nothin' white trash." I was mortified. What a terrible thing for anyone to do. What terrible timing!

"So what were we saying about Southern hospitality?" Simha said with a warm smile.

"I'm so sorry…" I began, with a profuse apology at the ready to be unleashed.

Simha laughed. "You don't need to be sorry or to make excuses for other people's behavior."

I wanted some of this calmness drug he was on. I wondered if it was available in bulk. I was quivering from head to toe while he was being totally Zen about the whole thing.

"Are you okay?" he asked, doing that freaky mind reading thing again, I'm sure.

"I'm swell." I was staring up at him again, lost in the warmth of those brown eyes and painfully aware that we had nearly kissed in front of God and everyone. *We* had nearly kissed. He hadn't just tried to kiss me. I hadn't just tried to kiss him. *We* had mutually been going for that kiss…and I still wanted it. I still wanted to kiss a man I'd only known three hours. I wanted to kiss him more than anything I'd ever wanted in my life.

"Charlie," I mumbled. I blinked and took a step back. "I've got to check on Charlie."

"Absolutely," Simha said. "I'm really looking forward to meeting him."

We took the Gateway Bridge back across the Cumberland River, lights glittering on the water below us, and then we were on Shelby Avenue. The car was silent because I was too nervous to think of anything to say. I was nervous about being so close and so alone with Simha in my car, nervous about taking him to my apartment, nervous about what he'd think of my apartment, nervous about what would happen when we got to my apartment.

Why was I driving him to my apartment? I never did this!

What did he expect when we finally got there? He couldn't think I meant to go to bed with him. We'd only just met, and I'd made it pretty clear I didn't want to get involved. But men don't think of one-night stands as getting involved. *A one-night stand?* I couldn't! I wouldn't! My hands had a death grip on the steering wheel.

Breathe, I told myself. Think. He knows you're a good girl. He must know. And he's a good guy. He may be hotter than sin, but he's a gentleman.

But we almost kissed!

The silence got longer, and I just felt so guilty. Simha was a visitor in our city, and he was a guest in my car, and it was my job to take care of him, make him feel comfortable, put him at ease. But I didn't know the right things to say to do any of that. He'd been complimenting Southern hospitality earlier, and I wasn't giving him any now. I was a failure. I didn't know what the best way to take care of him was. I didn't know what he was thinking sitting beside me, or what he was feeling. I was like that movie—clueless.

"Why is everything named Shelby?" Simha suddenly asked. "Shelby Avenue, Shelby Hills, Shelby Walk Park. I even saw a sign for the Shelby Golf Course. Who was Shelby?"

"He was John Shelby, a man who liked to keep busy. In addition to bein' a doctor, he was a farmer, a state senator, and a postmaster. He even helped build Tennessee's first insane asylum and a medical school here in Nashville. He bought a load of land, includin' a lot of what you see around us. He even built one of the first bridges over the Cumberland River just so he could get to all of his land."

"So he wasn't shy of dreaming big," Simha replied, duly impressed.

"Yeah, I imagine the phrase 'it can't be done' isn't one you would have tried out on John Shelby. He sure liked to get things done."

"What about you? Do you dream big?" Simha asked with the hint of a test.

"Why? You want me to build you a bridge?" I smiled.

"Maybe. Could you do it?"

"Well, my folks have a bit of land a little north of here. We raise chickens and grow apple and cherry trees and vegetables. I used to help take care of all that when I was a kid. Then, of course, with my daddy bein' a pastor, I'm always helpin' out at the church for Sunday service and weddin's and such. I'd call that buildin' a bridge."

"So would I," he replied with the most appealing candor.

I pulled into my apartment complex. "Here we are," I said weakly, my nerves skittering all over the place.

I parked in my assigned space in front of my apartment and then fumbled with my door like I couldn't remember where my door handle was. When I finally got out, I led Simha to my apartment door. I was so tense that my body felt like every muscle needed to be massaged out, but I wasn't about to suggest that. Who knew where that'd end up?

Charlie was already barking excitedly. I put my key in the lock, opened the door, and there he was, jumping straight up in the air like a kid on a trampoline as I flipped the light switch on. I squatted down to give him his ritual welcome home tummy rub.

"Hey, Charlie, I'm back," I said with a smile as I rubbed him all over. He threw himself onto his back, and I gave his spotted tummy some circular rubs.

Suddenly he stiffened, scrambled back onto his paws, and

glared at Simha, who was standing beside me.

"Charlie, this is Simha. Be nice," I said, standing up. "Simha, meet Charlie."

The only men my dog had ever met were my daddy and my brother Toby. He sniffed Simha's beautiful black leather shoes suspiciously.

"What a good boy," Simha crooned softly.

Charlie cocked his head and looked up at him.

"Such a good guard dog," Simha continued. "You take excellent care of your lady, I can tell." He held his hand out for Charlie to sniff. Charlie considered it. Then he licked it! "Good boy," Simha said with a smile as he rubbed the back of Charlie's ears.

Right then and there, my dog became Simha's best buddy. He threw himself onto his back, and Simha obligingly gave him tummy rubs. Charlie practically purred.

Dogs can tell so spontaneously if someone is trustworthy or not, kind or mean. Charlie's vote of approval for Simha was a welcome sight.

He stood up and smiled at me, and the living room just telescoped around us. "You're right," he said. "Charlie has the most…remarkable appearance."

"I'm glad you like him," I said, feeling that hypnotic urge to merge into the man. "He clearly likes you."

Simha chuckled. Then he slid his fingers through the hair at the back of my neck, and my heart just stopped.

"I'm not sleepin' with you," I whispered.

"Of course not," he said. Then he clasped my head and kissed me.

The floor tilted under my feet, and warm honey poured through my bones. With a moan, I wrapped my arms around his neck and kissed him back. My body molded to his, drinking him in, tasting the oak and vanilla of the Prichard's and something far more intoxicating that was all Simha Das.

He wrapped his arms around me tightly as our kiss went on and on. I could feel his heart pounding against me. He slid his hot tongue into my mouth, and my knees buckled. If he hadn't been holding me, I'd have hit the floor.

I gasped for breath. "I think we'd better sit down."

"Good idea," he murmured. He pulled me over to my sofa, and then he pulled me down onto it beside him.

Before I could think straight, he was kissing me again, and I forgot all about thinking. There was only this perfect man holding me and kissing me slowly, silkily until I was burning and tingling all over. He slid his tongue into me again, and it was so different from any kiss I'd ever known. So much better, so much more intimate, caressing, arousing. I tentatively slid my tongue against his, and his groan rumbled into the back of my spine as his arms tightened around me.

I couldn't stop kissing him. I didn't want to stop kissing him. His mouth was lush and hot, sometimes caressingly soft, sometimes demandingly hard.

Our kisses went on and on, saying so much more than words could say, connecting so much more than our bodies pressed together could do. The world had contracted into Simha's mouth caressing, sucking, kissing, brushing mine and his warm hands roaming over my back and his heart pounding against me.

Time disappeared. There was only Simha and me and endless kisses that blurred one into another and bodies that melted into one another. Our kisses became gentler, sweeter, more tender. I lay my head on his chest, and he embraced me so tenderly that I felt safe and perfectly at ease in his arms. He lifted his hand and began caressing my scalp as he ran his fingers through my hair. I can see why his touch won over Charlie so easily. I could feel myself melting against his chest.

My breathing slowed, and my eyelids became lead weights with the gentle stroking of his hands against my skin. The last I remember were his soft, warm lips against my forehead. "So beautiful…" he said, and I slowly drifted off to sleep.

*Your breath touched my soul
and I saw beyond all limits.*

✒ Rumi

Chapter Five

I woke slowly, wrapped in a warm, golden cocoon of happiness. The slow, steady beat of a heart below my ear filled me with perfect peace.

Simha's long fingers stroked through my hair again. I was in heaven.

"Good morning," he said softly.

"Morning?" I cried as I jerked myself up and off his chest. I had been lying half on him and half on the sofa. The throw from the back of the sofa was draped across my shoulders and hips. When did that happen? How long had we been lying there together?

I had never in my life slept the entire night with a man. My ex and I had hooked up some, but we'd never actually spent the night together. He always had to be somewhere else in a hurry.

But now, with all the evidence staring me in the face, I still couldn't quite comprehend that I had just spent the night in the arms of a man I'd known less than twelve hours. A man who could make my knees buckle with a single kiss or glance. A worldly man, a man who was flying out of Nashville and my life in only a few hours.

It immediately got worse. I stared at Simha's chest, hoping that what I was seeing was a dream that hadn't quite faded. Remnants of my lipstick and makeup were smudged right in the middle of Simha's white silk shirt where my face had been resting. There was also a damp circle on his shirt. "Oh Lordy," was all I could mutter. He followed my gaze and chuckled. I didn't know where to look or what to say or what to do. "I'm so sorry! I-I-I can't believe I ruined your silk shirt."

"It's fine—" he began.

In a panic, I grabbed the corner of the throw rug and started rubbing the stain frantically, hoping I could rub out the moment more than anything else. I slid my hand between his buttons to lift the material of his shirt. It was definitely damp. Please Lord, no. I had drooled in my sleep! Why couldn't the earth have just swallowed me up to save me from having to face this moment? My face flushed hot with searing embarrassment. I rubbed furiously at the stain, which just seemed to spread across his shirt.

I couldn't meet his eyes with mine. I was fixated on that cursed stain as my head started whirling through possible solutions. "Maybe seltzer water will get it out?"

"Honestly, it's not a problem—"

"Or a stain remover pen. I've got a stain remover pen!" I cried, jumping off the sofa.

He caught my hand before I could run off and stood up. With his other hand, he tilted my chin up so I had to look at him. "Mary, stop worrying. This isn't a problem."

I wanted to weep with embarrassment. Looking across Simha's shoulder, I could see that rain was pouring outside my living room window. Nashville's weather understood how I felt.

Charlie was sitting about five feet away, his tail thumping on the floor. His eager face said everything of his sole concern—he hadn't been fed yet.

I looked at my sunburst clock hanging on the opposite wall and blinked to make sure I was reading it right. Seven forty-two!

"Jeepers! I've got to get to work!" I shouted.

Simha smiled and calmly took control. "You get ready for work, and I'll call for a taxi."

"Right. Yes. Sorry," I babbled as I ran into the kitchen, so incredibly grateful to put some distance between me and the gorgeous reminder of last night's fever-inspiring kisses on my sofa.

I pulled open the pantry and scooped some dry dog food into Charlie's blue bowl. I saw Chloe's and Alice's wrapped presents on the kitchen table, and every moment of last night hit me like a brick wall. For a moment, all I could do was stand on the linoleum and feel nearly twelve hours of Simha Das packed into a single moment. Charlie charging past me to his food bowl helped bring me back to my senses.

"Thanks!" I whispered to my ravenous dog. I dashed to my bedroom, incredibly grateful to be doing something other than looking at Simha's beautiful, stoic face, thinking about something other than wondering what he must think of me, feeling anything other than the wild, careening emotions of waking up in his arms.

I stripped off my dress, pantyhose, and underwear and left them where they fell on the floor as I ran into the bathroom and locked the second door that opens up into the living room. It took every ounce of self-control I had to hold back a scream when I caught my reflection in the big bathroom mirror and saw what Simha had just seen. My hair looked like it had been mashed and then electrified. Most of the makeup on the left side of my face, the side that had rested against Simha's chest for most of the night, was gone. Mascara, eye shadow, rouge, and foundation were smudged across the other side of my face.

That was what Simha had woken up to.

I stood there staring after the blur of yellow in the downpour, feeling more confused than I had in the entire twelve hours I'd known the man. Had he been sincere? Oh, how could he be? He was a world traveler, and I was a small-town girl. That was probably just a line he used when he said goodbye to the latest girl in his newest port of call. That was all it was. A line.

Or was it? What if he'd been sincere? What if he really thought I was someone special?

I must have been holding my breath because it came out in a gust. What did it matter if he liked me, if he thought I was something special? He lived in another country, another world, and I'd probably never see him again.

Feeling depressed and blaming it on the rain, I got into my car and drove to work.

Goodbyes are only for those who love with their eyes.
Because for those who love with heart and soul, there is
no such thing as separation.

🕉 Rumi

Chapter Six

It's a good thing I'd been driving the same roads these last two years because my mind sure wasn't on the road or the traffic as I headed to work. It was on Simha Das and lush, endless kisses and the way he had looked at me when he'd said I was one in a million.

Oh, what was I doing to myself? The man was gone. He'd driven out of my life, and I had to stop thinking about him. Him and me, we just didn't make sense. We had nothing in common. Besides, what kind of a future could we possibly have with him in India and me in Nashville? None. And why was I even thinking about a future with him in it? We'd promised nothing. It wasn't love, surely? I'd locked my heart away in a steel safe, and I liked it there. No man could touch it there, not even a gorgeous filmmaker with addictive kisses and strong arms that could hold me as if they'd always hold me.

"Oh lordy!" I shouted. I had to stop thinking about the man. I'd never hear from him or see him again, and that was that.

The rain had slowed the traffic down like it always does, but I still had a chance of getting to work close to on time. I drove through the older residential neighborhoods on Shelby Avenue with their gabled, single-fronted family homes surrounded by trees whose green leaves looked heavy and forlorn in the rain and gray light. I thought about what I could do to keep myself distracted at work today. I wanted to stop thinking about Simha's hot mouth on mine. I planned how I could I get Chloe's and Alice's gifts to them. Long-distance relationships never work anyway, particularly when the guy in question lives in another country. I'd probably work through lunch to catch up. Simha should be just one of those things. A nice memory for my diary, if I kept a diary. He'd given me a single wonderful night, and I should just leave it at that. I mean, let's get real. What would I do? Drop everything and follow him back to India? That was ridiculous. Besides, I didn't want a relationship. No way, no how.

I turned left onto South Fifth Street, awash in two-story red brick apartment building complexes surrounded by grass and trees. A block down on my right was Annie's Diner with its shingle roof and welcoming front porch. Its parking lot was always crowded. Annie's served only breakfast and lunch, and I'd eaten a ton of both. The diner had some of the best cheese grits in town. Just a week ago, I'd had breakfast there with Mama to kick-start her day of door-to-door knockin' to spread the word about Daddy's church.

Passing Annie's Diner in the rain confirmed for me that I'd been right to let Simha go without a word. I wouldn't find cheese grits in India, or my Mama and Daddy, either. If I ever decided to unlock that steel box keeping my heart safe, I was bound to find plenty of reasons to do it right here in Nashville. I had no need to go flittin' halfway around the world.

A little farther down, half a block north of the Davidson County sheriff's office, was the two-story brown brick headquarters of Nashville Disability Housing Services. I pulled into the small parking lot running along the north side of the office and felt only relief.

I ran through the front door, just five minutes late. Considering I'd stayed almost an hour late the day before, I tried to feel righteous rather than guilty as I folded up my red umbrella and said hey to Stacey, our polyester-clad receptionist.

"Hey, Mary. Ain't that rain somethin'?" she said.

"It sure is," I said.

"George and I are the only ones who got here on time. I'll bet there's been an accident on the interstate."

"Probably more than one in this rain," I said as I headed to my desk.

"I'm sure glad I live in Maxwell Heights. I get to miss all that nonsense."

"I feel the same way about Lockeland Springs. Hey, George," I said to the short, stout dynamo whose desk was just a step from mine.

"Hey, Mary," he said without looking up from his computer monitor.

"How's the kids?"

"Samuel's got the chicken pox, which means the other three will get them soon enough."

"Sorry to hear that," I said as I hung my raincoat and umbrella on my coat rack and sat down. "I'll send some chicken soup on to your wife."

"Thanks, Mary. She'd appreciate that."

I stared at my desk with something approaching despair. I couldn't even see the desktop because it was covered with so many files, reports, papers, and phone messages. How was I ever going to catch up?

Sighing, I set to work. I called Fred Turnbull, the client I'd stayed late for yesterday, to see if he was comfortable. Then I called the contractors working on his house in Highland Heights. I said hey to Ed, Angie, Eli, Katherine, Tiffany, Lori, and Brooke as they straggled in and commiserated with them one by one about rush-hour traffic in the rain. I said, "Hey, boss" when Tammy stomped in, grumbling about rain, traffic, and her kids' dentist appointments after school. Tammy is the biggest, blackest go-getter in Nashville. If she can't get something done, it just isn't worth doing. I always tried to look real busy for her benefit.

Then Hannah shuffled into the office, looking like death warmed up. When Hannah loves, she loves with her whole heart. Her latest ex-boyfriend, Henry, hadn't been able to do the same. She was taking it hard.

"Get caught in the rain?" Tammy barked.

"Kinda," Hannah mumbled.

"You'll make up the time at the end of the day."

"Yes, boss."

"And grow some self-respect!"

"Yes, boss."

Hannah walked up to her desk to my right and just stared at it. George sat to my left. He took one look at her and went to get himself another cup of coffee.

"Tammy's right," I said.

"I know," Hannah said with a heavy sigh as she shrugged out of her raincoat and hung it up.

We'd been friends for six years, ever since we met in our freshman year in college. Her daddy is a white police officer, and her mama is a black Episcopalian minister. Hannah turned out to be a tall, brown astrology fanatic. Rather than follow the church, Hannah sought guidance from enthusiastically reading about what her stars had in store for her that day. She'd been the biggest thorn in my mama's side for six years because, despite all of Mama's best efforts, she couldn't convince Hannah that she should seek guidance from her husband, a Baptist minister, and not an astrologist.

"Venus is in retrograde which, for me, means I'm going to be struggling to stand up for myself at the moment," she said.

An "I see" would be the best I could offer in support. I didn't voice it, though. I wasn't about to challenge my mother's faith.

She opened her purse with a sheepish smile and pulled out three half-pound chocolate bars.

"Well, get to it," I said with a smile.

I reviewed the most recent field reports. I talked on the phone to contractors, most of whom thought rain was an excuse to take the day off, even though most of their work for the agency is done inside under a roof. I reviewed new client interviews.

Every few minutes, I'd feel Simha's mouth on mine or his hands stroking through my hair, or I'd hear him whispering in my ear, "Thank you for one of the loveliest nights I've ever had."

I could have said the same thing right back to him. I couldn't remember ever talking to someone and feeling so completely in my body, or feeling like such a *woman* when a man looked at me. Sighing, I gave up and fished his card out of my raincoat pocket. At the bottom was a website address. Looking all around to make sure none of my coworkers were watching, I typed the address into my computer.

I blinked at my monitor. There he was! A headshot of Simha stared out at me, commanding me to take him seriously as a filmmaker. One tab had a list of his films—he had made six shorts and four feature-length movies, and he was only twenty-nine! Another tab listed his works in progress—seven of them! The final tab linked to Reviews and Awards. I read these avidly. He'd been a semi-finalist at two film festivals, and he'd actually won a film festival award in Europe. All of the reviews spoke admiringly of his passion, his creative use of light and shadow, his compelling stories, his craft. Most of them called him a rising star.

I turned a little away from her and focused on a long black and white cocoon hanging from the narrow limb of a blue orchid tree. "Simha. Simha Das."

"Hm. Indian?"

"Yes," I said, stroking the cocoon with my index finger. I could feel a slight movement within. "He's a director. He was here for the film festival. He asked for my e-mail address, and I gave it to him. And now I think I shouldn't have."

"Why not?"

"He lives in another country!" I said, beginning to fidget with the cocoon. "It makes no sense to correspond with a man I might see only every couple of years or so, if at all. In a different life, it might be perfect, but I'm here, and he's there."

I started peeling away the opening of the cocoon for the struggling butterfly within.

"Mary, what are you doing?"

"I'm just tryin' to help this butterfly out of its cocoon."

"Stop!"

I turned to her, confused. "Why?"

"Darlin', it's a chrysalis, not a cocoon, and a butterfly needs to struggle within it to develop its wings, and then it needs to break out of the chrysalis by itself to get even stronger. If you open the chrysalis too early, the butterfly won't be ready. It won't be able to fly."

"Oh no!" I cried, turning back to the chrysalis I had partially opened. "I'm so sorry! I was just tryin' to help."

Aunt Sara hugged me from behind. "It's okay, Mary. It was an easy mistake to make. We've got lots more, and they're doin' just fine."

I pointed to a withered-looking chrysalis on a tulip tree. "Not this one, it seems. What happened to it?"

"Not every caterpillar becomes a butterfly. The chrysalis offers no guarantees."

"That's not fair."

"That's life, darlin'. This one will never know what it missed. Its life was complete as a caterpillar. That's all it was meant to be. This one, though," she said, pointing to a green and black speckled chrysalis, "is doin' just fine... And so if Mr. Das likes you, as any sane man would, I imagine he wants to further your... association."

"That's ridiculous," I insisted. "It was just one night, and he lives too far away. Besides, I don't know the first thing about India."

"Perhaps this is your opportunity to learn. You've always had a curiosity for the exotic."

"Anyway, it doesn't matter. I probably won't ever see him again."

I left my Aunt Sara, feeling disgruntled and unresolved for the first time in a long time. She hadn't given me what I'd wanted. She was usually like a crystal ball for me, full of wise directions and clear visions. But as I got back in my car, I was more confused about spending the night in Simha arms than I'd been when I'd arrived.

As I scooted down the road, I turned my car radio volume up full blast and sang "Emotional Girl" along with Terri Clark, and together we bellowed out all of the contrary emotions and extremes that made up our days and nights. It didn't help. I could feel Simha sitting beside me as he had last night, filling up my little car with his sensual masculinity. How could I have taken such a dangerous man home with me last night? What was I thinking?

I rolled my window down partway and let the warming afternoon air flow over me and blow some of the cobwebs from my head. I made myself focus on the road and the traffic. When Nolensville Pike forked, I drove onto Second Avenue South, which mouth open even though, in my mind, I demanded it stay closed.

Frigid water gushed into me.

I gagged. I choked. There was no air. Only water. Cold, demanding water.

Questions, so many questions, pierced my frozen brain like icepicks. Somewhere far away, I heard a muffled voice. "Where are you going, Mary Poser?"

"I'm goin' to the bottom of this river!"

"What are you doing?"

"I'm dyin'! Oh God, I'm dyin'."

"Where are you heading?"

I wanted to weep with frustration and terror and resignation. "Can't you see I'm busy dyin'?"

My vision blurred. I could feel my body go limp, become still.

"Did you find love?"

"What?"

"Did you find love?"

Was this to be my final confession? My vision was sliding rapidly into blackness. "No," I muttered to that insistent voice as I let go to the engulfing darkness, "I was too busy."

I relaxed and resigned myself to falling away forever to the overwhelming silence in my car that had become my tomb.

I felt something. I'm not sure what it was. With my last bit of strength, I forced my eyes open. There was a brilliant white light piercing the murky depths of my grave.

Reaching out of that light was a hand. Was this God? Was it an angel? Then I saw it. On the index finger was a silver ring with a glowing, mesmerizing moonstone.

The last thing I knew, the last thing I felt in the world that had been my life for twenty-three years, was that hand grasping mine and tugging me upward. Then the relentless darkness claimed me again.

There is a force within that gives you life. Seek that.

❧ *Rumi*

Chapter Seven

Even though my eyes were closed, I could see the challenge being proffered to the black shadows by that brilliant white light. I could make the light stronger by focusing on it and then see that strong hand with the gleaming silver ring within it. I knew the greatest joy, the most tremendous hunger, the utmost peace.

Light was streaming from the universe down into me. Then, out of my heart, this light poured out and filled the world. This intense gush of luminescence emanated in all directions, consuming every last hint of darkness in my inner and outer worlds. Like a river running its banks, with this torrent of light, I washed away all the shadows that had been clinging to my soul. I was clear of all doubt, all concern, and all fear. I could see myself and everything that could possibly be seen, and there was only love. When you wash away all that is, all that has been, and all that ever will be, there's only one thing left…

Then I started feeling things. My body…it wasn't cold anymore. It was warm.

In that moment, I distinctly remember the startling realization that I didn't know who I was. I couldn't imagine being the Mary I knew I had been before. The memory of her seemed to be a

relic from a different age or time. I couldn't tell whether I was
before her or after her or passing by her. She was both with me
but separate from me. I focused on her, and I could sense her
attention on me. I could hear her thoughts. Her breath became
my breath. Her body merged with me. Slowly, the feeling of
being Mary felt real again.

I started hearing things that had nothing to do with water
rushing over me. Voices. Human voices.

A woman's voice. "The good Lord is watchin' over us, and that's
a fact."

Mama?

And then a man's voice. "She's been touched by God. It's the
only explanation."

Daddy?

Another voice joined in, "Thank the paramedics. They saved
her, not some holy miracle."

Erin, my baby sister?

I focused all my energy on my breathing that was becoming
stronger by the second. I drew in air and challenged my vocal
cords to contract. I pushed air from my lungs, and a raspy noise
rattled from my throat in a single word, "Simha."

"She's comin' round!" Mama cried. "Oh, thank the Lord."

I tried and failed to open my eyes, but I could feel strength
returning to my voice.   "Where's Simha?"

"Who's that, darlin'?" Daddy asked gently.

I frowned. Why were they being so stupid? "Simha. Where's
Simha? I saw his ring. I saw his hand. I felt him pullin' me toward
the light." I could hear I was mumbling. Maybe they just couldn't
hear me properly?

"What are you tryin' to say, Mary?" Mama asked.

I managed to force open my eyes. Everything was blurry for a
moment, and then I saw my family—Mama and Daddy on one

side of me, Erin and Toby on the other, Aunt Sara and Grandpa Tom standing just past my feet. "Simha," I said crossly because they just refused to understand.

"What?" Aunt Sara said.

"Who?" Grandpa Tom asked.

"He was there, in the river," I said desperately. "He saved me. I have to thank him."

My family looked at each other blankly, not understanding.

Daddy took my right hand in his. "Mary, a couple of drivers who were on the bridge went into the river after you, and the paramedics pulled you out of the river and revived you. Is that who you're talkin' about?"

"No!" I said, tears filling my eyes. "No, it was Simha. There was all this light, and he took my hand. He pulled me out of my car and up to the surface."

"Of course he did, darlin'," Mama said soothingly. "The good Lord came to you and plucked you from the murky depths and saved you from darkness."

"Praise be to Jesus," Daddy said. "It *was* a miracle."

Erin and Toby looked at each other and rolled their eyes.

Erin piped in, "Guys, she fell into a river, not a whorehouse!"

"Erin Poser, you hush!" Mama retorted. "I'm ashamed of you, denyin' the Lord when the evidence of his mercy is lyin' right in front of you."

"Sorry, Mama."

Grandpa Tom hooted with laughter. "A whorehouse! That's a good one, Erin."

"It was a miracle," I mumbled insistently. "Simha came back and saved me." But no one was listening to me...

Mama was an older-looking version of me, a petite and slender blonde, but her eyes were hazel, not brown. She was trying her best to tower over her daddy, Grandpa Tom, looking no more

"We didn't know if she was going to wake up or not..." he sheepishly defended.

"When you've just woken from bein' hauled out of a river from your car, you're not too worried about these things," I assured him with a forced smile because he was working so hard to lighten things up, just like Daddy usually does. "So I reckon I wouldn't have minded at all if you took it."

"That's right...give him your only worthwhile possession!" Erin said.

"What about Charlie?" Toby retorted.

"Only if I could upgrade him to a real dog..."

Mama glared at all of us. "Toby and Erin Poser, you just stop that kind of talk right now!" she said.

"Now, now, Marjorie," Daddy said with a smile, "it's not a sin to be practical in difficult situations." He gave me a wink. "We're all just so grateful to have Mary safe and back with us that we're a mite giddy."

"Look on the bright side," Grandpa Tom chirped in with surprising energy and enthusiasm. He normally looked exhausted and about eighty-eight instead of sixty-eight. "You can be sure every single woman in Brian's congregation is bakin' and cookin' up a storm right now and leavin' casseroles and pies and ham hocks and greens on our kitchen table for us even as we speak. You're not goin' to have to cook for a week, Marjorie!"

Food and iPads? That's all my family could talk about? I lay there staring up at the white ceiling panels, lost in bitter whirlpools of thought and feelings, while my family debated the different dishes, good and bad, they could expect to find when they got home from the hospital. Then they talked about what they should give the drivers, paramedics, nurses, and doctors who had saved my life.

All of their talking and bickering and planning was just white noise for my mind as it tried to tune in to the fact that I was lying in a hospital bed and not lying dead feeding shrimp at the bottom of the Cumberland River. All of my family's talk and distraction was sucking me out of that glorious white light in the Cumberland River, and the warmth and strength of Simha's hand grasping mine, and the certainty that something miraculous had happened to me, the certainty that my life had been altered in a way I couldn't comprehend.

I was being dragged out of a profound miracle into a reality that felt foreign and limited to three dimensions. I began to drown a little again, this time in unshed tears.

I had flowers on bedside tables, dressers, and bookcases. They were crowding me out of my bedroom and out of my home. Beautiful as they were, they just didn't offer me any sense of connection to what I'd been through. They didn't give me what I needed. True, I didn't know what I needed, but I did know they weren't it.

I sat on my bed, holding Charlie, with one question burning a hole inside my head: why was I still alive?

Why had God chosen me to survive that terrifying plunge into the Cumberland River?

It had been three days since I had awakened in that hospital room, and nothing was right. I still couldn't feel myself entirely back in my body or my life. I felt almost foreign in my own skin.

Something had happened to me. I had experienced a cataclysm, an epiphany, or a divine intervention, and I could never explain it to my family, friends, and coworkers, and they would never understand. I felt like the Cumberland River had divided me from them forever, and that terrified me. The foundation of my life was gone.

I didn't know how to get it back. I didn't know what I was supposed to do to fix my life, or even if I should fix it. But if I didn't fix it, where was I? What was I supposed to do? Who was I supposed to be?

I felt exposed, as if stripped of ceiling and walls, clothes, and flesh. There was more to me than all these things. But nobody had ever said anything about this to me. I wondered if I'd ever experience what happened in the river again.

I pulled Charlie closer to my chest.

I prayed and prayed for someone to show me the way. But there was no one. Not even Simha.

I looked at the new cell phone Toby had gotten me that was sitting on my bedside table. I had checked it every hour these last two days I'd been home, but there were no e-mails from Simha. No texts.

How could he ignore me after saving my life? How could he be silent when he had lifted me into the light? How could he not feel and respond to my need for contact? We were connected, weren't we? We were linked by that brilliant white light, and death, and life.

Weren't we?

My phone beeped loudly against the bedside table, and I jumped about a foot off my bed, scaring the living daylights out of Charlie.

"It's okay. Everythin's fine," I told him as he resettled between my legs. I grabbed my phone. Someone had sent me a new e-mail.

Fingers trembling, I opened the app. Simha! Simha had contacted me at last! He must have been feeling all of my fear and doubt and confusion.

Simha: Dear Mary

He called me dear!

Simha: I haven't been able to stop thinking about the beautiful Southern girl I met at the Nashville Film Festival or that perfect evening we spent together. As I held you through the night on your couch, there was a voice inside my head saying "pay attention to this girl." So I did. I don't think I slept a wink. As I held you, your heart beating in rhythm with mine, I felt mostly overwhelmed by my intense attraction to you. It caught me by surprise, as did the entire time I spent with you.

Oh my!

My heart was pounding, and my face felt flushed. Charlie was looking at me like he was expecting something big to happen. Maybe he was still wary from almost being catapulted from my lap.

What could I say to that? It was wonderful...but why hadn't he said anything about what had happened to me, to us, in the Cumberland River? I just sat there reading and rereading his message again and again, and I still couldn't find even a veiled reference to what had happened to me. Maybe he needed a hint, a little reassurance that it was okay to talk about it.

> Mary: Hi, Simha. Thanks for the e-mail. Sorry I've been out of touch. On the day you flew out of Nashville, my car had a disagreement with the Gateway Bridge, and we ended up in the river for a little while. Luckily, I came out of it just a little sore and shaken up.

Two seconds after I pressed "Send," my cell phone vibrated angrily in my hand, making me jump again. Charlie scowled at me. I had a text.

> Simha: Tell me you're okay.
> Mary: My car is totaled, but I'm fine. Really.

He should know. He was there! Why didn't he remember? Why didn't he say something about his spirit reaching for me from halfway around the world and pulling me out of the river?

I waited and waited, but my cell phone stayed silent. I stared at it in disbelief.

How could he ignore that hint? How could he just...stop talking to me?

I was suddenly blazingly angrily. I couldn't sit still a minute longer. I got up, slid my feet into my sheepskin slippers, shoved my phone into my back pocket, and padded into the kitchen. Charlie trotted after me. We were having a family dinner tonight, and I'd told Mama I'd bring my homemade toffee-apple pie. For some people, chocolate is their comfort food. For others, it's ice cream. For me, pie fixes everything. I love cooking because it's so precise. Too much heat, and you burn something. Too little spice, and the dish tastes bland. If you cut up your apples unevenly, then the pieces will cook unevenly. With cooking, you always know where you stand. I loved this recipe because it was a delightfully surprising mix of toffee crunch and apple in light golden pastry. It was a bit naughty with all the added sugar, but I doubted I'd go to hell for making the most delicious apple pie in the world, and I was totally ready for a generous dose of delightful.

I pulled on my apron and turned the radio on full blast. An infuriated and sarcastic Reba McIntyre was demanding "Why Haven't I Heard from You?"

"Yeah, why?" I muttered as I started chopping apples. I drizzled lemon on the apples and put the sugar, honey, cinnamon, and water into a stainless steel pot and set it all to cooking. I loved watching tenaciously over the mixture, making sure it didn't boil, brushing down the undissolved sugar with a pastry brush as it darkened on high heat to a lovely golden toffee. Splitting the mix in two, I stirred in the apples, some butter, and a pinch of salt into one half before the mix hardened too much. The other half I left to solidify into lovely crunchy toffee. As the apples relaxed into the bubbling brew, I had ten minutes to roll out the pastry.

I added the sugar and beaten egg and chilled water to my ingredients, and soon I was rolling the gooey mix into a ball in my hands. In no time, my clay was ready for my masterpiece. The thirty-minute fridge time for the pastry was just enough for my toffee-apple mix to cool once a dash of vanilla had been added. It was also enough time for me to check my phone thirty times. I rolled out the pastry for the pie like I was punishing it for the crime of silence my phone had been committing. I laid half out in the pie tin and then poured in the toffee and apple concoction. Thankfully, the apples were keeping it together and hadn't ended up stewing as much as I was. I flopped on the pastry lid and brushed it with the remaining egg with some almond milk added. My masterpiece then needed to chill for a further thirty minutes. We both needed to chill, really. Thirty minutes of infuriating silence later, another brushing of beaten egg with a sprinkling of demerara, and my masterpiece was ready for glazing in the oven. I set the timer for forty-five minutes, wiped my hands on a kitchen towel, and tried to breathe a little more calmly. I picked up my phone and reread Simha's e-mail again. It was a really lovely message, but it wasn't what I wanted, or expected, or needed. In this e-mail and in his follow-up text, Simha hadn't said a word about the connection we had shared in the Cumberland River. He hadn't even said anything like "I knew something was wrong."

Grief washed through me as I realized that he *hadn't known* about my car accident or the river or the light or anything. I felt as though I had just lost something terribly precious.

Simha didn't know anything had happened to me. He didn't know anything about me.

I blinked back warm tears. I'd been so looking forward to discussing with him my terrifying, life-changing plunge off the Gateway Bridge. I wanted to relive the river with him, share the memory of the light with him, and tell him how safe I felt when he took my hand in his. Now, I was afraid to tell him any of that. I was afraid he'd just brush it off or, much worse, laugh at me, because he had felt none of it, seen none of it, known none of it.

I stood awash with confusion and anger. I'd been completely wrong about him. Who was this guy really, I mean, aside from being an Indian filmmaker? Even with all of the talking we'd done in those twelve hours, I had so many more questions than answers.

Was he just a player stringing along a girl in every port, including me? Or were his words sincere? If they were, what did he want from me? Sometimes he was so intense with me, and the next moment he felt so distant. Had some inner voice really told him to pay attention to me, and what did "pay attention" mean anyway? Begin active surveillance? Keep a safe distance? Romance?

What?

An answer was not forthcoming. I sighed gustily and got to work on the apple filling for the pie. I had just found the ladle I wanted when my phone vibrated against my butt. I jumped about a foot in the air. I really needed to calm down.

I set the pot down on the counter and cautiously pulled out my phone. Simha had sent me another text.

Simha: I get the feeling that your car accident was much worse than you first indicated. Would you like to talk about it? Would you like me to call you?

Oh lordy, no! Not yet. Not now when I didn't know anything.

Mary: That's nice of you, but I'm real busy and just don't have time to chat right now. I'll have to get back to you.

I pushed "Send" then carried my phone into my bedroom, holding it like it might burst into flames at any moment. I set it on top of my dresser and closed the door behind me when I headed back to the kitchen. Using a rolling pin, I smashed the toffee that I had set aside into shards that looked pretty much how I was feeling. When the oven dinged, I pulled out the pie and sprinkled the shattered pieces over its golden crust. The shards melted just enough to merge with the lid of the pie without losing their sweet crunch. My toffee-apple pie was perfect. I cried.

Lovely days don't come to you.
You should walk to them.

🐝 *Rumi*

Chapter Nine

Four hours later, I had exchanged my green sweatshirt for a white dress that Mama bought me that's covered with colorful butterflies. Cheerfulness is my family role, so I may as well look the part. I shoved my feet into red heels and started driving home to the bit of land Mama and Daddy owned just north of Nashville in the heart of wine country. I was also getting used to The Mule. That was the name we gave the big old yellow and tan Chevy Suburban my folks use as a sort of jack of all trades. It hauled everything from fertilizer to chicken feed. It towed Daddy's boat to the J. Percy Priest reservoir when he wanted to go fishing. Mama used it when she and five or six ladies from Daddy's church made their door-to-door visitations to spread the word in some not entirely safe neighborhoods. It felt and moved like a tank.

Daddy had loaned me The Mule to use until my insurance got sorted out to buy another car. On the drive to the farmhouse, I had the radio cranked up full blast. Tennessee-born Jessica Andrews was singing "I Know Who I Am," and I envied her because I didn't have a clue about myself. Not anymore.

Well, I did know one thing. I'd been thinking and acting like

a school girl. I had pretty much made up Simha Das. I had
invested him with all sorts of fantasy white knight qualities.
I had thought of him as being on a far higher spiritual plane
than I was. Now I knew he was just a guy. A nice, handsome,
long-distance guy. So anything happening between us other
than some occasional friendly e-mails was impossible. I had to
leave it at that.

I drove beside acres of vineyards that were already leafing
out. Finally, I turned left onto a narrow asphalt road, and then
right onto a single-lane dirt road. About a hundred yards down
the lane, there it was, looking familiar and welcoming in the
dwindling daylight.

The Yankees burned down the first house my family built here,
and our farmhouse was built by Mama's family just after the
end of the War Between the States. It's two stories of reddish-
brown brick, and dark green shutters hang on either side of
the tall windows. There's a cellar and an attic with a couple of
bay windows. A big gray porch with narrow white columns
runs across the front. Above it is a much smaller porch with
white columns that extends off of Mama and Daddy's upstairs
bedroom. A gray ground-floor porch and upper-floor porch
stretch across the entire back of the house. There's an old servant's
quarters out back. We use it for storage now, but it's a telling relic
of how our little society was structured not that long ago.

On either side of the house, we've got lawn and trees, lilacs,
and honeysuckle. The front yard is grass and towering elm,
oak, and maple trees, one of which has an old weather-beaten
treehouse high up in its limbs. When we were kids, Erin and
Toby and I used to play up there all the time. As teenagers, we
hid out among the tree limbs to escape all that came along with
being teenagers. Two years ago, when Erin was seventeen, she was
climbing up to the treehouse and fell. Whether the fall triggered

it, or it triggered the fall, we'll never know, but without any previous hint that she had a time bomb in her head, she burst a brain aneurysm. It was touch and go for a while, but she survived. The bleeding from the aneurysm damaged the nerves to her right arm. She did a lot of rehab, but her arm just hasn't returned to normal, at least not yet. She's self-conscious about it, and mad about it, and scared about it. Falling out of trees must be a family trait. I've done it plenty of times myself. I'm lucky not to have had the devastating consequence Erin has had to endure. I looked at the scars on my forearms. Some were still heavy-looking, and others were quite faint now, almost disappearing with time. I tell everyone that our treehouse has been a big part of our life for me and Erin, leaving its mark in so many ways.

The backyard has a bit of lawn, a couple of big old dogwoods and pink flowering crabapple trees, and a reddish-brown brick shed. Then there's a white picket fence, a half-acre vegetable garden that gives us food nine months out of the year, and a big wooden chicken shed. Farther back is an orchard where we grow apple and cherry trees. During the day, about twenty chickens go pecking their way around the fruit trees. At night, they roost warm and safe in the chicken shed. It was Erin's and my job to get those fool chickens out of the trees and into the chicken shed where they belonged. There's plenty of critters that would enjoy a tasty chicken dinner if we left them out at night.

This house was just about the best place in the world for a kid to grow up.

We used to have a lot more land. Up until about 1950, this was a forty-acre working farm that grew mostly vegetables, beans, fruit, and nuts. There was a big red barn for horses and cows. There was a pig shed. There was pasture. But my great-granddaddy Nathaniel wanted to be a lawyer, not a farmer, so he sold off all but three acres.

and there's no doubt."

"The hand of God," Toby intoned in a big booming voice, "reached down from heaven," he said, grabbing the top of my head with his free hand, "and plucked our little texting driver from the jaws of death!"

"Don't you go laughin' at one of God's miracles, Toby Poser," Mama said. "Git those plates into the dining room. Git!" she said, swatting him on the butt.

Laughing, he sauntered back into the dining room.

"Erin, go fetch your daddy," Mama said. "Supper's almost ready."

"Yes, ma'am," Erin said, sticking her tongue out at Grandpa Tom as she passed and making him laugh.

Mama walked over to the garlic bread resting on the cutting board and began slicing it.

"Mary owes her life to the men who saw her crash off of that bridge and risked their own lives diving into the river to rescue her, and to the paramedics who got her breathing again," Aunt Sara said as she stuck a serving fork and spoon into the big teak salad bowl. I didn't know what to say to this as I felt I wasn't there for any of it.

"Them bein' there was God's doin'," Mama insisted.

"Perhaps," Aunt Sara said, carrying the salad into the dining room.

"I hate to say it of my own sister, Mary, but your Aunt Sara is on the slippery slope to hell. 'Perhaps,' indeed!" Mama sniffed.

I was numb through and through as I slid the pie into the oven to keep it warm.

"Your sister is a good woman with enough sense not to turn her nose up at the workin's of the all-mighty Marjorie Collins Poser," Grandpa Tom declared as he scooped up the garlic bread in the bread basket and headed for the dining room. "Let's have no more talk of slippery slopes from you."

"Yes, Daddy," Mama said, looking peeved.

Toby walked back into the kitchen, and she handed him a big pitcher of sweet iced tea. He clicked his heels together, saluted her, and carried the pitcher into the dining room.

"That boy," Mama said with a sigh. She'd been saying "that boy" for most of Toby's life.

"Do I smell pie?" Daddy asked as he walked into the kitchen.

"You do," Mama said.

"The world is just simply a better place when there's pie!" Daddy cried, sweeping Mama into his arms and spinning her in a circle.

Mama was blushing. She never appreciated Daddy's affections in front of the family. "Brian, you fool!" she said.

"I'm a fool for you...and pie," Daddy said, sniffing rapturously at the oven. He turned and smiled warmly at me. "Is it yer toffee-apple?" My smile was the only answer he needed.

"And how is my little butterfly doin' today?"

"I'm fine," I said.

"Any bad dreams?"

"I'm sleepin' just fine, Daddy," I lied. I picked up and carried Mama's ravioli serving dish into the dining room.

"Hey, Mama, check this out!" Toby shouted. "You got a delivery!"

Toby was carrying a small square box. He set it down on the maple kitchen bench.

"Have you been orderin' raunchy videos in plain brown wrappers again?" he asked with a grin.

"That's your sin, Toby Poser, not mine," Mama said sharply.

He flushed and stayed silent.

"Burned..." Erin whispered to Toby.

Aunt Sara, Erin, and Grandpa Tom followed each other into the kitchen to see what Toby's excitement was about.

"What is it, Marjorie?" Aunt Sara asked as we gathered around her.

Mama tore off the paper, opened the box, and then beamed. "Oh good! They got here fast."

She pulled out a round sticker about five inches in diameter that read like it was shouting. "Fear God!" it said and had Daddy's church insignia below it.

"What on earth?" Aunt Sara said.

"What happened to Mary was a sign," Mama said. "I want you all to put these stickers on your cars to protect you. You should give 'em to your friends, too."

"But that doesn't make sense!" Erin said.

"Sweet Jesus, how could it not make sense to seek the Lord's protection?" Mama demanded.

"If Mary was plucked out of the Cumberland River without fearin' God last time, then clearly fearin' God is not necessary for a good pluckin'," Erin insisted, her lips fighting back a cheeky grin.

"*Erin Poser!*" Mama seethed, her face red with anger.

Toby laughed and hurriedly covered his mouth with his hand as Mama shot him a glare.

"Besides," Erin continued, "I thought we were supposed to love God, not fear Him."

"Careful, Niece, too much wisdom will just confuse yer dear Mama," Aunt Sara said.

"Don't you interfere!" Mama snapped.

"I think," Erin continued, rallied by our aunt's taunting of Mama, "under the circumstances, that 'Fear Drowning' would make a better bumper sticker."

"I don't drive no more, so I got no place to put these," Grandpa Tom said.

"I can't believe my own family is turnin' against me and God,"

Mama said, working herself up.

"Now, Marjorie, no one's turnin' against anythin'," Daddy said.

Mama opened her mouth to argue that, but Daddy distracted her by picking up a couple of soup ladles to use as drumsticks. He danced around the kitchen like he was the lead percussionist in a band, banging and clanging anything that would make a noise. Even Mama's butt got a tap with a ladle, which made her squeal and become an unwitting accomplice to Daddy's musical mayhem.

Mama grabbed the ladles from Daddy's hands. "Brian, you silly fool!" she said, desperately trying to hide her amusement. Daddy was indeed skilled at breaking Mama out of one of her moments where she gets all wound up, stressed, and serious.

"I like that song," Aunt Sara hollered.

"Don't you go encouragin' him!" Mama said crossly. She knew she was being deliberately distracted by Daddy's Jerry Lewis impersonations.

He kissed her on her forehead then took a sticker from the box. "I'll put this one on my sedan, Marjorie, and gladly. That was good thinkin'."

"Thanks for carin', Mama," I said, taking a sticker.

Toby, avoiding Erin's gaze, took his own sticker from the box. "Thanks, Mama."

Erin, glaring at all of us, spun on her heel and marched toward the dining table. "What we really need is a sticker that says 'Don't Text and Drive and You Won't Drive Off a Bridge.'"

"Erin!" Mama gasped then looked anxiously at me.

"Or how about one with a picture of Jesus that says 'Don't Look at Me. Keep Your Eyes on the Road,'" she continued from the other room.

"Erin, that's enough," Daddy called back to her.

Erin flushed and flounced into her dining chair.

hand, and his ring in the dark Cumberland…they were as present with me as the family dinner.

"Brian, I saw Jack Brady comin' out of that New Testament Ministry church the other evenin'," Mama said after takin' a sip of tea. "You gotta talk to him and set him straight. These Youth Movement churches are nothing but flashy rock concerts that insult traditional conservative values and religion. You talk to him, and you talk to his parents. They should know better than lettin' him wander off the true path like that. Oh, and you need to call on Lucille Harvey," Mama said as she helped herself to seconds of the collard greens. "She's back in the hospital again."

"What's wrong?" Daddy asked.

"The doctors still can't find the problem, and I'm not surprised. Lucille's been straying from the true path this last year, and I just know that's why she's havin' trouble now. I keep tellin' her that if she'd only get right with the Lord, then God would end her troubles and heal her."

"So what your sayin' is," Erin said hotly, "that anyone who is sick or hurt is a sinner, and God is punishin' 'em?"

"Well—" Mama began.

"Erin, your mama knows accidents and sickness and misfortune happen to good Christians all the time," Daddy said. "But for some folks, spiritual ills manifest in physical ills, just like some psychological problems can lead to injury or disease."

"Sounds like a good sermon for a Sunday," Mama said.

"Yes, dear," Daddy said. He took a long swallow of red wine.

Mama had always disliked the idea of Daddy drinking wine. She didn't believe it set an appropriate example for the Baptist community. I still vividly remember the terrible argument they had over it when we were children. Daddy had tried to defend his choice to occasionally imbibe by reminding Mama that a Baptist pastor, Elijah Craig, was famous for inventing bourbon whiskey.

That was our signal to vacate the premises. Even Toby had joined Erin and me in the sanctuary of the tree house that day. The yelling match that echoed across the yard to our ears had us all in tears. Whatever went down that day between them, it remains as the only instance I remember Daddy so sternly sticking to his guns against Mama's pious appearance preferences. To this day, she still made an audible sigh whenever he took a hearty gulp.

"We'd make real good subjects for a sermon or two, wouldn't we, Jenny?" Grandpa Tom said to Erin with a waggle of his bushy gray eyebrows.

"Uh-uh," Erin protested. "It's not my turn." She looked at me defiantly and said, "All yours."

"Oh lordy," I said under my breath. Grandpa Tom is in the early stages of Alzheimer's, and sometimes he mistakes one of us for his wife, my Grammy Jen, who died five years ago.

"Do you know what I was thinkin' about today, Jenny darlin'?" Grandpa Tom asked me with the innocence of a lamb.

I looked to Mama with pleading eyes, hoping she would let me tell my grandpa I wasn't his dead wife. Her glare said everything I didn't want to hear. I gave Grandpa Tom a bright smile. "Why, no, Tom dear, what were you thinkin'?"

He beamed at me, a twinkle in his gray eyes. "I was rememberin' that ol' Buick I had just before we were married, and how your daddy always insisted I get you home by ten. So I would get you close to home by *nine*, and then we'd climb into the back seat and—"

Daddy's knife clattered onto his plate. "Tom! You have to have some of these green beans. They're right out of the garden and just burstin' with flavor."

Grandpa Tom nudged me. "I'm lookin' forward to our little nap this afternoon," he said with a wink.

"Oh lordy," I said as I looked for an escape hatch in my dinner plate.

"How does that sound, Jenny?" Erin asked with a grin.

"You shut up!" I flushed with embarrassment.

"Girls!" Mama insisted.

Why she made us play this charade with my grandpa was beyond me. Keeping the peace seemed to be her highest priority, regardless of what lies had to be told to get there.

Erin clearly found the whole idea amusing. She leaned across to her brother and whispered, "I can't believe he can't remember any of us, but he can remember feeling up our grandmother in the back of a Buick!" Toby gobbled at his lips to stop from smiling. He was keen to deflect from any of Mama's attention. But he had failed.

"Speakin' of courtin'," Mama said to Toby, "I fail to understand, Toby Nathaniel Poser, how a handsome boy like you doesn't have half a dozen girls on his arm."

"I do, Mama," Toby muttered as he filled his plate with seconds of the ravioli on the table and didn't look her in the eye. "But I don't stay with any of 'em long enough to bring 'em home for a visit."

"You should have a *steady* girlfriend, Toby," Mama insisted. "Someone you can bring here for Sunday supper."

"Grandpa Tom didn't get married until he was twenty-six," Toby said defensively. "I'm only twenty-two."

"And that's my point!" Mama said. "You can't turn around one day, point to a girl, and say, 'Let's get married.' You gotta court a girl, Toby, and that takes time. Your daddy courted me my last two years of high school before we got married, and he was only twenty when we tied the knot."

"Best day of my life," Daddy said with a warm smile at Mama, which distracted her some, but not enough. She rounded on me. "If you'd stayed with Jason, you'd be married by now, Mary, and you'd have had someone to come home to when you left the hospital instead of an ugly dog."

I wanted to be anywhere but here. Just when I thought I was over the worst of the pain of the breakup, Mama had to make sure there was more hurting to be done. She wanted me married. I knew that. The whole of Nashville knew that. But why did she have to start back harping on it less than a week after I'd nearly drowned?

"Have you heard from Jason lately?" she asked hopefully.

"No, I haven't," I muttered.

"Toby, didn't you tell your friend what happened to your sister?"

"Jason's been real busy writin' new songs and talkin' to record producers, things like that," Toby said defensively before he shoveled about a dozen ravioli pieces into his mouth.

"I will never understand, Mary, why you broke up with such a handsome, hard-workin' boy," Mama said.

Jason had been her favorite since the day Toby had brought him home from grade school to visit and eat every cookie in our cookie jar, tellin' Mama he'd never known a cookie could be so good until he'd bitten into hers. She'd been putty in his hands, and she'd been determined to get me and him to the altar ever since.

"Hey, Daddy," I said desperately, "do you remember my friend Alice? She's come along to church with me a couple of times."

"The girl from New Zealand? Yes, I remember her."

"Is she the one with the funny accent?" Mama asked.

"That's her. I've been meanin' to tell you that she wants to join our choir. Is that okay?"

"Can she sing?" Daddy asked.

That stumped me. "Actually, I don't know if she can or not."

"Well, if she can't, she'll be in good company. Of course she can join the choir."

"Thanks, Daddy."

"I always wanted to sing in a church choir," Aunt Sara said, and I sighed with relief. My distraction had worked. "But one thing held me back…I sound like a bullfrog croakin' off pitch," Aunt Sara said with a grin.

"I wish Erin would get back in the choir," Mama said. "She has a such a pretty voice."

"No thanks," Erin said. "I don't feel like singin'."

"You don't feel like doin'—or *wearin'*—anythin' you should," Mama snapped.

"Marjorie, give the poor girl some air," Aunt Sara declared. "She's findin' her own way, just as we all have to do."

"Her own way?" Mama sputtered. "What do you know about her own way? You don't have any children. You don't even have a husband or attend church regular. You don't know what Erin needs or what she should be doin', Sara Collins, so stop stickin' your nose in where it don't belong!"

Daddy swallowed the rest of his wine and refilled his glass.

"You want Erin to be a pattern-card of *you*," Aunt Sara retorted. "You want her to twist and warp her soul into your image of what she should be. You're suffocatin' the child. Let her *be*, Marjorie!"

Their battle raged on while everyone else ate their supper and kept to themselves. Mama and Aunt Sara had been conducting variations of this battle for as long as I could remember.

I stayed silent, particularly because I had an almost overwhelming urge to shock Mama into silence by telling them all about Simha. I could just picture the horror in her eyes when I told her I had spent the night with an Indian, a man whose Hindu-based spirit had reached half way around the world to save my life—even if he didn't know it.

But I wasn't that brave. I didn't even feel safe thinking about him, let alone mentioning him. Besides, how could I tell her and the rest of my family about Simha when he was bound up inextricably with my car accident, and I couldn't even talk to them about my accident, not the way they were comfortable talking about it.

Something terrible and strange and miraculous had happened to me, and what I wanted more than anything was some help, some guidance to help me figure it all out.

But I couldn't ask for that guidance from my family. I didn't feel safe revealing anything that had happened to me in that river, or in my heart and soul and head since I'd awakened in that hospital bed, because this supper had made it crystal clear that they didn't want to hear it. If I forced it on them, they would duck, or laugh at me, or judge me, or ignore me, and right now I wasn't strong enough to take it.

So I just sat there at the dinner table, sipping my sweet tea and picking at my food.

I once had a thousand desires.
But in my one desire to know you
all else melted away.

⁂ Rumi

Chapter Ten

It was a long drive home after my first family dinner since my accident. I walked back into my apartment feeling a mixture of confusion, disappointment, and dissatisfaction. I had a headache that felt like it was pulling at the back of my eyes. I greeted Charlie, who was jumping up and down in front of me. We conducted our ritual of hugs and doggie kisses that apparently must occur at the front doorstep, then I gave him his dinner.

I walked into my bedroom, stripped off my clothes, and pulled on my flannel pajamas and wool socks. I looked at the florist shop my family and friends had made of my bedroom, and I'd just simply had it.

I grabbed the bouquets off of the bedside tables on either side of my double bed, carried them into the kitchen, and tossed them into the trash can. It took me five minutes to empty my bedroom and fill up my trash can, and I felt so much better.

I got a big garbage bag and emptied my living room and kitchen counters of every trace of flowery sentiment. I carried the garbage bag and my trash can out to the apartment complex dumpsters. I walked back inside with the empty trash can, and a big sigh of relief gusted out of me. I had my home back.

I kicked off my boots, returned the trash can to the kitchen, threw Charlie's ball for him for a while, then sat down on the sofa and grabbed the TV remote control.

The doorbell rang. I got up and headed for the door. I looked through the peephole and saw a skinny, pimply teenage boy holding a single rose in clear cellophane wrapping. Oh lordy!

I opened the front door. "Yes?"

"You Mary Poser?"

"Yes."

"Sign here," he said, shoving a pad at me with his left hand.

I scrawled my name then took the flower that he shoved at me. "Thanks," I said.

I kicked the door shut with my foot, carried my newest bouquet into the kitchen, and opened the lid of the trash can. Ravaged with guilt, I thought I had better read the card first. It's not other people's fault that their kind words wishing me good health were being read by someone who was feeling blind to beauty right now. A single rose was a curious choice by whoever was wishing me well. I searched for and found the little white envelope and pulled out the card.

You walk through fields of a thousand blooms, and none of them touch you. Then you discover a rose and your life is changed forever. - Simha

My legs got wobbly, and I sat down with a thump on my kitchen chair. I just sat there staring at the little card as my hand holding it began to quiver uncontrollably. The beautiful words blurred as my eyes began to swim.

It took me the better part of ten minutes to regain my composure. I dread a man who can so affect me with his words. I grabbed my phone and started texting.

Mary: Dear Simha—Thank you so much for the beautiful rose! Your lovely, kind words are flattering.

I pressed "Send," set my phone back down, and just sat there staring at my flower and mooning over it. Suddenly, my phone beeped on the coffee table. I picked it up, and happiness curled through me like smoke through a chimney. Simha had sent me an e-mail.

Simha: I'm glad you like it. I wanted to tell you how happy I am to know that you're safe after what you say happened to you. A life can be changed in so many ways. Sometimes an accident can have consequence beyond any physical impact.
          I have just spent an entire day editing my Bollywood-style film *Passion*. I kept surprising myself. I was trying to concentrate on editing the love scene, but my mind kept bringing up memories of my night in Nashville with you.
     P.S. Thank you for having this effect on me.

I stared at those words and felt my heart bumping against my ribs. I clutched at my chest with earnest disbelief. Why does he do this to me? Then the heat in my face and the spinning of my head just clouded everything over. He was being so charming and intimate and honest, and I just didn't know what to do with that. Should I believe him? I couldn't respond in kind, not when I felt so confused and conflicted and vulnerable.

What should I do with a man who saved my life and doesn't know it? What should I do about this running hot and cold that was doing my head in?

What would happen when Simha finally saw me for who I truly was—this confused, scared, fence-sitting, unholy mess? Would he hightail it for the nearest airport as any sane man would?

I reread his e-mail, and the same old question pounded at my temples: what does he want from me? Does he just want to be pen pals sharing thoughts and memories via e-mail? Maybe he had a bunch of people he wrote to, being all sweet and charming?

If he did...that might be okay. He hadn't even hinted that he planned to come back to Nashville ever, and I sure didn't make enough money to visit him in India. If we weren't going to see each other again, well, an occasional e-mail or text sharing our thoughts and feelings might be safe.

And I had to be honest, it was flattering that I distracted him from the work he loved, and it was admirable that he could tell me so. Not that I was anywhere near that admirable. No way was I going to tell him of my own incessant thoughts about him, let alone seeing him in the Cumberland River and the emotional aftermath of that near-death experience. I wasn't that brave. I took my time figuring out how to safely respond to him. I decided to lead with my head and not my heart.

Mary: Ha-ha. You're welcome. Unlike you, I wasn't working today. I was hanging out with Charlie, and cooking, and dodging the usual firestorm at the family dinner table. Mama knows just what to say to get us riled up.

Even though I'm fine, my boss ordered me to take the week off, and I hate it. I like working, I like my job, I like helping others, and she won't let me! One of my newer clients is a family coping with their daddy who's only forty-eight and was struck with early-onset Alzheimer's about three years ago. Now they need help making their house safe for him. I feel so sad for them because my Grandpa Tom was diagnosed with Alzheimer's a couple of years ago, and even though he's still really functional, it can be draining taking care of him, particularly because he's so worried about being a burden. I can't stop worrying about the progression of this terrible disease and dreading the day when we have to finally put him in a caretaking facility. I've seen too many families torn apart trying to care all by themselves for a loved one in the late stages of Alzheimer's. I don't want that to happen to my family.

I sent the e-mail, grabbed the remote, turned on the TV, and called Charlie up onto the sofa to cuddle with me. I began flipping channels, looking for something light and funny before I went to bed. I stopped at a *Will & Grace* rerun. The show always made me laugh. But I only got to watch about ten minutes of the episode when my phone beeped again and made me jump. (I've really got to stop doing that.) I opened it up, and there was a new e-mail.

Simha: It is your compassion for others and your kind heart that truly makes you one in a million.

Everything just seemed to melt in me. I turned off the TV and headed to bed.

This human being is a guest-house.
Every morning a new arrival.
A joy, a depression, a meanness,
some momentary awareness comes
As an unexpected visitor.

❧ Rumi

Chapter Eleven

I dashed into the Red Boot Café and searched the crowded tables for Chloe and Alice. Spottting them near the back, I began squeezing my way through good ol' boys in tan baseball caps with trucker logos, secretaries and clerks from the nearby office buildings, a few men and women in suits, and harried-looking waiters and waitresses, their arms loaded down with big plates of steaming food. Garth Brooks' rapid-fire "Ain't Goin' Down ('Til The Sun Comes Up)" was blasting out of the speakers, making everyone wish they could jump up and start dancing, but this was a lunch break, and people just didn't have time to eat *and* let loose...except for Alice, of course.

She was doing a lively Tush Push by our table and having a grand time. I couldn't help but smile. Alice is one of the most high-spirited people I've ever met...particularly when music is playing. She becomes an entirely different person with an open-hearted exuberance that lightens all the hearts around her.

Chloe looked up from her menu, looked pointedly at her watch, then looked at me. "You're late again."

"I know...I'm so sorry!" I said, sitting down opposite her. "I was walkin' out the door when Larry Brody called about a problem he was havin' with widenin' the doorways at Janet Walker's place. That boy can talk a mile a minute, but it takes him an hour to get around to the point. Hey, Alice."

"Hey, bro," Alice said with a cheerful grin as she plopped down on her chair. "We ordered you some iced tea."

"Thanks!" I said gratefully. I took a sip from the huge glass of sweet tea and settled on my chair.

"Larry Brody, my foot," Chloe said, narrowing her eyes at me.

I blushed. Larry *had* called, but he wasn't the reason I was late. Because it was an almost straight shot from Shelby Avenue, over the Gateway Bridge, and then right off of Eighth Avenue South onto Palmer Place, it used to take me just seven minutes to get to the Red Boot Café from my office. Now it took me closer to fourteen minutes.

"You still not seeing eye to eye with the Gateway Bridge?" Alice asked.

"I-24 gets me over here just fine," I insisted.

"I was bitten by a dog once," Alice said. "It took me a long time to trust dogs again."

"It's been almost a month since your accident, Mary. Get over yourself."

"Bro, she nearly died!" Alice protested.

"Everyone dies eventually," Chloe retorted. "She should be havin' fun, not mopin' around her apartment with that ugly dog of hers."

"I have fun," I said defensively.

"You've turned down every one of my invitations to go to the movies, to a club, or for a drink after work."

"I've been busy!"

"Busy avoidin' everythin' that smacks of happiness. You should be celebratin' the fact that you survived your car accident, not dwellin' at the bottom of the Cumberland River."

"I'm here, aren't I, havin' lunch with you?"

"For the first time this week," Chloe said darkly.

"I went bungee jumping once," Alice said. "Scared me to death. I was certain I was going to die. Of course, I didn't die, and that's what was awesome about it. There's something about glimpsing the edge so you know where you stand."

"Girl, you fell over the edge years ago," Chloe said.

"What do you mean by that?"

Chloe and Alice bickered while I sat there feeling miserable. Just like my family, my friends had their own take on what had happened to me and what it meant to them, and it just didn't have anything to do with how I felt.

"You girls ready to order?" our waitress asked as she walked up to us, order pad in one hand, pen in another.

"Chicken caesar salad," Chloe said.

"Hot turkey sandwich," said Alice.

"I'll have the brisket with mashed potatoes," I said without looking at the menu. Chloe, Alice, and I have lunch here a lot. It's halfway between Chloe's office and mine, and it's on the right side of the river for Alice to get easily to the Grand Ole Opry by two o'clock when her shift starts.

From out of the restaurant speakers, Hank Williams Senior sang out "Hey Good Lookin'" in his distinctive reedy twang, and I deliberately distracted Chloe from thinking about me by asking about her newest music video gig.

"It is so excitin'!" she exclaimed. "Such a creative process. The director is a genius. And Luke Bryan is just the cutest, sweetest man. He lost a couple of pounds for the shoot and, girl, he looks *good*. He could ride this pony. He knew my name right off, and he always smiles at me when he sees me. And you'll never guess who dropped by yesterday. Blake Shelton! He just thinks the world of Luke, and they're like the best friends ever."

Chloe gushed about her music video shoot for a while until

our food arrived and we dug in. Then she told us about all of the plans she was making for the Bugle Records promotion at the CMA Music Festival coming up next month and the event she was planning for the Yap IPO announcement a week after the festival.

"So Alice," I said when Chloe paused to take a bite of her salad, "how's your family back in New Zealand?"

"They're great!" Alice said happily. "No possums stripping the trees bare, no rabbit or mice plague, no drought, all good. Mom and Dad have been expanding the barn, and they bought two new bulls and a dozen new cows. They'll have the biggest privately owned dairy in the district in three or four years."

"That's great," I said. "You must miss your folks a lot."

"Well, I do, bro, but I don't miss the dairy. Cows stink."

I laughed. "Are you enjoyin' choir rehearsals?"

"Bro, it's choice!" Alice exclaimed.

"Choice?"

"Choice—awesome!"

"Girl, I swear you need subtitles sometimes," Chloe piped in.

"Everyone at choir practice has been so supportive," Alice continued, ignoring Chloe's comment, "and I'm feeling so much more comfortable singing out loud, you know, with actual people listening."

"Good for you," I said with a smile.

My phone vibrated loudly in my purse, and I pulled it out. Simha's newest text had my toes curling in my shoes. I smiled.

"Well, spank me, look at that smile, Chloe," Alice said. "You were wrong. Mary's got pleasure in her life for sure."

"What's goin' on?" Chloe demanded.

I looked up reluctantly. "It's a text from...a friend."

"*Which* friend?" Chloe demanded.

"Simha Das."

"Who?" said Alice.

"The Indian filmmaker we met at the film festival."

"Oh, *him*," Chloe said with a broad grin. "He was yummy. Gimme."

She grabbed the phone out of my hand and started to read Simha's text, stopped, then looked at Alice with wide eyes. "Listen to *this*." She started reading my text message. "I read this Indian proverb today: Only the nightingale understands the rose. You are as lovely as a rose. I am happy to brave the thorns to find the truth of your heart, for my heart is completely charmed by you."

Chloe burst out laughing, and Alice stared at me with wide blue eyes. "What's all this?" she asked.

"Simha and I have been tradin' an occasional text every now and then since my accident," I said defensively. "It's no big deal."

Chloe only laughed harder.

I was hurt and mad at Chloe for reading Simha's text without permission, and then for laughing at it. My "conversations" with Simha were private. I didn't want to share them, particularly when I had such a strong reaction to the things Simha wrote to me, about me. They were personal. They were important. They confused me and inspired me. I didn't want them ridiculed.

Sitting in the Red Boot Café, I realized for the first time since I'd met Chloe in grade school that I had to be careful about what I told her and cautious about the personal parts of myself and my life that I revealed to her. I had just learned that I couldn't trust her to treat something that was important to me with respect. My throat hurt like the devil. I poured some sweet tea down it.

Alice grabbed my phone out of Chloe's hand and gave it back to me. "Mary's lucky. I'll bet you don't have guys texting *you* romantic Indian proverbs, Chloe Corbett. So, Mary, Simha is that lion guy, right? He sounds pretty passionate. I'll bet he can't wait to get into your pants."

I choked on my iced tea. It took a moment of furious coughing before I could breathe again. Trust Alice to hit the nail bluntly on the head. Some of Simha's e-mails and texts did sound romantic, and I couldn't stop wondering: what *does* he want from me?

Our waitress provided a welcome distraction. We gave her our dessert orders—gelatin for Chloe, apple pie for Alice, chocolate cream pie for me—and she shuffled away as a busboy cleared off our table, using one arm to shovel all of our lunch dishes into a big gray plastic bin before heading off to another table.

Loretta Lynn was singing "You Ain't Woman Enough to Take My Man," and Alice suddenly jumped up and into an exuberant Electric Slide along with the music. Folks around us were watching her and laughing. Some were even clapping. Chloe sank low on her chair and tried to pretend she'd never met the Kiwi.

The song ended, and Alice plopped back down onto her chair, grinning happily. "I can't believe I never listened to country music before coming here. It's so grouse!"

"There's she goes again," Chloe muttered as she sat back up.

Our waitress handed out our desserts, and Chloe felt better.

"You're gettin' over your shyness, Alice," I said with a grin.

"Only with music, bro," Alice said with a loopy grin. "I just lose myself in it, and everything feels brilliant."

"Speakin' of music, the Nashville Musical Theater is holdin' auditions for *How to Succeed in Business Without Really Trying* next week," Chloe said. "The director used me in *Guys and Dolls* and *The Boys from Syracuse*, so I think I've got a good shot of at least gettin' a featured role. Maybe Smitty. She's got her own song. I'd kill it."

"That's great, Chloe," I said.

"Every credit helps," she said. "Music videos, community theater roles, local commercials. They'll all get me to Hollywood sooner than later."

She continued to talk about her current and future careers as we finished our desserts and paid our checks. Then the three of us kissed each other on the cheeks, headed out to the parking lot, and went our separate ways. I stared straight ahead as I took the I-24 back over the Cumberland River, got off at the Shelby Avenue exit, and returned to work seven minutes late.

"I'll stay an extra ten minutes tonight," I said to Tammy as I hurried to my desk.

"I know it," she said without looking up from her computer.

"The bridge?" Hannah asked as I passed her desk.

"Yeah."

I sat at my desk and tried to work, but I kept glancing at my purse. With a sigh, I gave up, pulled out my phone, and read Simha's text again.

> Simha: ...for my heart is completely charmed by you.

Alice was right. Simha was a passionate and romantic guy. I felt safe flirting over the internet with him now and then because I knew this wasn't going anywhere. He was in India, and I was here. We were just chatting. I checked to make sure my coworkers were all busy and ignoring me, then I started texting.

> Mary: I don't think I have too many thorns. I get along with everyone.

His answer popped up a minute later.

> Simha: I wonder if you get along with everyone and reveal your true self to few? I've been spending so many hours editing my film and watching the characters

reveal themselves frame by frame that it has made me think a good deal lately about human relationships: our relationship with ourselves and our relationships with others. I see so many people being busy together without ever touching. They know nothing of true connection: heart to heart, mind to mind. They just go about the daily business of living without actually *living*.

Mary: I know just what you mean. I've got a new client, an elderly woman who's all alone in the world, and my heart just breaks every time I talk with her. Her husband died years ago, her kids are scattered around the world, her friends are sick or in the grave. She has no one to hold her in her old age and tell her she's going to be alright. She has no one with whom she can share her memories, her fears, her joys. I took her a cherry pie the other day after I got off work and before I called on a friend going through a bad breakup, and Miss Lillian was so grateful to see me that I didn't have the heart to leave. She just sat there talking about her family, glad to have someone to hear her, even if it was just for an hour. I can't tell you how sad I felt when I finally drove off.

Simha: You treat your clients like family, and that is such a special quality. I'm curious about something. You talk so much about filling your days taking care of others, but you say nothing of the things you do for yourself.

Mary: I'm just pursuing what the Bible teaches— "You must help the weak and remember the words of the Lord Jesus, that He Himself said, 'It is more blessed to give than to receive.'" Acts 20:35

I got back to the work piled up on my desk, but I admit I wasn't exactly diligent. I kept checking my phone for a new e-mail or text. Sure enough, about ten minutes later, Simha wrote me back.

> Simha: Service to others and to our community is equally important in the Hindu religion. We have seva, which means selfless service. But Hinduism also celebrates and requires self-care, which includes daily practice to improve ourselves as we seek a stronger and clearer connection to divine bliss, the experience of infinite love. The heart soars most when we serve the light within us.
> So I hope you are leaving time in the midst of your busy days and caretaking to discover your heart's true light.
> My guru teaches that there are no coincidences. Everything happens for a reason. Has anyone asked you: why did you choose to drive your car off a bridge and into a river?

My jaw hit the floor. What the heck? First, he puts me on a pedestal, and then he does *this?* Angry, I started typing.

> Mary: I didn't choose to take a nosedive off the bridge and go swimming in my car!

I sat at my desk, arms folded over my chest, fuming. Who did Simha think he was? How dare he test me like that? I didn't know why I had that damn accident. I didn't know how I'd survived it, or why. I didn't know what I was supposed to do with my life now. I didn't know what direction to go in. I didn't know what I wanted, but I knew one thing I *didn't* want—I didn't want some Indian filmmaker pushing me on something he knew nothing about!

My phone beeped on my desk. I glared at it. It just sat there, looking innocent. I glared at it some more, then sighed and opened my e-mail app.

> Simha: Of course not. None of us consciously chooses to have a car accident, or open heart surgery, or a brain aneurysm. But each of those near-death events can be powerful, transformative experiences. They can change how we see ourselves and what we think and feel about ourselves. They can change how we see and act in the world.
>
> I am grateful that your accident was not physically catastrophic, but it was nonetheless a life-threatening event that may be working profound changes in you. Those changes can be positive and powerful if you wish them to be.

Oh! I hadn't been foolish and wrong after all. Simha *did* know what had happened to me. There was one person in the world who truly saw me, who understood the jumbled up mess of feelings inside me.

I felt warm all over. Cared for. *Seen.* Simha was giving me something I couldn't seem to get from my own family and friends, something I didn't even know I needed...until now.

I turned off my phone, shoved it back in my purse, and glared for a good ten minutes at the work still waiting for me on my desk until guilt got the better of me. I started reviewing the latest house inspections.

For a committed heart everything is possible.

🔖 *Rumi*

Chapter Twelve

The following Sunday morning, the church parking lot was full as usual, so I parked The Mule across the street from the Nashborough Evangelical Baptist Church where Daddy had been the pastor these last eighteen years. Folks who had been married by my daddy had kids going off to college in the fall, kids who had been baptized by my daddy when they were babies.

The church is one of the prettiest this side of the Cumberland River. It's a big three-story dark red brick building trimmed in white with four pairs of two-story-tall columns at the front supporting a big white triangular pediment. Tall windows fill the inside with lots of sunshine on most days. Today, though, dark gray clouds were crowding the sky, and the weatherman had promised rain later. The morning was already hot and muggy.

I tucked my emergency umbrella into my handbag, waited for a couple of cars to pass, then trotted across the street. I said hello to the folks on the front steps and to those chatting near the front door, even the ones I didn't know, and I knew most of these folks. Daddy had a loyal congregation that valued his wisdom, his big heart, and his occasional high jinks.

When you go to a Baptist church on a Sunday, you wear

child, my precious butterfly, to a terrible accident several weeks back when her car crashed off the Gateway Bridge and into the swollen Cumberland River."

I burned all over and tried to sink lower on the pew as every single person in that church stared at me. I couldn't believe Daddy was doing this. Taking something so incredibly personal to me and turning it into a public sermon.

"It's been nearly a month since the accident," Daddy continued. "I haven't spoken of it until now because I needed that time to think about what had happened and to pray for guidance and understanding. I've told you many a time that we all sit in the palm of God's hand, but I must confess that I didn't feel the security that knowledge usually gives me when I saw my child lyin' there in the hospital, not knowin' if she was goin' to wake up or not. Brothers and sisters, I was *scared*. I looked at her lyin' lifeless in that hospital bed, and I didn't think about God reachin' down into that river and pullin' my little girl back up into life. I thought instead about how I had failed her. I hadn't kept her safe. I hadn't even rescued her."

I stared up at Daddy, my eyes blurring with unshed tears, confusion nearly suffocating me. I wanted to shout, "That's not what happened to me!" I felt again the cold river water crashing into me, pouring into me. I saw that brilliant white light, Simha's hand reaching for me, the moonstone glowing its power and reassurance to me as I blacked out. Daddy and Mama said it was God or Jesus who had saved me. Aunt Sara said it was the men from the bridge who had risked their lives to pull me from the river. Some people said it was luck, some said it was a miracle, and others said I had freed myself and floated to the surface of the dark, cold water.

But I'd seen Simha's hand reaching for me. Hadn't I?

But how could it have been Simha when he had known

nothing about my accident? How could it have been Simha when we were, at most, remote pen pals, not two people sharing some kind of mystical connection?

What had happened to me that day in the Cumberland River?

"I stood beside my daughter's hospital bed feelin' scared, feelin' helpless," Daddy continued, "and I vowed then and there that I would never let anythin' endanger her again. I would give my life before I allowed anythin' to harm my little butterfly."

"Amen!" shouted Leroy Newsome in his big baritone.

"But there are two types of safety," Daddy continued. "There's the safety we seek with fear-based minds, and there's the safety we can only know with an open and courageous heart. If I had continued in the fear I felt in that hospital room, I would build a fortress around my daughter with walls a mile thick and towers as high as the sky. She would be protected from all harm, but she would also live her life inside a cold stone prison...and that would be no kind of life for a beautiful butterfly."

Daddy turned and looked behind him at the statue of Jesus on the cross. Then he looked back at his congregation. "But I did not continue to dwell in fear. God reached down and held me in the palm of His hand, and He reminded me that there is another kind of safety available to each and every one of us. And that is the safety we know when we open our hearts to Jesus Christ."

"Yes, brother!" shouted someone behind me.

"When Jesus was persecuted by his own people, whipped, chained, and left to die on a cross, he accepted every punishment, every wound, and every moment of suffering for us so that we may truly live. He could have built a fortress to protect himself, but he didn't. Jesus knew that, no matter what happened to him, he was loved—I said *loved*, brothers and sisters—and despite all the sufferin' he endured, Jesus never stopped loving *us*."

"Hallelujah!" cried Mrs. Beasely from the third row.

"Seein' my daughter lyin' unconscious in a hospital bed was my challenge, my wound, my suffering. I stood there, and for one terrible moment, I wondered: had God abandoned my family by allowin' that terrible accident to threaten my little butterfly? Well, the answer lifted up my heart, and filled my soul, and shouted in my head, and that answer was *no!*"

"Amen!" cried several in the congregation.

"The Passion of the Christ reminds us that God never abandons any of us, and that in times of trouble or doubt, we forsake fear and find our path back to love. With fear, I vowed to build a fortress around my little butterfly to keep her safe, but today, I renounce that vow. I have broken down the walls of fear, and I commit to you that I will live a new promise. I vow to open my heart in the name of Jesus Christ and to love my daughter, come what may. Now, I will tell you that I have also vowed to throw her back into the Cumberland River myself if I ever catch her textin' while drivin' again!"

That got a laugh.

"The same goes for all of you," Daddy continued. "You text while drivin', and I'm gonna throw you in that river, all except you Emmett Dawson."

Emmett sat in the front row on the other side of the aisle. He's a big man, tall and wide, with a pale red beard down to his chest.

"I'm not throwin' you anywhere, Emmett," Daddy said. "You'll have to throw yourself in the river."

Everyone laughed.

"You've already thrown me in once, Pastor!" Emmett shouted. "When I was baptized! That's all the dunkin' I need."

The congregation cheered.

"And that's what the river is best for, brother—personal transformation. So I will conclude today's sermon by vowin' to you, to all of you and to my precious butterfly, that I offer with an open and courageous heart the safety of sittin' in the palm of God's hand whenever troubles come. Thank you, Jesus, for your love and for showin' us the way."

I cheered and clapped with everyone else because that was what everyone expected of me, but I wasn't happy pretending in church to feel happiness when all I felt was confusion, humiliation, and despair.

Daddy cued Danny Green, and he began playing a lively version of "Joyful Joyful." The choir joined in, swaying and clapping a jubilant counterpoint to the organ music. Soon, folks started standing, singing, and swaying with the choir. I stayed where I was, not looking at Daddy, not looking at Mama standing beside me and singing with everyone else. I just couldn't. So I watched Alice. She looked transformed. For all her exuberance, she really was quite scared. Daddy said once that Alice hid her light under a bushel. But not today.

She looked blissful. She was totally immersed in the music, the words, the spirit. Then suddenly, Alice broke free into a rapturous and impromptu solo. Her rich, powerful voice and exuberance soared through the church and pulled everyone to their feet. Shouts of "Yes, sister!" and "Hallelujah!" rang out all around the church as the choir backed her up by continuing the main melody and lyrics.

As upset as I was at Daddy, I couldn't help but smile. Alice could really sing! She had a full, clear, and resounding voice that was perfectly on pitch and made the hair on the back of my neck stand up.

I glanced across at Chloe to share this stunning surprise and saw that her smile was strained. Oh dear. She heard Alice's talent, too. Chloe always got a little bit jealous when confronted by the brightness of someone else's star.

Daddy was so moved by Alice's singing that he burst

spontaneously into a routine from *Cinderfella*. He looked like the spitting image of Jerry Lewis as he started slow, running up to the choir and pretending to be Count Basie conducting his orchestra, then turned to the congregation and pretended to play the drums, then the saxophone, then the bass. He built the routine slowly, keeping it together at first, and then ecstatically flailing all around the altar as the music and the choir soared. Everyone laughed and cheered. The congregation had always loved Daddy's goofy, spot-on Jerry Lewis impressions.

But Mama didn't. She'd been beaming all through Daddy's sermon, hanging on his every word, her gaze glued to his face, fit to bust with pride. But now she was looking like she didn't know him from Adam, and she wasn't smiling.

I saw Daddy glance at her as the hymn was finally winding down to its close. Sadness flickered in his brown eyes.

If the heart is pleased with you, I am pleased;
and if the heart is opposed to you, I am opposed.

❧ *Rumi*

Chapter Thirteen

July in Nashville is hot, which is fine. What sucks is the humidity. It makes the days feel so much hotter, and it soaks you through with sweat. Air conditioners run almost all day long in the city.

They were keeping the Lean Machine comfortably cool. Even so, the paying customers were sweating like pigs on all of the different machines. The treadmills were placed up front looking out the floor-to-ceiling street-side windows. I guess their plan was to make passersby feel guilty for not coming in to lose their love handles, and to make members feel self-righteous for working out. More customers were sweating in the weight room and on the racquetball courts. Even more were sweating in the four exercise rooms where you could find classes in everything from jazzercise to Pilates.

I walked in after work on this Monday evening with Chloe and Alice for our weekly Zumba class. Zumba to the country music of Garth Brooks, Reba McIntyre, and Kenny Chesney, of course. I faltered only a second when I saw Toby talking with Jason, who looked wildly out of place in his jeans, sleeveless shirt, cowboy boots, and battered cowboy hat.

Toby had worked here for about a year at the front desk, welcoming customers, scheduling their classes and racquetball sessions, and helping to keep all of the exercise equipment in good shape. In his spare time, he worked out for like two hours a day, and he had the abs, biceps, and thighs to prove it. He spent the rest of the time with his band, The Nashbros. He played keyboards, Jason played lead guitar, and their high school buddy Scott played drums. They'd been together five years now, playing every roadhouse, juke joint, and bar that would have them. Their music career was going nowhere in a hurry, but they kept the faith.

That seemed to be the topic of Toby's and Jason's conversation when I walked in with Chloe and Alice. The boys were standing to the side of the front desk, oblivious to the panting, sweating, and flexing all around them. I'd grown impervious to seeing Jason by now. Toby and Jason were best friends. Toby had learned to play the keyboards because Jason had wanted to start a band, so they were always hanging out together. I didn't even mind when he barely flicked his eyes at me whenever we were in the same room. All the same, I couldn't help but eavesdrop while Chloe flirted with a personal trainer and Alice checked out the message board for upcoming classes.

"Jase, I don't know if you've noticed, but our band sucks," Toby said, looking uncertain.

"Are you kiddin'?" Jason said. "We're doin' great! I've got a ton of fans."

"Yeah, well I'm sure the two of them think you're the next Kenny Chesney. But I've had enough of this small-town rut we're in. Maybe it's just not our scene here. Listenin' to what some people say around here, even in my own family, leaves teeth marks in my tongue because I'm always bitin' it. It sucks listenin' to Mama flyin' off the handle about anyone who's not like her and doesn't bow down before her idea of Southern family values. And it sucks that Daddy just lets her."

"I like your parents."

"That's because they treat you like a rock star."

"Yeah," Jason said with his naughty boy grin, "I do like that."

"They're the two fans I was tellin' you about. Anythin' you do is gold as far as they're concerned.

"I've got more than two fans!"

"Okay, you've probably got three, but that's not the issue. Jase, I've gotta get out of this town. I've had it up to here with always havin' to do what's expected of me. I'm sick to death of Nashville. I'm so hungry for somethin' new, somethin' different, somethin' that fits me. I may not know what that somethin' is, or where it is, and it's drivin' me crazy not knowin', but I know it's out there somewhere, and I've gotta find it."

"You're breakin' up the band?" Jason demanded, looking scared.

"No, man. I'm sayin' let's take the band on the road! Let's go show the rest of this country what we can do."

"That's crazy talk," Jason scoffed. "This is *Music City*, dude! The producers and the record labels we need are right here! Bein' a hometown band gives us an edge we won't have anywhere else. This is where we catch the rocket, and once we do, we can ride it on out of here as superstars!"

That had been Jason's plan for as long as I'd known him. As far back as grade school, he'd been certain he was destined for country music stardom. He had copied the fashion and posturing of the stars of the moment, learned to play a guitar, and formed The Nashbros in high school.

I was brought in as their Number One Fan. Toby, Jason, and I had been the Three Musketeers for most of our lives. We'd gone to the mall together and to the movies, and we'd snuck out to concerts together. When they'd formed The Nashbros, I had sat in on most of their rehearsals and followed them from gig to gig—their most devoted fan, the one who applauded every song even if no one else was listening to them. Since I'd broken up with Jason, The Nashbros had been on their own. It sounded to me like no one else was applauding them yet.

Toby and Jason's conversation ended as it usually did—in horseplay. Jason casually put an arm on Toby's shoulder and then quickly moved in to wrestle him into a chokehold. My brother retaliated by getting his arms around Jason's waist and swinging him off to the side. He was about to flatten him like the Greco-Roman wrestler he'd been in high school, but Jason suddenly broke free.

"Chill, dude!" Jason snapped.

I must have looked just as surprised as Toby did.

"Come on, Mary," Chloe said, grabbing my arm, "class starts in a minute."

With a last look at my brother and my ex, I went with her and Alice down the hall toward the last exercise room.

"How'd it go with the trainer?" I asked.

"I've got a date on Friday night, of course," Chloe said.

"Of course," I said with a smile. Chloe had always been able to get any man she wanted. I don't know how she did it. I'd listened to her flirtatious conversations. I'd watched the way she'd arch her neck and cock her head and look at guys from under her eyelashes. I'd practiced all of that in front of my mirror at home, along with all of the other weapons in Chloe's large arsenal, and... nothing.

"Heard anything from the Lion King lately?" Alice asked.

"That's right!" Chloe said. "How is tall, dark, and yummy?"

"He's still editing his movie," I said.

Sally Iverson, wearing a low-cut sports bra and minuscule spandex shorts, brushed by me without a word. I shook my head at her inexplicable meanness and then followed her into the Zumba classroom with Chloe and Alice. Every wall was covered with mirrors, just to drive home how inadequate we all were.

"How goes choir rehearsals, Alice?" I asked.

"Brilliant, bro! We're learning a new hymn one of my friends back home sent me."

"That's great," I said as we took our accustomed places in the front row of students. Chloe always has to be in front. "I think the choir sounds so much better since you joined it."

"Cheers!" Alice said, blushing a little.

"My director pulled me aside after rehearsal for *How to Succeed* last night to tell me what a great job I'm doin' as Smitty," Chloe said.

"Of course you're doin' a great job," I said. "You're the best undiscovered talent in Nashville."

Chloe smiled happily as our instructor, who I was pretty sure was a former Marine drill sergeant, walked into the room.

Fifty minutes later, sweat streaming down our bodies and pooling in uncomfortable places, lungs straining for oxygen, muscles pleading for mercy, the class ended. Chloe, Alice, and I headed gratefully for the showers. They both had rehearsals to get to, so they cleaned up fast and dashed off.

I walked out of the locker room about ten minutes later, smiling as I thought again about the e-mail Simha had sent me today describing his mother's most recent and far from subtle attempts to marry him off.

There had been a deafening silence between us for two weeks that he'd finally broken with some "thinking of you and hope you're well" texts a couple of days apart. I guess he gets busy. A week after that, he'd sent a short text asking about Charlie's health and well-being. He followed that up a week later with a text about the disagreement he and his editor and producer were having over a particular scene in the movie they were working on.

A week after that, he sent me a long text describing his youngest nephew's sixth birthday party.

I couldn't stop myself. I wanted to wait, to appear cool, but I broke and texted him back in a flash to tell him about Toby's fourth birthday party. Mama and Daddy had hired a clown for the party, and Toby was so terrified of that clown that he'd run screaming into his room to hide, which set all of the other kids at the party to screaming, too. Things only settled down when the clown was sent home and cake and ice cream were lavishly doled out.

After that, Simha and I had settled back into texting each other once a week or so about our families, our work, the latest box office smash, that sort of thing. Not a word was exchanged about my car accident, my heart, or more importantly, us. We seemed to be settling into a pleasant pen pal association.

I stopped at the Lean Machine's front desk to say hi to Toby, but Toby wasn't paying attention. Frowning at the weight room, he was watching a crew cut blond guy who looked like a linebacker in spandex shorts, every inch of him glistening with sweat and rippling muscular rage. The linebacker seemed to be posturing and mouthing off to a shorter and leaner man in sweatpants and a sleeveless gray shirt, his red hair wet with sweat. It was Paul Mackenzie. I recognized him from high school. He'd been a couple of years ahead of me.

"What the hell do you mean by talkin' to Clay?" the linebacker demanded in a loud, belligerent voice. "You tryin' to recruit my brother, faggot?"

Toby started walking with quick, purposeful strides up to the two men. Worried, I followed after him.

"No," Paul said calmly, "I was answering his question."

"I was just askin' him to spot me, Junior," said Clay, a young, burly blond.

"Oh, he was goin' to do a helluva lot more than *spot* you, little brother," Junior sneered. He shoved Paul backward. "Weren't you, faggot?"

Even though Toby was six inches shorter and about fifty pounds of muscle shy of Junior, my brother put himself between Paul and Junior and looked the linebacker straight in the eye. "Back off, Junior Fenton," he ordered.

"This pillow biter was hittin' on my brother!" Junior thundered.

"Bullshit," Toby said.

"Junior, he wasn't!" Clay insisted.

"What the hell is he doin' in this gym anyway?" Junior demanded, his face red with fury. "We don't want your kind here!" he shouted at Paul.

"Yeah," Toby retorted, "we do. The Lean Machine has a no tolerance policy for intolerance, Junior. Read the membership regulations. Now, you can apologize to Paul, or you can get out. Your choice."

"I'm a frickin' member!" Junior bellowed.

"So is Paul, and he hasn't finished his reps yet."

Junior glared at Toby. Toby stood his ground. I wasn't really sure if Toby was there for gym policy or for just being pissed off with ignorance, based on what I heard him talking about with Jason.

Junior blinked first. "This sucks!" he shouted, storming toward the showers. "Come on, Clay! We're quittin' this queer-lovin' gym!"

"Sorry, Paul," Clay said to Paul.

"It's alright, Clay," Paul said with a smile. "We all know what Junior's like."

"Yeah," Clay said with a heavy sigh. He looked at Toby. "Junior may quit the Lean Machine, but I'm not."

Toby smiled. "See you tomorrow then."

Clay followed after Junior.

"You didn't have to rescue me," Paul said to Toby with a smile. "I was managing Junior just fine."

Toby rounded on him, mad as a wet hen. "I was just doin' my job. You were about to have your blood splattered all over the floor, and *I'm* the one who'd have had to clean it up while you were restin' easy in the back of an ambulance gettin' hauled off to the emergency room." Then Toby let fly on Paul with something I wasn't expecting. "What the hell are you doin' here, Paul? People like Junior hate you. It isn't even safe for you guys to have an annual gay pride parade here. Why do you put up with it when you can just get out?"

"This is my home, Toby," Paul said calmly in the face of my brother's frustration. "All of my folks and friends are here. Besides, the only way to change Nashville is to stay and change it from within so that it *is* safe and welcoming for me and everyone else who doesn't tow the white, Christian, heterosexual line."

"That ain't gonna happen," Toby said with certainty. He spun around, saw me, and stalked toward the front desk. I had to trot to catch up to him.

"Toby, what's the matter?"

"Nothing. Just doin' my job."

"No, you weren't! Paul is a good and courageous man, and he has as much right to live in Nashville as you or me."

"Courageous? He's dumb as a post. Riskin' his life by flaunting his homosexuality everywhere he goes."

"He isn't flaunting anythin'. He's just livin' his life."

"Well, he should live it somewhere else. This town's no good for him."

"What?"

Toby smacked the top of the front desk with his hand, his anger doubled. "I think he just set me off because I feel I'm trapped in a box that keeps gettin' smaller! And I don't know how to get out. I don't know anythin' except I've got to get out. Somehow."

"Oh, baby brother," I grasped his big hand with mine, "I don't want to lose you. This won't be home without you. But I can't stand seein' you so unhappy. If leavin' is the only way you can find the life you want, then I imagine you should...leave."

He smiled sadly and squeezed my hand. "But where do I go, Mary? What do I do?"

"I don't know."

"Yeah, neither do I."

My sweetheart, you have aroused my passion.
Your touch has filled me with desire.
I am no longer separate from you.
These are precious moments.
I beseech you, don't let me wait.
Let me merge with you.

❧ Rumi

Chapter Fourteen

The next day, I was still worrying about Toby, but I stopped when I walked into The General Store, six thousand square feet of pure bliss on Fourth Avenue South near Union Street. This place is country music nirvana. Huge signs hang down from the ceiling identifying each retail area. It has everything you could ever possibly want. The General Store is particularly known for its big vinyl record section with music going back to the 1920s. You can find recordings by legends like the Carter Family, Jimmie Rodgers, Gene Autry, Hank Williams, Patsy Cline, Buck Owens, Kitty Wells, and Porter Wagoner. One year, I bought Mama a copy of Al Dexter's 1942 recording of "Pistol Packin' Mama" on the A side, with "Rosalita" on the B side, and she cried all over me for ten minutes, she was so happy. Her grandma had played that record all during Mama's growing up years.

The General Store has an equally large CD section with more modern music, and a book section so big you think you're in a library. There's also a video section, posters from the 1920s to the present, and a souvenir section. The middle of the store has a stage. On Friday and Saturday nights, the best singers in Nashville perform here for The General Store Hour, a radio program carried all across the country.

The back half of the store is devoted to musical instruments autographed by country artists, performance costumes once actually worn by country stars, and museum-quality memorabilia. The General Store never has fewer than fifty customers, about half tourists and the rest locals, no matter the time of day or what day it is. This place feels like the lifeblood of country music, and it draws people from all over the world like a field of clover draws bees.

I wasn't here to buy anything today, though I was mighty tempted. I was here to pick up Erin. We tried to have lunch together once a week. I did a quick search through the crowd and found her pretty easily. On the side wall near the main entrance is a big community bulletin board that's always covered with posters and flyers announcing everything from a major upcoming concert to local band gigs, Nashville festivals and events, yoga classes, dog training, houses and apartments for sale or rent, and church notices. Below the bulletin board are four bookshelves full of flyers advertising all of that stuff, plus things like painting classes, automotive care classes for women, low-cost health clinics, and anesthesia-free teeth cleanings for dogs.

Erin was working the bulletin board—taking down anything more than two weeks old, putting up new flyers, and doing it all with body language that made sure we all knew she thought the task was tedious. She hadn't wanted this job. She hadn't wanted any job. She'd wanted to stay in her room and listen to music and feel sorry for herself. But Daddy and Mama had said that since she'd chosen not to go to college, she had to get out in the world and start pulling her own weight. One of the store managers was a member of Daddy's congregation, and she had gotten Erin this job.

A muscular woman in her fifties, wearing linen shorts and a

Grand Ole Opry souvenir tee shirt, was standing behind Erin. "Excuse me," she said in a German accent, "verr are the Dolly Parton music?"

Erin turned and blushed when she saw the woman staring at her weak and clumsy right hand. She put it behind her back. "Vinyl is on the left side of the store. CDs are in the middle section behind the cash registers," she said, her voice sullen.

The German woman thanked her and scurried away.

"Hey, Erin," I said, walking up to her.

"Hey," Erin said, turning back to the bulletin board. "I'll be done in a couple of minutes."

"Can I help?"

"I can do it myself!" Erin said hotly.

"I didn't mean it that way," I said, stung.

Erin sighed. "Sorry. Here, you can hold these for me," she said, handing me the stack of flyers she'd been holding under her right armpit against her body.

While I held the flyers, Erin used pushpins to put up a poster, pulled a flyer off the stack I was holding, pinned it up, then reached for another.

"Big crowd today," I said.

"It's summer," Erin said. "They're mostly tourists who think they know more about country music than we do."

"Lovely."

"Yeah," Erin said with a grimace as she put up a small color poster advertising the Shelby Avenue Baptist Church, one of Daddy's competitors.

"You interested in goin' to the Tim McGraw concert?" I asked, nodding at a poster near the top of the bulletin board.

"I'm over him," Erin said, posting a lost dog notice. "He just looks too skinny and hungry all the time. Makes me uncomfortable."

I chuckled. "How about The Band Perry concert next month?"

"That I'll do."

"I'll see if I can get us some tickets."

"You leave room for your daddy's church!"

Surprised, Erin and I turned to see Mama, wearing a powder blue suit and carrying big color posters advertising the Nashborough Evangelical Baptist Church, rushing toward us.

"Mama! What are you doin' here?" I asked, not really wanting an answer.

"Oh, I have been just everywhere!" she exclaimed. "Your Grandpa Tom has a doctor's appointment, and while he's there, I'm dashin' from hill to holler puttin' up the new church posters," she said, handing one to Erin.

Erin dutifully began to pin it up smack dab in the middle of the bulletin board, beneath The Band Perry poster and beside the Nashville Public Library's announcement of its annual Courtyard Concert Series.

"I've already been up and down Broadway," Mama rushed on, "and I've still got to make a start on the Arts District before I pick up your grandpa. Then I've got to scoot home to finish vacuumin' and icin' the cake for this afternoon's meetin' of the Buildin' and Grounds Committee. Then I've got supper to cook. Your daddy is bringin' home Carter and Faith Deerfield to discuss youth outreach strategies, and those two can *eat*. Tomorrow, me and Lurlene Newsome are gonna make some door-to-door visits in East Hill. Then I've got a meetin' of the Women's Ministry Committee, and that's gonna be hard because someone conspicuous in her absence from that meetin' will be Janice Thompson. She and her entire family have defected to the Marshall Street Baptist Church. That's right, the Thompsons! Butter wouldn't melt in their mouths—smilin' at your daddy and congratulatin' him on his sermon one Sunday and then runnin' off to a new church the next. After all your daddy and his church have done for those folks, that kind of betrayal just makes me *ill*. I'd tell you what I think of such traitors if I..." she snapped away from her own train of thought. "*Erin Jennifer Poser*, what in the name of all that's holy is *that?*"

Mama was pointing an outraged finger at a cheerful poster advertising the Visionary Heart Metaphysical Center, which sold books, music, crystals, candles, and magic supplies and offered psychic and Reiki classes.

Before Erin could say anything, Mama shoved the church posters into my arms on top of the other flyers I was holding, reached out with both hands, ripped the metaphysical poster off the bulletin board, and began tearing it into shreds.

"Mama, stop!" I cried. "You can't do that."

"I can, and I am!" she snapped. "I won't have perversion and paganism advertised on a *community* bulletin board right beside my church. I've never been so ashamed of you, Erin Poser. By puttin' this heathen poster up, you are betrayin' your daddy, your church, and God!"

"I am not!" Erin said, looking stricken. "Metaphysics can bring people to God just as surely as Daddy's church does."

I thought Mama's head would explode, it got so purple. "Don't you *dare* compare devil worship to your daddy's church!" she bellowed.

"Mama, I understand why you're so upset," Erin said desperately. "But I didn't put this poster up. Jimmy Holt, the assistant manager, did. I've...been takin' them down, too." She refused to meet my eyes.

Mama composed herself. "I should have known better than to think you'd allow this...this *evil*. You're a good girl, Erin, and a good Christian. But you gotta work harder at it."

Erin ducked her head. Her shoulders slumped. She was mute.

"Remember how God saved Mary?" Mama continued. "I wish you'd apply yourself like your sister does." It was my turn to cringe in response to Mama's backhanded compliments. "Erin, honey, what *are* you wearin'? You look destitute with that makeup and those dark clothes...and that top reveals much more than any right-thinkin' girl ought to reveal. I do wish you'd be more like your sister and wear clothes and makeup that are more flatterin'. How on earth are you gonna get a man lookin' like that? Tomorrow you're gonna show me what you're wearin' before you head off to work. Be sure and set these flyers out on the top shelf," she said, shoving a couple of dozen flyers into Erin's left hand, "and don't be late for supper."

She hurried out of The General Store to continue her rounds.

The minute the glass door closed behind her, Erin dumped the flyers in a nearby trash can, pulled down the church poster, and shoved it in the trash can, too.

"You mustn't regard the things Mama says, Erin," I said gently. "She doesn't realize—"

"I don't want to hear it!" Erin said, her face pinched. "I'm sick to death of everyone tellin' me Mama doesn't mean what she says, because she *does* and y'all know it! I've got a lot of work to do, Mary. I'm just too busy to have lunch with my *perfect* sister."

She stalked off toward the back of the store, so angry she could be shooting sparks off of her body.

The lump in my throat hurt worse than strep. My hands shook a little as I pulled the church poster out of the trash, pinned it back on the bulletin board, rescued the flyers, and set them back on the top shelf next to flyers for a new daycare center. Then I searched through the wreckage until I found the scrap of the metaphysical poster that had the contact information on it.

I called the Visionary Heart Metaphysical Center and told them they needed to bring a replacement poster to The General

Store. Then I left. When I got back to work, I knew the burger, shake, and fries I'd had for my solitary lunch had been a huge mistake. They sat like a boulder in my belly, a constant reminder of Erin's unhappiness and Mama's talent for making it worse.

I went back to reviewing the most recent field reports and scheduled renovation work for two houses and installations at three others.

"Hey, Mary, you ever work with Floyd Wilkins?" George asked me from his desk beside mine.

"A couple of times," I said.

"Reliable?"

"If you check in on him every hour or two, sure. Why? You havin' problems with him?"

George sighed heavily, his stout body sagging in his office chair. "He's two days late deliverin' a kitchen renovation, and he's makin' all kinds of excuses."

"I've been there, George. Here's what you do. You drive yourself out to that house. Have a clipboard, an official lookin' form on it, and a pen. You walk through that kitchen and pretend to inspect every square inch of it, makin' notes and check marks on that form as you go. That'll make Floyd sweat. Add some head-shakin' and tskin', and he'll get real anxious. Then walk up to him, look him straight in the eye, and say, 'Floyd Wilkins, accordin' to our contract, I start deductin' two hundred dollars a day from your fee for every day after the second day you're late completin' a project. I'll be startin' those deductions tomorrow.' Then you leave. You don't listen to his excuses. You don't give in to his pleas. You walk out of that house, get in your car, and you drive off. He'll have that kitchen finished for you by the end of the day tomorrow."

George grinned at me, stood up, and pulled on his jacket. He grabbed a clipboard, an official looking piece of paper, and a pen.

"I'll be back," he said as he sauntered out the door.

I got back to work. I scheduled interviews with two new clients, reworked a project budget and got Tammy's approval, and then checked in with Bobby Vance, a much more reliable contractor working on a bathroom installation.

My phone vibrated. I had a text. I took a quick look. Simha!

> Simha: An opportunity has come up that is bringing me back to the States, and I'd like to see you. I have scheduled a series of meetings in LA the third week of next month. I've booked my flight so I can fly into Nashville first. If it suits you, I'd like to have dinner with you. I'll stay in Nashville overnight and then fly to LA the next day. Will that work for you?

What? *What?* He's flying to Nashville to see *me?* Seriously? Why would he do that? I thought we were just being pen pals! Oh lordy, what should I do? Say no? But why should I say no? He's a nice guy. We've found lots of things to talk about these last three months. But he's coming to Nashville to see *me!* What does he want from me? He said he was planning to spend the night in town. Did he expect to spend the night with *me?* Oh lordy!

My phone vibrated in my hand. Simha had sent a follow-up text.

> Simha: I forgot to ask—Can you recommend a nice restaurant and a good, reasonably priced hotel nearby? I can make reservations from here.

Relief washed over me. Thank God. He hadn't assumed I'd share my bed with him. He was flying into Nashville to say hey, have some good food, and talk in person before flying off to Los

Angeles. Oh lordy, that was so much better!

> Mary: This is so exciting! I'm looking forward to talking with you in person for a change. Let me take care of the restaurant reservation. One of my favorite places is Kendrick's. It's nice, not too fancy, not too pricey, and it's got great food. Best of all for you, it's within walking distance of three hotels on Music City Circle in a neighborhood called Opryland. Take your pick. See you next month!

I couldn't stop smiling.

"What's up?" Hannah asked under her breath.

"Simha's comin' to visit."

She grinned at me. "From those pictures of him you showed me, I'd be smilin' too!"

George walked back in about an hour before quitting time.

"How'd it go?" I asked.

He grinned and high-fived me on the way back to his desk. My smile got bigger.

I knew I was more excited about Simha coming to visit me than I should be. We were pen pals. We were only going to have dinner together. He'd be flying to Los Angeles the next morning. It's just that I couldn't stop remembering his mesmerizing brown eyes, his lean muscular body so warm against mine, and his archer's-bow mouth that had been so hot and urgent on mine. I couldn't stop thinking about the fact that he was going out of his way to fly into Nashville just to see me. No man had ever done anything so flattering.

I was still grinning like a fool after work when I walked into Terpsichore, a dance studio where Chloe, Alice, and I take a contemporary dance class every Thursday. I love dancing, and I never would have known it if it wasn't for Chloe. Three years ago, she dragged me kicking and screaming to her dance class. I was hooked after two minutes. We've been going to class together ever since.

We were in the small locker room changing into our leggings and tees, and I couldn't help but notice that Chloe was nudging Alice and nodding at me. Alice sighed and turned to me as she pulled purple leggings up to her waist.

"Why are you such a box of budgies, Mary?"

I'd heard a lot of Kiwi slang in the little more than a year I'd known Alice, but that one had me stumped.

"Huh?"

"She means why are you smilin' like the cat that ate the cream?" Chloe said impatiently.

"I'm not!"

"Hogwash," Chloe stated. "Somethin's up. Spill."

I couldn't see any way of protecting myself on this one. "I just found out that Simha is flyin' into Nashville next month to have dinner with me on his way to LA."

"Choice!" Alice said, wide-eyed astonished.

"So he's finally makin' his move," Chloe said.

"He's not doin' anythin' except havin' dinner with me," I said hotly.

"Bugger me, that's some move," Alice said.

"It's not a move! It's dinner!"

"Flyin' thousands of miles to have dinner is a move, Mary, whether you want to think so or not," Chloe said. "All I can say is be careful."

"What? Why?"

"Long-distance relationships never work, bro," Alice said.

"We aren't in a relationship. We're just bein' friendly!"

"It's not just the long distance," Chloe said. "Simha's a director, and that usually has some egomania attached to it, at least from *my* experience. He probably figures with this big show of flyin' in just to see you that you'll be putty in his hands."

"He doesn't, and I won't," I said firmly.

"I've met a lot of blokes in my travels," Alice said, "and I've gotta say I'm with Chloe on this one. Too many blokes assume you'll shag them if they buy you a drink or two. Imagine what assumptions Simha must be making flying into Nashville to take you to dinner."

Chloe's dark almond-shaped eyes gleamed with wicked glee. "Just imagine what your Mama would say if she found out you're seein' an Indian filmmaker with no other plans on his mind than knockin' boots with you."

"Oh lordy."

"Forget her mum," Alice said with a grin. "What about her dad? Do Baptist ministers have shotguns?"

"That's enough, both of you," I said, slamming my locker door shut. "We're gonna be late to class. Come on."

Chloe looked at Alice in her purple leggings and yellow tee. "Are you really going to wear that?"

"I don't mind looking like a dag."

"What's a dag?" Chloe had to ask.

"Well, officially, it's the shit that dangles from a sheep's tail, but we don't think of it that way."

Chloe was speechless. Alice cheerfully led us into the dance class.

I wait with silent passion for one gesture,
one glance from you.

❧ Rumi

Chapter Fifteen

Charlie must have felt my excitement because he'd been practically tap dancing all through his morning walk. I headed back into my apartment, wanting to do a bit of tap dancing myself.

Simha was flying into town today. I would see him tonight, look into his warm brown eyes, maybe feel that sizzling laser beam start up between us again. I'd hear his sexy voice as we talked about anything and everything under the sun. I'd imagined our conversation a million times in the last month. In my imaginings, I was always sophisticated, clever, witty. I made him smile his heart-melting smile and laugh his delicious low laugh.

Was he excited about seeing me tonight? Had he imagined our conversation, too? Or was he busy with thoughts of his Los Angeles meetings? Was tonight really what he'd said it was—just a casual stopover on his way to the West Coast?

I hoped not. I hoped he was as excited as I was...and that worried me. A lot. I shouldn't be so excited about one dinner with a friendly correspondent, and neither should he. I shouldn't be worrying about whether or not I'd chosen the right dress for our dinner. Was it too conservative? Too revealing? What message did it convey? I needed it to say, "Hi, friend. Good to see you. Let's chat awhile and then say good night. We'll have a nice, friendly, safe time." That was a lot to ask of a sheer black sleeveless V-neck gown with a full skirt that wafted around my knees.

I stood in front of my closet, eyeing the dress critically, when my cell phone vibrated on my bed. Thinking it was Chloe sending another text teasing me about my "date" with Simha, I sighed and picked up my phone. *Simha* had sent me a text!

Simha: Flight attendants' union has just ordered a strike. Very chaotic here. My flight to the States could be canceled.

He wasn't coming? The depth of my disappointment shocked me. I hadn't realized until this moment how much I was looking forward to seeing him again. I'd thought I was just excited. This was something more, something stronger, something richer.

This was disastrous. I couldn't have *feelings* for Simha! Long-distance relationships never worked. I took a breath and sent a prayer of thanks to the flight attendants' union. When all was said and done, it was a very good thing Simha wouldn't be able to have dinner with me tonight. The more impersonal we kept our... well...relationship, the better.

Mary: Sorry to hear that. Everything happens for a reason. Avoid the chaos.

I tossed the phone back onto my bed and started getting dressed for work, but I couldn't shake the awareness that I was feeling down. This was so not good. I picked up my phone again and sent texts to Chloe and Alice telling them Simha had to cancel and asking them if they wanted to have dinner at Kendrick's with me tonight and maybe go to a movie after.

I got two quick texts back, both of them saying yes, and I felt a bit better. I still had something to look forward to tonight, just nothing that required a smoldering black dress.

I went to work, and I made myself focus on work, not on Simha and definitely not on disappointment. About mid-morning I called Kendrick's and turned my reservation from a table for two into a table for three. During my lunch hour, I checked out what movies were playing in town, found a comedy not targeted at fourteen-year-old boys, ran it by Chloe and Alice, and had something more to look forward to. That afternoon, I made serious inroads on the stack of files on my desk. Around four o'clock, my phone vibrated with a new text. If this was Chloe or Alice canceling on me, I was going to be really peeved.

Simha: Plane just landed. On way to hotel. Look forward to seeing you at 7:00 p.m.

What? He was here? In town? How? What about the strike? Hadn't his flight been canceled?

It took me a minute to realize that I was beaming—*beaming*—all over. Simha was here! In Nashville! He wanted to see me, expected to see me, tonight.

I was giddy with happiness for about thirty seconds, and then it hit me that I was giddy with happiness and shouldn't be. No, no, no, no, no! I could be pleased that he was in town. I could look forward to seeing him again. But, oh lordy, I sure as heck couldn't be *joyful* at the prospect.

But I was, and that rattled me to my bones.

It took a couple of minutes of being alternately elated and scared to death to remember Chloe and Alice. Oh no! I'd rearranged my evening. I'd made plans with my friends, plans they were looking forward to. I was going to have to disappoint them. I was going to have to cancel on them for a *man*, and that was a big no-no in the Girlfriends Code of Honor Handbook. But my feelings about seeing Simha tonight were too strong even for guilt. First, I answered his text:

Mary: Ditto. See you then.

Then I girded my loins and called Chloe. She answered, and I didn't give her a chance to say more than hello.

"I'm so sorry, Chloe, I'm so incredibly sorry, but I have to cancel on you tonight. Simha's in town. I don't know how he got here, but he's here, and he's expectin' us to have dinner like we planned, and I just don't have the heart to tell him I rearranged my evenin' because I thought he wasn't comin', and I feel just *awful* cancelin' on you at the last minute like this, especially when I'm the one who invited you and Alice to dinner and a movie, but he's flown all this way to have dinner with me, and I just wouldn't feel right turnin' him down."

I waited, panting, for her reply. I could feel Chloe's resentment scorching the air. Chloe hates being made second best.

"It's fine," she said. "Of course you should have dinner with Simha tonight."

I cringed. The word *fine* is something Chloe can say with a sweet smile and a dulcet tone that still rips a hole through your chest from the lance of her disappointment.

"Don't you give me a thought," Chloe continued. "I'll just make myself a grilled cheese sandwich and watch somethin' on TV."

I apologized for another five minutes, and she continued to be sweet as pie, so I gave up and hung up.

I took a couple of deep breaths, called Alice, and gave her the same apologies and explanations I'd given Chloe.

"Don't be a dag," she said cheerfully. "I'm not pissed off. Of course you should have dinner with Simha. You're probably due for a good shagging. I'm stoked you've got a date."

"It's not a date," I replied too defensively. I could imagine what she meant by "shagging" but wasn't game to ask what it meant.

"Get off the grass," Alice scoffed. "Good on ya, bro, for chasing after a flash bloke like Simha. If you do shag him, I want details tomorrow." I knew then what shagging meant to a New Zealander. Oh lordy.

"I am *not* chasing after him! And if shagging means what I think it means, Alice Doyle, you should be ashamed of yourself. I'm not that kinda girl!"

"I know, I know," she said soothingly. "You're a good Southern girl...who's all lathered up over an Indian guy with a *hot* body!"

I sank low in my chair, blushing all over. "Oh, shut up," I muttered.

I had to hold the phone away from my ear because Alice was laughing so hard. "Mary and Simha, sitting in a tree K-I-S-S-I-N—"

I hung up on her and glared at my phone for a while. But was Alice right? Was this a date? Worse, was I chasing after Simha? I hoped not. Oh lordy, I couldn't be, because it just didn't make any sense. Simha Das wasn't anyone I could imagine as a boyfriend, let alone a husband. He was a well-to-do international filmmaker, and I was a financially-strapped Nashville social worker.

And I didn't love Simha! We were just pen pals. Pen pals who were having a nice, friendly supper tonight. There would be no shagging! There wouldn't even be any kissing...although—No! No kissing! Just some pleasant conversation and that was it. End of story.

I found it really, really hard to focus on work for the next hour.

I got home around five-thirty, shoved sneakers on my feet,

My bones melted. It was nearly impossible taking that first step toward him. But the slight sting of the charm against my heel in my shoe pulled me back into my body and into reality. *Thank you, Aunt Sara.* I could breathe again. I walked toward Simha, and he stood up, his smile lighting his dark eyes.

"I'm so sorry I'm late!" I said when I was within five feet of him. "Traffic was worse than I expected."

"It's not a problem," he said in his sexy voice. Then he took my hands in his, and I felt their warmth streak through me. "It's so good to see you again." He kissed me on both cheeks.

It felt as if his soft lips had branded my cheeks.

"You're more beautiful than I had remembered," he said, "and I didn't think that was possible. That dress is lovely on you."

I blushed with pleasure. "Thank you," I said. I sat down, and he sat down in the dark red leather chair opposite me.

I was so happy. I just sat there smiling at the guy. He smiled at me. I blinked. Conversation. We were supposed to be here to talk in person. Anxiety returned. What do you say to a man you haven't seen in four months?

"So how did you manage to get to Nashville when all of the flights were canceled?"

"They weren't," he said, looking confused. "I said my flight could be canceled, not that it was."

"Okay," I said. Had I misread his text, or had he not been clear? I could feel tendrils of confusion and frustration curling through me. "But why didn't you text me and tell me your flight wasn't canceled, that you could make it after all?"

"Because my plans hadn't changed. I was only alerting you that they *could* change. I didn't think it necessary to text you about a nonevent."

I made myself smile, but I was a little ticked off. A text between "I may not make it" and "Here I am" would have been a huge help to my day. At the same time, why was I letting an irritation upset me? The big picture was that this man had flown thousands of miles to see me, and he deserved my courtesy. He was a guest on my home turf, and it was my job to make him comfortable.

"That's fine," I said.

"We seem to have had some miscommunication," Simha said with an apologetic smile. "I'm sorry if I caused you any confusion or difficulty."

"I'm good. Really. When I thought you weren't goin' to make it into town today, I made plans with Chloe and Alice tonight, but I canceled them to be with you after I got your last text, even though that made Chloe mad and disappointed Alice. I chose to do what I wanted...which is have dinner with you, in case you didn't figure that out."

He flushed. Good.

"I'm sorry it's taken me so long to return to Nashville to see you," Simha said apologetically.

"So you made a girl wait four months for a second date. But what's the rush anyway?" I smiled. I was trying to be clever, but I had just confirmed to us both that this was a date. Darn it.

"I *am* sorry, and I'm very very glad you wanted to have dinner with me tonight."

We smiled at each other and kind of got lost in that smile for a minute.

"I hope you like this place," I said hurriedly. "It's one of my favorite restaurants. I recommend the prime rib. It's amazin'."

"That sounds wonderful, but perhaps I should have mentioned that I don't eat beef. It's a Hindu thing."

"Well, they have chicken, fish, pork, and lamb here, and it's all great, too."

"I'm afraid they're not on the Hindu menu, either. We're

way with this direction of conversation.

"So why'd you change?"

"I guess I just grew up. Life's too short to sit at home feeling sorry for yourself."

Our waitress, a fifty-something short black woman in the Kendrick's uniform—black slacks and shirt, white satin tie—came up and took our orders. Thank God for that. I retrieved my arms from their hiding place to pick up my menu, and Simha deliberately didn't draw any further attention to them. Thank God for that, too. Well, really, thank you, Simha.

I went with the lamb because I remembered something about Hindus considering cows to be holy, and I just wouldn't feel right eating beef in front of Simha. He went with a bunch of appetizers and sides—salad, bread, rice pilaf, vegetables, that sort of thing. I was relieved. He wouldn't starve on my behalf.

"What I have found fascinating," Simha said when the waitress left, "are the things you've told me about your job. I would think working with people who have been physically maimed, people who are struggling with illnesses, and those who have been afflicted with some sort of dementia would make you sad for their loss. But you seem energized more than depressed when you speak of your work."

"I am," I said with a smile. "Most of my clients are incredibly upliftin'. They show me daily the strength of the human spirit in their courage, in their love for their families, in their sheer ornery determination to live their lives to the fullest.

, "I watch you, listen to you, and I see the feminine power of the goddess Shakti, who is equally creator, protector, and destroyer in the Hindu religion," Simha said warmly, "the one who keeps the wheel of life continually turning."

"Simha, I'm no goddess, and I have never considered myself powerful."

"Think of the plane flight I just took to have dinner with you—that's your power."

I had to catch my breath. "Okay, here's to a little bit of Shakti power in my life," I said, raising my wine glass in toast. "Guess who'll be Googlin' Hindu goddesses right soon?"

Our waitress, Rosalie, brought our salad and rolls, and we took a minute to get organized and start eating.

"You've been writin' me about your movie *Passion*," I said after a bite of salad, "and it sounds like you're wrappin' it up. So what movie are you goin' to make next?"

"That depends," Simha said, buttering half of his roll. "An independent filmmaker has to have six or seven projects in various stages of development at any given time because you never know which project is going to catch fire and secure financing. Right now, in addition to editing *Passion*, I'm also working on projects ranging from *Cinderella* to a contemporary Bollywood version of Jane Austen's *Persuasion* and a script we're trying to option that will break me out of the Bollywood box."

"So you're busy."

He nodded. "Very."

"What do you want to achieve in your career? A shelf full of Oscars?"

"Not really," Simha said, taking a sip of wine. "I made a few Indian-style films when I was starting out, and I got pigeonholed as the guy who makes Indian-style films. The money was coming to that box, and that was a problem because I hate being put in a box."

"You want to be more than a one-trick pony?" I was trying to be clever again. Did I just insult him? I had to relax. More wine. I reached for the bottle to top up.

"You could say that." He smiled. "There are so many different films I want to make, so many different stories I want to tell, such a wide variety of ways I want to reach the hearts and minds of my audience. So to break out of that box, I began by turning myself into the guy who makes Indian films for a Western audience."

"I'm fascinated by all of this stuff. I think it's admirable that you're puttin' yourself out there, explorin' new territory, takin' risks with your career and your heart."

While the waitress set our entrées on the table, I thought about all of the people in my life who were so completely different from Simha. They were playing it safe, doing the accepted things, staying on the same straight and narrow path that their parents and their parents before them had followed. I realized that I was just like them, and maybe, just maybe, I didn't want to be.

We ate our dinners and talked about boxes, movies, and favorite actors (he was old school—Brando, Peter O'Toole, and an Indian actress called Nargis). He told me hilarious stories about the week he'd been snowed-in in a small town in Germany that he'd been trying to drive through on his way to Frankfurt (he didn't speak any German), and I told him funny stories about all of the stray animals I'd rescued as a child—from feral kittens to raccoons and a baby owl with a broken wing—and my desperate attempts to hide them from my parents. The meal was fabulous, so we talked about food we loved, comfort food we had to have (he was a chocolate guy), and disastrous family holiday dinners we'd each survived by the skin of our teeth.

"It's so funny," Simha said with a smile after spooning the last of the chocolate mousse he'd ordered for desert into his mouth. "Before I came to Nashville, the only country singer I knew anything about was Dolly Parton, and that's only because of the films she's been in."

"Well, now you need to learn about the likes of Kenny Chesney, Tim McGraw, and Miranda Lambert. It'll be as awesome an experience for your ears as the mousse is for your mouth." That sentence didn't sound so provocative in my head.

Simha laughed.

Rosalie, who'd been real attentive all night, appeared again at our table. "Y'all want something else to drink?" she asked.

Simha looked at me. "Prichard's?"

I shook my head. I looked around the room. "No sign of Chloe. I'll just have a latte."

Simha looked at Rosalie. "Could I have a long black?"

"Us shorter staff not to your likin' sir?" our short African-American waitress replied with cool reproach.

"What?" Simha asked in confusion.

I had to work to find my voice. "What is it exactly you're askin' for?"

"A long black. You know, a double espresso with a little extra hot water."

Rosalie and I looked at each other and cracked up.

"What did you think I..." Simha asked.

"We weren't sure whether you were just declarin' your taste in women or..."

His eyes widened with sudden understanding. "Oh dear!"

"I'll be right back," Rosalie said with a grin, heading off.

Simha and I looked at each other and couldn't stop laughing until Rosalie returned with our coffee orders.

We sipped our drinks, giggling occasionally, and talked about some Southern words and phrases that confused Simha, like "caddywompus," "mind your P's and Q's," and "fit to be tied."

Rosalie gave Simha the check, and he gave her his credit card. "It's been a wonderful evening," he said to me. "I hate for it to end."

"I was thinkin'," I said a little shyly, "that it's real hot and muggy tonight. I could drive you back to your hotel and save you the walk if you'd like."

"That's brilliant," he said. "As it happens, I got you a small gift, but I forgot to bring it in my admittedly manic effort to get to the restaurant on time. If you give me a ride, I can get you your present."

"Perfect," I said, blushing a little. He'd gotten me something? I was wild to find out what it was. I was pretty certain it wouldn't be anything like the framed Nashbros' flyer Jason, my ex, had given me as a present to woo my heart.

Simha stood up and held out his hand to me, the moonstone of his ring glowing in the candlelight. "Shall we?"

It caught my breath seeing Simha's outstretched hand reaching toward me with that distinctive ring of his. I felt immediately lightheaded as I was transported in a flash to the only memory I had of my accident. That hand. That ring. I fought through the fog and commanded my legs to stand and, a little hesitantly, put my hand in his. My whole body sighed. "Let's go," I said.

When I am with you, we stay up all night.
When you're not here, I can't go to sleep.
Praise God for those two insomnias
and the difference between them.

Rumi

Chapter Seventeen

The butterfly charm was digging into my heel as Simha and I walked out to Kendrick's parking lot. I tried not to limp and, when that failed, I tried to hide my limp from Simha as I silently cursed Aunt Sara with every other step.

"I'm just over here," I said, pointing to our left. The charm dug in more and more as we walked across the black asphalt, the air hot and still and covering us like a tent. I had to let go of Simha's warm hand to pull my keys out of my purse. He started toward a blue hatchback. I pushed the unlock button on my car fob, and The Mule's lights flashed at us. "Over here," I said, heading toward the Suburban.

"That's your car?" Simha said in surprise.

"For now. This is The Mule. She's the farm workhorse. My folks loaned her to me until I get my insurance check and can replace my car which was...well, totaled."

We got in the Suburban, and I immediately felt the difference. The intimacy of my Mazda was gone. It felt like Simha was seated about a mile away.

"I'm glad you weren't totaled in that accident as well," he said as he fastened his seatbelt.

"I just had some bruising, mostly from the seatbelt."

"So how did you get out of a car that was in a river?"

I glanced at the moonstone on his hand. "That's where bizarre finds a whole new level."

"What am I missing?"

I smiled. "Never mind." I swung The Mule out of the parking space, and the box lid in back slid across the seat and caught Simha's attention.

He glanced at it, then stared a moment, then looked back at me. "That's a lot of cards."

I shrugged. "I like to give get well cards to my clients. It's more personal than an e-mail or a phone call. People don't write to each other enough anymore." I opened the glove box in front of him. It was bursting with cards. "I'm a bit behind gettin' these delivered."

"Wouldn't mailing them be easier?"

"Sure. But this is nicer, more personal, don't you think?"

He pulled some of the cards out of the glove box and sifted through them.

"Besides, deliverin' 'em by hand gives me a chance to eyeball my clients' homes and make sure everythin's okay."

Simha suddenly smiled and everything got brighter. "Let's get these delivered."

I stared at him. "Now? Seriously?"

"Absolutely. The night is still young, and we need to get these cards to the people who need them." His brown eyes held mine for a moment.

I took a breath. "You're a surprise a minute, Mr. Simha Das."

His grin crinkled his eyes, and I couldn't help grinning, too. I threw The Mule into Drive, and we headed off.

Unlike the brilliant lights of downtown and Broadway, we drove through darkened residential streets with pale streetlights and house lights, the trees along sidewalks and in yards creating

an image of silence and peace. But we had the windows rolled down, so we could hear dogs barking now and then as they defended their territories or worried about being left alone. Occasionally, there'd be the loud open-throttle rumble of a motorcycle or a car with a high testosterone muffler proclaiming to the world the macho prowess of the driver. Often we could hear TV programs and music leaking out of open apartment and house windows.

At apartment buildings, Simha and I would deliver the cards right into the hands of my client or a family member. At houses, we'd put them in the mailbox. As I drove, we talked, and as we talked, The Mule started feeling a lot smaller, and Simha somehow got a lot closer to me, even though he never moved from his seat.

We pulled up in front of a small dilapidated house in the low-income Edgehill Village neighborhood, and Simha put a card in the mailbox. "Wait a minute," I said, unfastening my seatbelt and getting out of The Mule. I walked up onto the sidewalk and stared at the house. Five sagging wooden steps led up to a small front porch. The aging screen door was covered with a picture of Jesus' face. I looked for any sign of an air conditioner, walked up the driveway to look at the back of the house, then walked back to The Mule bristling mad.

"Excuse me a minute," I said to Simha as I pulled my cell phone out of my purse.

"Anything wrong?" he asked.

"Plenty," I said grimly. I called the office phone of Tiffany, one of my coworkers, listened impatiently to her bored voicemail message, then finally came the beep. "Tiffany, this is Mary. I'm in front of Coralee Wayne's house. I'm lookin' at five dangerous front steps that she can't get up, and I'm not seein' an air conditioner anywhere. You signed off on a house that clearly you have never seen in your life. Otherwise, you would not have said it is in acceptable condition for a frail elderly woman with heart failure. First thing in the morning, you find our client proper housing or I go to Tammy about this!"

I ended the call and glared at my phone.

"Not powerful, eh?" Simha said innocently.

"I hate it when people lie about doin' their job, and an innocent, vulnerable person suffers because of it," I said, still mad as a hornet. "Tiffany's been at the agency for a year, and she's about as useful as a pogo stick in quicksand."

"Who's Tammy?"

"Our boss."

"Sounds like you should talk to her."

I sighed gustily. "Yeah. I just hate bein' the cause of anyone's trouble."

"Your clients are more important."

Startled, I looked up at Simha and smiled. "Yeah, they are."

We delivered the last of the cards—it felt so good not having them weigh on me anymore!—and I turned The Mule back toward Opryland.

"Are you still happy living in Nashville since your accident?" Simha suddenly asked.

No one had asked me that before. I took a moment to think about it. "It's comfortable. It's safe. That means a lot after my accident."

"Do you like to travel?"

I bit my lower lip. "I've gotta confess that I've never been out of Tennessee."

"Would you like to travel? Explore the world?"

"Yeah, but I've never thought about actually goin' out into the world to see them for myself. I'm a small-town girl. I like hearth and home."

I glanced across at Simha and saw he was frowning. Oh lordy,

I'd put my foot in it somehow. What had I said that concerned him? "My friend Caroline went to India on sort of a photo safari. She's a professional travel photographer, and she had an assignment from some big magazine or another, I can't remember which. Then she got married, and now she's expectin' a baby, so she works closer to home nowadays."

"Balancing a career and family is a challenge," he said, but his attention was clearly distracted. Perhaps he was still contemplating my lack of worldliness?

"I'll have you back at your hotel in just a few minutes."

"Before you do, I'd like to ask a favor."

"Sure. Shoot."

"I'd like to see the bridge where you had your accident."

I stiffened. "It's just a bridge."

"Please. Just a glance."

I sighed heavily then turned the car around and headed downtown. I turned on the radio and The Dixie Chicks were gleefully plotting the demise of a drunken wife-beater named Earl.

"That's...quite a song," Simha said with a smile.

"There's a reason Southern women are called 'steel magnolias.' It must have somethin' to do with that Shakti power you were talkin' about."

"I see."

We drove through the brilliant lights of Broadway, which made our first night together fully alive and almost vibrating inside The Mule. Tension was growing inside me. "How's Rob?" I asked, and Simha told me about their hope to work together on a film sometime in the next year or two.

I turned right onto First Avenue South and parked at the curb a block from the on-ramp to the Gateway Bridge. "There it is."

Simha leaned forward and stared through the windshield. He turned to me, shock on his face. "Seriously? *That's* the bridge? It's so high above the river. How on earth did you survive, let alone walk away with just some bruises?"

"Everyone has an opinion about that."

He reached over and grasped my hand. His warmth seeped into me. "Tell me what happened."

I took a shaky breath. "I was...distracted. I crashed into an oncoming semi, and it kind of flipped me up into the air and over the side of the bridge. The crash must've knocked me out for a minute, 'cause the next thing I knew, I was sinkin' into the river, and water was fillin' my car, and I couldn't get out. My seatbelt was jammed."

"My God," he said, squeezing my hand.

I looked at him, willing him to tell me what happened next, to tell me he knew he was there with me, savin' my life. But he didn't. The disappointment was like fog descending on my memories of the event. I stared through the windshield at nothing. "So there I was, completely submerged, drownin', losin' consciousness, hearin' voices in my head, and the next thing I knew, I was wakin' up in a hospital bed safe and sound."

"But...how?"

"Mama and Daddy say it was a miracle. My sister says it was dumb luck. My brother says I must have gotten my seatbelt undone and then floated up. My Aunt Sara says it was the guys who were on the bridge and saw the crash and jumped into the river to rescue me. My friends say it was the paramedics who got there just a couple of minutes after I hit the water."

"What do you think happened?"

I blinked. No one had asked me that before. "I don't know. Not for certain. What I do know I can't rightly put into words. It felt like a...a life force pulled me out my car and up out of that river." I braved a quick glance at him. "Then paramedics took me to the hospital, and I dawdled around in a coma for a day or so before I finally came back to my life again."

"A coma? Came back to my life again? Why didn't you tell me any of this?"

"I didn't want anyone to fuss. I'm fine. Back to life as usual…"

But it can't be life as usual. Not after that," Simha said quietly.

I felt exposed where I usually could duck for cover. I continued so as to appear in control of my mind that I was sure I'd lost since that accident. "Pretty much. I mean, there was nothin' else to do. The only thing that's really changed is that darned bridge. I still can't bring myself to drive across it."

"You've had a serious trauma, what some people call a near-death experience. It takes time to recover from something like that and, I guess, understand what it means to you."

I felt so much better to hear this. Everyone else just wanted to quickly find a story that suited them to deal with what happened to me, but Simha understood that, for me, understanding what really happened was going to take time. And he wasn't pressuring me to give him a story of certainty for his own peace of mind.

"Thank you for showing me your bridge, Mary." His smile grew. "Everything about it and you is so much more than I had imagined."

"My bridge? I'll be happy when my heart stops jumping out of my chest every time I see it." I could have said the same thing about Simha, but I don't think he needed to hear that.

He chuckled. "And thank you for Kendrick's, chocolate mousse, and get well cards. It's been a wonderful night," he said warmly.

"Yeah," I said with a smile.

"I hope the small present I got you in some way expresses my thanks for your friendship."

"I'd forgotten. What is it?" Friendship. Did he just say *friendship?*

He smiled. "You'll have to wait and see."

Ecstasy, not words, is the language spoken here.

❧ Rumi

Chapter Eighteen

"Thanks again for helpin' out," I said as we walked into the lobby of Simha's hotel. "I'm sure you didn't plan on runnin' around Nashville deliverin' get well cards in the middle of the night."

Simha smiled. "It's something I won't forget anytime soon. I had fun, Mary. Why are you limping?"

"I'm not," I said as we reached the elevator bank.

"Yes, you are."

"All right, I am, but it's not important."

"Did you hurt yourself?" Simha asked as the elevator doors opened.

"No."

"Then why are you limping?" Simha demanded as he pressed the button for his floor.

I sighed and looked up at the elevator ceiling as the doors swooshed closed. "I have a butterfly charm in the heel of my shoe."

Simha stared at me a moment. "Why?"

"I have no idea."

He chuckled. "But how did it get there?"

"I put it there."

"Why?"

I sighed. "Because my Aunt Sara told me to."

He stared at me a moment. Then the elevator dinged and stopped, and the doors opened. "I understand," he said, with unconvincing sincerity.

"No, you don't."

"You're right, I don't. This way," he said, taking my elbow.

The heat streaking through my body from that simple touch made me aware of something really important: I was walking toward a man's hotel room, and that man could melt my spine with just one sizzling glance. I looked down at my black dress. Vertical, I commanded within my mind. We are staying vertical tonight.

"Here we are," Simha said, stopping in front of a brown door. He swiped his card key, opened the door, and turned on the lights. I walked into his room with him as if walking into a man's hotel room was no big deal.

It was a standard hotel bedroom with a queen-size bed with charcoal and gray linens, bedside tables, charcoal drapes over the windows, a desk and chair, a wide dresser, a TV, a door to the bathroom. Sitting on the desk was a small box wrapped in silver paper with a red bow on top.

"First things first," Simha said, walking to the desk. He picked up the gift, turned, and held it out to me. "I saw this, and I just had to get it for you. I hope you like it."

I was nervous as I removed the wrapping and opened the box—what if I didn't like it? Nestled inside was a chain of small green tourmaline beads from which hung a carved circular green stone pendant. The pendant was two interlocking triangles, one pointing up, one pointing down. In the center of the two triangles was a moonstone.

"It's beautiful," I whispered. "Thank you."

Simha lifted the necklace out of the box. "May I put it on you?"

"Yes, please."

He stood behind me. I could feel every inch of him as if he was pressed against me. He slid the necklace around my neck and attached the clasp. "The symbol is known as shatkona," he said in a low voice, his lips close to my ear. "It represents the sacred union of Shiva and Shakti." He put his warm hands on my shoulders and turned me around, his dark gaze holding mine captive. "They embody the perfect unity of the changeless and the changeable, the merging of masculine and feminine duality into the divine one."

I could hear the passion in his words, feel the intensity of his gaze, and they set my heart to pounding against my breast. My head was reeling because I wasn't entirely certain why this was so important to him, and what he was trying to tell me.

I cleared my throat and tried to gather my thoughts. "Simha, as a Hindu, do you believe in God?"

"Yes, of course."

"But which one? I've seen pictures of so many different Hindu gods and goddesses."

"They are simply different aspects of a single Divine. Just like this pendant," he said, his finger brushing against my skin before he held the green shatkona up, "symbolizes the union of masculine and feminine into a single life force."

I had to take a step back so I could breathe again.

"Let's take care of that limp," he said with a smile. He took my hands, led me to the side of the bed so that my calves were against the silky bed cover, and gently pushed. My legs seemed too eager to buckle to have me sit on the bed before him. Perfect good looks could leave you cold, but this kind of sexy charisma went straight to your knees. The down feathers of the bedcovers received me with a soft and welcoming touch. His boldness was no surprise. I'm sure he was experienced in having women in his hotel room. The look of experience suited him, especially because somewhere deep in those eyes, there lurked a dangerous invitation to play.

I was just getting over the shock of sitting on his hotel bed when my shock doubled. He knelt on the floor in front of me. He pulled off my right shoe, found the charm, held it up, looked at it a moment, and then at me quizzically.

"I honestly don't know why I've been walking around with a butterfly charm in my shoe."

"Hm," he said. He set the charm on the bed beside me then raised my foot up. I had to lean back on my elbows. "It's made a mark on your heel."

He leaned forward and gently kissed my heel!

"Is that better?" he inquired.

I looked at him and laughed.

"What?" he said with an amused smile.

"I just figured out why I had a charm in my shoe."

"Good. Why?"

"Because my Aunt Sara is a schemin' matchmaker."

"I still don't understand." He pressed his lips to the sole of my foot.

"That's okay. No one really understands my Aunt Sara."

I felt so self-conscious. If I'd known Aunt Sara's plan, I would have put the charm somewhere more enticing. But as Simha's warm mouth caressed the top of my foot and finished off with little kisses on my toes, I learned for the first time in my life just how erotic a foot can be. I was feeling hot all over.

I hadn't known until this moment that Simha wanted me. He'd been such a gentleman before this. Perhaps he hadn't known it, either. He stood and then lay down on the bed beside me.

I hadn't known until this moment how very much I wanted him. I felt so conflicted. Holding up the charm around my neck, I asked, "So what made you think to get me this?"

He took the charm in his hand, and his expression seemed to harden. "May I ask you something?" he said.

"Shoot."

A smile teased his sensual lips. "What do you want in your life in the next twelve months? Or maybe the next two years? Even the next five years?"

I considered his beautiful, serious face for a moment. "Before my car accident, I don't think I could have told you. I was just livin' day to day. When I thought about my life and my future, I usually thought about what my family and my church expected of me. But now...I know that I want love, deep love. I want a family. I can't imagine a future without children, whether I have them or adopt them. And I'd like to continue workin' in some aspect of community service that helps people live with pride and independence, because it feeds my soul."

He was silent a moment. "Would you be equally honest about me? I want to know what you think of me. This isn't a test. There is no correct answer. I'd just like you to be open and direct with me."

I had to catch my breath. My fingers were shaking against the bed. "Wow. Well...I like that you're connected to your spirituality, and I admire your adventurous nature. I like that you're ambitious with your creativity, and that you're confident about your talent and your abilities. I appreciate your intelligence, and I love your sense of humor."

"Thank you."

"You're welcome."

"Mary, I need to know... How do you feel about me?"

My heart was hammering so hard, my jaw hurt. "I don't know. I'm not ready to be that brave."

"Fair enough."

"Speakin' of fair, what do you...think of me?"

He smiled warmly. "I think you're wonderful, Mary Poser. You're compassionate, intelligent, funny, kind, dedicated, loyal. You have a large and loving heart, and you're far braver and stronger than you know."

"Okay, brave. I can do brave. Maybe. How do you feel about me?" I asked in a rush.

His dark brown eyes held mine mesmerized. "I feel many things, some of which I don't yet understand, and some which... unsettle me. That lovely night we spent together on your couch... You are a wonderful kisser, Mary Poser. When you fell asleep, I had a constant feeling that I had to pay attention to you. It was such a strong feeling. But I clearly did a lousy job because I didn't notice you dribbling on my shirt."

"Oh lordy. Thanks for the reminder."

He laughed. "Just teasing. You slept so trustingly in my arms, and I couldn't sleep because I didn't want to miss a single moment with you. I felt as if I held something precious, something as delicate as, well, a butterfly, in my arms. I'd never felt that before. It's stayed with me all these months. I want to understand why I couldn't sleep that night. I want to understand this indefinable connection between us and why it's so attractive to me. Do you know what chakras are?"

I felt wildly off-balance, and my brain was going along for the ride. "Um, no."

"They're energy centers within our bodies. They're like spinning wheels of different aspects of our life force. Let me show you."

He placed his right hand against my pubic bone, and my whole body went into shock as his eyes held my gaze prisoner. "This is your first chakra, Muladhara, your root chakra, which is red. It acts as your physical identity and the center of your survival issues, your stability. People who have not advanced beyond this chakra only pray to God to help them survive."

He moved his hand slowly up my belly, his eyes never leaving mine. He stopped two inches below my belly button. "This is your second chakra, Svadhishthana, your sacral chakra, which is orange. This is the center of your emotional identity, your family, as well as your creativity, desire, and pleasure. People who are at this level pray to God to help and protect their family."

He moved his hand slowly up to my solar plexus. "This is your third chakra, Manipura, which is yellow. It is the center of your self-esteem and sense of community. Prayers to God are for benefits and approval from within the community."

He slid his hand to the center of my chest between my breasts. I stopped breathing, but my heart pounded on the inside of my chest to reach his touch. "This," he murmured, "is your heart chakra, Anahata, the chakra of unconditional love, which is green. Crossing the bridge to the heart is a particularly difficult task because we must have clarity of intent. We must clear our attachment to the first three chakras and connect to the God within our heart if we are to manifest the love that we desire. There are more," he said,

pressing his fingertips to the base of my throat. "The fifth is here. The sixth chakra," he said, touching the middle of my forehead, "and the seventh chakra," he said, touching the top of my head. "They are all important, of course. But the greatest work comes with the first three chakras. We must learn how to clear them and prevent them from controlling our lives before we can truly benefit from the others."

"But can't I pray for the first three and follow my heart as well?"

"Of course you can."

He pressed his hand against my pubic bone again, and I had to forcibly hold back a moan. "Does fear for our survival limit us?"

He slid his hand back up to my second chakra. "Is our desperate need to please our family holding us back?" His moved his hand to my solar plexus. "Are we contorting ourselves in an effort to conform to the values of our friends and peers?" He slid his hand up to the center of my chest, and I knew, I just knew, he could feel the wild beating of my heart. "When we free ourselves from the negative constraints of the first three chakras, we can cross the bridge to our heart chakra. When we identify our heart's desire, the positive energy of our first three chakras flows to our benefit."

He slid his warm hands up to cup my face. "I have worked hard to open my heart and to listen to what it tells me. I don't know what you and I are meant to be to each other, Mary, but my heart told me I had to return to you, connect with you, learn what we should be together. Do you understand?"

"Yes," I whispered.

He kissed me, hot and soft at first, then hungry and hard. I wrapped my arms around him, my heart shuddering against his.

Simha gently slid his hand, down from my neck, under my dress strap, pulling the strap over and off my shoulder. Breathlessly, I whispered, "We shouldn't," against the will of every cell in my body.

"I know," Simha replied with a soft and silky tone. He raised his other hand to my opposite dress strap and my black dress slid from my shoulders with his guiding touch. I had no choice. Even as I worried that we were moving way too fast, Simha's passion was merging into mine, growing and spiraling out of control. Desire poured through me, drenching every cell, demanding the wildest freedom.

I pulled his silver and lavender tie free. Then I destroyed another of Simha's shirts as I ruthlessly pulled it open, sending buttons flying everywhere. I groaned as my hands could finally sweep over his smooth, hard chest and then over ribs to cling to his broad back as his hot mouth scorched my arched throat.

"Yes!" I gasped. "Oh yes!" And Simha's wildness soared. Our clothes were shredded off our bodies like flimsy tissue paper as we traded hot, wet kisses that fueled my desire until I wanted to be just as wild as Simha.

He ripped the bedspread down the bed, and then we were kissing and writhing, body against body, trying desperately to get closer, feel more. We rolled deliciously over each other until he was on top of me, his nakedness sliding over mine, all silken skin and taut sinew and hard bone. I gasped from the shock of this new...everything. Then his hot, wet tongue drove deep into me, and I arched against him, my arms clinging desperately to him as vertigo sent me spinning out of control.

He slid slowly down my body, his lips pressing kisses to my collarbone. His tongue played across my nipple, and lightning streaked through me. He sucked my nipple into his mouth, and I shuddered against him, moaning his name. He caressed and teased and sucked my other breast as I writhed against him. Then he kissed his way further down my body, nuzzling my belly and making me shiver as I learned how sensitive my hip bones are.

With a groan, he slid his hands under me and lifted me to his mouth.

What? Wait! Oh my God!

His tongue stroked and lapped my dripping lips, and I couldn't breathe! Jason was the only man I'd ever made love with before this, and he'd *never* done anything like this to me. I couldn't think. I couldn't speak. I could only *feel* this shocking, instantly addicting, intimate caress. Simha's tongue slid and swirled, laved and licked. He was pushing me to places I'd never been before, pushing me, drugging me, enthralling me, driving me through every wall, and I couldn't... I couldn't...

He suddenly sucked hard on the engorged hub of my sex, and all of the tension that had been building in my body exploded into a hot white light, and I was crying his name as I threw my pelvis up against his mouth. He sucked again, and searing ecstasy tore a wail from my throat.

I collapsed back on the bed, and Simha followed me down, murmuring, "So beautiful, so passionate" as he kissed his way gently up my body and back to my mouth. I clung to him as little aftershocks rippled through me and against his warm body.

He was kissing my jaw, my mouth, teething my earlobe, his hands cradling my head. I was fully back in my body, in this heated moment. I could feel the hard length of his own hunger between us, and all of my desire surged up tenfold.

"Mary," he groaned, "I can't wait."

"Don't wait," I said, looking deep into his eyes. "I need you now. I need you so much, Simha. Now!"

His eyes never leaving mine, he shifted position. I watched as he pulled on a condom, making it a sexual act. I groaned. He moved back over me. I could feel him pressing against me, and I gasped. Then suddenly, he drove deep inside me.

"Oh, sweet Jesus!" I moaned as he stretched and filled me, awakening nerves in my body and synapses in my brain, opening me up in ways I had never known, never even imagined.

He moved slowly at first, murmuring my name, his gaze roaming over my face as I moved naturally with the rhythm he'd set, drinking in his taut expression, the fire blazing in his dark eyes, the hunger in his voice.

I could feel his control being methodically shredded as I pulled his head down to mine and kissed him, my tongue moving in him with the rhythm of our bodies, my desire coiling between us, in us. I wrapped my legs around his hips, and we both groaned as he moved even deeper into me, driving harder now, faster, his eyes telling me secrets and truths and longings for which there were no words.

A firestorm engulfed us, driving our bodies to move at fever pitch, wrenching cries without words from our throats, overwhelming every thought, every emotion, leaving only this frantic, pounding, desperate union that was carrying me deeper and deeper into the flames until their roar was all I could hear, their scorching heat was all I could feel wrapped in Simha's arms as he lifted me higher and higher.

"*Simha!*" I screamed as his climax crashed into me, flinging me up into his burning body drenched in perspiration, his ragged cry echoing in my ears. A second climax spiraled through me, bucking me against him, leaving me clinging to him like a buoy in this sea of flames.

We held each other desperately, shuddering with aftershocks, gasping for breath.

Minutes passed. Hours. I couldn't tell. Slowly, our bodies relaxed against each other. I could feel myself fully back in my own skin again. I could feel Simha's gentle lips caressing my shoulder, my throat, my mouth. With a soft moan, I returned his kisses over and over again.

He sat up, pulling me with him as our mouths shared lingering kisses. "Come here," he murmured, pulling me on top of his crossed legs so that we sat with my breasts pressed against his chest, my belly against his stomach, our arms wrapped around each other, and I was humming with pleasure. Our kisses went on and on as his warm hands slid slowly, caressingly over my back, and my fingers stroked through his thick, curly hair as they'd longed to do from the first time I'd seen him.

I felt desire slowly curling up through my body as his mouth kissed and sucked my arched throat, and his hands stroked my thighs and my bottom. "Oh!" I said just before his mouth claimed mine in a heated, hungry kiss. "Oh my!" I said as I felt him lengthening and hardening between us. I'd never made love twice in one night. I'd never put a condom on a man before, but that was what I was helping Simha do.

I started to lie back on the bed, but he shook his head. "Wrap your arms around my neck and your legs around my hips," he commanded.

My eyes widened. I'd never made love sitting up. But I did as he told me, feeling a little scared and very excited. We were connected again chest to chest, belly to belly.

"Now then," he said with a smile, his eyes burning into me as he slid his hands under me, lifted me up a little, and then slid into me.

"Oh my God!" I gasped, shuddering in his arms. This was a more intimate connection than anything I'd ever known before. I was both completely open to him and wrapped within him. All of those chakras Simha had talked about felt joined together.

He began to move in me, against me, in subtle, sensual ways that sent shockwaves through my body.

My head fell onto his shoulder. "I don't know what to do," I whispered. "I don't know what to do."

He nudged my head up and kissed me, slowly and deliciously. "Yes, you do," he murmured, his eyes holding mine captive.

And I did. We moved in perfect unison, and the pleasure grew, the need grew, rising between us like an island volcano surging up out of the sea, hot and powerful, rumbling between us, pushing us closer together, higher. Subtlety disappeared. Craving for *more* claimed us both. Carnality reigned as he crushed me in his arms and cried out my name over and over again.

"It's too much!" I gasped. "I can't. I can't!"

"Yes...you...can," he growled.

And I could. That volcano grew taller, stronger, roaring now in an inferno of lava searing us from within. The pressure was building and building, rocking us both, driving out all thought, consuming all of the oxygen. Simha knotted his hand in my hair, his eyes burning into mine. "*Now*," he groaned, and the volcano erupted between us, claiming us, scorching us to the marrow as we shook and shuddered in each other's arms, cries and moans and heaving gasps filling the air.

Every ounce of energy drained out of me as I followed Simha down onto the bed, my breasts against his chest, legs untangling, the most profound sleep claiming us both.

I woke an hour later to the delicious sensation of Simha nibbling on my toes. I chuckled, which made him chuckle. Then he began kissing and licking his way up my legs, bypassing my saturated sex, darn him. He caressed my hip bones, nuzzled my belly, which made me chuckle again, and then he settled in to feast on my breasts. I began by purring, but soon I was moaning, my legs moving restlessly against his.

I wanted so much more, so I rolled on top of him and began sucking and nibbling at his small, erect brown nipples. Soon, he was moaning and moving restlessly against me. I worked my way down his muscular, heaving abs, and there rising before me was full proof of my seductive abilities.

"Mary!" he gasped as I began to lick and feast on him and shred every bit of his self-control, loving that I had this power, loving that his pleasure and hunger were fueling my own.

Suddenly, he lifted my head up so that I had to meet his heated gaze.

"Take me into you," he said.

I stared at him. I had never done this before, and I wanted it. I wanted it so much.

A new condom was unsheathed as I shifted onto my knees.

I didn't think about how. I just did it. I straddled his hips and lowered myself slowly onto him, feeling him sink into me inch by inch. His hands were knotted in the sheets, his head arched back, a ragged groan lasting as long as this exquisite impalement. His dark gaze burned into me. "*Take me deep inside you.*"

I was gasping for breath by the time I finally had all of him in me. I just sat there for a moment, feeling Simha in the very core of my being. Then his hands swept up my legs and my torso to cup my breasts. His thumbs rubbed across my engorged nipples. I pressed my hands over his, and I rode him, gently at first, lifting slowly up inch by inch and then dropping suddenly down, both of us arching, moaning. I tormented us both again and again until I'd stoked the need and desire and the inferno to intolerable levels...and power exploded through me.

I took him deeply, riding him mercilessly, giving no quarter. Leaning down, I sucked at his mouth, bit into his neck, and felt him buck under me, his large hands moving feverishly over my back. I stared down into his dark, hungry eyes as I rocked against him and squeezed him within me, his shudder reverberating in my body. I clasped his head and sank my tongue deep into him, stroking him as I rode him, pushing him farther, harder, tamping down my orgasm, making it wait, making us both wait, as I gorged myself on Simha. I pushed him right to the brink and then pulled back, pushed him back to the brink again and pulled back as he watched me helplessly. His hips thrust up, driving him deeper into me, making me gasp. But I smiled and shook my head. "Not yet," I said. His groan made me smile even more.

I took him until he was shuddering with every rise of my body, every fall, every breath. I rode him until I could feel him grow even harder within me. Then I shocked him by rolling us over. I wrapped my legs around his hips. A glittering smile was on my lips. "*Now,*" I ordered.

He went mad. He plunged furiously into me, ruthlessly driving through my climax as it shattered within me. He was pounding into me, building a second climax, forcing it higher, broader, and then crashing it into me, blinding me, deafening me, leaving me helpless in his arms as he pushed so deep into me it felt as if he had reached my very heart. He was demanding my desire, commanding lightning storms and tornadoes to rise within me, and all I could say was "Yes!" All I could give him was everything he demanded. All I could do was surrender to this immense soul-shattering storm, my voice rising with his, merging with his, as I called his name, and he called mine, and the hurricane slammed into us, engulfing and claiming us both.

In the house of lovers, the music never stops.
The walls are made of songs and the floor dances.

🐌 *Rumi*

Chapter Nineteen

I woke slowly at first, as if I'd been drugged. I couldn't open my eyes. I couldn't hear anything, feel anything. Slowly, I became aware that I was naked. Then suddenly I could feel everything. My body was weak, boneless. Every nerve felt exposed, like my skin had been stripped from me.

And then I remembered *everything*.

Everything I had said, every wild sound I had made, everything I had *done*.

My eyes flew open, and I saw Simha lying naked beside me, deeply asleep. I skittered backward out of the bed and landed on the carpeted floor with a soft thump. Simha didn't stir.

Oh lordy, what had I done?

I was shaking so badly that I couldn't move for a moment. The desperate urge to flee finally galvanized my muscles. I scurried silently around the room, collecting my clothes. I tugged on my panties and put on my bra. I dragged my dress over my head. It took a terrible, desperate minute to find both shoes. I slid them onto my bare feet and began creeping to the door. Slowly, cautiously, I turned the door handle and pulled the door silently open.

I was almost free, almost safe. But something compelled me to turn around. Simha was lying on his belly on the bed, still deeply asleep, his black hair tousled, a thick tendril hanging on his forehead. His lean, muscular body was completely relaxed. I darted out of the room.

There was no one in the hallway. A window at the far end showed me that dawn was beginning to spread across the city. I hurried to the elevator, pushed the call button, and cringed when a moment later the elevator dinged, and the doors opened. Had the sounds wakened anyone? Had Simha wakened?

I hurried into the elevator, pressed the ground floor button, and the close doors button. Then I flattened myself against the side of the elevator, praying that Simha didn't awaken and come looking for me. The doors closed, and the elevator began moving down through the hotel. My legs nearly gave way with relief.

Just before I reached the ground floor, I realized I was about to be seen in public, and I knew I must look a wreck. I desperately combed my fingers through my hair and straightened my dress as best I could. As the elevator doors opened, I knew anyone seeing me would be able to figure out with a single glance what I'd been doing all night.

I used my longest possible strides for my walk of shame through the hotel lobby, knowing the desk clerk and the maid vacuuming the carpet saw me. They both knew.

I pushed open one of the glass lobby doors, and I ran. I ran just as fast as I could to The Mule. I fished out the car key from my purse, scrambled into the Suburban, got my seatbelt on, put the key in the ignition to start the engine. For a moment, I just sat there, overwhelmed by the enormity of what I had done, unable to understand how I could have forsaken every principle I lived by, terrified by the something in me I had never known existed that had ruled me all night long in Simha's arms.

I peeled out of the parking lot and broke every existing speed limit as I sped home.

When I finally reached the sanctity of my own home, I ignored Charlie's desperate pleas for attention and sat on my sofa, my knees drawn up, my arms wrapped around my shins. My heart was pounding against my legs. My hands were cold. I was scared. I was as scared as I'd been crashing into the Cumberland River.

I felt completely overwhelmed by Simha, by me, by everything. I had taken off Simha's necklace and hidden it at the back of my closet. I had taken a scalding hot shower that hadn't helped. I could still smell Simha, taste Simha, and feel where he'd been inside me. I sat there on my sofa for two hours in my bathrobe, feeling completely lost.

I still couldn't understand how I could have forgotten my morals and made love to Simha last night. I *really* couldn't understand how I could have made love to him so many times and in so many ways with such abandon.

I was scared by the wanton woman I'd been last night, a woman I'd never met before. I was scared that Simha could release her within me. I was scared that I had no control over her and that I hadn't wanted to control her. I had drenched myself passionately in every moment of last night.

The woman I had unleashed last night terrified me.

What scared me most of all, though, was the realization, the admission, that Simha Das had seduced me last night. He had brushed aside every moral and internal boundary I had as if they didn't matter. I was really scared at how easily I had said yes to that.

For two hours, I'd been calling myself every despicable name, beating myself up for being someone I didn't recognize. I was drowning in confusion. I felt just like I had after my car accident—something cataclysmic had happened, and I couldn't reconcile who I was and what I wanted. I longed for someone to give me the answers to all of the questions pounding in my brain, because if I couldn't find some way to understand what I had just done, who I had just been, I was pretty sure I'd end up as mad as a March hare.

I jumped when my cell phone suddenly began ringing. It was still inside my clutch purse, which I'd tossed onto an armchair when I'd fled into my apartment. I got up and walked to it as cautiously as someone approaching a rabid dog.

I pulled it out of my purse and looked to see who was calling. I cringed when I saw it was Simha. I just stared at it as it rang and rang. I set it on the coffee table, and it rang a few more times before the call went to voicemail.

Relieved, I sat back down on the couch. I couldn't talk to Simha. I couldn't face him. He wasn't safe. *I* wasn't safe, and I desperately wanted to be. I needed to be.

I jumped again when my cell phone suddenly vibrated against the coffee table. Reluctantly, I picked it up and cringed. Simha had sent me a text.

Simha: Are you okay?

I stared at his message and wanted to laugh hysterically. "Okay" was a far distant goal I hoped to achieve someday before I died.

I stared at my phone, and I knew, I just knew, that Simha would keep texting and calling until I answered.

Mary: I'm fine. Didn't want to wake you. Had to take care of Charlie. Meeting contractor at client's apartment in 20 minutes. Have to run.

I pressed "Send" and stood there staring at my phone and hating myself for my cowardice, for my inability to call Simha on his pretty ruthless seduction last night, and for the fog of confusion five feet thick all around me that kept me from seeing what I wanted...and how to get there.

An hour later, I was seated at my desk at the office (I'd lied to Simha), and all I wanted to do was run away and hide somewhere so I wouldn't have to pretend I wasn't a complete wreck.

"What's up?" Hannah whispered at me as she sat down at her desk.

I just shook my head at her and turned away.

The best I could do was work on autopilot. I answered calls from contractors and clients. I ignored Tiffany's glare when she walked in late as usual and listened to the voicemail message I'd left her last night. I worked on two new project budgets.

Every fifteen minutes, Simha called me or texted me. I let his calls go to voicemail. I didn't read his texts.

The minute the clock on the wall opposite my desk struck twelve o'clock, I raced out of the office as fast as I could without looking like I was running from a fire. I jumped into The Mule and gunned it for the one person who might be able to help: Aunt Sara.

The Pistol Annies were singing "I Feel a Sin Comin' On" in tight harmony from my radio, and I writhed in humiliation on the car seat. I wove in and out of traffic as I rehearsed in my head how to explain last night to Aunt Sara, a difficult task because I couldn't explain it to myself. I was so lost in my head that it took me almost too long to realize I was nearly at the approach to the Gateway Bridge.

Panic roared through me. I swung the steering wheel hard to the right and crossed three lanes of traffic, car horns blaring and tires screeching all around me, to escape onto South Second Street. I screeched to a stop at the curb and just sat there shaking all over from my most recent near-death experience. I sure hoped I wasn't forming a habit of nearly killing myself.

My greatest fear by far was the Gateway Bridge. Its silvery-white arch taunted me, tormented me. Four months, and I still couldn't look at it, let alone cross it, particularly after last night.

It took me about five minutes to pull myself back together. I turned The Mule around, wound my way over to the entrance onto I-24, and made it safely across the river. Ten minutes later, I pulled into a parking space at the Nashville Zoo, flashed my pass at anyone who looked official, and then ran. I ran through the summer crowds just as fast as I could all the way to the butterfly enclosure.

I searched desperately through all of the greenery and the dozen or so kids and grownups and finally spotted Aunt Sara in khakis and a purple blouse standing in front of a clump of blue jacarandas. She was misting the flowers with a plastic spray bottle filled with water and talking to some large black and white butterflies that were balanced on delicate yellow lily petals.

She saw me out of the corner of her eye and turned to me, beaming. "So how did your date go?"

"Thanks to your darn charm idea, things went a lot faster and a lot farther than I expected," I said grimly.

Aunt Sara laughed with pleasure.

"I wasn't ready!" I exploded, and she instantly sobered. "You set a cute little trap, and I fell into it, and I didn't want to."

"I'm so sorry, Mary," Aunt Sara said, setting down the water bottle and putting her hands on my shoulders, her concerned blue eyes searching mine. "I thought you and Simha had been talkin' since spring, that you knew each other."

"Texts and e-mails aren't the same as actually bein' face-to-face with someone! Simha knew that. That's why he wanted to see me.

He said so. He said he wanted to know what we are to each other and then he just...ignored who I am."

"How did he ignore you?"

"He ignored my boundaries and seduced me, Aunt Sara!"

"Mary, I know you through and through. You're a strong young woman. If you hadn't wanted to make love with Simha, he wouldn't have been able to seduce you."

"I wasn't ready!"

"I hear that. I believe you, and I'm so sorry that my idea of the charm aided pushing things too far too soon. But let's see if we can't put things into perspective. When you were with Simha, when you were just talkin', how did you feel?"

It took a moment to put myself back in the restaurant and then in The Mule. "I was happy."

"And were you happy when you made love with him?"

I blushed all over and looked everywhere but at Aunt Sara. "I was so much more than happy," I confessed miserably. "I felt like I was awake for the first time in my life. I felt connected to Simha in ways I've never been with another human being. I felt...consumed with passion. It was just pourin' out of every pore. I became this powerful wild woman, takin' what I wanted, doin' things I'd never done before, and lovin' all of it. I never wanted to stop."

"Oh my!" Aunt Sara murmured as she sprayed her face with the water bottle.

"Are you okay?"

"I'm just feelin' a little flushed from the humidity in here. Nothin' to worry about. So just so I understand correctly, you made passionate, uninhibited love to a man you've known for months now."

"Yes, but Aunt Sara, that wasn't me!"

"Really? Are you sure?"

I wanted to stamp my foot in frustration. "I know who I am,

and that woman in Simha's bed last night wasn't anyone I know!"

"I can hear that last night was an overwhelming experience for you," Aunt Sara said soothingly. "Did you and Simha talk about it afterward?"

"No. We fell asleep. When I woke up, he was still sleepin', and I...snuck out of his hotel room," I said, hanging my head. "I was just so confused and scared and angry and—"

"Overwhelmed."

"Yeah," I said, grateful that she understood. "I couldn't face him. I couldn't *talk* to him! I just couldn't."

"You weren't ready."

"Yeah, and I don't know if I ever will be for that again."

My phone started ringing in my purse. Despair filled me. I pulled it out and looked at the caller ID.

"It's Simha," I said glumly. "He won't stop callin' and textin' me."

"Sounds like he wants to talk to you."

I looked helplessly at my aunt. "I don't know what to say."

"How about tellin' him what you've told me? Tell him that as good as last night was, you weren't ready, and you're feelin' angry and confused. See what he does with that."

"Oh, I can't!"

My phone vibrated in my hand, and I jumped, feeling panicky and mad and overwhelmed by the last twenty-four hours. Reluctantly, I looked at my message.

"I got a text from Jason," I said, stunned.

"You mean that bum of an ex-boyfriend of yours?"

"Aunt Sara, he's not a bum!" I read the brief text in growing surprise. "He wants to get together for a drink to catch up or something."

"That sounds like a perfectly awful idea."

"Why?" I demanded angrily. "I've known Jason practically my whole life. We were friends once. Maybe he wants to be friends again."

Aunt Sara started telling me all the reasons why that wasn't a good idea, but I wasn't really listening.

"Mary Poser, that ex-boyfriend of yours never gave you anything you needed," Aunt Sara was saying. "This Simha, however, seems to have given you all of himself last night. You said yourself that you two connected in ways you've never experienced before. That's important. That's something you should pay attention to."

Simha had said his intuition had told him to pay attention to me, and look what had happened.

"Why?" I demanded. "Just because we connected doesn't mean that we should keep connectin'. How can I trust a man who doesn't respect my boundaries? And even if I could trust him, even if last night meant somethin' more than sex, so what? It's not like anythin' can come of it. He lives in India! He travels the world. I live here, and you know long-distance relationships never work. What am I gonna do? Move to India? I don't know anythin' about India, and heaven knows a white Christian girl would never fit in there, and I sure wouldn't fit in with his family. And besides, I couldn't just leave behind everythin' and everyone I know and love, and he couldn't just abandon his life in India to move here. So where does that leave us? Nowhere!" I thrust my phone back in my purse.

"Mary, darlin', don't run away from somethin' that could be—"

"I've gotta get back to work," I said. "Thanks for lettin' me fill your ear."

She stared sadly at me for a minute, then kissed my cheek. "Drive safely, and try not to hurt yourself with bad thoughts about this. Maybe you can explore your feelings more when you're not so, well, upset."

But that was the last thing I wanted to do. I drove back to the office with the car radio turned up full blast. I was thinking instead about Jason and what it would be like to be friendly with him again. I started scratching at the scars on my forearms. Were they itchy, or was I just a minefield of bad habits? I pushed away my aunt's words when they tried to break through the loud music. As I was crossing back over the Cumberland River, I suddenly felt Simha's lips brushing across my left breast, and I shuddered. Then I called myself every bad name in the book and ruthlessly shoved down everything I'd said and done and felt last night. I refused to be mired in sex and confusion. I didn't even glance at my purse when my phone rang again.

I pasted a smile on my face when I walked back into the office, but it faltered some when I saw Mama waiting for me at my desk wearin' her pale pink suit and a cross expression.

"Where on earth have you been, Mary?" she demanded as I walked up to her. "I've been waitin' here these last ten minutes."

"I went to visit Aunt Sara on my lunch break. How are you, Mama?"

"Worn to a frazzle, and the day's still young. I want to talk to you about you joinin' the church Buildin' and Grounds Committee."

"What? Why?"

"Because you deal with buildin's and grounds all day in your job, and you know a sight more about 'em than most folks on the committee."

Hannah walked into the office, saw Mama, and walked right back out again.

"Mama, I can't talk to you about this now," I said, exasperated. "I've told you a thousand times that my boss doesn't like employees takin' personal calls and havin' visitors durin' workin' hours."

"I'm not a visitor. I am your mother, and I have come here on important church business!"

"Mama, it isn't pressin' business. We can talk about it tonight," I said, casting an anxious glance at Tammy, who was frowning at me.

"Not *pressin'*?" Mama exploded. "Everythin' to do with the Lord's work is pressin', Mary Poser, and you'd know that if you weren't constantly shirkin' your responsibility to your church, your daddy, and God!"

"*Shirkin'*?" I said, steamed. "I haven't missed a church service or missed helpin' with a church event since I was a kid! And I only did then because—"

Mama knew my fishing hook story. "You're not doin' any door-to-door visitations. You're not a member of any of the church committees." Mama continued rattling off all of my shirking, and I was soon desperate. Tammy's frown had turned into a glare.

"Mama, I'll join the Buildin' and Grounds Committee, and we'll talk some more about it tonight! I'll come over for dinner. And speakin' of dinner, Jason sent me a text. He wants to get together for drinks."

Using my ex as a distraction, making it sound like his text meant more than it did, made me feel awful, but it worked. "Jason? Really?" Mama said eagerly. "Well, that's fine. That's just fine! I've been prayin' and prayin' for you two to get back together. He's such a nice boy. Any girl would be lucky to have him."

She finally left, Tammy stopped glaring, and I got back to work. Last night was still a storm in my mind that whirled its way in my chest, spinning my heart in all sorts of crazy directions if I let it. I had to keep my mind busy to calm the storm.

Love is not an emotion, it's your very existence.

❧ *Rumi*

Chapter Twenty

The next afternoon, Saturday, I dashed into the family kitchen twenty minutes late carrying two sugar-topped sour cherry pies. Mama was standing at the far counter, busy peeling potatoes. Chloe and Alice, who'd been invited to supper, were sitting at the kitchen table. Chloe was cutting the tips off of a huge pile of green beans, and Alice was pressing whole cloves into a big ham. Through one of the windows, I could see Grandpa Tom in the vegetable garden doing some weeding and talking to a couple of chickens.

"Hey, Mama," I said, setting the pies down on the counter nearest me.

"Those look just fine, darlin'," she said, barely looking up from the potatoes.

"Where have you been?" Chloe demanded.

"I was busy runnin' errands," I said defensively.

"Errands, huh?"

"Yes, errands! My neighbor Miss Olivia's cat was hungry and I had to feed him, but I'd run out of cat food, so I went to the pet store to get extra food, but they were closed, and the supermarket isn't near my place, so it took me longer than I thought it would.

Then I saw that the supermarket had a new delivery of the organic chicken feed our chickens like, so I thought I could get them both at the same time, but the bag of feed was too heavy for me, so I had to wait for a store clerk to help me load the bag in The Mule."

"So why do you have to feed the cat?" Chloe demanded.

"Is Miss Olivia away?" Alice asked, admiring her cloves handiwork.

"No, the cat was just hungry. It always comes to my apartment when it's hungry."

"That's because you keep feeding it!" Chloe said in exasperation. "Maybe if you let your neighbor feed her own cat, you'd be on time!"

"I said I was sorry."

"Why'd you need to get organic chook feed?" Alice asked cheerfully.

"It's better for the chickens," I lowered my voice, "and Mama doesn't buy it 'cause it costs more."

"I rest my case!" Chloe said.

"What case?"

"If you would stop worryin' about every single person on the planet, and their cats and chickens, you'd be *on time* instead of *late* all the time."

I didn't have a chance to defend myself because just then a car honked outside. Erin dashed into the kitchen wearing a white Alkaline Trio band tee shirt, a black miniskirt, a wide black belt with metal studs, about a dozen bracelets on each arm, neon pink nail polish on her nails, diamond-pattern black stockings, and pink Converse sneakers.

"I'm off to work," she said, heading for the back door.

"Erin Jennifer Poser, what are you wearin'?" Mama trumpeted.

Erin stopped and sighed heavily. "Clothes, Mama."

"That skirt is a sin to Moses. You go right upstairs and change into somethin' decent."

"Can't! Don't have anythin' decent, and I'm late!" Erin declared, running outside to the car waiting for her.

"That girl!" Mama said angrily as she glared at the kitchen door. "She hasn't had a boyfriend since her accident, and I don't see any on the horizon. How can she hope to get a man lookin' like *that?*"

"She's got good legs, and she's showin' 'em off, Mrs. Poser," Chloe said soothingly. "There are a lot of leg men out there."

"One look at that spiky black hair and raccoon makeup and they're scared off, and that's certain," Mama said. "I do declare I'm worried for her. She makes herself up queerer than a three-dollar bill and dresses like a hussy. She's piddlin' her life away at that store, resentin' her church duties, and spendin' the rest of her wakin' hours in her room listenin' to the most depressin' music I've ever heard. How's she gonna find a man? How's she gonna get herself a good husband, her own home, children? How is she ever gonna be *happy?*"

"She's got brains and the love of her family," I said soothingly. "She'll find her way to happiness, Mama, don't you worry."

"I'm her mother. I'll worry about her 'til the day I die."

"It's hotter'n a goat's butt in a pepper patch," Grandpa Tom said, walking through the back door into the kitchen and mopping his brow with his handkerchief.

"I've got a new pitcher of sweet tea in the refrigerator, Daddy," Mama said.

"You'll have to make a new one, 'cause I'm takin' this for myself," Grandpa Tom said as he pulled the pitcher out of the refrigerator, grabbed a glass from the cupboard, and headed for his room.

"That man!" Mama said as she filled the tea kettle with water and set it on the stove.

"Marjorie, are you in here?" Daddy called as he walked into the kitchen through the dining room door.

"Almost always," Mama said as the tea kettle began to whistle. She set it on a cooler burner.

"If you've got a minute, I'd appreciate it if you could take a look at my sermon for tomorrow," Daddy said. "It's not quite right, and I'm not sure where I got off track."

"I'll finish makin' the sweet tea, Mama," I said, standing up.

"Thank you, darlin'," Mama said, walking out of the kitchen with Daddy.

"Alone at last!" Chloe exclaimed. "All right, Mary Poser, *dish*. How did your date with Simba the Lion King go the other night?"

"It's Sim*ha*, and things went way too well," I said as I pulled a big blue glass pitcher out of the cupboard and put a pinch of baking soda into it.

"Ooh! You mean he gave you his Bolly-wood?"

"Chloe, please!" I said, my face flaming as I poured the boiling water into the pitcher, filling it halfway.

"You *bad* girl!" Chloe said proudly as I added six tea bags to the water and covered the pitcher to steep the tea.

"So you guys shagged," Alice asked quizzically, "and Simha filmed it?"

"What?" I squeaked. "*No!*"

"But you said Bollywood, and that's movie making, isn't it?"

I covered my face with my hands.

"Not Bollywood. Bolly-*wood*." Chloe stood up and pointed to her groin. "Wood." Alice still looked blank. "Oh, I give up." She sat back down.

"Okay, I'm confused," Alice said. "Did you guys shag, and did he film it?"

"Oh lordy," I said as I set the timer for fifteen minutes and sat back down at the table. "Can we please change the conversation?"

"Oh, there's no chance of that!" Chloe said with a grin. "Alice, it seems Mary and Simha *did* have sex and, unfortunately, he didn't video it."

"*Unfortunately?*" I squeaked.

"Bro, I told you he couldn't wait to get into your pants," Alice said with a grin as big as Chloe's.

I looked at them both helplessly. "It didn't seem like that at first. The evening started out great, and the next thing I knew, we were rolling all over his bed havin' the most mind-blowin' sex. But it was more than that. I don't know. It felt..." I sighed and shrugged. "I don't know. The whole night was just...overwhelmin'. The things I felt, the things I did...that wasn't *normal* for me."

"Wow," Chloe said, looking too cheerfully impressed.

"That isn't me!" I insisted. "He should have known that. But then how could he? But he shouldn't have assumed. Oh, I'm so confused."

"I hear ya," Chloe said, covering my fist with her hand. "Just because you liked what was happenin' in the moment doesn't mean it was right to be pushed into the moment. Sounds like he's one of those overconfident guys who knows his power and likes to use it. I'll bet he's used to gettin' any girl he wants into bed and only thinks about what he wants, not what it means to the girl. He's not worth a minute of your worry, Mary. I say drop him like a hot potato."

"Yeah, but if the sex was mindblowing," Alice said, "and if that night felt like it was about more than the sex, then maybe it's worth confronting him and working it out."

"Oh, I can't!" I said. "I don't know what to say to him. I don't know what I want from him. I don't know what he wants from me. I mean, what *can* he want? He lives so far away. I don't know his family and friends, and he doesn't know mine. I don't know if he'll always try to manipulate me into givin' him what he wants or if the other night wasn't normal for him, either. I just don't know."

"Sounds like he's too much hard work," Chloe said. "Anyway, why bother? There's plenty of wood in Nashville for you to burn between those thighs."

"Oh Lordy," I muttered. I'd never become accustomed to Chloe's startling candor.

"I don't know, bro," Alice said. "Sounds to me like Simha knows how to roar! If it was me, I wouldn't want to walk away from that."

I sighed heavily. "I'm walkin' alright, but I'm waitin' for my mind to catch up. I can't stop thinkin' about him. I don't mean the sex, although that's still pretty vivid in my head. I watch a sitcom and catch myself wonderin' if Simha would think it's funny, too. I go to a movie and wonder what Simha would think of it. I take Charlie for a walk and find myself talkin' in my head with Simha. And *now*, well, now I can hear him callin' my name when I'm takin' a shower. I can feel him touchin' me when I'm sittin' at work. I can see the fire in his eyes when I'm checkin' on a couple of pies in the oven."

"You've got it bad, bro," Alice said.

"But I *can't* have it bad! Simha and I don't make any kind of sense."

"None whatsoever," Chloe agreed. "Can you imagine bringin' him home to Sunday supper? Can you imagine what your mama would say? What she would do? An *Indian* man romancin' her daughter? She'd have a stroke."

"He's Hindu, too," I said miserably.

Chloe roared, laughing mercilessly. "That would kill her flat out," Chloe said with certainty.

"Is there any man your mum *would* like for you?" Alice asked.

"Jesus," I said wryly.

Alice smiled. "Seriously..."

"It's true," I said. "I'm pretty sure he's the only guy she can imagine me marryin'. I just know she expects me to walk into the house one day with him on my arm." I stood up to perform the introductions. "Mama, this is Jesus, my boyfriend. Jesus, this is my mother." Alice and Chloe laughed as I sat back down. "That'd make her happy the rest of her days."

"Jesus and Mary, together forever," Alice said, grinning. "Is that why she named you Mary?"

"You'd think so, but no. When I was born," I said, "Aunt Sara suggested to Mama and Daddy that they name me Mary, and they thought the same thing—what a good idea to name a good Baptist girl after the Virgin Mary! Except Aunt Sarah wasn't thinkin' religion. She was thinkin' sneaky. Aunt Sara is obsessed with butterflies. By namin' me Mary, I'd be Mary Poser, and *mariposa* is the Spanish word for butterfly."

"*Pequeña mariposa hermosa*," Alice said with a grin.

"What?" Chloe said.

"Beautiful little butterfly."

"Since when do you speak Spanish?" Chloe demanded.

"Since I spent six months in Peru a couple of years back," Alice said.

"You are so full of surprises," Chloe said.

"Did I tell you I've decided to get baptized?" Alice said.

"Really?" Chloe said. "More surprises."

"That's wonderful, Alice," I said warmly.

"Yeah, it is," Alice said with a grin. "I'm lovin' the choir, and your dad said in his sermon the other day that baptism is a 'personal transformation,' and I want that."

"Good for you," I said. "You're so brave always followin' your heart the way you do. First, you move to Nashville, then you join the choir even though you didn't really know how really well you can sing, and now you're deepenin' your spirituality. You're just... impressive."

"Thanks, bro," Alice said, blushing a little with pleasure. "I figured that if you can have a personal transformation driving your car into the Cumberland River, why can't I?"

Was that what had happened to me in April? Had I been transformed?

"So I'm going into the river, too!" Alice continued.

"I hope you're not plannin' on drivin' your car into the river," Chloe said, "'cause that's not how baptism works."

"No car, just some dunking in a dress. Although," Alice said, grinning at me, "I think your way was incredibly cool. Your dad's already put me on his calendar, and your mum is giving me all sorts of advice. I was hoping you'd both be my advocates. You'd have to be in the river with me. Are you willing?"

"I'd love to," I assured her.

"Me, too," Chloe said.

"Won't it bother you, bein' in the river again?" Alice asked.

"I don't think so," I said. "I've been fine with the actual river. It's that darned bridge that does me in."

"Huh," Alice said. "I think there must be something special about that river, Chloe. It almost took Mary's life, but she's not scared of it at all. Look how she's changed since she chose to go for a swim with her car."

"I didn't *choose*... What change?" I demanded.

"Come on, we can all see it," Alice said.

"See what?"

"I don't know what it is exactly, but you're different somehow."

"I'm not... And I did not *choose* to crash into the river," I insisted.

"Well then, maybe the river chose *you*," Alice said, "because you *have* changed, bro."

The kitchen timer began ringing, saving me from having to find some sort of answer to that. I got up, turned off the timer, scooped the teabags out of the pitcher, added sugar, ice, and a couple of lemon slices to the tea, and put the now full pitcher in the refrigerator.

Mama helped me a lot by walking back into the kitchen to finish peeling the potatoes. We had to change the subject now. I smiled almost triumphantly at my friends.

"So, Chloe, what event are you working on now?" I asked.

I didn't fool Chloe one bit. But she played along because she always loves talking about herself. She spent a good ten minutes talking about the different events her company was planning for a couple of local record companies, Yap, and a major winery. Then I helped Alice get a word in edgewise about being made a soloist in the choir. Then Mama shooed me and Chloe outside to herd the chickens back into the chicken yard and held Alice back to ask her about her baptism plans.

There's only one way to get our chickens back into their fenced yard. I divided some organic chicken feed into two bowls, handed one to Chloe, and we began shaking them and calling the chickens. The sound of easy food and our familiar calls brought chickens running to us from all directions, clucking and squawking and looking worried that they were going to miss out on the best food. We scattered some of the feed in the chicken yard for them, then began herding the stragglers inside.

"Jason sent me a text yesterday," I said with careful nonchalance as I encouraged Brick, a big Rhode Island Red rooster, to join the others. "He wants to catch up over drinks later tonight."

"Really?" Chloe said with wide eyes. "That is so cool! Mary's country rock star is back!"

"He's not back. We're just gonna talk a little. Old friends catchin' up with each other."

"Catchin' up," Chloe scoffed. "He's reachin' out, and you're reachin' back, and I'm glad. Any girl would be lucky to have that man."

"You're forgettin'—"

"No, I'm not," Chloe said, shooing one of the white broilers into the yard. "You were together a long time. It wasn't perfect, but it was good, and then he went stupid and cheated on you, I guess. But that's in the past. I'm sure Jason has grown and matured just like you have."

"Chloe, you're readin' way too much into this. We're just havin' drinks," I said as the back screen door slammed and Alice headed toward us.

"Don't worry, Mrs. Poser," she called back to Mama. "I'm an old hand."

"Your folks have always loved him, and he's been Toby's best friend forever," Chloe said.

"That's no reason to get back with the guy," I said as I nudged a black and white Plymouth Rock toward the fenced chicken yard. She flapped her wings in outrage, but she headed into the yard.

Suddenly, I heard a loud chicken screech behind me, and I turned just in time to see Alice wringing the neck of a fat broiler.

"Alice! What in the world do you think you're doin'?" I demanded, horrified by the sudden slaughter.

"Your mom needs a couple of chickens for dinner tomorrow night and doesn't have time to get to the store," Alice said matter-of-factly. "I used to do this all the time for my mum back in New Zealand. Usually, I used an ax to chop off their heads, but I don't want to get blood all over your backyard." She grabbed a second white broiler and dispatched it with equal calm.

"Oh lordy," I moaned, turning away hurriedly, feeling green all over.

Chloe laughed at me.

"You eat chicken, don't you?" Alice asked.

"Yes, but—" I began, not looking at her.

"Well, chooks don't grow in supermarkets, you know. A farm girl like you ought to be comfortable doing what it takes to add meat to yer meal. Can you get me a tub of hot water? It'll help me get the feathers out easier." Alice sat down on a green plastic chair and began plucking at the feathers of her first kill.

I had to press a hand over my mouth.

"Oh great," Chloe said in disgust, "you've just turned her into a vegetarian."

Alice chuckled. "You two crack me up. So did I hear you're seein' Jason tonight?"

"For drinks, yes."

"For drinks? Right." She winked at Chloe.

Chloe hooted with laughter.

"We're just catching up!" I said desperately.

Alice shook her head as the pile of white feathers in front of her grew. "You're okay. Just teasing. You'd be a sandwich short of a picnic anyway if you were silly enough to settle for the moon when you've got Simha offerin' you the stars."

"But Jason is a great guy," Chloe challenged. "He's handsome and talented. He's the lead singer and guitarist in The Nashbros, Toby's band. Mary used to go to all of their gigs."

Alice wrinkled her nose. "Toby's told me about The Nashbros' gigs, and it sounds like they're all in dive bars. Is that where you wanna hang out, Mary?"

"I'm not hanging out anywhere!" I defended. "We're just havin' drinks. We're just gonna *talk*."

"Sure you are," Chloe said with a grin, "and everyone knows

that nothin' ever comes from talkin'...except, wait a minute, didn't that Simha fella talk you into his bed?"

"Enough!" I growled as I closed the gate behind the last of the chickens scooting into their yard.

My friends were not helping today. Alice was cheering on amazing sex with a gorgeous guy who could blast away every good intention with a single glance of his dark brown eyes. Chloe was cheering on a reunion with my handsome, guitar-strumming, cheating ex. I could feel anxiety bubbling up in me. I dug my fingers into the scars of my left arm. It had a settling effect.

I needed someone to tell me what to say to Simha after what had happened between us, and to tell me how to feel about him. I needed to know how to tell him I was mad at him for seducing me, and how that night had scared me because of all the things I had felt and done that I'd never felt and done before. I needed someone to tell me what to do because I didn't know how to say those things to him and stay safe.

I needed someone to tell me if I should keep Simha in my life or if I should keep running. I needed someone to tell me if I was a coward or if I was simply keeping myself safe.

I needed to know what exactly Simha and I had shared two nights ago, if it was as important as it had felt, and what I was supposed to do about it if it was.

I needed to know why I could not get the man out of my head, why I couldn't silence the melting tone of his voice in my ear, why I couldn't stop feeling his mouth on mine, his hands caressing my body, his body moving so passionately in mine. I needed to know how to make all of that *stop*.

And I needed to know if I *should* make it stop.

"So where's my hot water?" Alice asked. She snapped me

out of my dizzying moment, and I rushed inside. I was happy for the escape. I couldn't ask Chloe and Alice about any of what troubled me because I was afraid they'd discover how frighteningly out of control I felt.

Live where you fear to live.

❧ Rumi

Chapter Twenty-One

A little after ten o'clock that night, I walked into Pete's Bar and was instantly transported back into all of the other small, dark, dank dive bars I'd been in as I'd followed The Nashbros from gig to gig before Jason and I had broken up. The smell of stale alcohol invaded my senses, and the noise hurt my ears. I appreciate company like anyone else, but I could never quite appreciate its appeal in this environment. The sole purpose of these gatherings appeared to be to get drunk and then laugh uproariously about nothing in particular. Despite the years of practice forcing laughter on cue, I always left with a hollow feeling of isolation and loneliness that seemed to seep into my spirit from the spirit-stained floors. The tiny stage at the back of the bar was barely able to hold the three Nashbros and their drum kit, electronic keyboards, and lead guitar, but that didn't matter. Cramped spaces filled with people was the recipe in these bars to approximate the flavor of close human connection.

I sat at the table closest to the stage and turned off my phone. I gave a thumbs-up to Toby and waved at Scotty, the drummer, and smiled at Jason. He was as handsome as ever in his faded, skintight jeans that emphasized his muscular thighs and hard butt. His sleeveless white shirt showed off his biceps, and his weathered cowboy hat completed the country rock star look. I sat through an entire set of music that sadly wasn't any better than the last time I had done this. But I was here to support Toby and Jason, so I kept a smile plastered on my face and applauded loudly at the end of each song, just like I used to do.

Sitting by the stage, sipping on a soda, I realized that I hadn't really done the bar scene since Jason and I had split about eighteen months ago. I'd done the clubs with Chloe and Alice and the quality honky-tonks like Tiny's and had gone to some great concerts, but I wasn't looking for this experience when I didn't have Jason to follow. Blessedly, Jason announced that the band was taking a break and would be back soon. Toby and Scotty headed to the bar for beers. Jason jumped off the small stage right in front of me.

"Hey, Mary!" he said, startling me by kissing me on the cheek. "I'm so glad you could make it tonight. Look at you! You look amazin'. I swear you get prettier every time I see you."

"Thanks," I said as I sat back down at the tiny table and Jason sat across from me. He'd surprised me. Jason hadn't been one for giving compliments when we'd been together. "How have you been?" I asked.

"I've been okay. Still workin' at Southern Fried Chicken and wearin' that stupid ass uniform for minimum wage. You're the one with all the excitement happenin' in her life. I haven't been able to stop thinkin' about you since I heard about your car goin' off the Gateway Bridge. I was worried about you."

"Really?" I said. "I don't remember seein' you at the hospital."

"Oh man, don't be like that. It was just bad timin' all around. I was workin' with a producer in Memphis writin' some songs, and we were kinda on a tight schedule. Sorry. There was nothin' I could do about it."

I said, "That's okay, Jason," but it wasn't okay. He hadn't sent me flowers, not even a get-well card. He hadn't said a word to me from April to today.

"I wrote a song for you," he announced.

"What? Really? That's so sweet."

Jason reached over and pulled his guitar off the stage. "I wanna play it for you."

"Here? Now?"

"Sure. Why not?"

Um, how about I don't want all of these people staring at me?

But I didn't get a chance to object because Jason was already strumming his guitar and beginning to sing:

"You're the apple of my eye,
You're the strings in my guitar.
When I'm strummin' out a tune
You're all the sounds I hear.
When we make music together
It's for the love we share together.
I could mark my world on any patch I choose
But the only patch I want is the skin that's coverin' you.
The skin that's coverin' you
It's the patch that's got my eye
The skin that's coverin' you
I can see from half a mile
On the skin that's coverin' you.
It's the only place I'd lie.
It's the skin that's coverin' you."

He finished with his big boyish grin. "It's good, isn't it?"

"Wow! That's so, um, special" was all I could get out. I instantly had a flashback that I had once found Jason's pitchy style endearing. I was struggling this time, particularly since the lyrics had me all confused.

"It took me only twenty minutes to write."

"I can tell."

"Yeah, I was so inspired."

"Um, yeah," I said with a bright smile. "But if you wrote that song for me, and it was really nice that you did that, how come you didn't mention my name in the lyrics?"

"You know it's about you, Mary, and a songwriter has to make lyrics sound like they're about whoever's listenin' to the song on the radio."

"I see," I said.

"And the line 'when we make music together, it's for the love we share together'—that doesn't really sound like me. I don't play an instrument."

He scoffed. "And you went to college. It's to create an image for my audience of us doin' somethin' really special together."

"Oh. Got it."

He suddenly covered my hand with his. "I wanted to sing you that song because I want you to know how much I've missed you, and how much I've changed. I can prove it to you. I'm much clearer now on what I want and what I need to do."

I stared at his hand for a minute. "And what do you want, Jason?"

"I want The Nashbros to take Nashville by storm with our new tracks. You'll love our new songs. They're great! We're debutin' 'em all over town, and I want you to be right there with us, like it used to be. Me and Toby up on stage, Scotty backin' us up, and you, our guidin' light, front and center in the audience."

I was floored. I blinked at him. "You want to get back together?"

"Sure! Isn't that what I've been sayin'? Why do you think I sang you that song? I know I made some mistakes in the past, Mary, but they're in the past. I was under a lot of pressure back then and, well, I just didn't realize what I had until you were gone. But I know it now. I want you at my gigs. I need your support. I can't imagine my future without my Number One Fan in it."

"Um..."

"Just trust me on this one, Mary. It'll be better than ever, I promise."

I could feel tendrils of unease winding through me. I remembered what it had been like being Jason's girlfriend before and the reasons I'd finally broken up with him. A lot had happened to me since we split up. I hoped I'd matured some. Had he?

I suddenly heard Simha asking me, "What do you want in your life in the next twelve months? The next two years? The next five years?" and desperately blocked out his voice.

I finally knew one thing: I didn't want to keep floundering around in all the overwhelming confusion I'd felt since I'd let myself get seduced two nights ago.

Jason had just said, "I need you." Simha had said, "I need to understand myself." There was a big difference between the two.

And there was a big difference between the familiar and the unknown. Every person has weaknesses and flaws. I knew the worst of Jason, and I remembered the many good times we'd had together. I remembered that I'd given him more than he'd given me, but there was sincerity in his eyes now as he stared earnestly at me. He said he'd changed, and it was only fair to give him the benefit of the doubt. He'd promised to do better. I had to believe he meant that he'd give as much as he got this time around.

At the same time, my mama didn't raise no fool.

"Let's try one date and see how it goes," I said.

"Great!" Jason said, and then he kissed me.

He caught me so unaware that I couldn't even register what I felt or thought about that kiss before he'd pulled away from me and jumped back on stage to start the next set.

He grabbed the microphone and pointed at the bar crowd as

the single stage light poured down on him. "Let's rock this joint!" he shouted.

I sat through the next two sets, applauding loudly every cover song and original song until my palms tingled from slapping them together so much. I finally slipped out the door to head home once I'd made enough of a gesture of support. I waved to Toby on my way out. I couldn't quite look at Jason. I wanted to avoid his eyes in case he wanted to ask me to stay. I needed to clear my head, and the noisy bar was just filling it with random clutter.

It was way too late when I walked back into my apartment. Charlie was at the door, his ecstatic leaps in the air tinged with anxiety. Pillow fluff coated the living room.

Guilt swamped me. I'd neglected my little dog. He'd made a point of letting me know by shredding cushions.

I couldn't be angry with him. It was my fault. "Oh, my poor baby," I said as I knelt down. "I'm so sorry I'm so late." He leaped into my arms with the most enthusiastic certainty that I was going to catch him. I envied his commitment. I wished I could just leap into Jason's arms, knowing with certainty that he'd never let me fall.

I walked around the living room, cleaning up the fluff, then I gave Charlie a new chicken-flavored rawhide chew. He threw himself onto the floor, held the rawhide twist between his two front paws, and began to cheerfully demolish it.

I remembered that I'd forgotten to turn my phone back on, so I turned the power on as I headed to the bathroom to wash off my makeup. I realized I smelled like beer, and I grimaced. A shower was in order.

Ten minutes later, I smelled better. I pulled on the shorts and sleeveless tee shirt I use for pajamas in the summer. "Time for bed, Charlie!" I called.

He trotted into the bedroom, carrying the last half of the rawhide chew. He got into his bed, turned around a couple of times, then settled down for the night.

I started to get into bed and picked up my phone from the bedside table to check it. No texts. I checked my e-mail and felt my heart thump in my chest. Simha had sent me an e-mail.

Excitement and fear warred within me so powerfully that my hand shook. Trying to feel brave and failing miserably, I opened my e-mail app.

Simha: Hi Mary, Please excuse my persistence, but I don't understand why you refuse to answer my calls or respond to any of my texts. I am just confused and trying to make sense of why you're not talking to me. Did I say or do something wrong?

My face was burning and my hand was shaking as I read his e-mail. I was swamped with the most awful guilt and shame. To share everything Simha and I had in his hotel room and then ignore him had been so incredibly wrong of me. But how could I have called him or texted him when I was overwhelmed by such conflicting emotions and thoughts? I still didn't know how to process what had happened, what I had felt and done, who I had been in that hotel room. But I did know one thing. I didn't feel safe within my own body and mind around Simha. I looked at Charlie curled up on his rug at the foot my bed. He could express himself so much better than I could. I knew exactly how happy he was to see me tonight and how much he was worried about me. I was seeking leadership from my dog. When did I become this wreck of uncertainty? I started typing.

Mary: I apologize for not responding to your calls

and texts before this. I have been real busy, and I also didn't know what to say to you because I was really upset. I don't sleep with someone I've only met face-to-face twice in my life. It's just not normal for me, and it goes against everything I believe about love and getting to know someone before taking this step. But you seemed not to care about my values or my boundaries. I've only slept with one other man in my life, and I'd known him for years, and I loved him. I barely even know you! I appreciate that you flew all this way just to see me, but you went way too far with me. I don't think we're even close to being on the same page, and I can't imagine a time when we ever will be.

I sent my text, turned off the lamp, threw myself back down on my bed, pulled the covers to my chin, and just lay there shaking.

Five minutes later, my phone vibrated against the bedside table.

"*God dammit!*" I shouted for the first and only time in my life.

Charlie leaped onto the foot of my bed and stared anxiously at me. He'd never heard me shout before.

I turned on my lamp and grabbed my phone.

Simha: You talk as though we are strangers to each other. I don't believe this. We'd been communicating with each other for months. I don't need to have you in the same room as me to feel your presence and, in your presence, I acted, or should I say we acted, authentically and truthfully. I am sorry I didn't know what your boundaries are, but I must place my ignorance at your feet because you never told me. I'm a simple man. I believed you when you were in my arms and you said 'yes' to my desire of you, to our desire of each other.

"*Aaargh!*" I yelled as I slammed down my phone on the bed beside me, which made Charlie jump again. I sighed heavily. "Sorry, darlin'," I said. I turned my phone off so I wouldn't have to know if Simha sent me another text. I turned my lamp off and flung myself back down on my bed.

Having boundaries and morals is normal. It doesn't make me conservative, or bland, or locked in some box. It's just how things should be and how I'd always known them to be. Simha was inviting me to be someone I didn't know, someone I didn't relate to. But when I met her the other night, this version of me he evoked, she seemed so certain and self-confident and outrageously wild. I couldn't be this woman. Not in this lifetime.

Simha may be free-spirited, unleashing his raw passions and sexual desires as he pleases, but that isn't my life. I don't know anyone who lives like that. Chloe says she does, but I know she's more talk than action and is just as conservative as the rest of us at the core.

He probably expected every woman in every city he visited to be eager to spread their legs for him whenever he passed through. How could I keep such a man? Why should I even try?

Jason was no knight in shining armor, but he offered me something safe and certain. I was tired of feeling scared and confused. I glanced at Charlie again, happily slumbering in his bed. He loves me because I provide for him. He shreds cushions when he feels unsafe. He knows he receives care and protection from me, and he loves me for that—at least when I'm not away in bars chasing after men. A sense of certainty through familiarity is comforting. Is that what I needed? I turned off my light and pulled the covers high over my shoulders. I was tired, and I desperately needed sleep, particularly because I realized I was seeking leadership from my dog again.

Love saw me and said,
"I am here. Wipe your tears and be silent."
I said, "Oh Love, I am frightened that it's not you."
Love said to me, "There is nothing that is not me. Be silent."

❧ Rumi

Chapter Twenty-Two

I packed the rest of August and most of September so full, I left little time to breathe. My excuses for being late to just about everything kept getting longer. I walked Charlie twice a day and took him to the dog park at least twice a week. I got to the office early and often worked late, except when I'd promised to meet Chloe and Alice at the gym or the dance studio. I filled my lunch hours with Chloe and Alice, or with Hannah (who was dating a new guy every week), even with Erin or Toby sometimes. Chloe and Alice and I went out to a club or a movie at least once a week. I supported Alice in her baptism. Erin and I went to The Band Perry's concert. I was having supper at home three or four times a week and helping out on the weekend with Grandpa Tom, the chickens, the vegetable garden, the orchards, and church business. I was attending the church's Building and Grounds Committee meetings once a week and helping to organize and run church events like a fundraiser for the choir and a Labor Day picnic.

My insurance check finally came in. I took Toby with me to go used car shopping and ended up getting a red Hyundai hatchback with low mileage at a fair price.

Every Friday and Saturday night, I sat in a different bar listening to Nashbro songs I'd heard a thousand times before and applauding loudly at the end of each one. The boys were getting steady gigs in the town's wide variety of dive bars, and sometimes other people applauded, too, which was a relief.

The hard heat and heavy humidity of summer were gone. Temperatures had dropped down into the low and mid-eighties during the day, and the September nights were downright cool and comfortable in the low sixties. It was a pleasure being outside again, whether I was walking Charlie, inspecting a new wheelchair ramp for a client, or working as a hostess at a church swing band dance in the park where Daddy did his *Cinderfella*/Count Basie Orchestra routine again, getting a lot of laughs and applause.

My stomach started acting up, sometimes hurting, sometimes queasy, never quite settled. I began buying Pepto Bismol in bulk and thought maybe I shouldn't be quite so busy, but I didn't do anything about it, figuring my stomach would adjust.

Every day, I told myself not to think of Simha. He was too far away. Whatever we'd had was over. Done. I'd never see him again. Never talk to him again. But if you tell yourself not to think of a blue elephant, guess what you think about? A couple of times a day, I argued with Simha in my head and pretended I didn't remember he was a constant presence in my dreams at night, and I ignored the grief that felt like a thick layer of fog in my soul.

"Girls! Come here!" Chloe hissed as Alice and I were walking into Terpsichore for our dance class on a lovely Thursday evening. She'd been lying in wait and now pulled us to the side of the front door so we wouldn't be trampled by the ballerinas, a tough crowd, leaving their classes and the ballerinas and tap dancers hurrying into the studio for their classes. "I've got big news!"

"What is it?" Alice asked, agog.

"You have got to promise not to tell a soul," Chloe said.

"We promise," I said. "What's up?"

"Friday night, The Bluebird Café," she whispered. "The Pistol Annies are sneakin' in to perform a set of new music to see what an audience thinks about the songs before they record 'em. And I've got tickets!"

"Blow me down, I'm in!" Alice said.

"Oh, darn it, I can't go," I said, biting my lower lip. "The Nashbros are playin' at the Bristol Saloon this weekend."

"Seriously? Do you know how many people I had to sleep with to get these tickets? You can miss one night of The Nashbros' music," Chloe said, glaring at me.

"But—"

"How many people *did* you sleep with?" Alice asked innocently, which only received an incredulous roll of Chloe's eyes in response.

"You are comin', Mary Poser, and that's that," Chloe stated.

"Look, you know I'd love to," I said. "If it was any other night—"

"Bro, you have to come," Alice said with pleading blue eyes. "It won't be the same without you."

"Jason and Toby need me," I said.

"*We* need you," Alice said. "You're our bro. Just because we don't play a guitar doesn't mean we aren't important."

"Of course you're important!" I declared defensively. "You're my best friends. I couldn't get through a week without you."

"And your rockstar boyfriend can get through a Friday night without you," Chloe declared.

"Jason isn't my boyfriend."

"Then why do you follow him around from one bar to another every Friday and Saturday night?" Chloe demanded.

"I'm just helpin'," I said.

"And what's Jason done for you lately?" Alice asked with a sudden intensity that caught me off guard. "He hasn't even asked you out on a date in nearly a month."

"He's just real busy right now," I said. "Between workin', writin' new songs, talkin' to record producers, and rehearsin' and performin' with The Nashbros, he doesn't have a minute to call his own. Jason will make it fifty-fifty between us when things calm down. I know he will. And for now, I can't let him down. Not when he's workin' so hard. He needs me at the Bristol Saloon tomorrow night. He *told* me so. I'll go with you girls to the Bluebird Café another time, I promise."

With a disgusted sigh, Chloe stalked off to our dance class.

Alice shook her head sadly at me. "You're gonna bust a gut tryin' to please everybody," she said before she followed Chloe.

At the farmhouse on Sunday evening, Erin, Toby, and I glared at Mama, but she didn't mind us. She was dashing back and forth between the kitchen and the dining room, happy as a lark because her three children had "dates." She'd invited Jason for me, Melissa Flynn, daughter of the head of the church Youth Outreach Committee, for Toby, and Vern Goosen, son of the church choir director, for Erin to Sunday supper. Daddy winked at me, Aunt Sara laughed silently at all of us, Grandpa Tom told stories of his courting days, and Erin, Toby, and I picked at our food.

I spent the next week doing what I always did. I took care of Charlie; took care of my growing list of clients; went to lunch, the gym, and dance class with Chloe and Alice; urged a distraught Hannah to take a break from dating for a while; went to the new Justin Timberlake movie with Erin; had supper at home twice with no extra men at the table; helped track down Grandpa Tom when he forgot he didn't have a driver's license anymore and took The Mule for a joyride; sat through an exhausting and useless church Building and Grounds Committee meeting; cheered on The Nashbros on Friday and Saturday nights at the Six Shooter Bar; and baked two pecan pies for family supper on Sunday.

I set the pies in a copier paper box lid on the back seat to protect them and then went to pick up Erin at the end of her shift at The General Store. I walked in just after five o'clock, and there was my little sister in tight black jeans, wide studded belt, a pink Escape the Fate band tee shirt, and new red and yellow streaks in her black hair. She was changing out the flyers and posters on the big community bulletin board.

She wasn't alone. Handing her a poster was a young man in his early twenties with short dark hair and a tee shirt with the logo for the New Testament Ministry, a Christian Youth Movement church in town known for its pretty raucous music-oriented services. He was cute, and he had a sweet smile that he was directing at Erin, who couldn't quite meet his eyes but was smiling shyly and blushing a little.

I sidled a little closer to hear what they were saying to each other.

"It's no problem, really," Erin said. "The manager approved your last poster with barely a glance. I'm sure he won't mind if I swap it out for this one."

"I really appreciate it," the cute guy said. "Rise Up is a hot Christian band, and we just got them at the last minute for the next two weeks of services. We really need to get the word out."

"Glad to help," Erin said, starting to pin his poster onto the bulletin board.

"Thanks. I'm Jack," he said, holding out his hand.

She looked at his hand a moment, and then awkwardly offered her left hand to shake. "I'm Erin."

"Why don't you come along this Sunday and hear Rise Up for yourself?" he said. "You'd really enjoy the service."

"Oh, I can't! My daddy's the pastor of the Nashborough Evangelical Baptist Church."

Jack grinned. "That's okay. We take anyone who wants to deepen their personal relationship with Jesus Christ. There's no commitment, Erin. You don't have to join or anything. People come and go all the time. Just come to one service. I think you'll enjoy it."

Erin, her face white beneath her makeup, jerked her hand free. "I don't think I will, and my relationship with Jesus is just fine, thank you very much!"

"Sorry," Jack said. "I didn't mean to push. Y'all have a good day." He headed out of the store, smiling at me in a friendly way as he passed me.

"You didn't have to be rude to the boy. He was nice," I said as I walked up to my little sister.

"I wasn't rude!" she said defensively. "And I get enough criticism from Mama. I don't need it from you, too!"

"Sorry, Erin. But why don't you want to go? It might be fun."

Erin stared at me like I had two heads. "The Ministry isn't Baptist, and you know what Mama and Daddy would say."

"Sure. But you haven't been happy in Daddy's church for a long time. Maybe you'll find somethin' you like at the New Testament Ministry," I said.

"You're crazy."

After she clocked out, we walked to my car in perfect harmony, one of the rare times I could remember in the last several years.

She glanced at the back seat as she got into the car. "You made pecan pie?"

"Yep," I said as I fastened my seatbelt.

"That's my favorite pie."

"I know," I said with a grin as I started the car.

"I appreciate that, Mary."

"I know."

Supper that night wasn't anywhere near as amicable. Grandpa Tom was in one of his fogs, and Erin had to be his Jenny, which she hates. Toby was sullen and silent for some reason. Daddy was unhappy with that morning's sermon. Mama and Aunt Sara argued all supper long about unimportant things: the newest Hollywood starlet to enter rehab, the appropriate length for teenage girls' skirts, and whether or not today's popular music promoted rebellion and promiscuity.

I drove off from the farmhouse feeling...unhappy... discontented... I wasn't sure. I couldn't find the right label for the gray feeling hanging over me, in me, like a mist. My stomach was queasy.

But I made myself smile as I walked into Hennessey's Irish Pub just before eight o'clock. I wouldn't have thought it possible, but it seemed seedier than any of the venues The Nashbros had played in the last six weeks. It was almost entirely dark. The only reason I didn't use the flashlight on my phone was to avoid drawing attention to myself. The bar was nearly full, mostly with hard-case guys determined to get hammered at the end of a bad week in a year of bad weeks. Tiny dark brown tables with a couple of chairs each were squeezed together between the bar and the stage. I found one that was empty. I sat down but soon found myself squeezed in between a potbellied drunk at the table on my left and a lumberjack-looking goliath on my right. When the waitress, a tough fortyish blond with colorful tattoos up and down her arms, finally managed to wriggle her way to me between the tables and heaving swell of patrons, I ordered a chardonnay. I should have asked for the bottle. It was going to be a long night.

On the stage opposite the bar, Jason and Toby were roughhousing as usual, cracking each other up, while Scotty shook his head at them and made some final adjustments to his drum kit. I waved to the guys, they nodded at me, then Jason grabbed the microphone, announced the name of the first song in their first set, "Lulu," and they began playing a song they'd been playing for the last four years. The chardonnays were going to help remind me how a pitchy rendition of a song I've heard more times than my own name could become endearing.

About two-thirds of the way through the first set, the potbellied drunk, who I could smell was fond of boilermakers, began to slump in his chair, sliding toward me. I was caught in a moment of confusing despair. Was I most upset that I could smell both beer and whiskey evaporating from his pores or the fact that I was now the only thing effectively holding him up as his legs had given in three drinks ago? I tried to avoid him, but I was too jammed in. I tried to shove him off, but he was too heavy. My waitress finally saw me trying to signal her. Between us, we were able to shift the drunk off of me and onto his table, where he began to snore.

I now smelled of beer, sweat, and whiskey.

"Isn't this great?" Jason shouted to me at the end of their song "Nashville Tangle."

I smiled encouragingly back at him.

"I told you we're gonna be the next big thing in Nashville," he said, and then the band swung into "I'll Have a Beer," a decent anthem to the ability of booze to take care of any problem that comes along. I was ready for my next chardonnay.

"We're gonna take a break in a minute," Jason announced in his sexiest voice, "but first we're gonna sing a special song to my girl."

He proceeded to sing "The Skin That's Coverin' You." I made myself smile through "my" song. I found myself envying the potbellied drunk who had found a means of disappearing through inebriation when the going gets tough.

At the end of the set, Scotty went to the bar for a beer, Jason headed over to the owner of the establishment to do some self-promotion, and Toby walked over to me and squeezed himself onto the chair opposite me.

"Well," I said with determined cheerfulness, "you must be excited about how things are going with the band. You guys are booked solid."

"I guess so," Toby said, slumping down in his chair and thrusting his legs out in front of him.

"You guess so? What does that mean?"

"Look at this place! It's not enough to be booked into every dive bar in town. At some point, we've got to head out into the big wide world and see what's out there for us."

"You'll get there," I said, covering his hand resting on the table with my own. "I know it. This is just the beginning, and the beginning is always the hardest haul. Today, Nashville. Tomorrow, the world."

"Oh yeah? Well so far, every single today has just turned out to be another cruddy version of yesterday."

"Oh Toby, how can every day be cruddy when you have a family and friends who love and support you?"

"This bar makes the point that sometimes all of that isn't enough. At least it isn't for me. I've gotta get out of here, Mary. I just have to. Sometimes I feel like there isn't enough oxygen left in Nashville for me. This town is stranglin' me." He looked at me for a moment, a worried expression on his face. "Is this," he said, indicating the bar, "what *you* really want?"

"This is just a way station, Toby, not the destination. I believe in Jason's plans. He's got it all figured out," I assured him with a determined smile as I rubbed my unsettled stomach.

The Nashbros finished their final set just after midnight. Scotty waved goodbye to me, Toby hugged me on his way out, and Jason spent five minutes enthusing about the referral the bar owner had given him to another bar that needed a band. Then he gave me a quick kiss and helped the other guys load their equipment and instruments into Scotty's van. I headed home, reeking of Hennessy's Irish Pub and worrying about my brother, whose unhappiness, I had discovered tonight, seemed soul deep.

At a stoplight, Miranda Lambert began calling out the "White Liar" in her life from my car radio. The moon was beaming on the hood of my car. There wasn't a soul around me as I waited for the red light to change. I sat there, staring straight ahead at nothing. I had only one thought in my head: Why had I survived that crash into the Cumberland River? Was it for this? The light turned green, and I had no answer.

I walked into my apartment just before one o'clock. Charlie was hysterical in his relief with his usual frenetic leaps in the air. Guilt swamped me again. I'd been away too long.

"It's okay, baby," I said soothingly as I rubbed his tummy. "You're safe, and you're very loved. I'll always come back, I promise."

Once he'd calmed down, he headed through the doggie door into the tiny patch of backyard, and I stripped off all my clothes, dumped them in the hamper, sprayed some air and fabric neutralizer over them and around the hamper, then took a shower. I scrubbed my hair and the rest of me until all of the hot water had run out. Then I dried myself, threw some lotion onto my poor, abused skin, and pulled on my pajamas. Charlie was already curled up in his bed at the foot of my bed. He thumped his tail, smiled happily at me, and then settled down to sleep.

I got into bed and plugged my phone into its charger on the bedside table. It suddenly vibrated in my hand. Oh lordy, I did not need another text from Chloe chewing me out about the Bluebird Café.

Then I turned to jelly. The most profound sense of déjà vu swept through my mind.

Simha! After a month of thinking I'd never see his name come up on my phone again, Simha had sent me a text.

Shock took my breath away. I was scared, too. But I was also happy, and that surprised me and scared me some more.

> Simha: Please let me apologize for my actions. It was selfish and wrong of me to dismiss your moral values and your feelings, and I am very sorry that I did so. I think neither of us knew each other as well as we mistakenly believed. I would like to rectify that. I would like to try again—if you're willing.

He'd had over a month to think about our last correspondence, and he clearly had.

Love has pierced with its arrow the heart of every lover.
Blood flows but the wound is invisible.

❧ Rumi

Chapter Twenty-Three

I read, and reread, and reread Simha's text. A wild rollercoaster ride of emotions careened through me. I was happy he'd contacted me and relieved he had apologized. I felt guilty I had shunned him so badly. I felt flattered that he thought of me and missed me. I was scared by how much I had thought about him and missed him this last month. I was anxious about where talking with him again would lead. I was sad every time I thought about texting just a one-word answer: "No."

There was risk in keeping Simha in my life, but slamming the door on him forever felt so much worse. I'd rather be a little scared talking to him than be miserable without him on the periphery of my life.

Mary: I'll accept your apology if you'll accept mine. I acted out of fear after our night together. I never properly considered your feelings. I'm sorry that I hurt you, and I'm sorry I wasn't communicating my feelings to you. I've missed talking to you, too. So yeah, let's try again.

It seemed like I'd been holding my breath this last month. I pressed "Send," then heaved an almighty sigh and felt so much better.

October is a tough month for Mama. She exhausts herself every year trying to convince the congregation that Halloween is a pagan holiday that should be shunned as surely as they shun the devil. The problem is, Daddy likes Halloween. He likes the opportunity to have a party and dress up like Jerry Lewis and do one of his routines from the old Jerry Lewis-Dean Martin movies. A lot of the congregation who have kids like Halloween, too, because they like dressing up in costume, bobbing for apples, and eating candy as much as their kids do. The rest of the congregation thinks like Mama, but it's a losing battle when the pastor won't speak out against Halloween from the pulpit. Mama and Daddy do a lot of arguing in October.

So my birthday, which is smack dab in the middle of October, has always been a bit tense. That's why, when I was sixteen, I insisted that we have my birthday party at the Ye Olde Ice Cream Shoppe where they serve banana splits in a trough two feet long and two feet wide. Milkshakes come in tall forty-ounce glasses. Sundaes are a minimum of five scoops of ice cream and about a gallon of hot fudge. We've had my birthday party there every year since. Mama is too much of a lady to argue in public, so she makes nice with everyone, no one says the word *Halloween*, and I get to enjoy my birthday in peace. Even Aunt Sara, who avoids the farmhouse like the plague in October, comes to my party and doesn't needle Mama once.

Chloe, Alice, and Hannah were there, of course, and so was Jason. He sat beside me, draped his arm over the back of my chair, and told funny stories about our high school courtship. He joked with Toby about their grade school and high school pranks, asked Daddy to do one of his Jerry Lewis impressions, complimented Aunt Sara on her recent picture in the local newspaper, and listened to Grandpa Tom's tale about making homemade ice cream for Mama and Aunt Sara when they were little girls. He teased Mama into a smile by complaining about how much weight he'd gained since he'd started eating her delicious food again. He was his usual charming, good-natured self, and I felt just like I had at sixteen when he'd come to my first party here, sitting between me and Toby and teasing me into giving him a kiss in front of everyone. My twenty-fourth birthday party was sweet and familiar, and I didn't need it to be anything more.

Everyone breathes a sigh of relief on November first because Mama puts aside her Halloween battle for another year and starts in on her holiday decorating and baking, even though Thanksgiving is four weeks away and Christmas is two months away. She doesn't care. She loves the holidays and does her level best to celebrate them for as long as possible. Since she makes the house look cheerful and beautiful and keeps stuffing us with amazing food, none of us objects.

I'm always glad to get to November first, too, but this year I was also a little sad...and worried. After we'd apologized to each other in September, I didn't hear a word from Simha in October. I didn't want to send him a text because I didn't want to seem too eager or mislead him into thinking of me as anything other than a long-distance friend. The silence made me think about him every day and wonder what he was doing and whether he was thinking about me. This made me worry, because I shouldn't be thinking about him so much when I was going out with Jason and everyone in my family and all of my friends were so happy about that (except when I couldn't go see The Pistol Annies with them).

One month stretched to two. No e-mails, no texts, nothing. Was I missing something? Was Simha expecting me to say something first?

On Thanksgiving, the mouth-watering aroma of roast turkey filled the house. It's a holiday I love because I have all of my family and friends around, talking and laughing and feasting cheerfully. Mama had commandeered the kitchen and chased everyone out except Aunt Sara, who was putting the final touches on her to-die-for maple sweet potato casserole. She had a brief verbal tussle with Mama about who was going to make the cranberry relish. It's a century-old family recipe that they both believe they do best, and it had been a source of competition between them for as long as I could remember.

The entire ground floor was decorated with Thanksgiving paintings, collages, and cutouts that Erin, Toby, and I had made in grade school, as well as pumpkins and gourds, vases of dried flowers, store-bought faux autumnal wreaths and vines, and paper turkeys and Pilgrims. Mama believes in decorating for every holiday.

Daddy had conducted his usual Thanksgiving service that morning, which meant he was free for the rest of the day. So he, Toby, and Grandpa Tom were sitting in the living room drinking beer and watching the third college football bowl of the day. They argued about plays in the game, which was this year's best college team, and whether or not another maple and pecan baked brie would fill them up too much before supper. Jason walked into the house without knocking, kissed me on the cheek, and then jumped onto the couch between Toby and Grandpa Tom, demanding to know what the score was.

Charlie was in heaven. I'd brought him along with me, and he'd spent the first hour sniffing every inch of the living and dining room, begging in the kitchen for scraps, and demanding constant human attention, which the boys and men were happy to give.

Alice rang the doorbell, and I let her in. "Hey, bro," she said. "Thanks for inviting me to your Thanksgiving again this year."

"Please. You're family. Consider it a standing invitation. What is *that?*" I demanded, curiously sniffing the casserole dish in her hand.

"Four-cheese macaroni and cheese," she announced with a grin.

"You're a goddess. Take it on into the kitchen, and don't get your feelin's hurt when Mama throws you right back out again."

Alice was back a minute later, and I took her into the living room.

"Happy Thanksgiving!" she called out to the men.

"Well, well, well, aren't you a pretty little thing," Grandpa Tom said, standing up and shaking her hand even though he'd met her many times before. "The name's Tom. Tom Collins. Did ya know they named a drink after me?"

"No, they didn't, Grandpa," Erin said as she walked into the room. He scowled at her. "Where's Jenny?"

"She ran off with the cable guy," Erin retorted.

"You mind your P's and Q's, young lady."

"I would if I knew what they were exactly."

"Y'all remember my friend, Alice?" I said with a determined smile.

The rest of the men gave her a vague hello, their eyes glued to the TV where a team in silver and red was at fourth down on the seven-yard line. Grandpa Tom sat back down on the sofa. I'd grown up on football, baseball, and basketball thanks to living with three generations of male sports fans.

"Let's try over here," I said, herding Erin and Alice to the loveseat and armchairs at the other end of the living room.

Erin shook her head disgustedly. "Segregation is alive and well in the South."

"You can watch the game if you want," I said.

"*Boring!*" Erin retorted, flopping down onto the loveseat.

"I still don't get why American football is so popular," Alice said as she sat down on an armchair beside me. "The players keep stopping to have a chat. What's with that? Back home, footy is a much faster game, and it doesn't have all of the Robocop helmets and padding."

"*Boring!*" Erin repeated.

"My little sister is not interested in sports," I said to Alice.

"What *are* you interested in?" she asked Erin.

"Nothin'," Erin said defiantly. I was worried that Erin's anger with the world was only getting stronger.

"Y'all turn off that TV," Mama ordered as she walked into the living room. "Supper's on the table."

"The game's almost over, Mama," Toby said.

"Record it," Mama said, turning on her heel and heading into the dining room.

Toby and Daddy exchanged a look. Daddy programmed the TV to record the rest of the game, and the men got up and followed Erin, Alice, and me into the dining room. Charlie trotted after us and settled himself under the extended maple dining table, ready to gobble up any tidbit that accidentally fell his way.

Just as she was getting ready to sit down, Daddy gave Mama an affectionate hug, lifting her off the ground in his arms. "You do Thanksgivin' proud, Marjorie," he said with a loving smile.

"Brian Poser, you behave yourself!" Mama said breathlessly, trying to sound cross. But she was blushing, and she couldn't hide her smile.

Everyone else was smiling, too, as we sat down. Even with its extra leaves, the table wasn't big enough to hold our meal, so bowls and casserole dishes were also packed onto the big maple sideboard. In addition to the huge twenty-five-pound turkey placed in front of Daddy to carve, we had cranberry and walnut spinach salad, honey glazed carrots, spicy braised collard greens, broccoli casserole, cornbread dressing, bourbon gravy, homemade cranberry sauce, Aunt Sara's maple sweet potato casserole, mashed potatoes, Alice's four-cheese macaroni and cheese, cloverleaf rolls, buttermilk biscuits, and for dessert, my contribution of a red velvet cake and two pecan-topped pumpkin pies. To drink, we had sparkling apple cider, bourbon, beer, and two different kinds of wine.

The Posers believe in feasting on feast days.

We also believed in dressing up for the occasion. All the men were wearing slacks and jackets. Even Grandpa Tom had exchanged his regular flannel shirt for a brown and red pullover sweater under a sports coat. All the women were wearing dresses or skirts. Of course, Erin's skirt was a black denim miniskirt, but the basic dress code was upheld.

We all held hands. Daddy said grace. We each said one thing we were thankful for and then, finally, mouths watering and bellies rumbling hungrily, we began serving the food.

While we ate, Mama talked about the success of the church's Thanksgiving food drive, which she had organized. Daddy praised Mama for her hard work. Grandpa Tom told us again the story of his first Thanksgiving with Grammy Jen as husband and wife, how her turkey was dry as sawdust and the pies were burned. She was so worried about everything being perfect, so Grandpa Tom had eaten everything on his plate to try to make her feel good about her efforts. He was bound up for a week after that. We all laughed even though we'd heard the story a thousand times. Erin told us about a new band she'd discovered, a female trio called Heartbreak. At least she was exploring new ways of feeling miserable. Toby talked about a member of the Lean Machine who didn't have the sense God gave a billygoat—he'd tried to lift too much weight without a spotter and broke his elbow and nearly crushed his throat for his stupidity. Alice told us all about a harvest festival and feast she'd attended in Peru. Where hadn't that girl been?

Jason spent his time talking with Toby, charming Mama and Daddy, and occasionally smiling at me as he had seconds and then thirds. He'd been spending Thanksgiving with us ever since we started dating in high school and had missed only one Thanksgiving during the year and a half we'd been broken up. His mama had died when he was four, and his daddy was a mean and dedicated alcoholic. Jason didn't have family, let alone a home, so he came here.

Aunt Sara mentioned that she was redecorating her house from top to bottom, and Mama was all over her like white on rice. She wanted to know design theme, colors, furniture, accessories, and she wasn't happy with any of Aunt Sara's answers, so they argued over them for a good long while.

Daddy and Toby debated Thanksgiving bowl games of the past. Jason was bragging to Alice about The Nashbros. Grandpa Tom teased Erin about her hair and makeup. Erin told him he was too old to care what girls wore nowadays, which made him laugh.

"You couldn't be more wrong," he told her. "That's young folks thinkin'. I'll tell you a secret…from the day they're born to the day they die, men enjoy watchin' girls."

"So what you're sayin' is you're a dirty old man," Erin said.

Grandpa Tom hooted with laughter. "And enjoyin' every minute of it," he assured her.

It was all very familiar and comfortable. So why was I having to work real hard to keep smiling? And why didn't I have any appetite?

My phone suddenly vibrated in my pocket, and I jumped a little, then looked a little guiltily at Mama. Phew! She hadn't noticed.

I snuck my phone out of my pocket and took a peek. Simha! He'd sent just two words, but he'd sent them!

Simha: Happy Thanksgiving!

I took a quick glance around the table to make sure everyone was preoccupied with their conversations and their food and quickly texted a reply.

Mary: Thank you! Happy Thanksgiving to you, too!

I started back in on Alice's sinful macaroni and cheese. I'd only gotten in a few bites when my phone vibrated again. Shoot! I looked hurriedly around the table, but no one had noticed. Mama would cut my arm off if she knew I was texting at the table on Thanksgiving. I glanced up at Jason. I was still safe.

Simha: The Hindu Thanksgiving comes in January, the traditional month of harvest in India. I imagine you are enjoying a great feast with your family. Unfortunately, I'm stuck eating Thai food out of a takeout container while I work late tonight.

I smiled, which was my undoing.

"Mary Poser, what are you doin'?" Mama demanded.

"Just takin' a peek at a text I got, Mama," I said.

"Family dinners are for family, not for work, young lady, and that is especially true on Thanksgivin'!"

"Yes, ma'am."

"Who's writin' to you?" Grandpa Tom demanded beside me.

"Oh, just a friend," I said.

Alice looked down at the name above my phone's message. "Oh, it's from Simha. What did he have to say?"

I nearly gasped aloud. Did she really have to announce to the entire table who the text was from? I was blushing all over. "He just wished me a happy Thanksgiving."

"Cool," Alice said.

Jason and Toby both shot me suspicious looks and probably would have pursued the matter further, but Mama started talking to Jason about a new member of the congregation who knew someone who was a cousin of someone who had a friend who worked for one of the record labels in town. Toby went back to talking to Daddy and Grandpa Tom about the current hockey season and the mixed play of the Nashville Predators. Alice was talking with Aunt Sara about the latest blockbuster action movie she'd just seen on a date with one of the techs from the Grand Ole Opry.

What would Simha make of my family and friends, I wondered. Would he appreciate their goodness, smile at their shenanigans, or be confused by the cacophony of too many people all talking at once? I didn't know, and I probably never would. I tried to imagine Simha sitting at our dinner table with us in Jason's chair. Would he wear the traditional Indian clothing he wore to the film festival? What would my mother say, having a Hindu at her Thanksgiving table sitting smack bang under the picture of Jesus on the wall? Bless her heart, but would that be a stretch for the boundaries of her thankfulness? I looked up at the picture of Jesus and sighed.

I seek no heart but yours,
I hurry only towards You.

❧ Rumi

Chapter Twenty-Four

The morning after Thanksgiving, Erin, Chloe, and Alice and I met at the southern entrance to Opry Mills, Nashville's biggest mall. Alice was to be initiated in our traditional Black Friday Christmas shopping frenzy.

Opry Mills sprawls just across the Cumberland River from East Nashville near the Two Rivers Golf Course. It's got everything from clothing stores and factory outlets like Ann Taylor and Banana Republic to a couple dozen shoe stores, jewelry stores, toy stores, sports equipment stores, all kinds of fast food and sit-down restaurants, and a multiplex theater. We get all our Christmas shopping done on one day, on sale, and then get to sit back for the next month and thank our stars we're not with the panic-stricken fools running around at the last minute trying to find the right present for a spouse, a child, or a coworker. We got swallowed up in a flood-tide of harried shoppers who were there with the exact same plan as us.

"Bugger me, this is insane!" Alice said when we were herded into the bright lights of the mall's western corridor. Big, sparkly snowflakes were hanging from the ceiling. Green wreaths with red ribbons dangled over every store entrance.

"We'll work off everything we ate yesterday without having to go to the gym," Chloe said as she recovered from being jostled by a determined pack of pimply fourteen-year-old girls. "Besides, it's fun, and it's worth it."

Three hours later, Chloe and Alice were having to hold their sides they were laughing so hard as Erin held up an outrageous tiger-stripe chemise with a wide black lace band running down the middle. Erin was trying to convince us that it would be the perfect Christmas gift for Mama. That girl was just getting more and more creative in discovering ways to wind up her mother. Heaven help us if she ever started messing with tattoos. Mama would flip.

Alice was in rare form, boogying every time the mall's sound system played a cover of "The Carol of the Bells"—and it came up at least twice an hour. Chloe, as usual, was finding more things for herself than for anyone on her Christmas list, for which she was soundly teased. Even Erin was in a good mood, joking with my friends and me, even gamely trying on a belted white dress Chloe insisted would look great on her and grudgingly admitting that it did.

Everything was great, but I felt…off.

We had lunch at a Japanese restaurant where we could sit down in comfortable booths, rest our feet and backs, and wrestle with chopsticks.

Chloe, Alice, and Erin compared the bargains they'd snatched up and planned their strategy of attack for what else they still had to get. I must have been looking too much like how I felt.

"What's the matter, Mary?" Alice asked after putting a whole tempura battered shrimp in her mouth and eating everything but the tail.

"Nothing," I said. "The food's great."

"This prawn's a rippa," Alice agreed, shoving more shrimp into her mouth, "but that's not what I meant. You seem off your game."

"I'm fine!" She looked skeptical. I knew I had to say something more, so I said the first thing that had come to my mind. "It's just, all of the things I've bought so far are the same old things I always get my family and friends for Christmas. I was hoping to find something different, something new and exciting."

"Daddy will love that new fishing pole, and Mama will probably wear that sweater and slack set every time she goes grocery shoppin'," Erin said.

"Toby will make every girl in town swoon when they see him in that fitted tee shirt," Chloe insisted.

"And your granddad said he needed a new drill," Alice said. "You got him just the kind he wanted."

"I know, I know," I said. "You're right. Of course you're right. They're perfectly fine gifts."

It was when I was buying a wristwatch with a black leather band for Jason an hour later that it hit me. All day long, I'd been buying the same old things for everyone else and seeing the perfect gifts for Simha! I'd seen a fifteen-hour documentary DVD set on the history of film at half price, and I'd thought how much Simha would love it. I'd found a two-CD set of country and western greatest hits from the 1960s and 1970s and thought how Simha would laugh if I gave it to him with a card explaining that it was time he learned about the best music in the world. Just beyond the wristwatch counter where I was standing was a display with a silver pendant of a tiger with emerald eyes, and I thought how beautiful it would look against Simha's smooth, brown chest.

Oh lordy...

I stood in that crowded store feeling just simply appalled. *What was I thinking?* Simha wasn't my boyfriend. He wasn't family. He wasn't even Christian! More importantly, he wasn't Jason, my boyfriend, the guy who had taken me to a real nice dinner only last week at Gabby's Burgers & Fries, which had the best cheeseburgers in town, and then to an action movie.

I shouldn't be thinking about Simha! I should be thinking about Jason.

I tried real hard during the last hour of shopping to think only about Jason, but I kept seeing things I thought Simha would like, overhearing conversations I thought would make Simha laugh, and wondering what Simha would say if he saw me in that red negligee in the Victoria's Secret display window. That one made me blush all over because it reminded me of the heart-stopping desire in Simha's dark eyes when we had made love last August. I'd been thinking more and more about that night lately, particularly when I was lying alone in my bed at night. I knew I shouldn't. I tried hard not to. But how do you forget the most passionate night of your life? It's like I'd had my first hit of an exotic drug, and now I was hooked, eager for more.

A week later, I was finishing putting up the last of my Christmas decorations in my apartment. There were colored lights around every window, every doorway, and the kitchen cabinets. There was a wreath on the door, a Santa Claus who danced to "Jingle Bell Rock" in the middle of my dining table, and Santa and Mrs. Claus figurines on my coffee table. I had hung Currier & Ives prints on my walls, along with Christmas tree and Santa Claus pictures. I had a six-foot-tall Christmas tree loaded down with lights and ornaments in front of my living room window. I'm like Mama. I love decorating for Christmas.

My doorbell rang just as I was climbing off my stepladder. I opened the door, and there was a Federal Express driver with a white international shipping envelope in one hand and an electronic signature pad in the other.

"Mary Poser?"

"Yep."

"Sign here."

I signed for the package, thanked the harried-looking delivery guy, and walked back into the house reading the label. Simha. First, a text on Thanksgiving, and now this. I guess he really was serious about staying friends.

I sat down on my sofa and opened the envelope. Inside was a small, thin square wrapped in green paper and a folded note on white paper. I'm not proud—I opened the gift first and found a DVD of the film *Bride & Prejudice*. Cool. I looked at the note and saw that it was handwritten. Even cooler.

Dear Mary,
Merry Christmas!
I hope you enjoy this film. It's a fun introduction to Bollywood cinema. And it's Jane Austen. What could be better?
Best wishes,
Simha

I should have finished my traditional Christmas Decoration Day by drinking eggnog and watching *It's a Wonderful Life* with Jimmy Stewart. Instead, I poured hot Darjeeling tea out of a Japanese teapot into a small round cup. Chloe had given the cups to me for my twenty-fourth birthday. I cuddled with Charlie on the sofa and watched *Bride & Prejudice*. I loved every moment of it. Jane Austen dressed in Bollywood charm was sheer genius. The only dark cloud was the guilt I felt. It was as though I was betraying Jason because I was watching something Simha loved. Worse, when the movie ended, I couldn't keep my pleasure to myself. I had to text Simha.

Mary: Thank you for my Christmas present! I just had to tell you how much I loved, loved, loved *Bride & Prejudice!* Yes, I opened it three weeks early. I couldn't wait. I loved the amazing colors and the energetic music. So vibrant, so much fun! I couldn't stop smiling. Every year, I watch *It's a Wonderful Life*. It's one of my Christmas traditions. Is there a Hindu holiday in December? Do you have holiday traditions, too? Thank you again and, assuming you don't celebrate Christmas, best wishes to you this holiday season.

I got myself some eggnog, gave Charlie a dog biscuit, and returned to tradition by starting to watch *It's a Wonderful Life*. Then my phone vibrated on the coffee table. I was happy to see it was Simha texting me.

Simha: I've seen *It's a Wonderful Life*. It's a favorite of mine, too.
We don't really have a major holiday in December. I suppose our closest holiday is Diwali, an ancient four-day festival of lights that celebrates the goodness of life and the victory of good over evil. It falls sometime between mid-October and mid-November. Each day honors a different god. On the fourth day, sisters invite their brothers into their homes, and we usually eat much too much on this day. On each of the four days, our homes and streets are brilliantly lit up, traditionally with oil lamps, and we use firecrackers to light up the night sky and express our joy.

Mary: Diwali sounds wonderful. If I was living in India as a child and the moon cooperated, I'd probably have thought all of the lights and firecrackers were celebrating my birthday. What fun!

Simha: Your birthday? Are you telling me you just had a birthday, and I didn't know?

Mary: Yes. Sorry. It never occurred to me to say anything. My birthday is October 15. No firecrackers, but lots of ice cream. It's the start of four months of good times: my birthday, Halloween, Thanksgiving, Christmas, and New Year's. The rest of the year seems pretty flat after all that. But right now, everything is fun. I just put up my Christmas decorations. Charlie is fascinated by my Jingle Bell Rock Santa.

Simha: I know that Santa! It makes me laugh every time I see it. Actually, I quite like Christmas. I like all of the decorations and the traditional movies like *It's A Wonderful Life* and *White Christmas*. I like some of the music and the spirit of giving and good blessings. It must be a special time for you. What are some of your holiday traditions?

Mary: On December 1, we all drive up into the hills to an old Christmas tree farm, spend about two hours finding just the right tree, then chop it down ourselves, load it onto The Mule, take it home, and decorate it and the rest of the house while listening to Christmas music, drinking hot apple cider, and eating all of the cookies and mini pecan tarts Mama made the day before. For most of December, Mama, Aunt Sara, Erin, and I are baking, mostly Christmas cookies, which we decorate and give to Daddy's congregation, neighbors, coworkers, and friends in baskets we've trimmed with red and green ribbons. We also bake fruitcakes, daily treats (like Mama's mini pecan tarts), and a lot of pies. On Christmas Eve, we're all together, and we get to open one present each. We watch Christmas movies like *White Christmas* and *How the Grinch Stole Christmas*. Aunt Sara and I spend the night, then on Christmas morning, we have breakfast (usually eggs, bacon, and fruitcake) and open the rest of our presents. Then we do all the church stuff and have Christmas dinner around four o'clock so we can eat leftovers around eight o'clock. The next day, we just lie around recovering from all of that food and savoring all of our presents.

I pressed send and stared at my phone screen, unhappy with my answer. It was accurate, but the excitement and joy I had felt as a child at Christmastime were not on that screen or in my heart. My phone vibrated again.

Simha: I thought *Bride & Prejudice* was an appropriate gift for you because it's all about family and cultural traditions and expectations. I can relate to this. Do you ever feel something like the pressure to conform that the daughters experienced in the film?

Part of me wanted to pour out all of my frustrations and fears, hoping Simha would understand and have some clever solution for my life and my world that I wasn't able to see from my perspective. But I wasn't ready for that kind of discussion with him, and maybe he wasn't really interested in finding out that ever since I drove my car off that bridge, I haven't stopped drowning.

Mary: Yes, of course. I think everyone does at some

point or another. I have to go to bed now. It's late, and I have to work tomorrow. Good night and a belated Happy Diwali.

I pressed "Send" and stared at our texts for a long moment. Then I pulled Charlie close and cuddled with him on the sofa as I stared at the frozen image of Jimmy Stewart and Donna Reed looking intensely at each other on the TV screen.

Love is not written on paper, for paper can be erased.
Nor it is etched on stone, for stone can be broken.
But it is inscribed on a heart and there it shall remain forever.

❧ *Rumi*

Chapter Twenty-Five

Christmas Eve and Christmas Day are working holidays for the Poser family. Daddy conducts three services on Christmas Eve and two on Christmas Day, and we're all there helping him. So we have to get up at dawn on Christmas Day to get our breakfast and open our presents before the morning service. Then we have an early Christmas supper so we can be back in church to prepare for the evening service.

This year, it all went by like a blur. The excitement and joy I had felt as a child were just a distant memory.

The next thing I knew, the house was full again with family and friends, including Chloe and Alice, and we were filling and refilling champagne glasses and watching the clock work its way slowly toward midnight.

A new year was almost here. So much had happened in the past year, but nothing had changed, and it felt like nothing was going to be any different in the coming year.

With thirty seconds to go, Jason had me under one arm and Toby under the other as he stared at the clock and enthusiastically counted down the seconds with everyone else, creating a swelling roar in the house. My phone suddenly vibrated in my pocket. I took a quick look. Simha! I smiled wryly. What was is it with this guy and timing? Since Jason was preoccupied with the clock, I took a chance and read the text.

> Simha: Happy New Year! I hope you have a wonderful year in which you step into your dreams, you love deeply, and are loved fully in return. I hope you will be wise when you need to be and laugh often. May the new year be filled with magic and surprises for you. Most of all, I hope in the coming year that you surprise yourself.
> Warmly,
> Simha

The countdown continued, with everyone shouting, "Ten! Nine! Eight!"

I felt like I was going to implode.

"Seven! Six! Five! Four!"

Outrageous? Magic? Full of surprises? Simha could wish all he wanted, but that wasn't my life.

"Three! Two! One!"

Nothing. I felt numb.

"*Happy New Year!*" everyone bellowed. Then they broke into a frenzy of hugging and kissing and laughing. Jason gave me a peck on the cheek and gave Toby a bear hug that lifted him off the ground.

I stood there in the middle of that happy crowd, making myself smile at whoever wished me a happy New Year because I didn't want them to see that something had shifted within me. I didn't know what that something was, and it worried me because it didn't feel safe. A lot of things didn't feel safe anymore.

The rest of that night, I worried about my stomach, which was acting up in a major way. All I could think about was how long I had to wait before I could escape back to my apartment without anyone caring. I saw an opportunity for escape when Daddy started one of his Jerry Lewis routines. While he kept everyone distracted with his antics, I slipped out the back door and headed home.

A week later, I dashed into The Carrot Bar fifteen minutes late. The lunch crowd had already packed the tables. It wasn't the usual Nashville crowd. There were a few business suits, but most folks were dressed casually—jeans and sweaters, loose long-sleeved dresses, skirts and leggings. There were potted ferns and other green plants everywhere. Murals on the walls celebrated the lush beauty of fruits and vegetables. I couldn't help noticing Taylor Swift eagerly reminding me to "Shake It Off" through the bar's speakers.

Chloe and Alice were seated at a table near the middle of the vegetarian café. Alice was looking around happily at the people of many colors and persuasions, and Chloe was looking glumly at the menu. It was the first time we'd all had lunch here together.

I weaved my way through to their table. Alice was telling Chloe about a backstreet café she'd discovered in Peru that she loved. Before I could apologize for being late, again, Chloe looked up at me and grimaced.

"How's the neighbor's cat? Full tummy? The chickens eatin' organic?"

"I get it!" I said, sitting down. "I'm sorry."

"You're always sorry," Chloe muttered, "but you never change."

"Hey, bro!" Alice said with her usual cheerful smile. "This place is so cool."

"I'm glad you like it," I said with an answering smile. "It's my new favorite lunch spot. The food is so fresh and delicious. You'll love it."

"Love it?" Chloe said. "There is nothin' to love, Mary Poser. I have been over this entire menu *twice*, and there's nothin' to eat!" She glared at Alice. "This is your fault, Chicken Killer."

"Oh, Chloe," I said, amused by her carnivorous outrage. "There's plenty of great food—you just have to open your eyes. The smoothies are lovely. The salads are huge and amazin'. The soups are out of this world. The tempeh burger and fries are incredibly fillin'. One of my favorite lunches is the quinoa salad. It's been helpin' my stomach."

"What on earth is quinoa?" Chloe demanded suspiciously.

"It's light and packed with nutrition, including vitamins, and it's a complete protein."

"You've been reading up," Alice said with a grin.

"I'm payin' a lot more attention lately to what goes into my body."

Our waitress, a cheerful redhead in a tie-dyed shirt and jeans, a short white apron tied around her waist, came up to us with a basket of crusty rolls and took our orders: the tempeh burger and fries for Alice, the quinoa salad for me, and, grudgingly, Chloe ordered the creamy carrot coconut soup along with a soba noodle vegetable salad.

"I can't believe you've gone all vegetarian on me," Chloe said as she buttered a roll.

"I haven't," I insisted. "I still eat a little meat...now and then. It's just that I don't think it agrees with my digestion anymore. Now fess up—isn't that roll delicious?"

"Yeah," Chloe conceded. She'd already devoured half the roll.

"So what happened with the music video audition you went on yesterday?" Alice asked.

Chloe grimaced. "Nothin'. Absolutely nothin'. They wanted blonde bombshells and said I looked too African."

"Bummer," said Alice.

"Don't worry, Chloe," I said. "This town is churnin' out music videos every day. You'll get another one."

"Yeah, but when?" Chloe demanded. "It's been two months since my last one. If it weren't for bein' cast as Gladys in *The*

Pajama Game at the Nashville Musical Theater, I'd be goin' out of my mind. That role made Shirley MacLaine a star, you know."

"You'll knock 'em dead, I know you will," I said. "So Alice, how goes the choir?"

"I'm loving the choir, bro, especially when I get to do a solo. It's not that I want to be a star, like Chloe. I just love feeling the music come alive in me and pour out of me like pure joy, and celebrating God, and inspiring people to open their hearts to God's love when they hear me. I feel...transported. I've even started taking voice lessons. But..."

"But?" I said in surprise.

Alice slid a little down in her chair, looking guilty. "But I'm not entirely happy."

"Why not? Is anyone bein' jealous and mean to you?" I asked.

"Not really. Well, not much. But that's not it. There's just so much pressure from *everyone* to conform to every single thing the church says, and what they think the Bible says, and how people think I should dress and talk and act. Your dad is great, Mary, but everyone else... I feel like they're trying to stuff me into a tiny box, and I *hate* boxes!"

I jumped a little. Simha had said once that he hated boxes, too. I suddenly had a flashback to my university days. We were taught that if you put a frog in a pot of cold water, and heat the water very slowly, the frog won't realize and it will eventually boil to death. If you put the frog in hot water, the frog recognizes the discomfort and immediately jumps out of the water. I was the first frog—no matter how much they turned up the heat, I'd always felt committed to this little pot of mine I called home. I guess that made Alice the second frog, thrust into a situation where she felt the "social" heat was too high. Simha was somewhere in the middle. He could tell that the heat was rising, the way he spoke about the pressures from his family and work colleagues. He was making an effort to explore his options of escape, but he hadn't quite found his way out of hot water yet. Chloe was just like hot water for the rest of us frogs.

I didn't want to tell Chloe and Alice that I'd randomly reduced us all to a group of frogs in a pot of hot water in my head. I hurriedly rummaged in the huge purse I was using and pulled out two pink heart-shaped boxes, each with its own white bow. I gave one to Alice and one to Chloe. "Maybe these will cheer you girls up a little. Happy Valentine's Day!"

"Ah, Mary, cheers. That's so sweet," Alice said, leaning over and giving me a hug.

"Yeah, thanks," Chloe said, hugging me, too.

They opened their boxes. Inside, Alice found a DVD of *Sleepless in Seattle*. I knew she was a romantic. I got Chloe *Coco Before Chanel*, hoping she'd be inspired by Coco's rise to success from obscure beginnings.

"Sounds like just what I need," Chloe said with a grin. Then she frowned severely at me. "But this doesn't mean I'm gonna sleep with you. Buy me a car, and I'll think about it."

"You're disgraceful," I said as Alice hooted with laughter.

Our waitress brought us our food. Chloe sampled the soup, and her eyes widened. "Okay, this is amazin'," she said.

"Told you so," I said smugly.

"What are you and Jason doing for Valentine's Day?" Alice asked me.

"Well," I said, a little uneasy and a little shy, "He's been actin' like he has a surprise for me."

"You mean, a ring?" Chloe asked excitedly.

I shrugged.

Chloe and Alice both squealed and peppered me with questions that I couldn't answer because I really didn't know what Jason was thinking, let alone planning.

"Bro, what's up with your stomach?" Alice demanded suddenly.

"What?" I asked then realized I'd been rubbing my unsettled stomach. "It's nothin'."

"Mary Poser, you've been havin' stomach trouble for weeks now," Chloe said. "Have you been to a doctor?"

"Yes, of course. She says it's probably just a virus or lingerin' upset from somethin' I ate a while back. Nothin' to raise a fuss over."

"So you're not pregnant?" Chloe said.

"What?" I gasped. "Oh lordy, *no!* Don't look like that, Chloe Corbett. I'm *not.* Jason and I aren't even sleepin' together."

"*What?*"

"But if you're not preggers, and this belly trouble has been going on for weeks—" Alice began, looking concerned.

"I'm fine. Really," I insisted with a determined smile. "Come on, girls. Our food's gettin' cold, and we have to get to work soon."

I drove back to the office half an hour later, hoping my stomach issue wasn't going to become an issue with my friends. The truth was, it had been going on for months, not weeks, and I *had* been concerned, which was why I'd gone to the doctor. But she couldn't find anything wrong with me, even after running all of her tests, and had finally asked if I wanted an anti-anxiety prescription, which was just insulting. I'm not stressed out about anything. My stomach is unhappy about something, and I'm dealing with it. Changing my diet has helped. A lot. I even started attending a Saturday morning yoga class at the Lean Machine, and that's helping, too, I think.

My stomach is probably unhappy because I must have picked up something at one of the dive bars I've been going to in support of Jason and The Nashbros. The food at those bars is, well, a challenge to the digestive system. I'm pretty sure the health inspector isn't even game to walk in. Once The Nashbros start booking better gigs, my stomach will probably start feeling better.

Work that afternoon went just fine. I'd been acting as a sort of mentor to Howard, the conscientious guy who'd replaced the useless Tiffany, and it made me feel good to be able to answer his questions, point him in the right direction, and give him some advice based on my experience. It felt good to be reminded about how much I really do know and how good I am at my job.

Hannah was happy, too. She was practically humming as she worked. Five months of celibacy had restored her good sense and returned peace and harmony to her days. She had vowed to stay celibate until she met The One and, though she had been mightily tempted by a couple of different very hunky guys she had dated recently, she had kept to her vow, and they had sought more...accommodating pastures. Hannah's experience was helping me to keep up my confidence that taking it slow with Jason was the right thing to do until we were sure, well, that it was the right thing to do. Things were getting better with Jason, and I was sure he had a surprise in mind for me for Valentine's Day.

The sun had already set by the time I got back home a little after five-thirty. I was thinking about the clothes I'd change into to stay warm while I walked Charlie, so at first I didn't see the box sitting in front of my front door. It was about two feet tall and wide, and when I finally did realize there was a box waiting for me, I got all fluttery inside. A present! On Valentine's Day!

I carried it inside, gave Charlie his tummy rubs, then inspected my box. It had a label from a toy company I'd never heard of before. Hm.

I gave Charlie a pigskin chew so he wouldn't fret at the delay to his evening walk. Then I pulled open my box. I removed a bit of brown packing paper, and there it was—an old-fashioned toffee brown teddy bear with gleaming amber eyes and moveable arms, legs, and head.

I pulled it out and held it up to admire it. "Aren't you cute?" I said. It wasn't one of the modern overly-sweet bits of fluff. This teddy bear had much more substance and a feeling of early twentieth-century design behind it. I started to fall in love then and there.

I rummaged around in the box and found a small card tucked into a white envelope:

This little guy said he belonged to you, so I thought I'd best send him along with my warm wishes for a happy Valentine's Day.

I knew I should be happy, and I did like the teddy bear very much, but what I felt most was relief. Not only had Jason remembered that this was Valentine's Day, he'd gone out of his way to get me a gift and compose a lovely note. If this was his surprise, it was a wonderful one. A reassuring one. He really did care about me, even more than I had believed.

I sat my teddy bear in the middle of my coffee table, changed my clothes, and took Charlie for his walk. When we got back, I relocated my teddy bear to my bed where it would be safe from Charlie's less and less frequent anxiety attacks. I gave Charlie his dinner and was just heating up some leftover vegetable stew for my own supper when my phone vibrated on the kitchen counter. I had a text:

Jason: Surprise, babe! I got us a last-minute gig at the Tipsy Turkey. I need you here. Can you make it?

Mary: Thank you for the surprise! Absolutely! I'll be there in 30 minutes.

The Tipsy Turkey was a major step up for The Nashbros, and Jason wanted to include me in his success! The relief I'd felt when I'd opened my Valentine's Day gift doubled. He cared about me. He needed to have me with him. Everything was happening just as it should.

I beat my own best time for changing my clothes and fixing my hair and makeup. But even though I broke a couple of speed limits, it was close to thirty minutes later when I pulled into the gravel parking lot of the Tipsy Turkey, a popular decades-old roadhouse northwest of town off the Ashland City Highway. It's a long, one-story building painted dark blue with dark yellow trim. It has a huge, gaudy electric sign by the road. The parking lot was full, which was great for Jason, and I knew they had some of the best Southern cooking in the state, which was great for me. It also has one of the biggest bars in town and a stage that can actually hold six or seven musicians comfortably. When they were starting out, a lot of today's country and western stars had been grateful to book a gig at the Tipsy Turkey. Music producers always dropped by to check out any potential talent.

Jason, Toby, and Scotty must be out of their minds with excitement, I thought as I walked through the door and nearly got knocked right back out by the wall of noise generated by a couple hundred people crowded together drinking, eating, laughing, and talking, plus the amplified music of The Nashbros performing under bright lights. They finished "Lulu," and at least half the people in the roadhouse applauded. Wow.

I found a table about a third of the way back from the stage, ordered some red beans and rice with a sweet moscato, and set out to get everyone, not just half the customers, to applaud The Nashbros by clapping loudly and shooting "Whoo-hoo!" at the end of each song. A couple of people looked at me like I was crazy, but most folks started applauding each song, too.

They liked "I'll Have a Beer" and said "Aww!" when Jason introduced "The Skin That's Coverin' You" and said, "This is for my girl who's here supportin' me tonight." Jason was in his glory, acting like he was Kenny Chesney in a stadium of 50,000 people instead of a roadhouse with a couple hundred folks. He strutted, he swaggered, he flashed his million-watt smile, and I noticed several younger women cheering him with way too much enthusiasm.

The Nashbros finished their set to decent applause, then carried off their instruments and equipment as a larger band started setting up on the stage. A couple of minutes later, Jason worked his way to me, grinning from ear to ear.

"Isn't this amazin'?" he exclaimed as he picked me up and swung me around exuberantly.

"Amazin's the word," I said, a little breathless when he finally set me down. "How did this happen?"

"The band that's settin' up now called in a couple of hours ago to say they'd been delayed, a car accident or somethin'. Management needed someone to fill in at the last minute, someone suggested us, and here we are!"

"A car accident? Was anybody hurt?"

"I'm sure they were fine. What a great surprise, eh?"

"Yes, and thank you so much for the Valentine's Day gift," I said, beaming as we sat down.

"Valentine's Day?" Jason said, his brow furrowed. "Oh yeah! I forgot. No wonder everyone's been so lovey-dovey. The crowd's emotion was just floodin' us on the stage and liftin' us higher and higher. It was amazin'."

"You didn't forget Valentine's Day," I insisted a little desperately. "You sent me a teddy bear."

"A teddy bear? Nah! I wouldn't give you somethin' so lame,

Mary." His eyes narrowed suddenly. "Did someone give you a teddy bear?"

"Um, yeah," I said, thinking fast. "That's right. It was from my boss, Tammy. She gets mushy about Valentine's Day. She usually gives all of us somethin'."

"That woman is downright weird. Well, Happy Valentine's Day. I'll treat you to a piece of red velvet cake, how's that?" He was back to looking around at his audience, practically glowing. "I'll bet there's a dozen producers in this crowd right now. We'll get ourselves a record contract out of this, you just wait and see."

I stared at him as he gushed about the stardom that was coming his way. *He hadn't sent me the teddy bear.* That could only mean one thing: *Simha* had sent it to me! *Simha* had written that card.

Oh lordy. I sat in the Tipsy Turkey as joy and disappointment battled it out inside of me. *Simha* had known the perfect gift to send me...and it was sitting on my *bed* right now! A man thousands of miles away had thought of me, reached out to me, and my boyfriend who said he needed me had forgotten me on the biggest day of romance on the calendar.

I sat there as Jason ordered a beer and talked on and on about the certain glory coming to him. I'd fended it off for months, but now I couldn't help but compare him to Simha.

They couldn't have been more different, and it wasn't simply a difference of age, social class, and clothes. Jason might talk of stardom and glory, but he was afraid to take the risk of leaving the little pond of Nashville to make his dreams come true in the great big world beyond. Simha, on the other hand, was traveling that great big world in pursuit of his dreams, exploring possibilities, taking risks. He was taking the biggest risk of all by making himself completely vulnerable as he put his heart and soul into his movies and then shared them with the world.

He shared himself with me, whether it was giving every bit of himself in one passion-soaked night in his hotel or in his platonic texts about the frustration he felt at his mother's constant matchmaking and his father's belittling of his career.

Jason forgot to kiss me half the time we were together and never talked to me about anything except his music. He never talked about us.

I refocused on my boyfriend sitting across from me.

"Scotty said he saw a producer from Bugle Records sittin' near the bar," Jason was saying. "Bugle is small, but it's up-and-coming, and it would make a great steppin' stone to somethin' bigger and better. I've heard—"

"Jason, I need to ask you somethin'," I said.

He turned to look fully at me. "Sure. What?"

"Where do you see yourself in twelve months?"

"Isn't that what I've been sayin'? I'll be playin' all the best stages in town. I'll have a record deal with Bugle or one of the other outfits, and The Nashbros' first album will be hittin' the charts."

"Sounds great. Where do you see yourself in two years?"

"Oh, babe, I'll have an awesome contract with someone like Big Machine or Paramount or Warner Brothers. The Nashbros will have the number one album in the country, and we'll be performin' on the Country Music Awards!"

"And in five years?"

"Five? Baby, there won't be a corner of the world where you won't hear my voice comin' out of the radio! I'll be big in England and Germany. Huge in Japan—they love country music, ya know. I'll be gigantic in Russia and China. Thousands of my Aussie fans will be comin' to hear me play!"

"You mean here in Nashville?"

"Sure! I can't desert my first fans, can I? Besides, I'll have a big old house on about fifty acres with my own recording studio. I've already found the land I want with good grazin' land for horses and cattle."

"Wow." I didn't hear my name anywhere in those five years of plans. A family wasn't there. "Okay, let me ask you somethin' else. What do you think of me?"

"What do you mean?"

"I mean, what do you think of me?"

He flashed his brilliant smile. "I think you're awesome, babe! You don't get jealous of the fans or my workin' on my music. You come to my gigs, and you're always there for me. A man couldn't ask for more. Why all the questions?"

"Just curious. Let me ask you one more. How do you *feel* about me?"

"Didn't I just tell you? What's with the third degree? It's Valentine's Day! We should be celebratin'!" He suddenly lifted me up and swung me around again. He put me back down, kissed me hard and fast, grabbed his beer, and shouted, "Happy Valentine's Day, y'all! Here's to love!" He took a long swig of his beer, then lit up when he saw my brother talking to someone he knew at a nearby table. "Toby! Get your butt over here! It's time to drink!"

Toby looked up, smiled, and began to work his way over to us, carrying a long neck bottle of beer in one hand.

I plastered a smile on my face and worked really really hard to hide from my brother, my boyfriend, and myself the dissatisfaction creeping up my spine, and how much that dissatisfaction scared me. I had a good life! I had a good family, a good job, a boyfriend who had big plans for his life, a dog who loved me unconditionally. I had nothing to be dissatisfied about. Nothing. Really.

Most of all, I tried to hide from my memories of Simha on that August night, but they shoved their way into the front of my head. I heard again Simha's thoughtful answers to the questions I'd just asked Jason, his explanation of the sacred symbolism of the green stone shatkona I'd buried deep in my closet. I saw his dark eyes looking so deeply into me as he said, "I don't know what you and I are meant to be to each other, Mary, but my heart told me I had to return to you, connect with you, learn what we should be together." My whole body burned as I felt the wild woman I'd been in his arms stirring.

"Isn't this great, Mary?" Toby said as he hugged me exuberantly.

With a gasp, I crashed back into the present, feeling dizzy and disoriented. "I'm so proud of you, little brother, and so happy for you," I said, hugging him back. "I'm sure this is the start of good things for The Nashbros."

"Man, it's about time," Toby said as he sat in the chair beside Jason. "We've been bustin' our guts for years."

"Yeah, but think about all of the 'paid my dues' songs you'll be able to write and record for your first album," I said.

Toby laughed and shook his head at me.

Jason grabbed his arm. "She's right," he said. "We've got to write some dues songs. They always get lots of air time on the radio and sell great."

Toby grinned and took a swig of beer. "I feel a song comin' on."

"Yeah, you do. Come on," Jason said, standing up. "Let's go back to my place and get to work. See ya later, Mary. Thanks for comin' out."

"Sure," I said. "Don't forget we're havin' brunch with Chloe and Alice tomorrow."

"We won't," Toby promised as he and Jason headed out.

Love asks for nothing and risks everything.

❧ Rumi

Chapter Twenty-Six

It took me forty-five minutes to get home. I wasn't speeding as I headed back. In fact, I was exhausted. Bone weary. Brain dead.

I walked into my apartment, ignored Charlie's welcome home ceremony, and changed into my flannel pajamas with the greatest relief. Simha's teddy bear was watching me from across the room.

I sighed. "Oh, what am I gonna do with you?" I asked.

I climbed into bed, sat back against the headboard, and propped the teddy bear on my unhappy stomach. "You're really sweet," I confessed. And it had been sweet of Simha to send him to me. The question was, what to do with him? I'd feel too guilty putting the bear in my closet. I'd feel like a neglectful parent. If I put him in the living room, someone was bound to ask questions I didn't want to answer, and there was always the problem of Charlie's occasional anxiety attacks. I sighed again. Teddy was in my bedroom to stay.

I glanced at my phone on the bedside table. I'd been raised to send thank you cards to every friend and relative who gave me anything, and you can't hide from something so ingrained in you. I picked up my phone and opened my text app.

Mary: Dear Simha, thank you so much for your Valentine's Day gift. The teddy bear is perfect. I have to smile every time I look at him, which is a blessing on a long hard day like today. I assume Valentine's Day is not on the Hindu holiday calendar, so thanks for thinking of me.

I didn't even bother putting the phone back on my bedside table. Sure enough, a few minutes later, it vibrated in my hand.

Simha: You're very welcome. I'm glad you like him. I rather like a holiday symbolized by a heart pierced by an arrow, because love can hurt sometimes. No, Valentine's Day is not on our calendar, but Hinduism does have several love-related festivals. We have Shivaratri, which celebrates the marriage of Shiva and Shakti in February/March. We put offerings of food and drink on the altar and spend the night in prayer and meditation. Not a great idea for a date night, I suppose. In its defense, Shivaratri is romantic in *what* it celebrates rather than in *how* it is celebrated. For us, the coming together of Shiva and Shakti is both sexual and spiritual—a divine union— which something each of us hopes to replicate in our own marriages. I can think of nothing more romantic.
How did you celebrate Valentine's Day today? Are you tired because you worked long hours, or because you spent a romantic night out with someone?

My eyes widened at that. The man was not afraid of being blunt. I read his question again, and I couldn't help but smile. Romantic? Jason? Ha!

My smile faded. I reread Simha's text. His people sought a divine union in their marriages? Really? Even in the arranged marriages?

Wow. That was kind of...mind-blowing. When I thought about marriage, I thought about the best I had seen around me—marriages that were comfortable, safe, companionable. That's what I had hoped for myself. Now here was Simha saying that marriage could be so much more, and I just didn't know what to do with that information.

Mary: Yes—hard work. No—date. Plus a late night. My brother's band, The Nashbros, had a last minute gig tonight at an important venue, and I went to support him. Just got back. Exhausted. Heading to bed. Thanks again for Teddy.

I didn't get much actual sleep. My stomach was upset again and kept me awake... and I couldn't stop thinking about Simha, and Jason, and how incredibly different they were. If they were standing in the same room, they'd still be worlds apart.

The next morning just after eight o'clock while I was still in my pajamas, my landlord knocked on the door.

My landlord is a big, beefy guy with a beer gut hanging over his belt and a comb-over of about six strands of dyed brown hair that emphasizes his baldness. A half-smoked cigar is always shoved into the side of his mouth.

"Mary Poser?" he growled when I opened the door.

"Yeah," I said warily.

"You've got a dog."

As Charlie was poking his nose between my ankles, I couldn't deny it. "Yeah, I do."

"Rental agreement states no pets. No exceptions."

"Well, I had to make an exception for Charlie! The animal shelter was gonna euthanize him!"

"Not my concern. You're breakin' the terms of your rental

agreement. Either you get rid of the dog or you're evicted."

I didn't even have to think about it. "I would never get rid of Charlie! Not for you. Not for anyone."

"Then you've got thirty days to get out, or I'll sue."

"Fine!" I said defiantly. "I've been wantin' to move closer to my job anyway."

"Here's your chance," he said indifferently as he handed me an eviction notice. "Thirty days." He turned and walked back to his battered white pickup.

I closed the door. I was shaking with outrage and a little fear. I'd never flunked an exam at school, I'd never been fired from a job, and I'd never been evicted in my life. Charlie was looking anxiously up at me.

I squatted down beside him and began to rub behind his ears. "Don't you worry. I'll find us an even better place to live, some place where they *like* dogs and have neighbors who don't rat you out to the landlord."

By the time I'd showered and dressed, I felt better. It *would* be great to find a better place to live. Maybe closer to the dog park as well as the office. Maybe an apartment with a larger back garden for Charlie. Even a covered carport! I'd start looking as soon as I got home. I took Charlie for his morning walk, and then I headed for Jason's apartment.

Chloe and Alice were there ahead of me, of course, waiting at Jason's door.

"Don't say anythin'," I said, holding up my hand. "Let's just grab Jason and go. Toby's probably holdin' a place in line for us at The Pancake Pantry right now."

I knocked on Jason's door, but there was no answer and no sound of movement. I tried ringing the doorbell and then knocked again. Nothing. I looked at Chloe and Alice, and they looked at me.

"Probably hungover," Chloe said.

I sighed and knocked again. Then, with a shrug, I tried the doorknob, and sure enough, the door was unlocked. When Jason gets busy with his music, he often forgets the practical details of his life.

We walked into Jason's wreck of a studio apartment. Dirty dishes, some of which had been there a week ago, covered the formica-topped kitchen peninsula and counter. Dirty clothes were strewn across the floor and on the ratty green sofa and matching armchair. A sock was hanging over a framed buddy picture of Jason and Toby, their arms slung over each other's shoulders as they grinned at us. Music sheets and empty beer bottles littered the coffee table and the floor around it. An old acoustic guitar leaned against the end of the table. The old PC on the battered desk in the corner was still on. A video game was paused on the TV screen. Jason, wearing last night's clothes, was sprawled unconscious on top of his unmade bed. My brother was crashed out on the sofa.

"Ah, the glamorous life of the country western star," Chloe said with a wry grin as she shook her head at the mess.

"I never ever want to see his loo," Alice said with a shudder.

Chloe walked over to the computer, took one look at the screen, blanched, and hurriedly turned away. "Porn, of course. No wonder girls nowadays don't stand a chance."

"Why?" Alice asked.

"Guys are either gamin' their brains out, makin' love to their beer, or havin' sex with their computers."

Alice snorted with laughter. The guys didn't even stir. "This is how the night went," she said, going back to the door. "They walked in last night and were just too tired after taking off their jackets to get them to the closet or even drape them over a chair." Pretending to be exhausted, she stepped over the jackets lying on the floor. "They staggered a little further before their shoes were just too tight to keep on." She pretended her sneakers were pinching as she walked around Toby's black army boots and Jason's cowboy boots. "They worked on their music for a while, but their inspiration just refused to pay a visit, so they played a video game to stir up the creative juices, and when that didn't help, they switched to porn to stir up...other juices."

"*Alice!*" I gasped, blushing beet red.

"I'll bet I know why Jason's coat was just too heavy to hang up," Chloe said, picking up the jacket and rifling through the pockets. She pulled out his wallet, and Alice trotted over to see what she'd found. "Yep, I was right," Chloe said, pulling a trio of condom wrappers out of the black leather wallet. "These made the jacket way too heavy."

"Chloe, stop!" I said, trying not to giggle.

"Bro, look!" Alice hissed. She and Chloe stared at something in Jason's wallet then looked at each other, puzzled. They looked around the room a moment, and then looked at each other again.

"What?" I demanded, walking back toward them.

"Nothin'," Chloe said, shoving Jason's wallet back into his leather jacket. "Your boyfriend's just broke as usual. He probably expected you to pay for his brunch today."

"The point is moot," I said, turning to look at Jason and Toby, who hadn't moved an inch since we'd been in the apartment. "These guys aren't goin' anywhere. Looks like it's gonna be a girls' brunch today." My stomach gurgled unpleasantly, and I rubbed it.

"What is wrong with that thing?" Chloe demanded.

I grimaced. "It's just upset 'cause my landlord called on me today to evict me 'cause of Charlie. I've gotta move in thirty days."

"I'll help, bro," Alice said instantly. "I'm great at packing and shifting boxes."

"You can count on me, too," Chloe said warmly.

"Thanks, girls, I appreciate it," I said sincerely.

"*What about you boys?*" Chloe shouted.

Jason and Toby stirred. Barely.

"What?" Toby mumbled into the sofa cushion.

"*Mary has to move!*" Chloe bellowed. "*Are you gonna help?*"

"Yeah. Sure," Toby mumbled, then he rolled over on the sofa and went back to sleep.

Jason waved randomly in our general direction. "I'll try to help, but I can't guarantee anythin'. My music." He was snoring a moment later.

*Your body is away from me, but there is a window open
from my heart to yours.
From this window, like the moon,
I keep sending news secretly.*

❧ Rumi

Chapter Twenty-Seven

It was the end of a long, hard Friday workday, and I was standing in the middle of my living room, exhausted and overwhelmed as I looked helplessly at the half-empty boxes all around me. There was still so much to do, and I was moving tomorrow morning. I'd never be done packing in time!

I had to keep telling myself to stay calm and only think about one room. That way it wouldn't seem so overwhelming.

I headed for the kitchen. I had Chinese food in the refrigerator that I could heat up in the microwave and eat straight out of the carton with a plastic fork. Everything else in the kitchen could go into boxes.

One by one, I wrapped my dinner plates and put them in a heavy cardboard box, followed by salad plates and bowls. I worked my way around the kitchen, one cabinet at a time. Charlie lay half in the living room and half in the kitchen, watching me anxiously.

"It's okay, darlin'," I told him periodically. "You're comin' with me. We're just movin' to a better house. All of your things will be there, I promise."

I finally finished packing up the kitchen. I left the living room for last because, aside from the DVDs, throw pillows, and pictures, there wasn't a whole lot to pack. Moving slower than molasses in winter, I headed for my bedroom. I saw my bed and groaned. Oh, how I wished I could just hide under the covers and sleep for the next decade!

Instead, I started packing as Charlie lay in his bed and watched every single thing I did. At this point, I didn't care about wrinkled clothes. I just pulled out a drawer from my dresser, dumped the contents into a box, replaced the drawer, and pulled out another one. I pretty much did the same thing with my closet. I didn't even take my clothes off their hangers. I just scooped everything up and threw it into boxes.

The shatkona Simha had given me last August slipped to the floor. I picked it up and looked at it for the first time in six months.

I'd forgotten how green the small beads were, how beautiful the circular green stone with the interlocking triangles was, and the way the small moonstone glinted in the light. The pendant was small, but it had weight and heat as it rested in the center of my palm. I had a sudden urge to put it on. Instead, I tucked it into a corner of my purse and started packing up the things in my bedside table. My phone suddenly vibrated in the back pocket of my jeans. I glanced at my clock radio. It was a little after eleven at night.

Simha: Hi, Mary. I thought you might like to know that I'm attending the Nashville Film Festival next month. I wasn't meant to be attending, but we just got notification that my feature, *Passion*, has been scheduled for a prime slot. Manal, my producer, booked our tickets today. I'll be staying at the Green Hills Hampton Inn. I'm hoping to see you again while I'm in town. How about lunch one day?

I had picked up the shatkona, and he texted me in that instant. I'd heard about people calling each other at exactly the same moment, but this guy's timing was becoming uncanny.

So Simha was coming back to town, and he called me the same day he found out. I couldn't hide from the fact that it scared me, a lot, to have Simha so near...and it thrilled me. I couldn't hide from the images filling my head of how Simha and I could spend the ten days of the festival together. Most of those images were a replay of how we'd spent the time in his hotel room last August. Thank God he didn't ask me to meet him at the hotel! He knew I'd feel safer with lunch. But I couldn't have a lunch date with Simha. What about Jason? We could casually run into each other at the festival, but the idea of lunch date had me weak in the knees. I just couldn't.

My heart was pounding and I was blushing and my hands were cold and clammy. Danger seemed to be closing in on me. It was squeezing the oxygen out of my lungs. I was rattled and overwhelmed, and what I wanted most as I stood in the middle of my disaster area of a bedroom was safety. Seeing Simha, particularly in my current condition, was *not* safe. But I couldn't just ignore him.

Mary: I'm so glad to hear your film is being shown. Congratulations! Unfortunately, the film festival is coming at the worst possible time for me. I'm way busy. I'm swamped with work and family stuff, and I have to move into a new house next month, so I'll have to see how I go. Sorry.

I felt like such a coward. I knew Simha would react poorly, but I didn't want to go into the details of my relationship with Jason, and seeing him would turn my safe little world upside down. Two minutes later, my phone vibrated again.

Simha: Disappointed of course, but I understand that you're busy. Perhaps after your move, which I know can be quite stressful, we could see each other if I'm still in town?

I avoided eye contact with Teddy, who I'm sure was frowning at me, and I got back to work.

The next few weeks passed by in a flash, and the film festival opening night raced closer on the calendar. Saturday morning, working on just four hours of sleep, I was helping Erin stuff the last of my bedding into boxes while Chloe finished packing up the living room. Toby and Alice carried furniture out to the U-Haul truck he'd backed up to my front door, and Charlie was scratching at the back door. I'd put him in the tiny backyard to keep him safe while people trooped in and out of the apartment.

"Oh lordy, I didn't give Charlie his breakfast!" I suddenly cried in the middle of folding up my comforter.

"You take care of him," Erin said, taking my end of the comforter out of my hands. "I've got this."

"Thanks," I said gratefully.

I hurried into the kitchen, grabbed some food out of the refrigerator, dumped it into Charlie's bowl, and then let him in.

"I'm sorry, darlin'," I said soothingly as he dashed for his bowl. "I won't forget again, I promise."

Charlie looked despondently at the food in his bowl.

"What's the matter with Charlie?" Chloe asked as she peeked into the kitchen. "Is he off his food?"

"No," I said. "I'm just tryin' to switch him to a new diet."

Chloe peered into his bowl. "What is that?"

"Tofu with a bit of vegetable broth."

"Seriously?" Chloe demanded. "Just because you've turned vegetarian, your dog has to be vegetarian, too?"

"It's worth a try. A girl in my yoga class said her dog's been on a vegetarian diet for years and is doin' fine, so I thought I'd give it a go with Charlie."

"You really did fall off a bridge, didn't you?" Chloe said, shaking her head and heading back into the living room.

I ignored her snide humor and squatted down beside my dog. "Come on, Charlie, give it a try."

He looked pleadingly up at me.

"There's a dog biscuit waitin' for you if you try," I promised him.

He started eating, not a lot, but some. Clearly, I would have to think twice about putting tofu on his future menus.

With the furniture loaded, Toby and Alice had started packing the remaining boxes.

"Look at this," Alice said, holding up my bottle of laundry detergent with a sticker of a dolphin on it that read 'protecting our oceans.' "You even use dolphin-friendly washing powder. That's so sweet!"

"Yeah, when was the last time you saw a dolphin in Nashville?" Chloe scoffed. Thankfully, Chloe wasn't in charge of saving the planet. She spotted Toby in the kitchen and headed his way. "Toby, rescue me from this madhouse!"

My brother shook his head. "Well, you work out how to pack all this stuff of hers, and then we can all leave."

"Hey, Toby!" Erin called from my bedroom. "Give me a hand."

"I'll give you two," he said, heading down the hall.

He came right back, carrying a big box packed with most of my bed linens. He dropped it on the floor near the open front door and pulled the teddy bear Simha had given me out from under his arm.

"This thing's too big to fit in this box, and all of the others are almost full," he said. "You might as well just bin it."

"No!" I shouted in a sudden panic as I grabbed Teddy out of his hand.

"It's just a teddy bear," Toby said, exasperated.

"He's a gift, and he's important to me."

"Is that the pressie Simha gave you on Valentine's Day?" Alice asked, coming over to take a look. "What a cracka of a teddy!"

"Yes, it is," I said tensely, wishing Alice didn't say everything that came into her head. It dawned on me, from the mention of Simha's name, that he was probably in town by now.

"That Indian dude gave you this?" Toby demanded incredulously.

"That Indian dude was just bein' friendly," I retorted.

"You're with Jason," Toby argued defiantly, holding up the teddy by the ankle. "That darn foreigner's got no right sendin' you gifts, *especially* Valentine's Day gifts."

Simha's gift was looking to take the fall for my blatant oversight of not telling Simha about Jason as Toby looked ready to rally a lynch mob for my teddy bear. "Simha is a friend," I said, squaring off with my brother. "He gave me a gift. I gave Chloe and Alice gifts on Valentine's Day, too. They didn't mean anythin' except friendship. You gave Jason a new cowboy hat for Christmas. It doesn't mean you want to marry him."

"That's different!" Toby said furiously.

"How?" I demanded.

Toby glared at me. I glared at him.

"These boxes aren't gonna pack and load themselves," Chloe said mildly.

With an oath, Toby grabbed the linens box and carried it out to the truck.

"Thanks," I said gratefully to Chloe.

She shrugged. "Stringin' along two guys at the same time. I

didn't know you had it in you."

I gasped in outrage. "I'm not stringin' anyone along!"

"That's not what I'd say if I was Jason or Simha."

I glared at her then looked at Teddy. His amber eyes regarded me calmly. Stubbornness welled within me. I wasn't stringing anyone along, and I wasn't giving up Teddy. Jason had given me exactly zip for Valentine's Day, and I deserved something.

I carried my teddy bear out to my car and put him in the front seat.

Nine hours later, I was officially settled in my new home: one-half of a duplex just three blocks from Shelby Park and only eight minutes from work. It was a hundred dollars more a month, which ate up the raise I'd gotten in January, but it had a bigger kitchen with a lot more counter space compared to my old apartment, a bigger bathroom, and a large fenced and shared yard for Charlie to run around in. The landlord had even said I could install a doggie door in the back door off the small laundry room.

Chloe and Alice had helped me unpack my kitchen boxes, and then they'd had to go. Erin had helped me unpack my bedroom things and insisted on helping me make my bed. "You'll feel like you're home if you walk in here tonight to find everythin' all set up nice and cozy and waitin' for you," she had insisted before she left for work. Toby had stayed, helping me arrange the furniture and finish unpacking.

I was dead on my feet as I started organizing my DVD collection. Charlie was bristling with energy as he sniffed his way from one room to the next and then started all over again.

Toby walked into the living room after having installed the doggie door in the back door. He was shoving his phone into his back pocket. "I just ordered you some pizza. Don't worry, it just has veggie toppin's," he said. "You need to eat, and then you need to go to bed."

"You are a saint, and I don't deserve you," I said, giving him a hug.

"Someone's got to look after you," he said gruffly as he awkwardly returned my hug, "'cause when it comes to takin' care of yourself, you don't have the sense God gave a gnat."

I chuckled. "Today every inch of my achin' body agrees with you a hundred percent. I am never movin' again for as long as I live."

"Hey, guys," Jason said, walking into my new house, "sorry I'm late, but I've got great news! A producer at Wildcat Records caught one of our sets at Sophy's Place last week, and he really likes our music. He's gonna produce a demo for us and then run it by the owner to see if he'll go for makin' an album!"

"That's fantastic, dude!" Toby cheered as he and Jason gave each other bear hugs and then high-fived each other. He had a hundred questions for Jason about the deal.

I ignored them both as I sat back down on the living room's hardwood floor and continued organizing my DVDs. When that was done, I carried the last box of clothes into my bedroom.

"You managed to miss the main event here," Toby said to Jason as I walked back out. "We're pretty much done here."

"Looks good, man," Jason said. "Why do rental walls always have to be white?"

"It's a law or somethin'," Toby said. He picked up my teddy bear from the top of my box of toiletries and held it out to Jason. "Turns out Valentine's Day was a little extra special for Mary this year. Say hi to Mary's boyfriend, little fella."

"Huh?" Jason said. He turned on me. "Who gave this to you?"

"It's none of your business," I said as I snatched Teddy out of Toby's hand and started carrying him to my bedroom.

Jason followed me. "Did that foreign guy who keeps textin' you give you that doll?" he demanded.

I put Teddy on top of my pillows and turned on Jason with a feast of fury I didn't know I had in me. "Why weren't you here today? Everyone else came to help except you. Even *Erin* was here packin' and loadin' and unloadin' boxes!"

"You shouldn't have let her. She could have blown another pipe in her brain, and it would have been *your* fault."

I had never been so close to slapping someone in my life, but I kept my hands clenched in fists at my sides. "You are the most ignorant, selfish person I've ever known!"

"Don't try to change the subject," Jason growled as he grabbed Teddy and held him up in front of me. "I am not happy about this!"

I yanked Teddy out of his hand. "I don't care," I said.

"You *lied* to me, Mary. You said Tammy gave this to you."

I blushed. I'd told the white lie to protect Jason's feelings, and it had backfired on me big time. "When I said that, I didn't know who had sent me the teddy bear. I had originally thought you had been a great boyfriend who had remembered Valentine's Day and cared enough to give a teddy bear to me. When you told me you'd forgotten, that was the first I knew that someone else must have sent it to me. I was just guessin' when I said it could have come from Tammy."

"Well, you were wrong, weren't you?" Jason sneered. "And you worked real hard to keep your secret admirer a secret!"

"Simha is not an admirer. He's a friend. A *long-distance* friend."

"That foreigner has no right sendin' you anythin'!"

"It was just a friendly little gift that doesn't mean anythin'!"

"Mary, you can't be takin' gifts from other men."

"Fine," I retorted as I stormed into my new kitchen with Teddy. I threw off the lid of the rubbish bin that I'd placed in the corner of the room and shoved Teddy in. "Happy now?" I challenged Jason who was watching me from the corridor.

"Yes! You're *my* girlfriend!" Jason roared.

"Well, I don't *feel* like your girlfriend!" I shouted right back at him. "You gave me a ticket to a concert you wanted to go to for my birthday. You gave me exactly *nothin'* for Valentine's Day. We haven't had a date in two weeks, and you didn't even help me move. You never help me with anythin' that's important *to me!*"

I stalked back into the living room with Jason dogging my heels. "I turned up tonight, didn't I?" he demanded.

"Yeah! After all the work was done."

"Mary, I was workin'! I'm devotin' every wakin' minute of the day to The Nashbros, except when I'm workin' at that damned minimum wage job. You know that! You know how important it is to sacrifice everythin' for The Nashbros right now! We're on the verge of breakin' into the big time."

I ignored him. Instead, I got up right up in Toby's face and jabbed my finger into his chest. "Happy now?"

"I didn't mean to start a fight," he said, not meeting my eyes.

"Didn't you?" I said bitterly.

"I just don't want anythin' comin' between you guys. You two belong together. We've all been best friends and family since we were kids. I didn't want some foreign guy messin' that up."

I stared up at my brawny younger brother, stunned by the connections my brain was suddenly making. "Last August, when Simha came back to town and we had dinner...did you tell Jason?"

"Well, yeah—"

My eyes widened with mingled fury and horror. "Is that why Jason asked to get together over drinks and catch up?"

"Maybe," he said, flushing and still not meeting my eyes. "I can't remember."

"I do not *believe* this!" I exploded as I flung away from him. "My own brother conspirin' against me! And *you!*" I said, jabbing a finger into Jason's chest. "Suddenly decidin' to jump back into my life. What was the matter, Jason? Were you jealous because I might be movin' on from you?"

"No!" he insisted earnestly. "Well, maybe. It's just that havin' some other guy chasin' after you made me realize that I couldn't stand losin' you to someone else and never bein' in your life again."

"You're barely in my life *now!*"

"I know it's been hard on you, babe. But just as soon as we get this album deal signed, you and I will do some celebratin' together, just wait and see."

"And if the Wildcat deal falls through? How much longer do I have to wait?"

"Mary, what in hell do you want from me?" Jason demanded.

"What do you think I want?" I shouted. His blank look only enraged me more. "Get out of my house. Both of you. Get out!" I turned on my heel, stalked into my bedroom, and slammed the door behind me.

"Geez, Toby, are all the Poser women so high-strung?" Jason asked my brother.

"I heard that!" I shouted through my bedroom door. "*Get out!*"

A moment later, I heard them walk out of my new house, slamming my front door behind them. I stormed back into the living room. The only male in my new house was Charlie.

"Are all men pigs?" I demanded of my dog, who was watching me anxiously. "Are they all stupid, ignorant, selfish brats? What's with the boys club, sticking up for each other and not givin' a damn about anyone else's feelin's?" Charlie sat through my tirade, just looking at me. I'm sure he was totally interested in everything I had to say. "Tell me, Charlie, are male egos so fragile that they can't stand having a woman they cheated on and haven't talked to in nearly two years even look at another man?"

Charlie clearly understood that this wasn't going to end well. He scuttled off to the safety of his bed in my new bedroom. I folded my arms over my chest and glared after him. Now I felt guilty for yelling at my dog.

Of course, there was the little matter of the white lie I'd told

Jason on Valentine's Day. I'd known the teddy bear hadn't come from Tammy the minute Jason told me he hadn't given it to me. I'd known it was Simha. I'd known Jason would have a conniption fit if he knew...and I'd sure been right. Had I been wrong trying to protect him? Would it have been better if I'd been honest instead? He'd still have been mad, but maybe he wouldn't have been as mad? Maybe it would've inspired him to show me a little more affection on Valentine's Day?

Fortunately, I was saved from coming up with an answer when my doorbell rang. I jerked it open, planning to blast Toby or Jason or both of them for daring to come back. I snapped my mouth shut when I saw that it was a gangly pizza delivery guy. He took two steps back when he saw my face.

"You ordered a pizza?" he asked tentatively.

"Yes."

He shoved the flat white box into my hands.

"Thanks. What do I owe you?"

"It was paid by credit card when it was ordered, ma'am," the boy said, backing away. "Have a good day!" He turned and quickly headed to his car.

The pizza didn't stop me one iota from hating Toby and every other man, and it didn't make me feel less guilty about my little white lie, but it did remind me that I hadn't eaten anything since some leftover Chinese food for breakfast, and I was starving. I carried the pizza over to my dining table and didn't bother with a plate or a knife or a napkin as I usually would. I opened the lid, pulled a big slice of veggie-covered pizza free, and shoveled it into my mouth. I couldn't resist the satisfying relief of a moment of gluttony.

I was about to grab a second slice when my phone vibrated on my coffee table. I glared at it. Then I ate another slice of pizza, walked into the kitchen, wiped my hands on a paper towel, and went to see who had dared to bother me on tonight of all nights.

Simha: I hope your move went well and that you're now relaxing with Charlie cuddling beside you. Now that all that hard work is done, how about celebrating your new residence with lunch with me tomorrow?

So much for perfect timing! The last thing I needed to think about right now was an inappropriate date with Simha. I glared at my phone then ate another slice of pizza. Which helped. With my stomach filling and my fury ebbing, I felt bad about turning Simha down and making him wait to see me. I mean, after all, he'd flown thousands of miles to attend a film festival in my home town. He'd given me a month's notice he was coming, which was considerate. I should schedule a time to get together. The truth was, part of me really wanted to see him, too.

But I shouldn't. Simha would be dangerous to my world and to my life. His timing was just too wrong now. I was dating Jason, even though I still really wanted to slug him. It wouldn't be fair to Jason for me to see the man who'd sent me a teddy bear for Valentine's Day...would it?

My belly was now full, and the exhaustion from thirty-six hours of hard work and just four hours of sleep left me like a limp rag on the chair. There wasn't an ounce of energy left in me. I had nothing left to support the walls that usually kept me safe. I realized for the first time how much every cell of my body responded to the idea of seeing Simha, of being alone with him. And I felt a surging hunger to see him again, hear his sensual voice, drink in his rich laugh, watch his smile that lit up his dark eyes when he looked at me. The fear and the desire battled it out for a couple of minutes, and then I just gave up. I was too tired to deal with anything or anyone, even me.

Mary: I'm sorry, Simha, but I'm just too exhausted to make any plans right now. You're sweet for wanting to celebrate my move with me, but I can't do lunch tomorrow because I'm planning to pretty much sleep all day long. I may even skip church for only the second time in my life tomorrow. Enjoy Nashville, and I'll check in with you later.

Wearily, I stood up and slid my phone into my back pocket. I closed the lid of the pizza box, carried it into my new kitchen, and put it into my refrigerator. I turned off the living room and kitchen lights and began trudging down the short hall to my new bedroom. My cell phone began vibrating against my fanny.

"Oh no!" I groaned. I waited until I'd walked into my brightly lit bedroom before I pulled out my phone and looked at my newest text.

Simha: Is there something wrong I need to know about?

A tear trickled down my cheek. Oh lordy, what was I going to do?

There is little one can say about love. It has to be lived, and it's always in motion.

❧ *Rumi*

Chapter Twenty-Eight

I didn't spend all of Sunday in bed, but I spent all morning in there. I only got up when Charlie insisted he was really really hungry and he'd eat anything, even tofu. I eased myself out of bed and shuffled into the kitchen. I opened a can of vegetarian dog food, put a big scoop into his bowl, added in some bits of leftover pizza, and put the bowl on his kitchen mat. He attacked it like he'd gone weeks without food instead of hours.

I took my time in my new shower, using the heat to wash away all the tension that had been building up in my shoulders. When I got out, I felt human. I got dressed and looked at my room and saw that Erin had been right. Having everything in place, without a box in sight, did make me feel more cozy. I walked out to my living room and looked at my familiar furniture and the pictures of family and friends all around. My picture of Jesus was hanging on the far wall. I felt more at home. I liked this new house.

I took Charlie for a nice long walk in Shelby Park. The sun was warm on my head and shoulders, and the scent of growing things filled my lungs. We got back to the duplex an hour later, and Charlie settled down happily for his afternoon nap.

I grabbed my purse and my keys. "I'll be back," I promised him. Then I walked back outside to my car, which was in my one-car garage. I now had a garage!

I drove out of my new tree-filled neighborhood and onto Shelby Avenue and headed for the Gateway Bridge. Yes, I knew what I was doing. Every Sunday for the last six weeks, usually after church, I had tried to make myself cross that bridge. Every Sunday for the last six weeks I'd failed.

I had the front windows of my hatchback down about three inches each. Warm spring air poured over me as I drove through the old residential neighborhoods on either side of Shelby Avenue with a few teenaged skateboarders riding the sidewalks. My Carrie Underwood CD poured soothingly familiar music into the car as she sang "Jesus, Take The Wheel."

I would have liked Jesus, or anyone else for that matter, to take the wheel, as I could feel my heart starting to pound as I passed South Fourth Street and drove across the overpass above I-24. My hands were clenched on the steering wheel. I passed Interstate Drive, and nausea roiled within me.

A red light at South Second Street stopped me. I'd have stopped anyway. I looked in my rearview mirror. No one was behind me. I stared ahead at the sloping, slightly curved on-ramp that Shelby Avenue became. I could barely see the silvery-white arch of the bridge over the river. I was shaking.

I couldn't do it. I still couldn't cross the Gateway Bridge, and I didn't know why. It had been almost exactly a year since my accident. I should be over it by now. I should be able to cross this bridge. But something life-changing had happened to me here, something I still didn't understand. And because I didn't understand it, I couldn't do anything about it, and that just made me so mad and scared that I didn't have words or room for it all. I hit pause on my Carrie Underwood CD. The wheel was in my hands, and I just wasn't ready to steer it toward something that scared the bejesus out of me.

A car blasted its horn behind me, and I jumped. I quickly turned right onto South Second Street then turned around at Victory Avenue, grateful that football season had ended, and LP Field, its vast asphalt parking lots, and surrounding streets were deserted. I turned on my car radio as I took Shelby Avenue back to the entrance to I-24 and merged cautiously onto the highway. Jo Dee Messina began singing her bleeding-heart ballad "Bring On the Rain."

"Oh, shut up!" I said, turning off the car radio. I was no longer in the mood for a song preaching my destiny from the dashboard. My stomach twisted and clenched, and I knew it had nothing to do with changing my diet. I did feel so much better eating vegetarian, but my stomach was refusing to settle. I knew I was also feeding on a heavy serving of anxiety, and it was becoming a meal I could no longer digest with any sense of ease or comfort. Erin was unhappy at home and starting to argue with Mama more and more. Daddy was doing his Jerry Lewis impressions more frequently, and Mama was starting to argue with him about that. She insisted that life should be serious and that fun for fun's sake was just plain wrong. I knew Aunt Sara and Mama weren't speaking at the moment because of a flare-up they'd had about Mama accusing Aunt Sara of setting a bad example for her nieces by choosing not to get married. Mama choosing to get married right out of high school is something she feels dutifully obliged to advertise as God's plan for all of us. Heaven knows how she really feels beyond this sense of duty. Everyone was aware that Grandpa Tom's memory was starting to get foggier, too. That always worried me.

The icing on my indigestible cake of anxiety was worrying about how Jason really felt about me, wondering what he wanted from me, and fussing over what I wanted from him. The fog in my head concealing the road of where we were going made me feel scared, guilty, and uneasy. It seemed like discontent was always bubbling inside me just below my skin, not just about Jason, but about everything, and that worried me most of all.

Ouch! Nothing clears the mind like a jolt of pain. I looked down at my left forearm at the deep indentations I was leaving from my nails digging into the skin. I quickly commanded my right hand to leave my left arm alone. I felt so out of control.

When the pain settled, I could feel what I wasn't prepared to think about. Simha was in Nashville, I was doing everything in my power to avoid him, and I didn't want to know why. I know a lot of things scare me, but I've never realized how frozen I can be with fear.

I pulled into the crowded parking lot at the Nashville Zoo, flashed my pass at the ticket clerk, and headed for the butterfly enclosure. I walked into the manmade rainforest. The warm, humid air engulfed me, filled my lungs, and eased a little of the tension in my shoulders. Hundreds of butterflies were flying around dozens of people, more than half of them children who were talking excitedly and loudly about everything they were seeing and touching, which was a lot.

It was easy to spot Aunt Sara standing at the far end of the enclosure. Her new short haircut, the catalyst for her argument with Mama, made her stand out in a crowd of mostly long-haired women. Mama had insisted it made her look mannish and was sure to chase off any prospective husband. Aunt Sara had whipped out her reply with a sharpened tongue, saying that she didn't want to be like Mama, prettying herself for some man's approval. That didn't go down so well with Mama.

Aunt Sara was trying to referee three kids—all of them under ten, no parents to be seen—who were trying to catch the butterflies flittering around them. Two of them listened to her and backed off. The third, a dark-haired boy of about nine with a stubborn expression, did not. He made a grab for a big blue and black butterfly, and my rebel aunt squirted him right in the face with her water bottle.

He let out a howl of surprise and outrage, which quickly brought his errant parents to his side. He faked some tears and pointed an accusing finger at Aunt Sara.

"Oh, I'm so sorry!" Aunt Sara said with a plausible smile. "I was tryin' to mist some of these orchids, and I must have accidentally squirted your son by mistake. I'm so glad you're here," she said to the suspicious parents, "because the butterflies are such delicate creatures, and children can sometimes ignore the rules of the enclosure and try to grab them which would, of course, kill them. The butterflies, I mean. The zoo counts on parents helpin' their children to learn to respect nature, and I just know you'll do a great job with your three wonderful children. Y'all enjoy learnin' about these beautiful gifts from God on this lovely Sunday afternoon."

The parents herded their three children away from my treacherous aunt, who turned to me with a smile.

"Hello, Niece!"

"Hey, Aunt Sara," I said, kissing her on her cheek. "That was an interestin' solution to your problem."

"Wasn't it?" she said, beaming. "Respecting nature sometimes comes with the need to establish boundaries."

"Boundaries established." I smiled warmly.

"How are things?"

"Daddy wants you to make up with Mama."

Aunt Sara scowled. "Compassion for my dear sister and her need to control everyone has its boundaries as well."

"Well, just don't go squirting her in the face with water too much. She just worries about you. She wants you to be happy."

"I *am* happy! And *everyone* has been complimentin' me on my haircut."

"It makes you look ten years younger," I assured her.

Aunt Sara laughed. "Did you see that huge tree trunk stuck under the Gateway Bridge?"

"It's a big-un," I said, not meeting her gaze.

"Mary, there is no stuck tree trunk. You're still takin' the long way 'round, aren't you?"

"Yeah," I said, blushing a little.

She cupped my face with her hands. "Maybe part of you is still stuck under that bridge? Relax. Don't force it. The day will come when you'll be ready to cross the Gateway Bridge, and you'll just do it. You'll see."

"But when?" I could hear the trembling in my voice. Surely Aunt Sara could, too. "It's been a year! I shouldn't still be scared of it. It's embarrassin'."

"Facing what makes us feel threatened or unsafe shouldn't be embarrassin', child. That's where our strength of character develops."

My phone started ringing. "Sorry," I said to Aunt Sara. I pulled my phone out of my purse, checked to see who was calling, and nearly dropped my phone. Simha! I shoved my purse back into my purse as it continued to ring.

"Don't you want to get that?" Aunt Sara asked, watching me closely without looking like she was watching me closely.

"No, it can go to voicemail. I'll check it later." I finally met her eyes. "It's Simha. He's in town for the film festival. He wants to get together."

"That's wonderful!"

"No, it's not!" I sighed.

"Why not?"

"Because I'm with Jason!"

"Jason? Don't get me started on that—"

I glared at her.

"—interestin' boy," she said with a smug smile. "Are you goin' to see him while he's in town?"

I bit my lower lip. "I don't know. Toby and Jason act like I'm a two-timin' hussy because of him."

"Are you?"

"No! Simha and I are just friends."

"With benefits," Aunt Sara added wickedly.

"No! No, I'm not gonna sleep with him again. Oh lordy, do you think he thinks he's gonna sleep with me again?"

"I have no idea. I've never met the man. But after the night you two shared last August, I wouldn't be surprised if he was thinkin' about it. Maybe not on this visit, though," she added hurriedly, "but at some point in the future. I wouldn't be surprised if you were secretly hopin' for the same."

"What?" I said, blushing all over. "No! Of course I'm not."

"My poor niece," Aunt Sara said with kind eyes. "You don't know what you want, do you?"

"No," I said miserably.

"Would you like to know?"

"Of course I would!"

"Okay. Close your eyes then. Go on, close them!"

I considered her a moment. Then I closed my eyes.

"Okay," Aunt Sara said, "now I want you to think about Jason. I want you to picture him in your mind, from the top of his cowboy hat to the tips of his cowboy boots. Can you see him?"

"Yep."

"Good. Now, still holdin' that picture of him in your mind, I want you to think about all of the things about your interestin' young man that appeal to you. Now, where in your body do you feel him?"

I placed my hand flat against my solar plexus.

"All right," Aunt Sara said, "leave your hand there and shoo Jason out of your mind. Now, I want you to think about Simha. Picture him in your mind, from the top of his head down to his toes."

I couldn't help but smile as I remembered Simha the first time I'd seen him at last year's film festival. I saw again his tall, lean, muscular body draped in that perfect black suit, and his thick, curly black hair brushing past the collar of his white silk shirt. I saw his archer's-bow mouth that had once moved so hungrily over mine and his dark brown eyes framed with thick black lashes that seemed to burn into my very soul.

"Now," Aunt Sara said quietly, "still holdin' that picture of Simha in your mind, I want you to think about all of the things about your Indian filmmaker that appeal to you."

Oh, where to start? I loved his sexy voice and low laugh. I liked his intelligence, and I liked being challenged by ideas that were different from mine. I admired his courage in pursuing a career no one in his family believed in, and I admired his willingness to make himself vulnerable by putting his heart and soul on a movie screen. I liked that he was interested in what I thought and that he cared about what I wanted and needed. It secretly pleased me that he had overwhelmed me and had taken me too far too soon, and I even loved his passion which had sparked something wild and powerful inside me.

"Good," Aunt Sara murmured. "Now, where in your body do you feel Simha?"

I raised my other hand to my chest.

"Okay, keep your hands where they are, open your eyes, and take a look at your hands."

I looked down and saw that my right hand was resting on my solar plexus, where Simha had said we house our third chakra, and my left hand was right between my breasts. I hurriedly dropped them to my side.

"What's all this supposed to mean?" I demanded.

"That's up to you."

"I don't know! All you did was remind me of my stomach, and I'd gone almost a whole hour without thinkin' about it."

"Your stomach? What's wrong with your stomach?"

I absent-mindedly rubbed my belly. "I don't know. It's been actin' up for the last couple of months. The doctor says nothin's wrong. Stickin' to a vegetarian diet is helpin'."

"Are you sure?"

I avoided her prying eyes and turned to look at several butterfly chrysalises hanging from the slim limb of a young African Tulip tree. It took a minute to shift my focus from my belly and my aggravating aunt to what I was actually staring at. "Hey, look!" I said in surprise. "One of the butterflies is wrigglin' in its chrysalis."

Aunt Sara peered at the grayish cocoon. "That one's still a caterpillar. It's not quite a butterfly yet, but it's gettin' there."

"How much longer does it have to wait?"

"That's hard to say. Each caterpillar, and each butterfly, is different. When it's ready, it will transform, break out, and fly free."

I looked at her suspiciously. "Are you talkin' about me or the butterfly?"

"My dear little *mariposa*, all butterflies, of course!" Aunt Sara said with a smile.

I had to laugh. "Mama's right. You are incorrigible."

"And you wouldn't have me any other way."

"No, I wouldn't," I said with a smile as I kissed her on her cheek.

I walked slowly back to my car, thinking about caterpillars, butterflies, bridges, bellies, and men. Only when I was safe in my car did I pull out my phone and, reluctantly, listen to Simha's voicemail.

"Hi, Mary! I hope you're getting all your work done that's keeping you busy."

The shock of hearing Simha's warm, sensual voice for the first time in six months made me feel like all of Aunt Sara's butterflies were fluttering around inside me, and that rattled me. How could just listening to his *voice* have this effect on me?

"I want to invite you to something that is both special for me and hopefully fun for you. My film will premiere at the festival next Wednesday night, and I want very much for you to come. I'd also like you to come with me to the presentation dinner that Thursday night, the concluding night of the festival, when all of the awards are handed out. It's a lot of fun, and the food is great. Let me know if you can come. Enjoy the rest of your Sunday!"

The voicemail instructions began droning into my ear, and I hurriedly ended the call.

I stared at my steering wheel for a while, not knowing what to do, what to say, what I wanted, or what I secretly wanted. I couldn't give him the answer he wanted. Not right now. I needed time to think and pray about this.

I chewed on my lower lip for a minute, then I sent him a text.

Mary: Thanks for the very kind invitations. I'll see what I can do.

I stared at my text for a long time after I sent it. Then I called Jason. He answered on the fourth ring.

"Hey, babe!" he said in a hopeful voice. "Are you talking to me again?"

"I am if you take me out for somethin' to eat," I replied.

He chuckled. "And you eat the craziest things these days. I'll pick you up in an hour."

"Great. See you then."

Then I drove back to my new house, the long way, as usual. On the way, my stomach started munching on a big piece of homemade anxiety pie.

Once I have seen your face
I shut my eyes to others.

❧ *Rumi*

Chapter Twenty-Nine

I was sitting about halfway back from the movie screen in the stadium seating of the largest of the Green Hills Regal Cinema's theaters. Chloe and Alice were on either side of me. My ears were filled with the cacophony of hundreds of conversations all going on around me at the same time. The place was packed, mostly with well-dressed locals, but I recognized some even more dressed-up local celebrities, some Nashville Film Festival organizers, a half dozen or so movie actors, and foreigners who, Chloe whispered, were Hollywood movie producers and directors.

I hadn't told Simha I was coming. I thought that I should tell him what was going on in my life face-to-face—about Jason and, well everything—but not in a situation where I felt trapped and couldn't escape easily. Perhaps we could just casually cross paths in the lobby, and I could tell him then?

I hadn't realized just how big a deal Simha's film was until now.

"I told you *Passion* had a lot of buzz," Chloe said, practically vibrating with excitement. "They're sayin' it should walk away with the prize in the narrative feature competition. There's a load of prestige that goes with that and benefits for anyone who knows the director for the next project." She'd come tonight to support me and because she was curious about Simha, but now I could see the wheels whirring in her brain. Tonight had suddenly become a stepping stone on her way to movie stardom.

"Bro! Pretty soon you'll get to say you knew Simha when," Alice said with a grin.

"Yeah," I said weakly. This was becoming bad déjà vu. My palms were sweating.

I shouldn't be here. I shouldn't have agonized twenty minutes trying to decide what dress to wear tonight. I shouldn't have taken twice as long doing my makeup and hair. I shouldn't be sitting here anxious for Simha's success. I shouldn't be sitting here remembering every single moment of that first night we'd met and spent together a year ago.

Simha walked into the theater looking impossibly gorgeous in a charcoal suit that molded itself to his lean frame, a white shirt, and a black and white striped silk tie. He'd cut his hair. It was short on the sides and in back and cropped short and thick on top. Long sideburns emphasized the planes of his face. He was standing next to the most ornately robed Hindu woman I could imagine. Everything about her glorious outfit glittered in a sparkling display of colorful red and white silk and golden trim. Dazzling gold jewelry was layered up her arms. An ornate decoration of beaded pearls and precious stones adorned her forehead and neck, and even more precious stones dangled from her ears. Even the piercing in her nose sparkled in the dimly lit theater. She was made up so heavily and impeccably under her intricately patterned head covering that I couldn't tell how old she was. I thought Nashville women knew how to dress to the nines. This outfit must have taken hours to prepare. Who was she?

They walked into the theater, and Simha sat down next to the gorgeous Middle Eastern woman I'd seen him with last year, Manal, his producer. She beamed at him then tilted her head back and laughed at something he said. He seemed so relaxed and comfortable between these two pillars of beauty and grace.

I was starting to feel more comfortable about keeping my distance from Simha. If I had to replace one of those beautiful feminine pillars, Simha's house would soon crumble to the ground. Waves of inadequacy were thundering through my head. Anyway, Jason was my boyfriend. I had no right to be having feelings about a man I hadn't seen in six months and had worked so hard not to see this week. Oh lordy, I shouldn't have come tonight.

"If Courtney Cox can get a hit series and a TV career out of appearing in some old Bruce Springsteen music video," Chloe was saying, "then if I can get myself on Simha's arm, I'll be meetin' the producers and directors he's meetin', and I'll be able to give 'em my resume."

"What?" I glared at Chloe with an immediate anger I wasn't quite accustomed to. "Chloe, no! You can't use Simha like that."

"Why not?" she asked. "In this business, it's who you know that gets you where you want to be. With Simha, I could be walkin' the red carpet at my own movie premiere next year."

"That's so you, Chloe," Alice said. "You always dream big, and you've got the balls to back it up."

"Balls?" Chloe said in amusement.

I was watching Simha talking with Manal and worrying about Chloe's plans for him and how those plans might drag me back into his company, and that idea just plain scared me, which helped me better understand why I'd worked so hard to avoid him this last week. Simha scared me. He was dangerous because he provoked something inside me, something I wasn't prepared to see or know.

The lights in the audience suddenly dimmed, and everyone quieted down. A big, barrel-chested man in a tailored light gray suit walked to the center of the stage carrying a wireless microphone.

"Howdy, y'all," he said with a big smile. "My name's Ted Carmichael, and I'm one of the Directors of the Nashville Film Festival. I want to welcome you to the final night of film screenings. Tomorrow, of course, we'll have the awards ceremony, and I hope you'll come to that very special event, too. Now, though, you're gonna have the pleasure of watchin' the world premiere of a truly excitin' film called *Passion*. To tell you more, I want to introduce you to its executive producer, Manal Amiri."

Everyone applauded, and I made myself clap, too, as the gorgeous producer, wearing an immaculate white pantsuit, her head covered in an emerald green scarf, stood up and walked onto the stage. Ted Carmichael shook her hand, gave her the microphone, then went off into the wings.

"Good evening," Manal said in a lyrical English accent. "Thank you for coming. It is my great honor to introduce *Passion*, a wonderful independent feature film crafted with the passion of its title by its amazing director, Simha Das, and featuring a truly superb cast. Our film explores the internal and external conflict of people who are motivated by their hearts and people whose motivation comes from their heads. In our film, the head-based decisions are often fear-based decisions. Our head-based hero is ruled by his need to conform to the values of his society. Heart-based choices, in contrast, are personal and usually challenge social values, often in the pursuit of personal growth. *Passion* explores each kind of decision-making and their impact on relationships and, while it does not advocate one form over another, it does suggest some possibilities for a union of the two. At its core, *Passion* is the story of alignment within ourselves and in our relationships. There is also a deep irony at the core of the film, because it was made within the strict censorship rules of the most conservative Bollywood standards that, for example, prohibit showing an actor and actress kissing. Our challenge was to make a film about passion without being able to show the physical manifestations of passion, very much like the limitations American moviemakers faced in the 1930s, 1940s, and 1950s when even married couples had to be shown sleeping in separate twin beds."

Manal went on to discuss the making of the film, but I wasn't paying attention. I was looking for Simha, but he'd disappeared with the ornately dressed woman. What were they doing?

"Now," Manal was saying, "I'd like to introduce you to our director, Mr. Simha Das."

Simha stepped forward from behind the walled theater entrance with the beautiful woman. Great, he was about to introduce us all to his beautiful new Indian bride.

Chloe leaned into me, "I bet that's his mama. Here for her son's big night."

"His mama? You really think so?"

She turned Simha slightly toward herself and brushed at his jacket lapel as if removing some hint of dust or dirt that would likely not have been there in the first place. She kissed his cheek. My body relaxed instantaneously. Chloe was right. That's what mothers do. She was preening her son with pride to let everyone in the cinema know he was her son. Some behaviors make their way into all cultures. Mama would be doing the same thing, claiming her territory and looking immaculate as ever, if Toby ever did anything audience-worthy.

Startled by my own relief to discover Simha wasn't recently married, I applauded with everyone else as he walked on stage from the wings in all his masculinity and grace. He kissed Manal on both cheeks. Surely one cheek was enough. He took the microphone and then walked to center stage with Manal a little to the side of him.

"Thank you for your very kind words, Manal, and thank all of you for coming tonight," he said, his sensual voice inundating me from every speaker in the theater. "*Passion* is a project dear to my heart. It, um, it began with a wonderful script by, um, Hugh. Hugh Jahsti."

Was I the only person in the theater who saw that he seemed distracted by something? He kept talking about the movie, and I couldn't take my eyes off him. Six months. It had been six months, and I could still feel every inch of him imprinted on my body, my mouth, my heart. The passionate, powerful woman I'd been in his arms in August stirred within me, and I desperately shoved her back down into the darkness where I'd been hiding her.

"I'm happy to announce," Simha was saying, "that Manal and I have recently finalized financing for our next film, *Persuasion*, a contemporary version of the classic Jane Austen novel, which we will be making..." He looked up from the microphone right at me. His beautiful brown eyes pierced through my flimsy armor of anonymity and struck me in the chest. "...right here in Nashville. Production will start in a few months," he concluded.

Manal nearly fell over as she spun around to look at Simha. Her stunned expression said everything of her surprise from Simha's clearly unexpected announcement. Simha was going to be in Nashville? Making a movie? Making a movie took *months!* He was going to be in Nashville for *months!*

He had known I was in the audience all along. Was that why he seemed so distracted? Oh lordy. I turned into jelly right there in the middle of the theater.

"Before we run *Passion*," Simha was saying, "I'd be happy to answer some of your questions."

Manal looked like she had plenty of questions, but she had to wait her turn because a woman in the sixth row raised her hand, and Simha called on her.

"Mr. Das, why are you making your next film in the US?" she asked.

He smiled. "I like the US. It doesn't matter who you are or where you're from. If you believe in yourself, then America truly is the land of opportunity. Yes, the gentleman in the denim jacket."

"Why Nashville?" the twenty-something denim-clad gentleman asked.

"Inspiration comes from many things, many places, many people," Simha replied. He looked at me! He was looking right at me! "Nashville offered me something beautiful, something special that I just felt compelled to return to."

Simha took other questions, but I wasn't listening. I'd been deafened by all the conflicting emotions clamoring for attention inside me. How in the world had he spotted me in the crowded theater? The things he'd said, they'd been directed at me, they were *about* me, I just knew it, and that knowledge was overwhelming. My face was burning and my heart was pounding and my hands were trembling.

If I was a wreck now, how was I going to survive having Simha in town for *months*?

He finished taking questions, thanked the audience again, and then walked off stage with Manal Amiri, who seemed to be quietly fuming, giving him a serving of her thoughts and concerns all the way back to their seats. His mother grabbed at his arm with a frown of consternation that said everything about what I couldn't hear her saying to him. I wanted to keep watching as Simha's steadfast pillars of femininity transformed into hissing snakes of disapproval for him, but the theater darkened completely, and then *Passion's* credits began playing across images of London.

They went by in a blur for me. Then Simha's name flashed onto the screen, and it seemed to stop there. I stared at it, mesmerized by the letters of his name as surely as I'd been mesmerized by his dark brown eyes a year ago. Time suddenly jump-started, and the movie began to play. I pulled my purse up from between my feet, pulled out my bottle of Green Life, and took a sip.

"I can't believe Simha is makin' a movie in Nashville!" Chloe whispered excitedly. "Mary, you've gotta remind him that he knows me and that I'm your best friend. I've gotta get a part in that film."

"Chloe, I do not have that kind of influence with Simha," I hissed.

"Don't be daft, bro," Alice whispered loudly. "He just told the entire audience that you're beautiful and special."

"He wasn't talkin' about me!" I insisted.

A dozen people loudly shushed us. Embarrassed, I scrunched down in my seat.

"Yes, he was," Alice said obstinately.

"You've definitely got some sort of magical influence over that guy, Mary Poser, and you are going to use it to help your best friend in the whole wide world get a part in his movie," Chloe insisted.

Oh lordy. "I am not askin' him for any favors, not even for my best friend in the whole wide world!" I whispered.

"Bless your heart, aren't we the shrinkin' violet today," Chloe hissed.

Alice looked at me with dread. Chloe was getting worked up, and I spent the next ten minutes trying desperately to placate her, earning an occasional "Shh!" from folks nearby.

I sipped from my Green Life bottle.

"Still a bit funny in the tummy, bro?" Alice asked.

"Yeah," I said. "My yoga teacher recommended this stuff. It's pretty good."

"Shh!" said the woman behind me.

On the screen, the hero was coaxing a beautiful young woman in a turquoise sari to stay with him, but she seemed torn by some internal conflict.

"I love Indian clothes," Alice whispered to Chloe. "They're so colorful and sensual, and they look so comfortable. I've always wanted to buy some, but I'd feel funny wearin''em in Nashville. I could get away with it on the East Coast or the West Coast, but not in the South."

The hero and heroine on the movie screen had advanced to physical romance, but they weren't kissing, and they were wearing all their clothes. They finally made it to be horizontal together. The hero even pushed up the heroine's blouse and began blowing softly on her concave belly.

"Why is he blowing on her?" Alice asked.

"That's what they do in Bollywood films," Chloe whispered.

"Huh?"

"Shh!" said half a dozen people around us.

"So blowing on someone is sexy?" Alice quietly persisted.

"It can be," Chloe insisted, "if you've got the right guy and you're in the mood."

I wasn't really listening to my friends, or watching the movie screen. I was remembering every minute of making love with Simha in that hotel room. I sat in the cinema, burning with a perpetual blush of rekindled passions as I watched Simha's film called *Passion*. Squirming uncomfortably with embarrassment in my seat, I felt like I was being personally provoked by him as an entire audience comfortably accepted his ostentatious comfort with passion.

The next time I glanced at the screen, the hero and heroine were with about a hundred other people, the women dressed in gorgeous Technicolor saris, and the men wearing equally colorful knee-length tunics and slacks. They were singing and dancing joyously to some fast-paced complex choreography.

"I wonder if we can get to learn a class in Indian dancing, or at least Bollywood dancing," Chloe whispered excitedly in my ear.

"I'd sign up. It looks like fun."

"I'm confused," Alice whispered. "Weren't the hero and heroine just in the bedroom blowing on each other?"

"Yes, they were," Chloe whispered.

"So why are there suddenly a hundred people dancing all around them?"

"Because it's Bollywood—everyone gets in on the act."

"What? In the bedroom?"

"No!" Chloe hissed. "In the story."

"Huh?"

"Dang girl, you've been all 'round the world, but you sometimes act like you just landed here yesterday."

Alice stared at the screen, trying to figure it all out. I distracted her by whispering to her and asking her about the dancing she'd done on her world travels. I was doing my best to avoid the association of Simha with passion, and watching his film wasn't helping. Then I thought about the fact that Simha had traveled all over the world, and I'd never left Tennessee. Could any two people be more different than him and me? It was simply ridiculous to be nervous about having him in town, and to be jealous of Manal, and to be wondering why Simha was making his next movie in Nashville when, despite the passion that had once sizzled between us, we had nothing in common and no hope of anything resembling a future.

The audience's thunderous and lengthy applause as the closing credits began to play jerked me out of my thoughts. I realized that Simha's movie was over, and I wouldn't have been able to tell anyone about what had happened in it.

I had to get out of there. But I couldn't stop looking at him. He was arguing with Manal. She looked mad as a wet hen.

"Come on!" Chloe said as she took my right arm and Alice took my left. "Let's go mingle."

"Mingle? Oh lordy" I said, but I was ignored. Chloe, Alice, and the crowd pulled me out of the theater, down the hallway past sponsor booths and posters, and out into the tiled ground floor lobby of the cinema with its pink, purple, and lavender neon lighting. Huge movie posters hung from the ceiling and decorated the walls, press booths, and local and national sponsor booths. A huge disk of multicolored neon rings was suspended over our heads. The crush of moviegoers was exhausting. My feet were stepped on. I was bumped and jostled. The noise level was painful.

"Pedestrian and pedantic," one man declared loudly. I turned and recognized Virgil from last year, his red hair still shaggy, his face ruddy, his voice bombastic as he gave his critique of Simha's film to anyone who would listen. "It's a criminal example of pompous self-indulgence. Just another overbaked movie musical. *Anyone* can and does do Bollywood nowadays. Now, if you'd seen my film, *A Question of Honor*, that premiered this morning, you'd have seen a real, honest, gritty, emotional film."

A few people took the bait and began telling Virgil how much they enjoyed the film. I'm sure he was just looking for a way to turn the attention of some of the patrons back on himself.

One of those people was Alice, who, feeling obliged to defend Simha and a film she didn't quite grasp, was giving Virgil a piece of her mind. Chloe had scurried off to "mingle" with the directors and producers she recognized in the crowd. She'd driven us here. I couldn't leave without her. I looked around desperately for an island in this ocean of moviegoers and saw, of all people, my Aunt Sara, dressed up in an actual little black dress and heels and talking to the barrel-chested Ted Carmichael. Sanctuary!

I politely pushed and shoved my way toward her.

"I loved it," Aunt Sara was saying to Mr. Carmichael. "Such a mature understanding of the heart and human relationships for such a young director, though of course some credit must also be given the screenwriter. What did you think, Ted?"

"Nice visuals, but I didn't really understand it."

"That, my dear, is because you remain hopelessly locked inside your head," Aunt Sara said with a smile. "I can't thank you enough for pulling strings to include *Passion* in your festival, even though you don't understand it."

"I'd like to be the hero in this, Sara, but I didn't really have to pull anything," Ted confessed. "The film got unanimous thumbs-up from the three pre-screenings and then from the programming staff. I just had to say thank you. Next time, give me something harder to deliver. You know I'd do anything for you, Sara. You were always my favorite."

"Ted, you're a darling," Aunt Sara said, kissing his cheek, "but I can't help but think that I'm not the first woman to hear that."

"Why don't we go get a drink together so I can correct that assumption?"

Aunt Sara shook her head, smiling broadly. "Thank you, no. Once was enough."

"Aw, Sara…"

Blushing, I spun on my heel and quickly headed off in the opposite direction. I could talk to Aunt Sara later.

The crowd had thinned by about ten percent, which was why I was able to see Jason walk through the glass lobby doors, looking completely out of place in his getup of scuffed cowboy boots, faded jeans, sleeveless shirt (pale red this time), and the big off-white cowboy hat Toby had given him for Christmas. He stood a little taller and strutted a bit as he walked toward me.

"Hey, babe," he said with his devil-may-care grin, and then he kissed me.

"Jason! What are you doin' here?" I said. He was the last person I had expected to see at the film festival.

"I thought I'd surprise you and pick you up and take you to

tonight's set at the Tipsy Turkey."

"That's so sweet," I said, but I knew Jason just wanted to whisk me away from anything having to do with Simha just as fast as he could.

I'd been rethinking my initial anger when I'd learned why Jason had wanted to start going out again last August. It was flattering that he was jealous of other men and of Simha in particular. If that jealousy had taught him the truth of his feelings about me, and he had acted on them, then that was a good thing.

That's why I had to hold back a grin at Jason acting at being considerate tonight. Fake it 'til you make it, I guess. "I'm ready to go," I said. "I just have to tell Chloe and Alice—"

"Just a minute, babe," Jason said. He wasn't looking at me. He was looking at a skinny man in his forties wearing an ill-fitting brown suit who was standing a couple dozen yards away. "That's Cal Hornsby, the head of Wildcat Records! I've been tryin' to see him for weeks to move The Nashbros' demo forward. I'll be right back!" He was already working his way through the crowd.

Shoot! I'd been so close to getting safely out of here, and then Jason had to go off chasing the scent of a music producer.

"So," said an all too familiar voice, "what did you think of my film?"

Sorrow prepares you for joy. It violently sweeps everything out of your house, so that new joy can find space to enter. It shakes the yellow leaves from the bough of your heart, so that fresh, green leaves can grow in their place. Whatever sorrow shakes from your heart, far better things will take their place.

❧ *Rumi*

Chapter Thirty

It took everything I had in me to turn to face Simha.

He was smiling. "Hello, Mary," he said warmly, his dark eyes searching my face.

"Hello, Simha," I managed. "Congratulations on *Passion*. Everyone in the audience loved it."

"And you?"

"Oh, I loved it, too!" I said, blushing with my lie. How could I love a movie I hadn't actually watched? I had been too busy discouraging Chloe's crafty stardom strategies.

"So it looks like I'm going to be in town for a few months."

"Yeah," I said, my blush deepening. "It's, um, excitin' that you're makin' your next movie in Nashville. It should bring a lot of new business to town."

"Business?" Simha said with a puzzled frown. "Mary, what's going on?"

"Nothin'!" I said, searching anxiously for Jason. I didn't want him anywhere near this. He was standing with Cal Hornsby. Thank God.

Simha's dark gaze held my eyes captive. "I have been in town eight days. I've sent you texts. I've sent you e-mails. I've left you voicemails. And you haven't answered even one of them. You know the presentation dinner is tomorrow night, don't you?"

"I'm sorry. I've been busy."

"Busy?"

"Look, I've got this slightly awkward situation," I said helplessly. "That guy I was talking to just before you came up... Well, he's *kind of* my boyfriend."

"Kind of your boyfriend? So I invite you to a very important night for me. The last I hear from you is 'I'll see what I can do,' and now you tell me you have a slightly awkward situation called a *boyfriend?*"

"Sorry. I didn't know what to do."

"How long have you been together?"

"A while."

"A while—days?" he pressed. I couldn't look at him. "A while—weeks?" My lack of confirmation wasn't helping me out. "A while—months?" I finally looked up. His eyes widened at my blush. "*Months?* He's been your boyfriend for *months* now, and you didn't tell me?"

"I'm sorry," I said with the worst sensation of guilt I could imagine.

"Why didn't you tell me?" Simha demanded. "Did you think I couldn't handle it?"

"No, of course not. But you've been kind to me in the past, and I wanted to protect you. I didn't want to upset you."

"Well, you have failed. Spectacularly. Hiding the truth upsets me. Just tell me one thing—are you certain that he's the one you want?"

"I think so," I said, feeling pushed against a wall.

"You *think* so? What does your heart say? Are you happy with him?"

"I *am* happy," I said defensively. "I'm content. I'm in love. I'm supported and protected. So there! You've made me say it. Does that make you happy?"

"No, of course it doesn't make me happy!"

"He's actually my ex. The guy I'd told you about." Now I was standing in a grave and just digging deeper.

"Your ex? The guy who cheated on you? I can't imagine that he makes you happy or that you really prefer him."

"Jason is a hard-workin' man pursuin' his dream, just like you."

"From what you've told me about him, that *cowboy* is nothing like me."

"There you are, Niece, I've been lookin' all over for you," Aunt Sara said with a determined smile as she walked up to us. I must have hit her ears with some of the grave-digging verbal mud I was shoveling out in response to Simha. She looked at me sternly. "It's not fair of you to monopolize our guest of the night, you hear?"

I think I just got rescued. I took a breath and retreated into the safety of my Southern manners. "Aunt Sara, this is Simha Das. Simha, this is my aunt, Dr. Sara Collins."

"How do you do?" Simha said with a bit of effort. He clearly had more to say to me.

"I'm glad to meet you at last," Aunt Sara said heartily. "Mary has told me so much about you that I feel like I know you."

"Really?" Simha said as he looked at me, his eyes like daggers.

"I must say that I'm thrilled to meet such a talented director," Aunt Sara continued. "It gives me the chance to tell you how much I enjoyed your movie. There was such beauty and humor in *Passion*, and honesty, too. As far as I'm concerned, life without honesty just isn't worth livin'."

Simha shot me a frowned look. "I agree with you wholeheartedly."

Aunt Sara managed to calm us both with her charm. She

continued talking to Simha about the first films she'd fallen in love with. I just stood there, mute, with desperation growing inside me. I couldn't stand seeing my Aunt Sara talking happily with Simha. Everything felt out of kilter, me most of all. I grabbed Aunt Sara's arm anxiously.

She cast me a knowing smile. "Oh good heavens, where are my manners?" she said. "I've got to learn let other folks get a word in edgewise."

"I really must return to my team. They're expecting me. It was lovely meeting you, Sara," Simha replied.

"It was delightful meetin' you at last, Mr. Simha Das. You seem just as wonderful as Mary described you." I could kill her. Simha looked at me again, his expression finally softening. "Come along, Niece," Aunt Sara said, guiding me away from any chance of further bad behavior.

We pushed our way through the crowd.

"Oh, Mary, I like him!" she exclaimed. "I mean, not only is he just about the best-lookin' young man I've had the pleasure to see in real life, he's talented, smart, well-educated, passionate about his career, thoughtful, well-spoken—"

"I know all of Simha's good qualities," I said impatiently.

"I'm not so sure about that," she retorted. "What did I interrupt? You two looked ready to slug each other."

"We were talkin' about Jason," I said as I looked again for my boyfriend.

"Jason? That redneck bull with straw for brains?"

"Aunt Sara!"

"Pardon my candor, Mary, but I can't help feelin' the fire that's still burnin' in you for Simha."

"Aunt Sara, *stop!*" I hissed. "There's no fire except the one that's fuelin' your imagination. He's in town for his film. Nothin' more."

"Now who's the one with a flamin' imagination?"

"Jason!" I called to my actual boyfriend as he started heading back into the crowd. "Over here!"

"That boy sticks out like a wart on a toad. Give him my regards. I'm sure I have somewhere else to be," she announced as she headed off in the opposite direction.

I closed my eyes for a moment and prayed for just a moment of peace. Did everyone have to be so in my face tonight?

"Who was that?" Jason demanded as he finally reached my side.

"Aunt Sara, of course."

"No! I mean that guy you and she were talkin' to."

I bit my lower lip. "That was Simha Das, the director of the movie I just saw."

Jason's face got red. "Is he the teddy bear guy?"

"Jason, let's just go."

"In a minute. Wait here," he ordered as he turned and started shoving his way toward Simha.

I struggled after him. "Jason, no!"

He didn't listen, of course. He went straight up to Simha and confronted him. Who should I run to? Which shoulder do I stand by? The indecision had me frozen in my tracks. I couldn't hear what Jason was saying over the din of the crowd in the cinema foyer, but I could see that both men were in each other's face like warring peacocks. It would have come to fisticuffs if Alice hadn't intervened. Both men seemed to calm down instantly in response to whatever pearls of wisdom she had to add to the hostile brew. I couldn't just stand aside like a stunned mullet while Alice did what I should have done, so I weaved my way through the crowd toward the trio.

"What's goin' on here?" I demanded as I reached Jason's side.

"I was just leaving." Simha gave me a disappointed look that just cut me to the soul, and then he walked away.

"Oh, Jason, what did you do?" I said anxiously.

"I told him to stay away from you, and he got the message, believe me."

"You shouldn't have done that. You had no right."

"'Course I did," Jason scoffed. "He's just lucky he walked away when he did. Come on, babe, let's go," he said, reaching for my arm.

Spontaneously, I pulled away. I looked at Alice, but I had no real plan. "I forgot that I promised Chloe and Alice I'd join them for a few minutes at the after-party," I lied, but Alice smiled approvingly, "I'll have to meet you at the Tipsy Turkey."

"What? But I drove all the way here to pick you up!"

"I didn't ask you to," I said. "Go on now. You don't want to keep Toby and Scotty waitin'. I'll get there in time for your set, I promise."

Jason glared at me and even pouted a little bit, but he finally left. As soon as he was out of earshot, I spun on my heel toward Alice, "What did they say?"

"Well, the part I caught was when Jason called Simha Gandhi and then threatened that he'd better stay away from you otherwise he'd make him bleed. Simha, that is."

"Oh, lordy." I sighed. "What did Simha say?"

"You're gonna like this. He looked Jason straight in the eye and said, 'I am quite prepared to bleed for Mary.' This, of course, left Jason a little stumped."

"And then what happened?"

"Simha decided to put icing on the cake by saying," she broke into her best impression of Simha's accent, while puffing herself up to imitate Simha's solid frame, "'If Mary seeks for me, and you try to stop her, then you had best be prepared to bleed for her as well.'" She returned to her normal dimensions. "That's when it looked like the blood was about to start pourin'."

"Seriously? So what did you say?"

"I told them that if they both didn't pull their heads in, I was goin' to kick them both in the nuts so hard that they'd wish they were bleeding. That seemed to settle them down."

I slapped my hand over my mouth. I wasn't sure if I was covering a squeal of laughter or shock.

"I'm sorry you had to witness that."

"I'm only sorry they weren't squabbling over me," she laughed, hooking her arm in mine. "It's time to party!"

My night was about to spin into an entirely unexpected direction. Simha and Manal had pulled out all the stops by hosting their after-party at the Schermerhorn Symphony Center, a big white neoclassical building downtown with tall columns topped by a huge carved pediment out front. Inside, the shoebox style concert hall has two tiers of box seats fronted by carved white stone. Above them is a gallery, the cheap seats, which is topped by two tiers of white columns and windows. Eight huge chandeliers hang from the white molded ceiling. The orchestra seats in the middle of the hall between the box seats had been removed. In their place were some white sectional sofas and round tables and chairs scattered around on the cherry and hickory parquet floor, a large buffet running down the right side, and a large bar running down the left side, leaving room for dancing and conversations in the middle.

There were even more people here than there had been at the theater. Apparently, the film festival folks were using this as their end of the festival pre-party.

As far as I was concerned, there couldn't be too many people here tonight. The more people, the harder it would be for me to see Simha, and the harder it would be for him to find me and continue berating me for my lack of honesty and transparency. I wanted to be around him, but I wanted to hide from him at the same time. I felt like a mobile contradiction when I hadn't offered Chloe any protest when she declared that we simply had to attend this party. Indian music was playing, including music I vaguely recalled from Simha's movie. The environment kept every moment we'd ever shared and every ounce of guilt I felt for dodging him this last week front and center in my thoughts. Behind those thoughts were discomforting reminders that I'd have to leave fairly soon to make it to the Tipsy Turkey in time for Jason's set. I tried to massage my stomach out of its current unhappiness.

"Still achin'?" Chloe asked.

"It's not a problem, really," I insisted. "Just feelin' a bit bloated, that's all. I'm on a really strict detox."

"Again?" she said in surprise.

"I think it's helpin'," I said.

"Bro, get real," Alice said. "Look around. There's a bunch of people scoffin' down all sorts of crap tonight, and none of them have a gut ache. Maybe your problem has nothing to do with what you're eating and drinking. I'm just saying…"

My phone suddenly rang in my purse. "Sorry, guys, let me just check if it's important," I said, grabbing the phone and its heaven-sent opportunity to change the subject. I looked at the caller ID and answered it on the third ring.

"Hey, Hannah, what's up?" I asked.

"*I'm gettin' married!*" she squealed loudly, forcing me to recoil from my phone's speaker.

"Gettin' married? How? Who to?"

"To Kevin, of course."

"Kevin?" The short, skinny guy she had met only recently? "How can you marry Kevin? You've only been datin' him five weeks!"

"When it's right, it's right. We knew that the first night we met. You've gotta be one of my bridesmaids, Mary."

"Well, of course I will."

"You're an angel! Talk to you later!"

She hung up before I could even say goodbye.

"Hannah's gettin' married," I announced.

"We could hear," Chloe said wryly. "I'm gonna find Simha. Let's meet back here in twenty minutes."

She was gone before I could say, "No! Don't!" Alice went off a minute later to dance with a cute actor I think I recognized from a poster for one of the competing feature films I'd seen at the movie theater.

So there I was. All alone in a beautiful room with a rumbly tummy that I was really tired of, music that made my feet want to dance, and obsessive thoughts about a man I didn't want to think about. Worse, I found myself searching the crowd for him. Much worse, I smiled when I spotted him standing near the middle of the room, a glass of whiskey in one hand, talking with someone I recognized—Rob Barrett, his fellow director from New York. Chloe apparently spotted them at the same time because she was suddenly there in front of them, talking and flirting—flirting with *Simha*. I couldn't watch a second more.

I turned away and, to distract my thoughts, started counting all of the round bulbs hanging from a chandelier over my head. When I'd done that, I started counting all of the pipes in the concert organ at the far end of the hall.

"I'm back!" Alice announced happily. "That boy can dance! We're goin' out tomorrow night to do what he calls boot stomping."

"You're goin' out with an actor?" I asked in amusement.

"Yep."

"Don't tell Chloe."

"Right."

"I wish Chloe would hurry up. I've got to get to the Tipsy Turkey in time for The Nashbros' set."

"Mary, can I ask you something?"

"Sure."

"How sure are you of Jason's interest in you?" Alice continued tentatively.

I stared at her. "He's bein' faithful," I said.

"That's not what I mean. Well, a little of it is, but how into you do you think he is?"

"He nearly beat up Simha he was so jealous," I said wryly. "He's into me."

"But why?" Alice demanded.

"What on earth do you mean?"

"I mean, have you ever seen the pictures in his—"

"Girls!" Chloe said, pouncing on us. She was practically vibrating with excitement. "Girls! You won't believe it. Simha's asked me to read for a featured role in his new film!"

"Bugger me, that's awesome!" Alice said.

Chloe sighed heavily. "I wish you had nicer ways of expressin' your happiness. Now that I know what that means…"

"Congratulations, Chloe, that's fantastic news," I said.

"I haven't got the part yet, but I *will*. And it gets better," she said, grabbing Chloe's arm and mine. "Do you remember Simha's friend, Rob, from New York? He's gonna help produce the film and, ladies, he needs extras for the dance scenes! How much fun is that gonna be? The Three Amigas dancin' together in a movie! Auditions are in three weeks, and they'll have rehearsals in the evenin's after that 'cause they know most folks have day jobs."

"Sounds fun, Chloe, but I really can't do it," I said.

"What do you mean you can't?" she demanded.

"You know how busy I am. Most nights I'm at The Nashbros' gigs."

"So busy means sitting on a bar stool and listening to songs you've heard a thousand times before?" Alice said. "Bro, you are so coming with us to Bollywood! It'll be so choice!"

"Mary, how many times in your life are you gonna have the chance to be in a real movie?" Chloe pressed.

"That's your dream, Chloe, not mine," I said.

"Mary Poser, you are gonna audition for this movie if I have to twist both your arms off gettin' you there!"

I know that look of determination in Chloe's dark eyes. There's nothing that can stand up to it, particularly not me. I caved. "Okay," I said with a heavy sigh. "I'll go to the auditions. But I probably won't get in. This is Simha's movie, don't forget, and we don't exactly see eye to eye anymore."

"If he's willin' to audition me for a featured role, he won't think twice about hirin' you as a dance extra. You'll see!" Chloe said happily.

"Come on," I said uneasily as my stomach spasmed, "I've *got* to get to the Tipsy Turkey."

You have to keep breaking your heart until it opens.

❧ Rumi

Chapter Thirty-One

Simha had rented a three-hundred-seat theater downtown for auditions on Monday and Tuesday evening in the second week of May. The wooden stage was wide but a bit shallow. Black curtains hung down on the sides, hiding the wings. A plain white screen hung down, hiding the far back stage and back brick wall of the theater. A dark orchestra pit separated the stage from the first rows of seats. Sitting in the tenth row was Simha, with Manal and Rob sitting on either side of him, along with Jimmy Smith, their local producer, Vidya Hamada, their choreographer, and her assistant Ramón Ortega.

The theater lights and the stage lights were on. We could see them. They could see every inch of us.

Simha had auditioned actors last night, and tonight he was putting the actors he'd chosen for callbacks through a dance audition because all of the actors with speaking parts had to be able to dance, too. Simha was also auditioning dancers for four different group scenes in his movie. More than two hundred of us had turned up. Chloe, wearing a red long-sleeved leotard, red tights, and a semi-sheer white chiffon skirt that fell just above her knees, stood in the wings, watching everything avidly. She was practically clawing at the black wing curtains as she waited for her chance to get on stage and show everyone what she could do.

She was in the second group of actors to be called to dance. She was the first to walk out on stage. She put herself smack dab in the middle of the first row of actors. She was "on" for every single moment of the rehearsal, and then she blew everyone else out of the water during the actual dance audition.

She high-fived me and Alice as she walked off stage with the other actors who were panting for breath.

The choreographer and her assistant then began teaching the audition routine to batches of twenty dancers at a time. The dance looked complex and exhausting as I watched it from the wings with Alice at my side. She'd been given number thirty-five. I was thirty-six.

Alice was in an emerald green unitard that barely reached mid-thigh. She had straightened her hair into silky ebony strands. She was her usual cheerful, laid-back self, chatting in a whisper with anyone and everyone backstage. I wore my usual dance class clothes—blue and purple tie-dyed leggings and a turquoise tank top—and I'd pulled my hair back into a ponytail to keep it out of my way. I'm sure I looked a wreck.

Simha was right there, just ten rows back. He'd be watching everything I did. He'd watch me make a complete fool of myself. He'd probably assume that I was auditioning just to get his attention, and I wasn't! I was only here because Chloe and Alice had made me come. I hadn't heard from him since the film festival, and that was a month ago now. He'd pretty much ignored me ever since. I hadn't gotten a single text from him the whole time he'd been in town. Jason, on the other hand, had taken me on dates twice a week since the film festival—talk about marking your territory!

Well, Simha Das couldn't ignore me tonight. Whether I made

a fool of myself or not, he was going to see me and, and when he did, I wanted him to…well, I'm not exactly sure what I wanted him to do. I was there to dance, to support Chloe, and to deny any feelings I may have for Simha in the process.

The first group of dancers completed their audition and walked off the stage, and then my group was called. Alice and I walked on stage. She headed for the front row, but I pulled her back and planted us in the second row on the left side. The choreographer, a stately Indian woman in her forties, began rehearsing the routine with us, and I had to give it all of my attention to learn the steps and arm movements. But out of the corner of my eye, I couldn't help noticing that Simha wasn't looking at me. He wasn't even looking at the stage. He was deep in conversation with the rest of his production team.

Really? He was just gonna sit there working and ignore me? Well, I could ignore him, too!

The rehearsal went by way too fast, and then the choreographer and her assistant returned to their seats. Now, I thought, now Simha will look at me. He'll try to catch my eye. Maybe he'll look distracted or uncomfortable when he sees me—and I hoped he would.

The music began playing, and he didn't even glance at me! He spent the entire audition headlocked with the choreographer, who *was* watching us, and talking. I hated myself in that moment. I wanted Simha to notice me. I wanted him to be impressed by me. I wanted him to admire me. I was furious with myself because I shouldn't be wanting any of that.

Before I knew it, the dance routine was over, and the choreographer's assistant, a buff young man in sweatpants and a sleeveless white tee shirt, was shooing us off the stage. A little dazed, I walked off with Alice and was immediately enveloped in Chloe's bear hug.

"You girls were fantastic!" she shouted. "You outshone everyone on that stage. Alice, you were on fire out there, and Mary, you were electric. I've never seen you dance with such intensity before." Little did she know that my intensity was fueled by self-loathing and regret.

To be honest, I was so consumed within my own errant thoughts, I couldn't even remember doing the audition. So how could I have done it well? But sure enough, I got a call the next day from the choreographer's assistant. I was in. I was going to be one of the dancers in Simha's movie.

A week later, I still couldn't believe it, but everyone at the Lean Machine was so excited for us. Alice was also chosen to dance in the movie. We were starlets as far as the other members were concerned, except for Sally Iverson, who ignored us as usual. Chloe was a bona fide star. She'd been cast in a featured role as Louisa. Whenever we were working out or taking one of our classes, folks would come up to congratulate us and ask us questions about the movie we couldn't answer because rehearsals hadn't even started yet.

Daddy and Aunt Sara were the only ones in my family who were happy about it. Toby was jealous on Jason's behalf, Erin was jealous on her own behalf, and Mama was worried that I'd be corrupted by all the foreigners and the lure of Hollywood. I tried to tell her I'd only auditioned because Chloe and Alice made me. I tried to tell her I was just doing it as a lark and had no intention of ever following it up with another movie, let alone relocating to Hollywood. But she kept on worrying.

My friends were all happy for me, including Hannah after I assured her that rehearsals and filming wouldn't interfere with her bridal shower and wedding. She gushed daily at work about seeing me soon on a movie screen before diverting conversation to her newest wedding plans, which were growing to mammoth proportions. She was planning the wedding of the century for herself. Even my boss and coworkers were happy for me and teased me about soon becoming the next Julia Roberts, or Kristen Stewart, or Miley Cyrus.

It seemed everyone else in Nashville was talking about the movie, too. It had been a couple of years since we'd had a movie with any level of buzz this film had had. *Passion* had won at this year's film festival, and now Simha had cast Catherine Moore and Henry Tate, two rising independent film stars as the leads in his new movie, *Persuasion*. That was serious buzz news.

With everyone talking about it, all I could think about was the movie, but for entirely different reasons from everyone else. All I could think about was having Simha in Nashville for the next three or four months and how scared and happy that made me. Every night, I lay in bed wondering if Simha was going to ignore me every minute of the dance rehearsals and the shooting of the four scenes I'd be dancing in. Every night, I told myself that was the best-case scenario. Every night, I confessed to myself how badly I wanted him to notice me, like me, want me. Every night, I fell asleep feeling guilty, because Jason's girlfriend shouldn't be wanting such things.

Before I knew it, it was already June. I told Chloe I'd come support her event promotion for Bugle Records, which had four of its up-and-coming country artists performing at the massive Day in the Park at the boomerang-shaped Centennial Park in the West End district. Starting at dawn, the park was packed with tens of thousands of people who came for the free music at the bandshell, the food, the arts and crafts fair, the miniature boat races on Lake Watauga, the carnival, and the final three laps of the Tour of Nashville bike race.

I made Jason get up early and take me out for pancakes, followed by Charlie's morning walk, even though Jason and

Charlie don't really get along. Jason likes bigger dogs. Still, it was a nice thirty minutes of talking about The Nashbros, and the new exercise routine Toby was teaching Jason, and Kenny Chesney's newest hit single. Then I headed for the park.

Chloe was managing the Bugle Records booth near the bandshell. She was on stage introducing Bugle artists during the day-long concert. She was backstage making sure the Bugle artists stayed clean, sober, sane, and on pitch before they performed. She was selling Bugle CDs and tee shirts and caps to the huge concert audience like a peanut vendor at a baseball game. Alice was helping out in the Bugle Records booth except when she felt compelled to break out dancing to the music. She was soon drenched in sweat, topped by the sweetest grin of a girl having the time of her life. I was an unofficial assistant, helping Chloe and Alice stay hydrated on this hot and humid day, shoving protein bars into their hands and reminding them to eat, and acting as Chloe's shill by applauding loudly whenever a Bugle artist performed. It wasn't a far cry from my usual Nashbros' duties.

Clem Hawthorn, the third Bugle artist, was a hunky guy with abs for days and a devastating smile that had several girls in the audience hyperventilating. He had the crowd in a frenzy of heaving dance and cheering. The energy of the crowd was infectious, and part of me just wanted to lose itself in the resulting fever. I headed back to the Bugle Records booth and joined Alice, laughing and dancing wildly in my best version of crazy girl losing her sensibility. I bounced around in front of the booth with Alice and, as I spun around, my flailing arm connected with someone's chest. I turned to apologize but lost the words.

"Mary!" Simha said happily with an enchanting smile. "You really are on a mission to ruin my shirts aren't you?"

I just stood there like an idiot, staring at him, hyperventilating, and trying to ignore how hard my heart was thumping. He was looking gorgeous in his body-hugging, short-sleeved white shirt and Dockers. How much of my crazy dancing had he witnessed? I drew a breath to blurt out an embarrassed apology, but then my embarrassment nose-dived into mortification as I realized that Manal Amiri was standing at his side, smiling politely at me. She looked stunning in her white muslin slacks and shirt, her black hair covered by a white silk hijab. She was everything an elegant and refined lady should be—and everything that was opposite to the unruly flailing wreck I must have appeared to be. She looked like she'd just stepped off a Paris catwalk. I didn't even bother trying to fix my hair that I'm sure looked like fairy floss having a bad day. I just cleared it from my face enough to look at them clearly.

"Hi, Simha," I managed, "what are you doin' here?"

"Chloe told me about Day in the Park the other day at rehearsal, and it sounded like a good way to discover more Nashville culture," he said. "I don't believe you've met my producer before. Mary, this is Manal Amiri. Manal, this is my friend, Mary Poser. She'll also be one of the dancers in our film."

"How do you do?" Manal said in her beautiful English accent. She held out her slender hand, and I shook it, feeling more judged by another woman than ever before in my life. Southern women could be snooty, but this woman was in her own stratosphere of cold aloofness.

"Pleased to meet you," I lied.

"I remember you from the dance auditions," Manal said as she looked me up and down. She looked at my sleeveless pink cotton empire waist dress with perfectly restrained disdain. "You have a knack for Indian dancing."

"Bless your heart," I said with my brightest smile. I desperately needed to extract myself from this woman's self-esteem-draining vortex. "Chloe and Alice are just over here, Simha," I said, directing my smile at him. "I'm sure you want to say hello."

Chloe beamed him her most flirtatious smile, and Alice was as cheerful as usual in greeting him and was even genuinely happy to meet Manal. Chloe started talking nonstop to Simha about all of her hard work today, while Alice pestered Manal with questions about her travels.

With their attention diverted, I stood back and tried to gather myself and get my feet planted back firmly on the ground, my heartbeat back into a regular rhythm, and my head back in the game.

Then Simha turned to me and knocked me flat with his brilliant smile. "Mary, I'm so glad I found you today because I want to show you something very special. They're celebrating Sitalsasthi today at the Sri Ganesha Temple. It's a festival, a carnival really, that honors the marriage of Shiva and Shakti with music, dancing, food, and even brightly decorated floats. I know you'll love it."

"It sounds great, but I can't," I said automatically. "I'm busy here helpin' Chloe and Alice."

"I'm sure Chloe and Alice can spare you for an hour. It's not too far away." Simha turned to Chloe. "Can't you?"

"Absolutely," Alice replied promptly, which ticked off Chloe. "That Hindu thing sounds beaut, bro. You should go. Have fun. Don't worry about us...we'll be fine. We've got this thing managed, don't we, Chloe?"

My best friend gave me a glittering smile. "Don't give us a minute's thought. Go...have fun. We can get by without you for an hour."

"Terrific," Simha said. "Manal, you are welcome to stay here and enjoy Day in the Park with Chloe and Alice."

Manal was clearly not accustomed to Simha dumping her with strangers, particularly not in exchange for the company of a straggly-looking country girl.

"Of course. Have fun." There was a definite tightness to her smile.

Simha took my arm and began to lead me away. "Just as long as I'm back in an hour," I said weakly.

"Absolutely," he said with his brilliant smile.

One minute, I was applauding Clem Hawthorn's set, and the next minute, I was off to a Hindu festival with Simha? How in the world had this happened?

I was parked nearby on Twenty-Fifth Avenue North, and I had the remarkable good sense to ask Simha about his impressions of Day in the Park as we walked to my car, which kept him busy so I could gather my thoughts. I glanced at the tall, determined man talking animatedly as he walked by my side.

Simha had wanted something, and he'd gotten it. The worst part was, I didn't mind. I was so flattered that Simha wanted to spend time with me rather than Manal, so happy to be with him again, and so curious about this festival of his that I couldn't—and didn't want to—complain.

I walked up to my red hatchback and unlocked the doors. Simha stared at it in surprise.

"The Mule has been retired?" he asked.

"Grazin' happily back at the farm," I said as I got in. He got into the passenger seat, and there we were again in close, intimate quarters. I was hyper-aware of the man sitting beside me and praying he couldn't hear my pounding heart. "This is your hijacking, so which way?"

He chuckled. "This isn't a hijacking," he said innocently. "I'm not that ruthless, and you could have said no."

"I did say no."

"But you didn't mean it."

I had to laugh. "Where are we goin'?"

Woman is the radiance of God.
She is not a creature.
She is the creator.

꩜ *Rumi*

Chapter Thirty-Two

While I drove, Simha told me the four-hundred-year history of Sitalsasthi and the ways it was commonly celebrated. He directed me to a hilly, forested enclave due west of Centennial Park off Charlotte Pike. We wended our way down a two-lane road through green trees that made me feel cooler just looking at them on this bright summer day.

I turned left onto a long, sweeping driveway that ended at a large parking lot crammed with cars. I had to drive around a couple of minutes before I found a space I could squeeze my hatchback into. Once we got out of the car, I could actually look at the temple. It was huge! It was a big, rectangular, dark red brick building with white trim and a monumental entrance of intricately carved white masonry that rose three stories. It was an Indian oasis sitting in the middle of lush gardens surrounded by forest.

"*Wow,*" was all I could say.

Simha smiled, took my hand, and led me into the lofty entry hall covered in richly colored tiles in mosaics of different animals. Elephants, bulls, peacocks, tigers, and even bees adorned the walls in colorful motifs among trees and flowers. We walked through the entry hall and outside into a vast courtyard.

I gasped. The colors were stunning—deep reds and golds and oranges, brilliant turquoise, vibrant green, hot pink—not only in the clothes people wore, but also in the garlands decorating the arcade running around the outside of the courtyard and on the stage. On that stage was a tall golden altar or throne that looked like a giant golden peacock tail. Around the arch of the throne were carved images of a dozen different Hindu gods and goddesses. Seated together on that golden throne covered in bowers of flowers were the young man and woman chosen from the community to represent Shiva and Shakti this year, dressed in their wedding best.

All around the huge courtyard were bigger-than-life Technicolor representations of Shiva and Shakti, along with table after table loaded with food and drinks, and big planters with lemon trees. In the shaded arcades that encircled the courtyard were large colorful statues of Hindu gods and goddesses.

In the middle of the brick and mosaic tile courtyard were three or four hundred people. Some were dressed in casual Western clothes, so I didn't feel like I stuck out like a sore thumb. The rest were in traditional Indian clothes. The women looked gorgeous in their elaborately bejeweled robes. They were all watching the performance of six young women dancing to what Simha said was a traditional northern Indian dance called the Kathak. Their fast footwork, lyrical arm movements, and intricate turns were fueled by exuberant music of drums, cymbals, trumpets, and wooden flutes. There was an instrument that looked like a cross between a lute and a banjo and a dozen other instruments, even violins.

The air was electrified. One breath, and I felt like I'd just gulped down a dozen energy drinks. Simha led me across to the food tables. Most of it was new to me. I think I ate one of everything on the tables in a gustatory expedition into foreign delicacies. All of it was delicious. I couldn't help but ask the women supervising the tables about recipes while Simha looked on, laughing and shaking his head. I stuck my tongue out at him and memorized the recipe for rajma, a vegetarian chili served with rice.

Simha disappeared for a minute while I was getting tips on how to make naan, a delicious Indian flat bread. He came back carrying plastic cups filled with mango lassi, a wonderful Indian drink made with milk, yogurt, sugar, a dash of cardamom, and of course mango. He offered me the drink with the most boyish smile. I'd never Simha looking so happy.

"Oh my...this is amazin'!" was all I could muster.

"I knew you'd like it."

"Like it? I love it!"

Simha barely gave me enough time to even touch my drink as, like a kid in a candy store, he pulled me into the happy crowd.

"Come on," he urged as he plucked my drink from my hand and placed it on a table with his.

"But I don't know how to do this dance!" I protested weakly.

"Of course you do!"

The music thrummed in my veins. My body ached to join in the dance of the six sari-dressed young women. I wanted to hug everyone around me. Simha held my hand as we jumped and jigged and spun and twirled with all the other people dancing in the audience. Simha was dancing with graceful exuberance in front of me, using his arm and handwork to coax and tease me into joining in. I had never in my life thought I'd see Simha so carefree and *dancing*. There wasn't anything for me to do but laugh and join in. Almost instantly, the music lifted me out of self-consciousness and into pure joy. My feet and arms and body knew just what to do as Simha and I danced, and laughed at each other, and teased each other, and danced and danced. Time ceased to exist. There was only the boisterous crowd around us, the compelling beat of the drum, the rocket-fueled music, and joy. Simha swung his free arm behind my waist and pulled me in toward him, and we continued to swirl together in a magical moment where everything foreign melted away into the most perfect feeling of connection and harmony with the music, the people and, of course, with Simha.

"Simha Das!" a commanding woman's voice called from somewhere nearby.

Simha clearly knew the voice, and he stopped abruptly, his body stiffening as he released himself from our embrace. I turned to the source of the voice and recognized the woman immediately. She was again the most impeccably dressed Hindu you could imagine. It was the woman I had surmised to be his mother from the cinema.

"Mother? What are you doing here?" Simha's tone was guarded and defensive.

"I'm a Hindu stuck in Hicksville. Where else would you expect me to be?" she replied, concealing nothing of her disdain for my home town in her tone.

"Mother, please," Simha continued, clearly embarrassed by his mother's austerity, "I'd like to introduce you to my friend, Mary Poser. Mary, this is my mother."

"Pleased to meet you, Mrs. Das," I replied as warmly as I could without giving away that she was intimidating the bejesus out of me.

"Yes, a pleasure, dear. You're making friends, Simha? How quaint, when you should be working on your film. It's okay—I understand you're easily distracted."

So now I was ready to slug the smug tart right in the red dot between her perfectly plucked eyebrows. As I mentally prepared my right hook, she jabbed at me with a verbal counterpunch that I simply didn't see coming.

"Considering the mess you made of the wedding plans we

arranged for you, I've got some great news. I'd like to introduce you to Abha."

Mrs. Das turned to reveal Abha, a beautiful young Hindu girl who had been standing obediently behind her. She smiled shyly at Simha.

"Abha is the daughter of a dear friend who lives here in Nashville. A chance to redeem yourself," she smiled smugly at Simha and then looked to me with the most menacing "go away" look in her eyes.

"Hello, Abha," Simha said politely.

"Hello, Simha," Abha replied, just as politely.

"I think I should maybe…" I just wanted to die, to run away, to be anywhere other than in this situation, witnessing Simha being introduced to his potential new bride.

Instinctively, I backed away. I could see that Simha was conflicted and speechless in response to the surprise card his mother had just played.

"Mary, I'm so sorry. I had no idea…" he whispered with deflated exasperation.

"It's okay," was the opposite of everything I was thinking and feeling, but the words came out anyway.

I knew Simha felt compelled to allow his mother to play matchmaker with his life, but I couldn't bear to witness it. I turned away and hurried through the crowd, away from Simha, his mother, and that lovely girl. Outside the courtyard, I broke into a run along a narrow corridor which led to another and then another. I kept running in a maze of confusion.

The corridors led to a room that was lined with a multitude of statues of gods and goddesses in various poses. The idols in brightly colored clothing, adorned with flowers and beads, distracted me from the mayhem of thoughts that were still eager to race with my legs. I wanted to feel that all the statues were looking at me, judging me, but they weren't. It was obvious that each of the statues was there to tell its own story and, in that moment, I was just another statue with a story. Each of the statues had a small plaque below it. The temple clearly expected clueless visitors like me who needed an explanation of all the deities. They should put me on a shelf, too, and give me a plaque—the goddess of stupidity.

I walked around the room, calming my breathing as best I could. Reading the plaques below the idols helped. One had three faces. It was called Brahma. One was blue and had four arms, named Vishnu. One, labeled Ganesha, had the head and trunk of an elephant. A four-armed goddess, Lakshmi, stood on a big lotus and held lotus flowers in two of her hands. Kali, written as the goddess of time and change, was downright scary with her dark blue body and red tongue poking out at me. Her ten hands each held a different object. I recognized one as fire. She rested one foot on another god with the label of Shiva, who was apparently lying in her way to drain her anger. The idea of standing a foot on Simha to help me drain a little anger was mighty appealing in the moment.

On any other day, the image of Kali would seem terrifying and scary. But today, she was everything I was feeling. I was feeling majorly blue, and if I could throw some fire around, I certainly would, and the more I thought about the idea of standing on Simha's head, the more I liked it. Were these deities meant to reflect our own tumultuous world back at us in faces and forms we could identify with? What did this say about Christianity? Was I meant to relate to being nailed to a cross and made to suffer for the sins of those around me? I'd always separated myself from Jesus. His suffering was for my benefit. It's what I'd always been told. I'd never considered relating to his suffering as a roadmap for dealing with adversity or disappointment. Kali dealt with being pissed off by standing on some guy's head. I could relate to that. How did Jesus deal with his torment?

"Mary?"

I turned to see the shadow of a man in the doorway to the room. Simha stepped into one of the bright rays of daylight that streamed through the temple windows.

"I'm so sorry."

"It's fine. It seems you're under a bit of pressure from your mother."

"I didn't tell her why I called off my engagement. She was very embarrassed and angry with me. I chose not to reveal to her my ex-fiancée's infidelity."

"I understand. Aren't you old enough to choose your own bride, though?"

"Could you please have this conversation with my mother?"

"Hell no."

He approached me, and I could see in his expression that he was exhausted from what he was having to deal with. I didn't want to go over the details of what either of us had experienced anymore.

"You've got so many gods and goddesses. I'd forget who's who."

Simha visibly relaxed as he realized I wasn't actually going to stand on his head. He'd probably just been through that experience anyway.

"The different gods and goddesses are reflections of the one Divine," he replied. He looked at the beams of light that were shining into the room like spotlights in a theater. "If the Eastern wall was Hinduism, and I described how the light falls on what I see, and if the Western wall was Christianity, and you described how the light illuminates what you see, our descriptions would probably be very different. But it's all the same light. The only difference is in what we are able to see."

"Okay, so if I love the Tennessee Titans, and they're the only ones for me, but y'all are mad for the Jacksonville Jaguars and can't follow anyone else, we're all yellin' from a different side of the pitch, but we all still love football!"

The furrows of despair crumbled away from Simha's brow, and that smile that kills me every time returned to his lips. "Go Jaguars!" he declared warmly.

"Go Titans!" I smiled in reply. We understood each other.

I couldn't help but notice what appeared to be a very intimate embrace of a male and female deity beside us. It was not a freestanding statue, but a sculptured motif embedded in the wall.

"Who are these two? They look like lovers."

"That's the divine union of Shiva and Shakti in yab-yum."

"What's that?"

"Oh, nothing really."

"Seriously, I want to know."

Why was he being so coy all of a sudden?

"Well, yab-yum is their sexual union. It reminds us that when we embrace sexually, we become as they are, cosmic creators… You asked."

I flushed slightly, but he had my curiosity aroused, for want of a better word.

"A cosmic sexual union? I can't think of anything similar in Christianity. If anything, my religion is quite devoid of sexuality. For a woman to get credibility in the New Testament, she has to be a perpetual virgin or a repentant prostitute."

My mother would kill me if she knew I just said that. I looked closer at the motif. The woman was sitting on the man's lap. She had her legs wrapped around him, and there was a long shaft that extended from his…

"Is that his…?"

"Yes."

"Oh lordy, I thought it was. Actually, I don't know what I thought it was. We definitely don't see *that* in Christianity!"

Simha shifted awkwardly. I was becoming accustomed to identifying his quirks, particularly the ones where he was about to ask or say something disquieting for him.

"On that note, about the night in my hotel room. I'm sorry for, well, being so eager to get all cosmic."

"Mama always says everything happens for a reason. Although I'd never tell her about that."

"And at the film festival, when you told me about your boyfriend, I was upset and jealous. I reacted poorly."

I appreciated the effort he was making.

"Don't be so hard on yourself. You've been very straightforward with me."

I couldn't help but look at the phallus of Shiva again. I must have flushed brighter than a beet. Simha sought diligently to conceal his smile at my embarrassment. He reached into his back pocket.

"I got you something."

He pulled out an envelope. I opened it, and there was a card inside. On the card, there was a love heart on the cover. Inside, the card read, *To Mary*—that was it. It just said, *To Mary*. I looked on all the other surfaces of the card for a clue to the next line, but there was nothing.

"That's it? To Mary?"

"There's so much I wanted to say. Today, I want the card to say 'I'm sorry.' On a different day, I want it to say something else."

I was speechless. In front of me was the most humbling expression of openness and vulnerability I'd ever experienced from a man, and to my right was an erect deity with an oversized penis being ridden by his goddess.

"I really should go." I wasn't used to any of this.

"Of course." Simha nodded politely. "I'll walk you to your car."

"How are you gettin' home?"

"I can get a cab."

I assumed he meant hailing a taxi and not ordering a bottle of wine. Although the latter would likely have done us both a world of good.

"Don't be silly. Your apartment is only a couple of miles away from my duplex. I'll drive you there."

So I drove him home. We crossed over the Cumberland River on the I-65 bridge and took Woodland Street past the businesses, bars, and apartment buildings. Then Woodland turned east, and I drove us through older residential neighborhoods with pale streetlights, big single-family homes, front yards, and trees. Several yards had small signs that read "Jesus Loves You." I wondered what that meant to Simha, but I wasn't game to ask.

We kept it to small talk all the way. We talked about my job and his movie. We talked about our families, his father's unhappiness with the career he'd chosen, my brother feeling trapped in his life but not knowing what he wanted or needed, his mother's desire for grandchildren, and how my sister was fixing to be a thorn in my mother's side.

I finally pulled to a stop in front of a newish white two-story building with a slate gray roof. It looked like a big farmhouse, but it was actually an apartment building with a dozen or so units. It had a covered wraparound porch supported by white columns on the ground floor, a row of bay windows on the upper floor, and a row of white chimneys sprouting out of the top of the roof.

"Nice," I said, setting the brake.

"I like it," Simha said.

"I am not gettin' out of this car," I informed him.

He looked at me with the best impression of innocence he could muster. "I never thought it would be otherwise."

"Whatever."

He grinned at me, leaned over, kissed me on the cheek, then stepped out of the car in one fluid movement. "Thanks for joining me at the temple."

"Thanks for an absolutely fantastic day."

"Ditto," he said as he closed the passenger door. He waved at me, I waved at him, and then I scooted back down the road, grinning from ear to ear. I could still feel the warmth of his lips on my cheek.

I was still smiling when I walked through the front door of my duplex, the festival music thrumming in my veins, the incredible food filling me with wildly exotic tastes and smells, and Simha's smile, the most exotic pleasure of all, still fresh in my mind.

I gave Charlie his welcome home cuddles, trying to match his enthusiasm, and a new vegetable-based chewie to apologize for being gone so long. He settled down on the floor, propped the chewie up between his front paws, and began chomping.

I stretched and sighed happily, then caught a glimpse of myself in the mirror on the wall by my dining table. I looked rumpled, suntanned, and as happy as I felt, and it finally occurred to me that I shouldn't be. I blinked. *I'd just spent the entire day with Simha!*

I looked at Charlie. "Why can't I say no to that man when I'm with him?" I demanded.

Charlie looked at me, offered no comment, and returned to his chewie.

"I shouldn't have said yes," I said aloud. "I shouldn't have gone to the festival. I had no excuse at all for goin' with him, and I most definitely shouldn't have offered to drive him home!"

But the truth was that I had loved everything about the festival, and the restaurant, and every moment I'd spent with Simha. I knew I should feel guilty, but I just couldn't. But then my phone rang.

Today I am like Solomon
with the ring of abundance on my finger
and the divine crown on my head.

🌿 *Rumi*

Chapter Thirty-Three

I pulled my phone out of my purse. Chloe was calling me. I swear I could hear her anger in the ringtone alone. Yes, I believe she has that sort of power.

"Hey, Chloe," I said feebly, answering the call.

"Don't 'hey Chloe' me!" Chloe yelled in my ear. I cringed and held the phone a couple of inches away from my head. "You promised you'd be back in an hour, *and you never showed!*"

"I'm so sorry, Chloe! I've got no excuse. I was havin' a good time, and I forgot."

"*You forgot?* You forgot your best friend? You forgot your promise to help me today? I needed you there. That Manal woman lasted five minutes before she answered her phone and wandered off. Bless her heart—the stuck-up bitch."

"Chloe, I can't apologize enough," I said hurriedly. "I'll make it up to you, I swear. The next event you plan and manage, I will be there. I will handcuff myself to your side, and I won't leave it all day, I promise."

"It was Simha, wasn't it? Did you sleep with him again?"

"What? *No!* No, it was nothin' like that. We just went to the festival and stayed late, so we had dinner and I took him home and that's all. Nothin' happened, I swear."

"Nothin' except spendin' the whole day with a man who isn't your boyfriend! How could you do that to Jason?"

"I didn't do anythin' to Jason. Chloe, nothin' happened! It was completely innocent."

"Seems to me you're havin' a hard time rememberin' where your allegiances lie."

"I'm not! I was just distracted. It won't happen again. Let me take you to brunch tomorrow at Mad Donna's to make it up to you."

"Well..." Mad Donna's was one of Chloe's guilty pleasures. "Okay. But don't think you can get around me with one good meal, Mary Poser."

"I don't. I won't. I'll meet you there at eleven."

"Okay. Don't be late."

"I won't. I'll be there early."

"That'll make it a day of miracles," Chloe said sourly, and then she hung up.

I heaved a huge sigh of relief. Having Chloe mad at me for longer than a day could make my life a living hell. She'd see to it. Mad Donna's would mollify her some. I had a chance of getting out of today with all of my limbs intact.

Then my phone vibrated in my hand. I had a text.

Jason: Where the hell are you?! We've just finished our second set. You said you'd be here!

Oh lordy! I'd completely forgotten The Nashbros' gig! My guilt doubled. Then it tripled when I discovered Simha's card was still in my hand up until now. The love heart looked up at me, silently demanding my attention. I only noticed because I had to put it down to write a text back to Jason. I had to admit the truth to myself: I'd had a much better time at the Sitalsasthi festival with

Simha than I'd ever had at any of the dive bars I'd gone to for The Nashbros. I put the card on my dresser and hurriedly began texting.

Mary: I'm so sorry! I've been incredibly busy today. I just got home.

Jason: You'd better turn up for our last set. I'm counting on you.

Mary: I will. I'm on my way!

I didn't even think of taking time to change. I grabbed my purse, told Charlie I'd be back, and dashed out of my house and back to my car. I zoomed through the Saturday night traffic, watching out for drunk drivers and trying to figure out what excuse I could give Jason about why I was late without having to mention Simha. I didn't need to be yelled at twice in one night.

I pulled into a parking space right in front of Billy Bob's Bodacious Bar and ran inside. The place was packed. When you arrive late at a bar, the roar of the drunkards seems so much more confronting. I usually arrive early and develop a tolerance to the gradual escalation of inebriated hollering. I squeezed and shoved my way to the one empty stool at the bar and ordered a club soda and lime, which probably annoyed the bartender who knew sober is not good for tips. Glass in hand, I turned around on my stool. Only The Nashbros' instruments were on the tiny stage. The guys were still on break. I heaved a sigh of relief and took a sip of my drink.

Nothing so far had come of The Nashbros' demo at Bugle Records or the casual interest of Wildcat Records. The Tipsy Turkey only booked the guys when it was desperate for a last-minute replacement band. But Jason's belief in himself and The Nashbros never wavered.

The band returned to the stage, and I clapped loudly and got about a quarter of the customers to join in.

Jason smiled and waved at me, and I smiled and waved back. Any red-blooded woman would have smiled at him. He was looking particularly hunky tonight in his faded jeans, sleeveless black shirt, and white cowboy hat. His smile seemed lit by a million watts as he swung into the first song of this set. The Nashbros sang a couple of new songs, a couple of covers of Kenny Chesney and Luke Bryan songs, and some old Nashbros standards, and then Jason silenced the tepid applause and looked right at me.

"I'd like to sing this next one to a very special lady here tonight. Mary Poser, here's your song."

He got a couple of "ahs" from some of the more sober ladies in the bar and then began singing "The Skin That's Coverin' You."

I kept a smile plastered on my face, though to be honest, I was disappointed with myself for not appreciating the song more. I must have heard it a hundred times and, although Jason said he wrote it for me, I simply couldn't connect to the lyrics. It didn't help that I always anticipated the same note that Jason enthusiastically slid around without hitting in the second verse.

At the end of the song, I applauded loudly, and a lot of the women joined in.

"Like I said, folks, I wrote that song for the special lady in my life," Jason said, using his sexy, husky voice. "I especially wanted to sing it tonight because...well, tonight is a real special night for the both of us, and I want all of you to help make it even more special." He fished around in the front pocket of his jeans and pulled out a small jeweler's box. "Mary, darlin', you ain't ever gonna be able to say again that I never give you anythin' worthwhile." He opened the box, and the stage lights sparkled on a small diamond.

The world suddenly tilted. I nearly fell off my bar stool. Then Jason got down on one knee on the stage. "Mary Poser, will you marry me?"

The blood drained out of me. I stared at him, stunned.

He gave me his sexiest smile.

Meanwhile, every single person in that bar was whooping and hollering loud enough to raise the roof. "Say yes! Say yes! Say yes!" they chanted, getting louder and louder until there wasn't any oxygen left to breathe and no place to run.

"Well, babe?" Jason said.

I stared helplessly at him. He'd just laid himself bare in front of everyone for me.

Oh lordy!

"Say yes! Say yes! Say yes!" the audience howled, demanding satisfaction. It came at me from all sides, trapping me, boxing me in.

"Yes!" I said.

The crowd went wild, cheering and yelling as Jason stood up and grinned like a little kid who's just successfully ridden a bicycle for the first time. He shoved his way through the crowd, folks slapping him on the back, and then he was standing in front of me.

"Here you go, babe," he said, grabbing my left hand and shoving the ring on my finger. It was a little big.

All I could say was, "Oh lordy, how will I keep it from falling off before I can have it resized?"

Then Jason hauled me into his arms and gave me a big wet kiss while everyone in Billy Bob's Bodacious Bar went absolutely nuts all around us.

Jason never asked me why I'd been late getting to the bar. I was going to have to get rid of that card Simha gave me. I was probably going to have to burn it, just to be sure.

If the sun's light is not a sign in your heart,
space does not expand, doors do not open.
The grave would be more pleasant for you.
So come, arise from the tomb of your heart!

❧ Rumi

Chapter Thirty-Four

I gunned my hatchback into the parking lot just after nine on a Friday morning, turned sharply into a parking space between an old sedan and an older pickup truck, and hit the brakes. A hundred yards away sat the hulking sound stage where Simha would be filming the first of four group dance scenes for his movie.

Alice was standing next to Chloe's gold Camry, watching me. Chloe was pacing.

I stepped out of my air-conditioned car, and the July heat and humidity hit me like a massive sauna.

"What a surprise," Chloe said, arms folded over her chest. "You're late!"

"Hey, bro," Alice said with a smile.

"Sorry," I said as they joined me. "I was busy. I had to feed the new neighbor's cat and I'd run out of cat food so I went to the store to get extra food but they were closed and the supermarket isn't near my place so it took me longer than I thought it would. I had to get food for Charlie anyway—"

"*Whatever!*" Chloe said impatiently.

"What does Charlie think of you feedin' cats?" Alice asked innocently.

"The first time was a helluva raucous 'cause I was holdin' the cat and Charlie came up from behind an' it was on for young and old…"

"Who cares!" Chloe roared.

I'm glad she didn't want more detail because I didn't want to tell her the truth about why I was late. I'd been home to show Mom and Dad my engagement ring. Jason had done the right thing and spoken to Dad first, so they were both chewing at the bit to see the ring. Mama was as proud as punch, and probably mostly relieved, that I was *finally* getting married. I didn't want a twenty-questions session, and I'd made excuses to be alone for a while by disappearing into the treehouse so I could gather my thoughts. I was rattled. I was scared, and I was confused. I didn't want anyone to see me like that, so the treehouse was my first choice, as it had been all my life, to hide away while I tried to pull myself together. I didn't always succeed, and I don't think I had effectively succeeded this time, either. Old habits can be hard to break, and hiding out in the treehouse had taken me back to coping strategies and ideas I thought I'd suppressed long ago.

Chloe glanced in my car and did a great double-take. "Did you seriously put your makeup on in the car while you were driving?"

"Well—"

"How many bridges do you need to fall off before you learn not to do that?" she demanded.

I was actually quite glad she was focusing on the car. I didn't want her to focus on me to discover how anxious and exhausted I was.

"I knew I was gonna be late, and I didn't want to be later and disappoint you even more," I said, hoping to placate her, again.

"You are such an idiot!" Chloe said. "You need special makeup for the film lightin' and cameras, not somethin' you bought at a drugstore and put on in your car. Honestly! You're gonna have to wash all that stuff off. Come on," she said, spinning on her heel and heading for the sound stage. "We're late for makeup, hair, and costuming. We're gonna get yelled at."

"Sorry," I said in a small voice as Alice and I trailed after her. I was going to need a whole truckload of makeup to hide the way I was feeling.

"*Busy,*" Chloe muttered.

"Bro, what's going on?" Alice asked me in a low voice. "You look like a train wreck."

Startled, I looked at her and then looked hurriedly away. I didn't have an answer for her. I just kept walking. As we got closer to the sound stage, I had a pretty good idea about what I was hoping to achieve today: I was eager to see Simha from a distance so I could prove to myself that I shouldn't be interested in the man. I was engaged to Jason. I was going to marry Jason and have a home and raise a family with him. Simha was just flat-out dangerous.

I didn't have to feel guilty. I didn't have to worry. Today, it was going to be strictly business. I was going to be seeing Simha in his element, and I'd be able to do my part and dance with Chloe and Alice as I'd been instructed because he would be focused on making his movie. I'd just be one of a hundred people on that sound stage. I was safe. He always ignored me when he was working anyway. I'm not exactly sure how I feel about that.

Chloe stopped us at a long row of RVs that had been parked in front of the sound stage and had us check in with a friendly woman wielding a clipboard. The RVs were set up to handle the makeup, hair, and costuming for the thirty dancers and eight actors in the scene being shot today, most of whom, like me, had taken vacation days from our day jobs to be here. It looked like a series of constantly revolving doors as actors, dancers, and extras walked in and came back out prepped for filming. Because Chloe was one of the featured actors in the scene, she got shunted off to the first three RVs. Alice and I got sent into the cattle cars.

Amazingly, we walked back out twelve minutes later, ready for filming. The makeup-hair-costume crew had an assembly line that, I'm sure, worked better than anything Henry Ford could have ever hoped for. Somehow, we found Chloe amidst a colorful, chatty mob of sari-clad dancers. She, of course, looked fabulous in her sparkly turquoise dress, which had calmed her down a lot. She smiled at us, looped her arms through ours, and walked us into the sound stage.

"Welcome to moviemakin', ladies," she said proudly.

"Wow!" I said.

"Bugger me! You look awesome!" Alice said delightedly.

"Darn it, girl, remind me to teach you some great Southern expressions to show enthusiasm..." Chloe couldn't help but offer in reply.

"Chloe, leave her alone..."

The cavernous building was a dozen different worlds of brilliant lights and deep shadows. It had a three-story-high ceiling with catwalks running all around it and a dozen folks running around them putting the last touches on the massive lighting rigs above us.

The set took up about two-thirds of the space. It was an elaborate Technicolored fantasy exaggeration of the living and dining rooms in the Musgrove family's Federal-style manor, including 1980s-style décor. There were portraits of generations of Musgroves on the walls. It was all stunningly different from the drab rehearsal hall where I and all of the other dancers had been rehearsing every evening these last four weeks.

The song and the dance we were going to shoot today were intended to showcase the determination of the Musgrove sisters, including Chloe, who played Louisa, to best each other in their contest to win internet tycoon Frederick Wentworth's heart. Their parents' hopes for a future wedding and a wealthy son-in-law would be juxtaposed by the bitterness of Mr. Wentworth toward Anne Elliot, and the sadness and embarrassment of Anne as she coped with the Musgrove sisters, her rivals. Anne's selfish sister and hunting-obsessed brother-in-law were part of this cast, and her still deep and now clearly hopeless love for Frederick Wentworth was the focus of the scene. Surrounding these central characters was a large chorus of servants, neighbors, and distant relatives, of which Alice and I were a part, that was commenting on all of these characters and relationships through lip-synced song and dance.

I was trying to see everything all at once. The movie camera was a surprise. It wasn't the big hulking beast I'd seen in older movies about filmmaking. It was black and compact, and its only outstanding feature was its hefty lens. Right now, it was perched on a tripod, but I saw a man wearing a Steadicam harness rig waiting on the sidelines. I had learned that these Steadicam rigs allowed the camera to move in and out of the dancers in the scene. The operator had his own choreography to move within our troupe of dancers without bumping into any of us.

Dozens of technicians worked around us and above us on everything from electrical cables to the soundboard. Chloe pointed out other people crowding the sound stage, including the Director of Photography. He was a short Asian guy in his late forties who was looking at the set through what seemed like a dozen different lenses. The First Assistant Director was a thirty-something tan and lean athletic woman with short hair wearing shorts and a tee shirt. The technical director, camera operators, construction manager, set designer, script supervisor, the loader standing around with the clapboard, a paramedic, and young unpaid interns eagerly learning their crafts all had their place on the set.

I saw Manal, gorgeous as always in khaki slacks and a red silk shirt, a beige hijab on her head, as she talked with the script supervisor. I saw Rob Barrett in jeans and a green tee shirt with a smaller digital movie camera glued to his eye as he walked around the stage filming everything. But I did not see Simha. The disappointment that surged through me annoyed me. I hate how our emotions sneak up on us sometimes, just as the memory of Simha's intense gaze as he danced with me at the temple catches me unaware more than it should.

Fortunately, the First Assistant Director distracted me by ordering all of the actors and dancers onto the set.

"Ready?" Vidya, the choreographer, asked us.

"You betcha!" Alice replied, beaming as though the question was directed solely at her.

"From the top!" Vidya commanded us as she clapped her hands together in the timing she wanted for our performance.

The movie techs watched with enchanted smiles as we sung out loudly, slapped our thighs, pumped our fists, stomped our feet, and built the power into an explosive final shout. Applause erupted all around us, and we all grinned like fools.

With Vidya and Ramón, her assistant, standing in front of us just off the set, we rehearsed the number one last time as the playback filled the soundstage with music. I couldn't stop smiling. It was so exciting to be dancing in full hair, makeup, and costume on the actual set with all of the movie technicians standing around watching us! I was so glad that Chloe and Alice had talked me into doing this. But most of all, I just loved dancing this choreography. I loved how natural these Indian dance movements felt. I loved their sensuality. I loved the fun of dancing Indian steps to country and western music.

The run-through ended, and we stayed on set as all of the actual moviemakers stood in a large clump in the shadows near the camera, conferring on the scene.

"Hey, Alice, did you see Rob?" I asked as we stood under the bright stage lights together. "He was filmin' the rehearsal. He's filmin' everythin', but I think he's given you some extra camera time."

"Oh, I know," Alice said nonchalantly.

"You do?" I said in surprise.

"Oh yeah. He's taking me out to dinner tonight."

"Does he know?"

"Not yet," Alice said with a grin.

Alice always made me laugh, and I admired her wacky, cheeky self-confidence. My laughing was interrupted by Simha, a Simha I'd never experienced before. He was wearing sneakers, jeans, and a crisp white Oxford shirt, and he was simmering with anger.

"Harvey!" he yelled from the middle of the clump of people standing near the camera. "Those amber spots still aren't right. You said you'd have them fixed twenty minutes ago."

"Sorry, Simha."

"I need them fixed. *Now.*"

"Yes, sir!" Harvey, a thickset man, scrambled up onto the catwalk to talk to his lighting riggers.

Simha wasn't watching him. He was looking through the movie camera and shaking his head. "No, I don't like it, Keung. It's a half meter too far back. I want a tighter focus on the building for the wide-angle shot."

"This is the exact setup we used for 'Touching Me, Touching You' in *Passion*," Keung said placatingly, "and you loved that shot."

"This isn't *Passion*," Simha snapped.

Keung sighed. "Okay, okay," he turned to his camera operator, "move it forward."

"Susan, have you checked costume continuity?" he asked the script supervisor, a black woman with glasses and an iPad in her hand.

"We're good, Simha," she said in a surprising English accent.

"Are you sure? What about the scarf on Roberta? Wasn't it knotted on the left side?"

"Nope, right side," she said, showing him an image on the iPad. "Good."

"Harvey!" the First Assistant Director shouted into the rafters with her own English accent. "We're waiting on you."

"Almost there," Harvey shouted back.

The First AD walked up to Simha, who was looking through the camera again. "Lighting's almost ready, boss."

"Good," Simha snapped.

The lighting shifted subtly on the set. "How's that?" Harvey called.

"What it should have been twenty minutes ago," Simha retorted under his breath. "All right, everyone, take your places!"

I moved into line with Alice, feeling unsettled. I'd wanted to see Simha at work, and I'd liked seeing him so completely in charge, but I'd never expected to see him impatient, terse, and as a perfectionist. I remembered how he'd responded to his mother's presence at the temple. He was under a lot of pressure from so many angles, and I had to remind myself that he was a mere mortal with flaws like everyone else. No one belongs on a pedestal. It's a lot of pressure meeting lofty expectations.

I got distracted when Simha walked to the edge of the set. "Actors, everyone clear on motivation? Any questions?"

No one said anything.

"Good," he said. "Henry and Catherine, I want to see the angst behind the smiles and choreography."

"We'll angst our brains out, boss," said Henry Tate, the tall, ruggedly handsome Frederick Wentworth to Catherine Tate's plainly costumed and made up Anne Elliot.

"Thank you," Simha said with a wry smile. "Dancers, I want bright, high energy in every step and arm movement. I know

Vidya has taught you not only the steps but the emotion of this scene, and the facial expressions needed to reflect that emotion. Don't forget that when you're going through your choreo. I want to see all of it on the first take. Clear?"

"Yes, sir!" we all said as one.

Simha stepped back into the shadows. "Ready," he said to Cecily, the First AD.

"Silent on the set!" she shouted. A hush fell over everyone. "Sound!"

"Sound on!" one of the technicians called.

"Camera!"

"Camera on!" said Oscar.

Cecily nodded to the clapper. He moved in front of the camera. "*Persuasion*, Scene Nineteen, Take One." He clapped the board at the camera then stepped back.

"Actors and dancers," Simha said, "I won't be saying 'Action,' because the music is your cue. You'll hear an eight-beat countdown first. Cue music!" he called.

A moment later, I heard eight beeps, and then music that I now knew as well as my own name filled the soundstage. Right on cue, I began to dance and lip-sync with everyone else. Adrenaline poured through me—I was dancing in a movie! In *Simha's* movie!

The scene went by in a blur. We all held our final poses until Simha shouted, "Okay, that's a take!" and then we relaxed. For less than a second.

"Good," Simha said. "Everyone settled now? Let's do it again. Original positions."

We all scrambled back into our starting positions.

The clapper walked back in front of the camera. "*Persuasion*, Scene Nineteen, Take Two." He clapped the board then stepped back again.

"Cue music!" Simha shouted.

Eight beeps, then music filled the soundstage, and we began dancing again. And again. And again.

After the fourth take, Simha announced himself satisfied. But we weren't done. Not by a long shot. While the actors and dancers mobbed the craft tables and grabbed water bottles and drained them, the crew reset the camera and some of the lights.

And we did the scene again, twice, for the new camera angle. Then the crew reset the camera and some of the lights, and we did three more takes. The camera and lights got reset again, and we did two takes with close-ups of Frederick Wentworth, then three takes of close-ups of Anne Elliot.

In between the takes, I caught my breath, drank water, and watched Simha. I couldn't take my eyes off him. I was obsessed. I felt like a stalker. I watched everything he did, worked to overhear everything he said, studied every expression that flitted across his face. I didn't tell myself that I shouldn't. I didn't even ask myself what I was doing. I just did it.

He was like the confident captain of a three-masted clipper ship. He was in perfect command of every sailor, every detail, even the wind and the sea.

And sometimes during the breaks, when everyone else was doing their jobs, and he just stood there watching and sipping from a water bottle filled with sweet ice tea, he talked to Chloe. He smiled at Chloe as she arched her neck, cocked her head, and looked up at him from under her eyelashes. Once, he even laughed, and I died a little inside.

Was the flirtation mutual? Had this been going on during all of the rehearsals and filming that had already happened? Even the questions sank me into misery. I told myself I had no right to be depressed, let alone jealous. I'd made my choice. I was marrying Jason. Simha was a friend.

It didn't help.

Alice suddenly appeared at my side and nudged me. "He's making a documentary."

"What?" I said, turning and trying to focus on my friend.

"Rob. I've been chatting with him. Not only is he one of the producers on this movie, he's also filming a documentary about the making of an independent feature film. This one."

"Cool."

"And he's taking me to The Palm tonight," she said with a grin.

I smiled back. "Good work. That's a pretty high-end restaurant."

"I'm worth it," Alice said nonchalantly as she headed to the craft table for a doughnut.

A couple of minutes later, Vidya and Ramón called us all back to the set and rehearsed us for the coming Steadicam shots so we knew how to move, or stay put, as the Steadicam operator and camera glided through the dancers and actors. The rehearsal, followed by five different takes, required all of my focus and attention. Still, I had to work hard to give Simha the bright, high energy he wanted, because my depression just kept growing.

Chloe knew Simha was my friend, so why was she pursuing him? And Simha knew Chloe was my friend, so why hadn't he mentioned to me even once when we'd bumped into each other that they were dating? *Were* they dating? Or were they just in the flirtation stage? If they were, it wouldn't last long. When Chloe wanted something, she got it, especially when it was a man.

My misery deepened.

After the fifth Steadicam take, Simha called a break and huddled with Manal, Rob, and some of his crew. Everyone stood around me chatting, laughing. I felt like a tiny black island in the sea of their good humor.

The conference started breaking up. Soon, it was just Simha and Rob talking as Rob played back some of the documentary footage he'd shot today. Suddenly, Simha looked intently at Rob's screen, and then he spun his head around and stared right at me, his dark gaze piercing through my heart like a javelin.

Then he walked toward me.

The dark thought, the shame, the malice,
Meet them at the door laughing, and invite them in.
Be grateful for whoever comes.
Because each has been sent
as a guide from beyond.

🌿 Rumi

Chapter Thirty-Five

"Hello, Mary," Simha said.

"Hey," I said, feeling oddly shy.

Without any delay or expression on his face, he lifted up my left hand. "Congratulations."

The blood drained out of me.

"Thank you," I said, awkwardly pulling my hand free.

"It must be recent," he said. "You didn't mention it at the temple."

"Yeah, it's...um...recent," I said, too embarrassed to look him in the eye.

"Hi, Simha!" Alice said, coming up to us with a big smile.

"Hello, Alice," he said with a much smaller smile. "Are you enjoying making the movie?"

"Oh, it's choice, bro! But I've been meaning to ask you—when do we get to blow on each other?"

"Blow on each other?"

"Don't people blow on each other in Bollywood movies?"

"Oh lordy," I said under my breath.

Simha's smile grew. "Only sometimes, and usually in the love scenes. I'll make sure you get your chance to blow on someone."

"Awesome!" She thought for a moment. "Am I missing a double meaning that's goin' to gross me out?"

"Oh, lordy…"

"Hey, girls!" Chloe said brightly as she strode up to us, planting herself at Simha's side, taking his arm, and smiling flirtatiously up at him. "So, Simha, what do you think of my work today? Am I giving you everything you want for Louisa?"

"You've been great," Simha said. Was it wrong of me to think, perhaps even hope, he said it without any real enthusiasm?

"I'm so grateful for this opportunity, and I'm enjoying this movie so much!" Chloe gushed with a determined smile as she leaned a little against Simha. "It's the greatest education watching a talented filmmaker work. I've learned so much about film acting from you. And I've enjoyed learning about *you*, too," she said, with a coy look up at Simha.

"Well," I said with my own determined smile, "you two look happy."

"Oh, I feel like I've known Simha forever," Chloe said while Simha stared at me. "He just has to look at me, and I know what he wants from me. We have a wonderful connection."

"Yeah, but you and Simha aren't—" Alice began.

"Has Mary shown you her engagement ring?" Chloe hurriedly asked Simha as she glared at Alice. "She and Jason have set a date in September."

My stomach clenched.

Simha went very still. His face was stone. "That's fast."

"Well, it's just gonna be a simple weddin'," Chloe said brightly, "so there isn't much plannin' to do. It's not like makin' a *movie!* You know, I just love this script. It has such a depth of character and emotion, such truth in the relationships. I can really relate to Louisa's eager search for love."

A sudden hard, sharp spasm made me cringe and press my

hand to my stomach to try to push it back into calm. Darn it, I'd left my goji berry juice in the car, and I could usually count on it to settle things down.

"Louisa is a great role," I said, trying to cover a second twinge. I didn't cover it well enough for Simha. He looked at me like he was scanning my bones.

"How have you been recently, Mary?" Simha asked.

"Oh, I'm just real busy," I said, trying not to cringe as my stomach spasmed.

He stiffened. "You have an interesting culture here. When you ask people how they are, they say they're 'busy.' But if you're in love or following your heart, 'busy' seems like such a disappointing description of how you are, don't you think? But then, perhaps for some people, the word 'busy' is their code for unhappy."

Then Simha took me completely by surprise. He took my hand, that he was still holding, and flipped it over to expose my forearm. Alice and Chloe gasped at the fresh scratches on my forearm that were still weeping.

"Fall out of the tree again?" Simha pried coldly.

"It was the cat! He scratched me when Charlie scared him. It was an accident!"

Simha glanced at Keung, the Director of Photography, who was signaling him. "Excuse me. My DP needs me." He strode over to Keung like he was eager to escape us. To escape me. I just stood there, mouth open, speechless.

Alice looked at me wide-eyed and confused. "How did you let the cat do this to you?"

"It didn't mean it. It was scared because of Charlie."

"I think it's time you let people feed their own pets, Mary Poser," Chloe concluded with a hint of jealousy that Simha seemed more interested in my cat-wrestling story than her acting.

We did one more take and then, seven hours after we'd started our moviemaking day, Simha shouted, "That's a wrap for today, ladies and gentlemen. Thank you all for your hard work."

He didn't even glance my way as I collected my things and left the sound stage with Alice and Chloe. Chloe was chattering about what good friends she was becoming with Catherine Moore, the compliment Henry Tate had given her the other day, and how well she and Simha were getting along and how much he admired her hard work and professionalism. I think that's what she said, anyway. I wasn't really listening.

We climbed back up into the RVs, turned in our hair ornaments and other accessories, changed our clothes, and handed our costumes back to the wardrobe folks. Then we headed to our cars. Chloe air-kissed Alice's cheeks and then mine and drove off with a cheerful wave of her hand.

"Enjoy your date," I said to Alice as we reached the ancient Nissan Sentra sedan she'd bought used almost two years ago and that still, miraculously, started every time she turned on the ignition.

"I plan to," she said with a grin and a wink.

I got into my car and rolled down the windows to let out the suffocating heat. Fortunately, I had a box of makeup remover wipes in my makeup bag. I used three wipes to get rid of the heavy movie makeup and put some lipstick back on. Then, I turned my hatchback toward The Black Hat, a downtown dive bar. The Nashbros were playing there this weekend, and for once, I was eager to get there. I needed a drink.

I arrived just as The Nashbros finished setting up. I waved at the boys as I sat down at a sticky table near the back of the bar. I asked the waitress to wipe it off and got a weary glare and a lifeless swipe of a dirty, damp rag for my pains. I ordered a Prichard's. Yes, I really needed a drink.

"We got Jack," she said and brought a single shot of Jack Daniels. Cheers to the worst day of my life. I threw back my head and gladly let the spirit scorch my throat on its way down.

Jason joined me during the break after the first set. He talked the entire time about a gig he was trying to line up at The Peach Orchard, a more upscale juke joint. During The Nashbros' second set, my phone vibrated in my purse, and I hurriedly turned it off. Once the set was over, Jason, Toby, and Scotty gathered at the bar next to me for a round of shots. I turned my phone back on and checked my messages. Oh lordy, Simha had sent me a text!

Simha: I hope you're okay.

I couldn't think. The whiskey already had me swimming, and now, with my inhibitions dulled, all sorts of different emotions started battering me from every side. I couldn't stop the tears that started welling in my eyes.

"What's that?"

Startled, I turned to see Jason standing by me. "Nothin'," I said hurriedly, shoving my phone into my purse. "Just a message from a friend."

"What about?" he asked, sitting down beside me.

"Oh, um, just a query if I'm okay. I was tired today."

"Who was askin'?"

I had just settled on saying it was from Chloe, but then Jason grabbed my phone from my purse and lit up the screen. The name 'Simha' reflected in his eyes from my phone.

"That movie guy?" Jason exploded. "What the hell is he doin' textin' *you?*"

"It's nothin', Jason," I said placatingly. "We just chat with each other now and then in a text or e-mail."

"Are you seein' him on the side?" Jason demanded.

"What? No! Of course not. We bump into each other now and then, but it's no big deal. He took me to a Hindu festival one time…"

"A *Hindu festival?*" I had never seen Jason so angry. His face was red, and he was shaking. "You are marryin' *me*, babe. You got *no* right hangin' with some foreign dude. I don't know him, and I don't trust him. I don't want you *ever* seein', talkin' or textin' that foreigner again!"

"Jason, that's so unreasonable!"

"I don't give a damn. I haven't been runnin' around on you, and you are gonna stop runnin' around on me right now!"

"But I'm not runnin' around on you! We haven't done anythin' wrong. Simha's just a friend."

"Are you so dumb that you can't see that he wants to be a helluva lot more than *your friend?*"

Memories of that August night in Simha's arms flooded through me. I hung my head to hide my blush. Never chug down a Jack before arguing with your fiancé. The liquid spirit exposes all the cards you usually hold hidden against your chest.

"I want your promise, Mary, right here, right now, that you're gonna have nothin' to do with that man from this moment on."

"But I've committed to dancin' in three more scenes in his movie with Chloe and Alice," I said in a small voice. "I signed a contract. I can't back out."

"Well then, all you're gonna do is *dance*, is that clear? You don't talk to him, not one word. Not one text. I want your promise, Mary."

I sat there feeling like a couple of tons of iron were pushing me down into the wood chair. It had been wicked of me to encourage Simha. It had been sinful to let him talk me into outings that I'd kept secret from everyone, including Jason. I couldn't let it happen anymore if I was going to make my life with Jason. Jason was absolutely right. I couldn't communicate with or see Simha again.

Tears welled hot and heavy in my eyes. The grief of never talking with Simha again, never feeling his smile warm me, was so enormous that it shocked me.

"I promise," I said in a low voice, not looking Jason in the eye.

"All right then," Jason said. "I've got to go play another set." He stalked off toward the stage, shoving chairs angrily out of his way.

I wrapped my arms around myself to try to stop the shaking, but it didn't help.

I got home a bit more than two hours later. Charlie was leaping up to my eye level. I gave him the bare minimum of returned enthusiasm, even though he hadn't seen me in sixteen hours. I ignored the throw pillow filling that he'd clearly made an effort to decorate the living room with. I walked numbly into my bedroom, sat down on the side of the bed, grabbed Teddy, held him tight to my chest, and finally let myself cry.

Hot, plump tears poured down my face as I sobbed out the wrong I'd done Jason, the hurt I was going to hand Simha, and the loss of something I hadn't let myself know how much I wanted until right now.

I had scattered half a box of tear-soaked tissues around my feet before I finally got myself back under control. I was back to following my dog's lead and making an awful mess in an effort to feel better. I washed my face, reassured Charlie that I was okay. I was even lying to my dog now. Grabbing my phone from my purse where I'd dropped it on the living room floor, I walked back into my bedroom and sat back down on the bed. After turning my phone back on, I just stared at it for a good ten minutes. Finally, I worked up enough courage to start texting.

Mary: Dear Simha, I don't want to hurt you or upset you, but I've done harm, and it has to stop. I've got to stop seeing you, stop talking to you, stop texting you because I've hurt and upset the man I'm going to marry by seeing you and talking to you. You're a wonderful man.

I have loved the time we've spent together and the things we've shared together. But I have to do right by Jason. Duty is as important to Baptists as it is to Hindus, and I've been shirking mine this summer. You're a good man, and I'm going to miss you, but I've got to do my duty and say goodbye now and forever. I wish you all the best. Mary.

With a trembling finger, I pressed "Send" and immediately dissolved into wracking sobs again.

Swim out of your little pond.

🐉 *Rumi*

Chapter Thirty-Six

"I swear, Mary, your salads get more elaborate each time you come over for supper," Mama said as she stuck a couple of serving forks into the big wooden salad bowl I'd brought to family supper.

"I'm just bein' creative, Mama," I said as I pulled the plastic wrap off the large porcelain bowl of potato salad I'd also brought. I put a heavy serving spoon in the bowl. "This is just the usual recipe," I said, lifting up the potato salad.

"No need to be embarrassed by creativity, Niece," Aunt Sara said as she picked up a serving tray loaded down with corn on the cob.

"I was not criticizin' her, Sara," Mama snapped.

Fortunately, before Mama and Aunt Sara could get into an argument, Erin walked into the kitchen. I was sure her miniskirts were getting shorter and her makeup darker. The way things were going, I was going to have a Goth for a sister in no time at all. Mama's conservative guidance didn't stand a chance against Erin's overt efforts at defiance. What had me stumped, though, was on her back.

"Erin, why are you wearin' a backpack to supper?" I asked.

"It's not a backpack," she said. "It's a parachute."

I blinked. "Okay, so why are you wearin' a parachute?"

"Because when I had my aneurysm, I fell about twenty feet to the ground."

"But now you're standin' on the ground. In fact, you're indoors. Why on earth do you need a parachute?"

"You're such an idiot."

"I'm not the one wearin' a parachute in the kitchen!"

"Erin! Explain it to your sister," Mama ordered.

Erin sighed heavily at me. "I'm gonna learn how to skydive. Skydivers use parachutes. Because of the weakness in my arm, I can't reach the rip cord to open the chute. So I'm wearin' this parachute to remind me to exercise my arm every day so it can reach the cord and pull it when I finally do jump out of that plane." She tried to raise her right arm up to the rip cord and could only lift it about halfway. "See?"

"Oh lordy, Erin!" I said. "What if you jump out of a plane and can't lift your hand up to the rip cord, or you don't have enough strength in your arm to pull it?"

"Well, I'll have about two minutes to think about my relationship with Jesus Christ before—" She smacked her left hand on the kitchen table.

I cringed. "Where on earth did you get such a crazy idea? How can you even think of jumpin' out of a plane? You've been scared of heights ever since you had your aneurysm and fell off the treehouse ladder."

"I know. That's the challenge. I'm killin' two birds with one stone. I'm gettin' my arm stronger and gettin' over my fear of heights at the same time. I'm gonna book a tandem jump first, and if I can handle that, then I'm goin' solo." She tried to reach for the parachute rip cord again and failed.

"Mama, how can you let her?" I demanded.

"Your sister doesn't listen to a word I say," Mama said, shooting Erin a glare. "Come on, folks are hungry," she said, grabbing the platter of fried chicken. "Erin, have you got the rolls?"

"Yes, Mama," Erin said wearily as she lifted the big bread basket with her left hand and lowered it so her right hand could help support it.

We carried the food into the dining room where all the men—Daddy, Grandpa Tom, Toby, and Jason—and Aunt Sara were already seated.

"At last!" Toby said. "I'm starvin'."

"You're always starvin'," Erin said as we set the food in the middle of the table.

"I'm still a growin' boy," Toby said with a grin.

"Best biceps on any stage in town," Jason agreed, nudging my brother, who shoved him back. They'd have started wrestling if they weren't seated at the dinner table.

I went back into the kitchen with Mama to get the pitchers of sweet tea and lemonade. Once we were all seated, Daddy said grace, and we began serving.

"I always eat better at this table than anywhere else in town," Jason said, helping himself to two pieces of chicken. "No one fries up chicken like you, Mrs. P."

"Oh now, Jason, no need to flatter me," Mama said with a pleased smile. "I'm practically your mother."

"Just another six weeks," Daddy said, scooping some potato salad onto his plate.

"I can't believe it's August already," Mama said. "There's still so much plannin' to do for the weddin'. Did you choose your tuxedo yet, Jason?"

"Yes, ma'am," Jason said after a sip of sweet tea. "I took your advice and went with black."

"Oh good!" Mama said. "You'll look so elegant."

"It's a good thing you're marryin' this good lookin' boy, Mary," Daddy said with a grin. "Toby needs a brother."

Jason laughed, and Toby flushed.

"It's a good thing she's finally gettin' married, period," Mama said, handing around the bread basket.

"Mama!" I protested. "I'm only twenty-four."

"Don't worry, I've had her in my ear most of my adult life for not finding Mr. Right. I've always preferred his mischievous brother, Mr. Right Now," Aunt Sara said with a grin and a wink as she poured herself some lemonade.

"Toby's written a great new song about love and marriage," Jason said before Mama could get on her high-horse about her sister staying stubbornly single and disconcertingly polyamorous. "We're gonna debut it tonight at Gilligan's Lagoon—that's a bar on Briley Parkway—and I know it's gonna be a hit with the arrangement I've given it. Great potato salad, Mrs. P."

"Mary made it," Mama said proudly.

"Well, I'm just glad she has time to cook again now that she isn't rehearsin' for that damn movie. 'Scuse me, I mean that darn movie," Jason said.

"Me, too," Toby said with a sour look at me.

My stomach churned, and I passed the potato salad to Grandpa Tom.

"You filmed your last scene, Mary?" Aunt Sara asked.

"A couple of days ago," I said. It had been misery. Just like the second and third dance scenes. I'd had to spend hours on the same sound stage as Simha and not look at him except to notice Chloe virtually hanging off him. I'd had to walk in the opposite direction if he came anywhere near me, not say a word to him, not even "hello." My misery was made worse by knowing there'd be no text or e-mail from him when I finally got home.

"And I'm glad," Jason said flatly. "I never liked her associatin' with those foreigners."

"Oh, me either!" Mama said. "It seems everywhere I go

nowadays, I see all these foreigners in town wearin' strange clothes and talkin' what sounds like gibberish. They even smell different! And there's not a white face in the bunch. I think we oughta have a say in who's allowed into Nashville and who isn't. What if those godless foreigners want to stay? If we don't say somethin' now, we'll soon be overrun by Indians and Arabs and Muslims and such, and this is a Christian town!"

"Mama, there are Jewish synagogues, Muslim mosques, and Buddhist and Hindu temples in Nashville," I said in exasperation.

She ignored me. "It's bad enough we have all these Mexicans who insist on speakin' Spanish, but soon we could be rubbin' elbows with folks speakin' some strange language that isn't anywhere near American."

"Mama, nobody speaks 'American,'" Erin said. "We speak English. If you'd poke your head out of the church doors, you'd see that thousands of foreigners already live in Nashville, and they help to make it a lot more interestin' place to live than *you* do."

"Erin Poser!" Mama gasped. "Where in the name of the good Lord did we go wrong with you? How can you say such things to me?"

"*How can I?*" Erin stormed. "I'm not the one seedin' prejudices. We reap what we sow, Mama."

The room hit that post gunshot silence in an instant. I'd never heard Erin stand up to Mama before. Only Aunt Sara ever did that. Occasionally, Grandpa gave it a go. I looked to Daddy to see if he was going to choose a side. He spontaneously did what he always does in these situations and broke out into one of his Jerry Lewis routines. He started pulling faces and flailing his arms around manically, and that made all of us, even Erin, laugh...but not Mama.

"Brian, you shouldn't make fun of a serious conversation,"

Mama said, frowning. Daddy turned away and took a long swallow of wine. I had my hands clenched under the table, trying to find half the courage my little sister had just shown.

"Now, now, Marjorie," Grandpa Tom said loudly, "there's no need for a hissy fit. You could start an argument in an empty house."

"I will not sit here and be insulted in my own home!" Mama said.

"If *you're* gonna insult everyone who isn't *just like you*, then I'm gonna say somethin' about it!" Erin said.

"Erin, that's enough," Daddy said. "This is a family supper."

"*She* started it," Erin said, slouching back in her chair and folding her arms over her chest.

"And I'm finishin' it," Daddy said. He took a swallow of wine. "How are your butterflies doin', Sara?"

Aunt Sara grinned at him. "Just fine, Brian, and thank you for askin'. We should have another release sometime in September, and then you'll have yourself a sight. Thousands of multicolored butterflies fillin' the sky is somethin' that still thrills me down to my socks."

"I get that kind of thrill every time I set foot on a stage," Jason said.

"I just wish the stages were a bit bigger...and cleaner," Toby said. Jason frowned at him.

"Jenny has always been my biggest thrill," Grandpa Tom said.

"I'm takin' my vacation next spring in Kenya," Aunt Sara continued. "It's kind of a butterfly microcosm for the entire continent. I should be able to see most of the African species in one visit."

Mama choked on a sip of sweet tea. "Kenya? *Africa?* You're goin' to *Africa?*"

"Yep," Aunt Sara said.

"*Alone?*"

"Probably. I'm not datin' anyone seriously, and I don't figure that'll change before my trip."

"You can't go traipsin' off halfway around the world all by your lonesome!" Mama insisted. Mama sometimes made her fears of stepping out glaringly obvious. How she and Aunt Sara could be sisters always puzzled me. There must have been a mix-up at the hospital back in the day.

"I am fully capable of takin' care of myself, Marjorie," Aunt Sara said, glowering at Mama. "Kenya is one of the more stable countries on that continent. It also has some of the best wildlife reserves in the world."

"I'm just sayin' it'd be safer for you if you had a husband to go with."

Aunt Sara gasped. "Are you ever goin' to let up on that?"

"The Bible is clear. God says women are supposed to *marry*," Mama declared. "It's the natural order. Without a husband, you are denyin' Jesus' vision for your life. Look at Mary—she has *always* done God's biddin'."

My stomach clenched. How did this suddenly become about me?

"She has always been a dutiful daughter," Mama continued, "and a good Christian, and that's why God saved her from that terrible car crash and why he sent her a good boy like Jason to marry. I'll bet God has sent you lots of good husbands, but you just wouldn't open your eyes and your heart to see 'em. You're so all-fired determined to be independent and a *career woman* that you don't even see the path God is tellin' you to follow!"

"Why you sanctimonious harpy!" Aunt Sara exploded. "Just because *you* married early and had children doesn't mean that God wants every single woman on the planet to do the same! I have a *brain*, Marjorie, a brain given me by God to *use*, and I am usin' it to honor His creations! You're so damned rigid that I'm amazed you haven't squeezed the life out of Mary and Erin and Toby! You've certainly been tryin' hard enough to do just that!"

That crack made Mama spitting mad. Right then and there, she and Aunt Sara entered into a royal battle for the souls of Erin, Toby, and me. We three just looked at each other, a little amazed, a little embarrassed. I was also queasy. I didn't like being held out as the poster girl for conformity, duty, and obedience. The labels felt too heavy on my shoulders, too confining, too true—and none of that felt like a good thing. My stomach was twisting and knotting and clenching so much that it was impossible for me to eat.

"Girls, girls, girls," Grandpa Tom finally said, "that's enough. This is a supper table, not a battlefield."

"*She* started it!" Mama and Aunt Sara said at the same time.

"And you're both in the wrong," Grandpa Tom said. "Usin' my grandchildren for your weapons, rippin' up at each other for the good choices you both made in your lives, throwin' God's name around like you've got some kind of a direct line to the mind of the Almighty himself. You should be ashamed of yourselves. Why, I wouldn't blame Jason for havin' second thoughts about marryin' into such a family."

"No, sir," Jason said stoutly. "You folks are the best people I know. I'm not goin' anywhere. Besides, I'm used to family fights."

"Well, son, you'll get plenty of 'em around here," Grandpa Tom said. "Sara, you go off to Kenya if that's what you want and send us lots of postcards, and Marjorie," he said looking at Mama, "you let your sister go with your blessin' and be happy she inherited your mother's strength. I may wear the pants," he said with a wink at Daddy, "but Jenny always called the shots."

Daddy's lips quirked in a rueful smile. He raised his wine glass in toast and took a swallow.

"I think it'd be excitin' to visit another country," Toby said. "I'm not so interested in Africa, but I've always had a hankerin' to see Australia. Remember that Crocodile Hunter dude? He was crazier than a hoot owl, but he sure had some good times down there."

"No pullin' a crocodile out of somebody's backyard for me," Erin said. "If I wanted fun, I'd go to Rome. From what I've heard, those Italian boys know how to treat a girl right."

"*Erin Jennifer Poser!*" Mama gasped.

Daddy chuckled. "It's the Posers' Latin blood, Marjorie. You can't fight it. *I'd* go to France and drink coffee in cafés with folks who appreciate a good comedy movie."

"I don't know why y'all want to travel," Jason said. "Nashville has everythin' you could ever want right here."

"I couldn't agree more," Mama said. "We're each of us born in a particular place for a reason, and we oughta stay put."

"If that was true, we wouldn't be sittin' at this table right now," Grandpa Tom said. "This whole country was settled by folks born one place and choosin' to move here. Heck, even the Indians came here from somewhere else…Russia or Mexico or some such thing."

"Indians," Mama muttered, and I groaned inside. "Why on earth did they have to make a Bollywood movie in Nashville anyway?" she demanded. "We don't have any elephants or tigers except at the zoo."

"Mama, the movie has nothin' to do with jungle animals," I said in exasperation. "It's a contemporary tellin' of a Jane Austen novel, and there aren't any elephants and tigers in the book! Simha is makin' the movie here because he thinks Nashville is beautiful. He's inspired by some of our landmarks like the Parthenon, and he really likes all of the Southern hospitality he gets from everyone except *you*."

"There you go, stickin' up for that Gandhi again!" Jason said furiously.

"I am *not* stickin' up for him," I said with enforced calm. "I'm explainin' why he chose to make his movie in Nashville!"

"You sure seem to have an *intimate* understandin' of his thinkin'!"

"I do not! I wish you would stop imaginin' somethin' that isn't there!"

"*You're* the one who was hangin' all over him!"

"I was not!"

"You *texted* him!" Jason said, pointing an outraged finger at me.

"I send texts to everyone! And, because of you, I no longer send any to him." Erin's bravado must have wafted over my way, giving me a sniff of courage. "Simha is in town to make a movie, *not* to sleep with me, and when he finishes makin' his movie, he will *leave!*" I yelled. "And if you're gonna keep actin' like a jealous jackass, then I'll leave, too!" I could stand up to Jason, but not usually in front of the family. It felt sinful.

"Mary!" Mama said, shocked. "That's no way to speak to your fiancé!"

I threw my napkin down on the table, shoved my chair back, and stormed out of the dining room, bristling with fury that Jason would dare throw Simha in my face after I'd given Simha up for *him*. I stalked out the front door, saw the wood ladder going up the trunk of the tree that had our treehouse near the top, and suddenly that seemed like the best place in the world to be. It was the refuge of my childhood and teen years, and I was finding myself drawn back to its sanctuary again. Jason and Mama wouldn't follow me *there*, and I didn't have my cellphone on me, so they couldn't even call me.

I climbed up twenty feet and heaved myself into the treehouse through its entrance in the floor. It was just seven feet deep and four feet wide on the inside. It had a small window in the wall facing the house. A history of two young girls growing up in pictures lined the walls. My drawings were almost exclusively of butterflies. Erin's work on the walls was far more eclectic and interesting, ranging from horses to waterfalls and majestic mansions—the likely fantasy of her future life in the years beyond our humble treehouse. We both had wooden boxes with hinged lids in which we would store our toys and treasured possessions. The boxes doubled as seats for imitation tea parties that we shared with our dolls and any imaginary friends we chose to invite on that day. The treehouse was always shadowed and relatively cool on the hot and humid evenings with cool breezes finding their way through the entrance and every gap in our scantily clad hideaway. As the sun descended in the sky in the evenings after school, and the birds sung their final chorus, we would sit together and share our adventures of the day and reveal most of, but not all of, our secrets to each other.

The only new addition to our little abode was a big brown teddy bear sitting in the corner of the room that looked like he was there to watch over the entrance to ensure only invited guests entered. It was the teddy Simha had given me. Although I risked being lynched by my fiancé, I simply couldn't throw him away.

I lifted the lid to my toybox. I knew exactly what I was looking for, but for the life of me, I couldn't find it. I could feel the panic rising in my throat, and I started hurling dolls one way and the other to frantically search the entire box.

Erin's head suddenly poked up in the entry. "Can I come in?" she asked.

I spun around from my futile search with a wild rage in my tone I rarely allow. "How dare you!"

"What are you talking about?"

"Who said you could go through my stuff?" I was in no mood to tolerate any shenanigans from my sister. I didn't doubt that my blood was boiling with fury.

"I don't know what you're talking about!" Erin pleaded with fear creeping into her eyes.

"What have you done with it?"

"With what? What are you talking about?"

"I swear Erin, I'll—"

"I don't know what you're talking about! What's missing?"

I searched her face for a clue that she may be lying to me. But she was never one for stealing in the past. I didn't understand why she would start now. "It doesn't matter. What are you doing up here anyway?"

"Comin' to see what's up with you. Are you okay?"

"I'm fine."

"So can I come in, or are you goin' to beat me to death with Barbie?"

"Sure," I said, glancing at the Barbie doll still clenched in my fist. I scooted over to give her room.

Erin pulled herself awkwardly in through the entrance. She hadn't been in the treehouse since her accident. It was hard for her to pull herself up and in because of the weakness of her right arm, but I knew enough by now not to offer to help. She shifted over to my side. The parachute was still on her back. She looked around the floor at the carnage of dolls and toys, and her eyes settled on the one item she wasn't expecting to see.

"Nice teddy bear."

I sighed, but I didn't want to talk about it. I was simply ready to weep, so I did what I usually do when I feel helpless and distraught. I changed the topic of conversation. "Erin, you just climbed twenty feet straight up!"

"Yep," she said with a grin.

"What about your fear of heights?"

"Still got it," she said, inching away from the entry, "but it's a mite more manageable."

"Wow."

"Yeah," she said wryly. "Thanks for comin' up here. You've given me a great idea. Climbin' this tree every day should make my fear of heights even more manageable *and* help strengthen my arm." She chanced a peek out the entryway. "This could even be a good jumpin' off place to test my parachute arm once it starts to get stronger."

"Do you think you can get the strength back in your arm?"

"I know, I know," Erin said, her face darkening. "I've been sayin' that I'd gone as far as I could go with my rehab, but I know now that I can go a lot further. I don't know if I can get my arm back to normal, but I'm determined to at least get it close. I have to."

I shook my head. "You're the bravest person I know."

"Nah. I'm just desperate for a better life than the one I've got."

"Yeah, but you're doin' somethin' about it. Most people sit around talkin' about what they want, how they want to change, and here you are doin' it. I think you're admirable for that."

Erin preened herself. "I guess I am pretty spectacular."

I laughed, and she grinned at me. Then she leaned back on her left elbow and looked me straight in the eye.

"So Mary, arguin' with Mama *and* Jason at the dinner table. What in hell is goin' on with you?"

She could see that my anger had subsided, and she was eager for answers. We had always confided in each other, and today should be no exception. "They just know how to push all my buttons, I guess."

"I know Mama acts like she's the door bitch to heaven, but you know she means well. She just gets threatened by what she doesn't understand, whether it's my dress sense or Indian filmmakers. It's exhaustin', but it's understandable. What I don't get is why Jason's nose is so out of joint."

I sighed heavily. "He's just jealous because Simha and I are... were...friends."

"Were?"

"Jason got upset about me spendin' time with Simha and talkin' with him, and he..." I sighed again. "Well, he put his foot down. So I told Simha we couldn't be friends anymore. The thing is,

I feel so bad, because the last time we actually spoke together, Simha was upset and angry with me."

"How could he be mad at the most perfect girl in Nashville?"

"You have got to get over this misconception you have about who I am," I urged her before I continued. "I am the most *im*perfect girl in Nashville. You have no idea."

"What made him so mad?"

"He saw my engagement ring. I hadn't said anythin' to him. I mean, what could I say? An' then he…"

"What happened?"

"He asked me how I was, and I said I was 'busy.' That's when he lost it."

"Okay, now I'm real confused."

I was too emotionally exhausted to do anything other than come clean with Erin. "I've always used the word 'busy' as an excuse to explain why I'm always late, why I'm never organized, why I'm so easily distracted. It sounds so much better than admitting I'm a train wreck."

"Train wreck? You?"

"Yes, me," I said with another sigh. "I don't know who I am, what I'm doing, or where I'm going. I just go around telling everyone I'm busy to keep *them* happy. They ask 'How are you?' I reply 'busy' and get a pat on the back. If I say 'really busy,' I get two pats on the back. If I say 'sooo busy' while doing the busy dance, I get a cheer."

"The busy dance?" Erin said. "What busy dance?"

"It goes like this," I said, demonstrating. "You slump your shoulders dramatically, drop your head a little to one side, and give your face a real exhausted, exasperated expression while you say 'I'm sooo busy!'"

Erin laughed.

"The thing is, it seems like I've been lyin' to people for years to just to keep them happy. Does everyone go around saying they're busy just to save face when they're feelin' lost and confused, or is it just me? I don't know what the truth is about anythin' anymore, especially *me*. I think this is what upset Simha. He could see I was hidin' behind the word 'busy' to avoid bein' honest with myself."

"Perhaps you should try being more honest with yourself?"

"Well, maybe if everyone else was more honest with me."

"I don't think that's how it works. What are you so afraid of?"

Thankfully, I didn't have time to answer, as we were interrupted by the sound of the slam of the house's front screen door. We peered out of the treehouse and saw Aunt Sara plop herself down on the front porch swing. She lifted a cigarette case and lighter out of her slacks pocket. She pulled out what appeared to be a spliff of marijuana from the case, lit it, and took a long drag that she let out slowly, happily.

Erin and I looked at each other. Erin giggled. I had to grin.

The front screen door opened again, and Grandpa Tom came out on the porch, looked at Aunt Sara, and sat down beside her. She offered him the joint, and *he took it!* He inhaled like a pro—*my grandpa*—and handed it back to her.

"Grandpa is always so full of surprises," Erin whispered with wide-eyed astonishment.

Aunt Sara and Grandpa Tom passed the joint back and forth as the distinct aroma of marijuana wafted its way up to the treehouse. They chatted together in low voices.

"Daddy, are you out here?" Mama called as she walked out the front door. She froze when she saw her sister and daddy. Despite their efforts to conceal their smoking, the realization of what they were doing nearly knocked Mama over.

"What in tarnation do you think you're doin'? On my porch!" she cried.

"Just relaxin'," Aunt Sara replied without buying into Mama's angst.

"Relaxin'! You call that relaxin'? It's the devil's work, that's what you're doing."

"Oh Marjorie, get a grip," Aunt Sara said. "It's just a little joint, and a little grass never hurt anyone."

We hadn't realized that Grandpa had been holding his breath the whole time to hide his last inhalation from Mama. He lurched forward, coughing and spluttering as smoke came billowing out of his nose and mouth.

Erin and I had to clap our hands over our mouths to keep from laughing out loud.

"Daddy! How could you?" Mama declared with the most exasperated expression on her face. Grandpa looked at her sheepishly, but he clearly couldn't think of any viable story that would make Mama understand. She spun on her heel and stormed back inside the house. Grandpa Tom and Aunt Sara looked at each other and shrugged. She handed him back the joint, and they continued smoking together like nothing had happened.

Erin and I sat back from the window so we wouldn't be heard. "You're so like Aunt Sara. You do what you want and say what you feel. Just like she does. I've never done that. I'm the 'good girl' like mom. We run around doin' what everyone expects us to do. My accident was like a glimpse of my life from outside myself. I've been so busy seeking approval from my family, my friends, even God, that I forgot to ask myself what I want."

"What do you want?"

"I don't know." The answer was that simple.

Erin looked at me with a hint of hesitation in her eyes. "Do you really think you were saved by the hand of God?"

No one had asked me so directly before. "No. Maybe. I don't know. What do you think?"

"Well, I'd like to offer my opinion but," she slumped her shoulders theatrically, "I'm sooo busy."

"You're busy?" I doubled her efforts to over dramatize my words. "I'm crazy busy!"

Erin wasn't about to be beaten, and she was clearly enjoying herself. She flailed her arms around mocking hysteria. "Well, I'm super crazy busy!"

We laughed so hard that we had to lean against each other for support.

Every leaf that grows will tell you:
What you sow will bear fruit.
So if you have any sense my friend,
don't plant anything but Love.

❧ Rumi

Chapter Thirty-Seven

Everyone was so keen to tell me how wonderful the party was. I kept smiling and thanking them until my jaws ached. I'd been smiling for hours. That's what I was supposed to do when my family, friends, and a good chunk of Daddy's congregation who had known me most of my life gathered together to celebrate my engagement to my high school sweetheart. So I smiled even as my stomach twisted itself into a perpetual cramp.

To save money for the wedding reception, Mama and I had planned a casual outdoor engagement party along Sevier Lake in Shelby Park. It was more of a fancy picnic for folks wishing Jason and me well. Charcoal fires were cooking up some tasty barbecued pork and beef that I couldn't eat. A white tent was spread over the buffet tables with their platters of meat, pigs in a blanket for the kids, deviled eggs, ten different kinds of salad, three different kinds of coleslaw, rolls, vegetables, bowls of beans and bowls of rice, cookies and cupcakes. It was probably just nerves, but I had no appetite. There were big sweet tea dispensers, pitchers of lemonade, and barrels of ice and champagne, beer, sodas, and water. Outside, we'd set up round rental tables with pink tablecloths and chairs where people could sit and eat.

We also had a sound system playing country music and a relatively flat area where people were dancing. We'd strung some big white paper lanterns on wires over the tables and dance area to light up the night. We'd stuck tiki torches all around the party to give some more light and chase away the mosquitoes.

Over a hundred people in their casual best were dancing, and talking, and laughing. I was circulating through the crowd to make sure everyone was having a good time, that they had enough food, and that even the oldies were getting up on the dance floor. I was thanking them and showing off my engagement ring and answering questions about the wedding and where Jason and I were likely going to honeymoon. Jason had suggested Branson, Missouri, the live music capital of the world, but we hadn't decided yet. The next big question was where Jason and I were going to live. My duplex was likely to be our little love shack until Jason's career outcomes neared his expectations. From this followed the next question—when could they expect to see our first baby? This was when I usually excused myself to move on to the next guest to start all over again at the first question.

I wasn't really having a good time, and I had to work hard to hide the truth from everyone, particularly my family and Jason, especially because my fiancé was having a great time. He was roughhousing with my brother, laughing with his buddies, drinking one beer after another, dancing with every woman who asked him, and charming every single person at our party. He and Toby and Scotty did an acoustic version of "The Skin That's Covering You" that had everyone going "Aww!" and applauding loudly when Jason pulled me into his arms to kiss me. Then I went back to being a good hostess.

I lost my smile completely when I saw Chloe walk toward us about an hour and a half into the party with Simha cradling her arm.

It had been two weeks since I'd last seen him on the day of filming the final dance scene. I noticed every curl of his thick black hair, his chiseled jawline, his dark eyes glowing in the lamplight, the casual white jacket draped over his broad shoulders, the emerald green shirt open at his throat, the black slacks outlining his long, muscular legs. His hooded eyes met mine, and I felt the air rippling toward me from his gaze.

"Hey, y'all!" Chloe said cheerfully to my guests as she made her entrance in a white sundress with spaghetti straps.

I turned and walked, though I wanted to run, in the opposite direction. It wasn't simply that I didn't feel safe around Simha, or that I had promised Jason I would never talk to him again. I just couldn't bear seeing him and Chloe as a couple, and I didn't want to spend one second thinking about why. Most of my family was standing in a clump watching the dancers, and I tried hiding myself in the middle of them. It didn't work.

"Hey, Mary!" Chloe said from right behind me. "Congratulations again on your engagement. What a cute party."

Groaning inwardly, I plastered a smile on my face and turned. "Thanks," I said. With my heart pounding furiously, I made myself look at her date. Was he glad to see me? Mad as hell? Indifferent? I couldn't tell. His face was a mask.

"Hello, Simha," I said. "It was nice of you to come. This is my daddy, Brian Poser. Daddy, this is Simha Das."

"The man who's got the whole town talkin'," Daddy said with a smile as he shook his hand. "It's good to meet you at last."

"The pleasure is mine, sir," Simha said. "Mary has told me so much about you that I feel we met long before this."

"Has she?" Daddy said, looking at me curiously.

"Simha, this is my mama, Marjorie Poser," I said hastily.

"Oh, I know you!" Mama said as she shook his hand. "Mary showed me your picture a while back."

"Did she?" Simha said with a pleased smile.

"You're the friend of the young man she was correspondin' with last Thanksgivin'."

I cringed, and my stomach seized up when I saw Simha's puzzled expression.

"Have you met Mary's fiancé?" Mama asked.

"We spoke at the film festival last April," Simha said with a wry smile.

"Simha, you remember my Aunt Sara?" I said hastily.

"Of course," he said, turning fluidly to her with a smile. "We also met at the film festival."

"It's good to see you again," Aunt Sara said with a smile as her blue eyes watched the both of us with eager intensity. "How goes the movie?"

"On schedule and on budget," Simha replied. "I can't ask for more."

"And of course you remember my brother, Toby," I said, pulling Toby closer.

"Hello," Simha said, holding out his hand. "Thank you again for the help you gave us when we filmed at the Lean Machine."

Toby shook it while watching Simha suspiciously. "Just doin' my job," he said. "I've been hearin' a lot about you lately...from *Jason*."

"Toby!" Mama said. "Melissa Flynn is standin' over there all alone. You go ask her to dance this minute."

"Yes, ma'am," Toby muttered as he headed off.

"Jenny, when are you gonna introduce me to this fine-lookin' young man you've been flirtin' with?" Grandpa Tom demanded playfully.

Oh lordy, I couldn't be Grammy Jen on top of everything else tonight! "Now Grandpa, you know I'm Mary. Your wife Jenny is over there," I said, pointing to Erin, "dancin' with Scotty."

"Is she now?" he said, peering into the crowd of dancers. Then he jabbed me with his elbow. "And who's this fine young man?"

I gave him and Simha my most determined smile. "Grandpa, this is Simha Das, the filmmaker. Simha, this is my grandpa."

"The name's Tom," the old rascal said, beaming as he shoved his hand at Simha. "Tom Collins. Did ya know they named a drink after me?"

"No, they didn't!" Erin called out as she danced by with Scotty. It's the first time I noticed she was still wearing her parachute over her dress.

"Seriously?" I called out to her pointing at the bulky accessory on her back.

"You've got your dreams, I've got mine," she replied contently as Scotty whisked her away on the dance floor.

Grandpa Tom chuckled. "Women are fickle critters."

"Totally incomprehensible," Simha agreed solemnly.

Grandpa Tom peered up at him and chuckled. "Watch what you say around the Collins women, son, or you'll be busier than a one-legged man in a butt-kicking contest makin' your apologies."

Simha grinned at him. "You bred a strong-minded family, sir."

"Naw. Our daughters and granddaughters got all their sass and fire from my Jenny. Cuter than a basketful of puppies, but prickly sometimes like a bag of nails."

"To be handled with care either way," Simha replied.

I wasn't sure whether us Collins girls were being complimented or castigated. I think men speak to each other about us in code sometimes. It left me stumped as to how I should respond, with gratitude or dispute. Thankfully, Alice bounded toward us and gave Simha a cheerful hug. She'd been hugging him since the first day she met him. I hoped he was getting used to it. She announced that Rob was "in the loo," then dragged Grandpa Tom off to dance with her. Music was playing, so Alice had to dance.

I looked hesitantly up at Simha.

"Chloe invited me," he said stiffly. "I hope you don't mind."

"No, not at all," I said. "How have you been?"

His lips twisted into something resembling a smile. "Busy."

Chloe suddenly turned to me and looped her arm through Simha's arm. "Oh, we are *so* busy right now with *everythin'* involved with filmin' his movie, *you* know."

"Yes," Simha said, his mouth hard. "Very busy."

"Oh," I said. "Well, congratulations."

"For what?" Simha asked.

"Chloe's been telling me that everythin's goin' really well with you."

"She's doing a fine job as Louisa."

"No, I mean—"

"Simha!" Chloe said suddenly. "There's someone you've just *got* to meet. Come on!"

She dragged Simha off with her toward the buffet tent, and I was glad, even grateful. It had been misery standing with him and feeling so distant from him. But I still watched them walk off longer than I should have.

I finally turned away, and Alice caught my eye as she danced with Grandpa Tom. She didn't have her usual smile. In fact, she looked worried, and I had no idea why.

"Mary, you go get that young man of yours," Daddy said. "It's time for me to make a toast."

My stomach spasmed. I covered it with a smile and went to dig Jason out of the throng of his best buddies—a group of hard-drinking, sports-playing, blue collar guys, including Toby.

The line dance ended, and Daddy took a cordless microphone and stepped up onto a small five-foot-square platform about six inches off the ground. "Folks, could I have your attention, please?" he said into the mic, his voice booming out of the two big black speakers.

The party guests gathered in front of him and quieted down. My family and I stood in the front row. Jason had hold of my hand, and there was a big smile on his face. There wasn't a spotlight at the party, but I felt one shining on me anyway.

"Folks," Daddy said into the microphone, "you know I'm not one for speeches…"

Everyone laughed.

He smiled good-naturedly. "… but I have something to say tonight. We are here to celebrate the engagement of Mary, my little butterfly, to her country star, Jason Purdett. This is a joyous occasion, and we're glad y'all are sharin' it with us tonight. Jason, you've always been like a son to me…ever since I first caught you climbin' out of Mary's bedroom window early one mornin' seven years ago."

I blushed, the crowd laughed, and Mama directed one of her glares at me that said everything about the conversation we were likely to have later. I made myself look only at Daddy.

"Her mama and I welcome you into our family as we celebrate your engagement to our daughter," Daddy continued. "You're now welcome to use the front door after you—"

"*Daddy!*" I interrupted, a little too enthusiastically, which made everyone laugh again.

He grinned at me. "I was goin' to say, after you spend the night singin' to our butterfly," he said innocently. He raised his plastic glass of champagne into the air. "To Mary and Jason!"

Everyone around us raised their drinks in toast and shouted, "To Mary and Jason!"

The music fired up again, and Daddy launched into his Jerry Lewis-style dance routine for everyone to enjoy. I laughed and applauded with everyone else, the knot in my stomach easing a little bit. Then folks went back to their drinking, eating, dancing, and talking. Jason gave me a kiss on the cheek and headed off with Toby to get another beer. I started walking up to Daddy to thank him for his toast, but I stopped. Mama was arguing with him.

"How could you?" she hissed. "At your own daughter's engagement party!"

"How could I do what?" Daddy asked, confused.

"Act like a fool in front of all these people!"

"I wasn't foolin', I was clownin'," Daddy retorted, "and everyone enjoyed it, includin' our daughter."

"How many times do I have to tell you that it isn't seemly for a Baptist pastor to be paradin' all of that foolishness in public?" Mama demanded.

"Marjorie, why do you fight so hard against good humor, when God celebrates it throughout the Bible?"

Mama stared at Daddy, shocked.

"Bringin' laughter to others is a gift from God and a callin'," Daddy continued, "and it's one I intend to start pursuin' as I should have done these last four years and more."

Mama looked shaken, as if the foundation beneath her feet was crumbling. "Brian, no!" she said hoarsely.

"Marjorie, yes. We'll talk about it at home. Tonight is about Mary and Jason."

I backed up hurriedly before they could see me. I turned and collided with my sister.

"Whoa! Where's the fire?" she said, smiling and looking amused and pretty, despite the parachute, in her pink and black dress and fishnet stockings, pink stripes running through her spiky black hair. "I think Daddy missed his callin'," she continued. "He should've been a Jerry Lewis impersonator in Vegas."

"Mama doesn't agree," I said, troubled and sad as I watched Daddy walk away from her.

"Somethin' wrong?" Erin asked.

"I think there's gonna be a revolution in the Poser household."

"Huh?"

I smiled at her. "It appears you aren't the only rebel in the family."

She looked at Daddy talking now with the Goosens. "Really?"

"Yeah."

"So," she said, pointing to the other side of the dance floor where Simha and Grandpa Tom were talking up a storm, "is that the Simha I haven't heard near enough about?"

"Yeah," I said cautiously.

"He's gorgeous. Should I tell him where you keep his teddy bear?"

"If you say anything about that to anyone, I'll tear your arms off and shove them down your throat!"

"I guess that's a no then." She smiled cheekily. "Well, if he's at your party, I reckon he can't be too upset with you."

"I don't know," I said miserably. "I can't tell what he's thinkin' or feelin' tonight. When I asked Simha how he was, he said he was 'busy.'"

"Really?" Erin said. She slumped her shoulders, tilted her head, and adopted an exhausted expression. "Did he do the busy dance?"

"No. But Chloe did. It doesn't make sense. Simha hates it whenever I use that word. The last time I saw him, he said that 'busy' was code for bein' unhappy." I stopped. "I'm such an idiot."

"No. Just a little slow," Erin replied a little too eagerly.

"Shut up."

She laughed at me. I scowled at her, which made her laugh harder. "I think it's time I met the man who's makin' you hotter than a horndog," she said, heading off toward Simha and Grandpa Tom before she had time to witness me blush shamefully.

All I could do was silently watch Simha as Erin walked up to him, introducing herself. He smiled warmly at her. Erin and Grandpa Tom and Simha talked together a good five minutes, then Grandpa Tom pushed Simha and Erin onto the dance floor, and they danced. They danced like they'd been friends forever. Simha made subtle accommodations for Erin's weak right arm as he danced a graceful two-step to John Michael Montgomery's equally graceful "Sold" about the girl he'd found at the Grundy County Auction. Simha chatted and laughed with my little sister and looked happier than he had all night. When that song ended and The Dixie Chicks' began singing the slower, more lyrical "Cowboy Take Me Away," they stayed in each other's arms and kept dancing.

It wasn't until Vern Goosen accidentally bumped into me with plates full of food for his folks that I realized I was paying more attention to Simha than to my own party. I bit my lip and tried to decide who I should go up to and talk with when Grandpa Tom took the decision out of my hands.

"Hey little lady!" he said with a grin. "How about a dance...and I won't take no for an answer."

"As if I could ever say no to you," I said fondly. I gave him my arm, he led me out into the middle of the dancers, and we began a gentle rumba.

"I like your young man," Grandpa Tom said.

"Jason likes you, too."

"No, no. I mean your other young man. Simha."

I blushed. "Simha is *not* my young man!"

"I see."

At least one of us wasn't being convincing, so I pressed on. "Grandpa Tom, I am marryin' *Jason*. Simha is clearly with Chloe."

"Is he now?"

"Yes!"

"Well, if you say so. She's got herself a fine man."

The dance ended. Grandpa Tom kissed me on the cheek, walked into the dancers, collected Erin, and led her off to get some lemonade and a cupcake. Simha was left standing alone, looking at me. I was looking at him, and the pounding in my chest arrived on cue. Taking a deep breath, I made myself walk up to him. "You've made quite a hit with my Grandpa Tom," I said and tried to smile.

"He's a charmer," Simha said. "Your grandmother probably didn't stand a chance when they met."

"That's what she told me."

"Speaking of which, how is it that your sister, his granddaughter, is also his wife he calls Jenny?"

"Yeah, that must be confusing. Grandma Jenny died five years ago, but he always forgets. His mind isn't strong anymore. So we all take turns being his loving wife. But not as loving as, well, you know. It does get a bit awkward sometimes."

"Is that how it is with you and Jason?"

I blanched. "What?"

"Is it an act?"

"How dare you?" I retorted, anger bubbling up from my throat.

"It's just that I haven't seen you two spend more than a couple of minutes with each other since I've been here. This is your engagement party. You're supposed to be in love. You two should be glued together."

"You have no right to judge us or to tell us what we should be doin'," I said flatly.

"That's right," he said just as flatly. "I forgot. I'm not allowed to speak with you. You caved faster to him than a house of cards in a gust of wind. Apparently, Jason can't handle the competition."

"You are not competition," I said grimly. "You are—you *were*—my friend."

"Your friend? From the moment we met, I have been so much more to you than your friend. As you have been to me. How many more ways will he oblige you to bend and compromise to make this work?"

"Hey, Mary!" Erin said, walking up to us. "Do you..." She ground to a stop when she felt the tension crackling between me and Simha. She just stood there, uneasy and unsure what to do. I ignored her.

I squared off with Simha. "You come to *my* engagement party, you parade around with Chloe on your arm, charm my family, put down me and my fiancé, and act like *you're* the injured party?"

"What's goin' on?" Jason demanded as he walked up to us, glowering. "What's *he* doin' here, and what in hell do you mean by talkin' to him?"

"Chloe brought him, and I'm not talkin' to him, I'm yellin' at him," I retorted.

Simha softened in response to the building tension. "Mistakes are bound to be made when you put an arrogant filmmaker and a steel magnolia together in the same room."

All of my anger evaporated. I just stood there staring at Simha, his dark eyes holding mine captive.

"We ain't in a room, we're in a park," Jason spat out, "and you two aren't *together*, and you sure as hell aren't friends. Mary has more self-respect than to be friends with *you*. She knows damn well that if you lie down with dogs, you get up with fleas. Get your mangy ass out of my party. We don't want your kind here."

"*Jason!*" I said, utterly embarrassed.

"His *kind?*" Erin gasped. She grabbed Simha's arm. "Come on, let's go get a drink. I've gotta wash the Jason stank out of my mouth." She took a couple of steps, then turned her head and glared at my fiancé. "You are such a tool!"

She started to walk off with Simha, but Toby suddenly blocked their path.

"What the hell are you doin' here, imposin' yourself on my sister and upsettin' my best friend?" he demanded.

"I was getting a drink with Erin," Simha replied calmly.

"Don't you dare go anywhere with this guy, Erin," Toby ordered. "It isn't safe."

"Safe?" Erin said in amazement. "Are you drunk?"

"No, and I know what I'm talkin' about," Toby insisted. "This guy can't be trusted. He's been makin' eyes at Mary for months now, ignorin' the fact that she's an engaged woman, and ignorin' Jason's rightful claim."

"I'm not a gold mine," I said grimly.

"Don't you go talkin' to him!" Toby ordered Erin. "The guy's a foreigner. We can't trust him. He isn't even a God-fearin' Christian. Isn't that right, Mr. Famous Filmmaker?"

"Toby, please stop," I said, my stomach roiling.

"Well?" Toby demanded. "Are you a God-fearin' Christian?"

"Simha, I am so sorry," I began.

"Don't you go apologizin' to him," Toby barked. "It's a fair question. It's a question you should be concerned about."

"Toby, what in the world has gotten into you?" Erin demanded. "It's like you've suddenly been possessed by our mother!"

"I want an answer!" Toby yelled, ignoring Erin.

"No, I am not a God-fearing Christian," Simha said calmly.

Admitting to not being a God-fearing Christian wasn't the most popular statement you could make around these parts. The smug silence from Jason and Toby was deafening in reply.

"Toby, can I ask you something?" Simha continued, being sure to speak as calmly as possible.

"What?" my brother asked, looking fiercely suspicious.

"Do you believe that God *is* love?" Simha asked.

"What kind of question is that?" Toby said. "Of course I do! God is our salvation. God is our guidin' light, dude!"

"I agree," Simha said. "So tell me, Toby, if God is love, why would you fear love?"

"What?" Toby said. He looked around the group for support,

but everyone looked just as stumped as he felt.

Simha continued, "I don't mean to embarrass you. But I will tell you what I believe. I believe that religion and society often train us to fear everything. Fear God, fear authority, fear persecution, fear humiliation. We are trained to conform through fear. But this serves its purpose. Toby, when you find love, it will be such a contrast to all this fear that you've been conditioned to endure. When you identify it, you will want to surrender to its majesty. So live in fear until you're ready to love."

Erin looked at me in amazement. "Whoa," she said softly.

"I know," I whispered, "he always talks like this."

Toby, meanwhile, was staring at Simha, his face red, his chest heaving. "Whatever!" he said, shooting a glance at Jason. He strode off, nearly running, pushing his way through the other guests without apologizing.

"I'm sorry to have caused such an uproar," Simha said to me, holding me captive with his dark gaze again. "I think I should make things easier on everyone and just leave."

"Yeah!" Jason blustered. "You should! *No one* talks to my best friend like that!"

"A crime for sure," Simha replied ambiguously.

I could see my enraged fiancé gearing up to start throwing punches. "*Jason,*" I said desperately, trying not to gasp in pain as my stomach twisted inside me, "don't start a fight, please! Simha is our guest, he is Chloe's date, and he isn't goin' anywhere."

"Except with me," Erin said, taking his arm again. "Come on, Simha, you promised me a drink."

"Of course," he said, smiling down at her.

Erin looked over at me. "I promise not to wear my parachute at your weddin', 'cause you're the one who's gonna need it!"

She walked off with Simha before I could think of anything resembling a cutting reply.

"What the hell did she mean by that?" Jason said, fuming.

"She was just makin' a joke," I said, "and what the hell did you mean by bein' so obnoxious, causin' an uproar in the middle of our engagement party?"

"Me? I didn't do nothin' except defend the woman I'm gonna marry from that damned curry-muncher," he declared defensively. "I'm gonna go see if Toby's okay."

He then strode off after my brother.

I stared after him, my emotions as jumbled as my internal organs, which felt like they were seizing up in a vise. I clenched my eyes shut and started breathing long, slow breaths.

"Such an entertaining party!"

My eyes flew open. Aunt Sara was standing before me, beaming.

"Do you need an ambulance?" she inquired pleasantly.

I closed my eyes again. "No! I'm fine!"

"Of course you are," Aunt Sara said. Laughing merrily, she walked off to inflict herself on someone else.

"Mary! Oh, there you are!" Mama exclaimed as she hustled over to me, wreathed in smiles. "Pastor Nighby is here, and he's askin' after you. Come along. You can talk over your weddin' plans with him."

"Swell," I muttered, forcing a smile as I let Mama drag me over to the man who was going to marry me to Jason in five weeks.

Drunken with love, I sail like a boat.
Anchored to mind, I fail to float.

❧ *Rumi*

Chapter Thirty-Eight

I basically didn't sleep for the next month. I couldn't. There wasn't time. I was working full-time, going to The Nashbros' gigs, turning up at the farmhouse three or four times a week for family meals, trying to support Erin's rehab, worrying about Toby who was both jittery and withdrawn all the time, coping with Grandpa Tom, going to church, serving on the Building and Grounds Committee, running my usual errands, and taking care of Charlie.

But that wasn't all, not by a long shot. I was finalizing my wedding plans with Mama and reining in her hourly efforts to explode my simple wedding into a giant fantasy Disney extravaganza. I was choosing the wedding cake and working with the Hyatt to organize the reception (and going over and *over* and over the seating arrangements with Mama). I was meeting with the caterer to be sure there'd be something that everyone, even vegetarians, could eat at the reception. I had to choose and pick up the wedding rings (Jason was busy), pick out the tuxedos for the groomsmen, and make sure the four guys, including Toby, actually picked them up. I had to organize and keep track of the wedding gifts that were pouring in. I had to confirm the honeymoon reservations. I was also reorganizing my duplex so Jason could move in with me after the honeymoon and feel like it was his home, too.

There was more. I had to help Chloe run her lines for *Persuasion* three or four times a week and listen to her rhapsodize about her relationship with Simha. I had to let Alice tell me all about filming the choir singing for a concert in the movie and all of the wonderful things Simha had said about her voice. Everywhere I went—the grocery store, the bridal salon, the Hyatt—I had to listen to folks all around me talk about Simha's movie and try to pretend they weren't driving knives into my heart. I stayed true to Jason and did my level best to avoid Simha. I turned in the opposite direction whenever I saw him at the grocery store, or the park, or on the street. But I couldn't avoid feeling hurt that he had stopped texting and calling me even though I had told him to do so.

It infuriated me that I still couldn't bring myself to drive over the Gateway Bridge.

Five days before the wedding, I drove up to the farmhouse to finalize the last of the wedding plans with Mama. It wasn't until I stepped out of my car that I saw Erin. Still wearing her parachute, along with black leggings and a long pink tee shirt, she was climbing up the treehouse ladder, slowly, because her right arm was still weak. About halfway up, she turned, looking scared and determined at the same time. Then she jumped onto an old mattress at the base of the tree. She picked herself up and, as I started walking toward her, she began climbing the tree again. She went two rungs further up, turned, and jumped, landing cleanly on the mattress in front of me.

"Erin, isn't that kind of dangerous?" I asked in my most nonconfrontational voice.

"It's fine," she said impatiently. "I've scheduled my first

tandem sky jump. I've only got three more weeks to get ready, and by God I will!"

"Erin, don't get me wrong," I said, stopping her from climbing back up the tree. "I think you're so incredibly brave to climb this tree after what happened to you, but isn't there a safer way to strengthen your arm and get over your fear of heights?"

"Brave?" Erin practically spat. "You really don't get it, do you? This isn't about this stupid tree! You want to know why I'm doin' this? It's because when you walk into a room, all the guys look at you. You're beautiful. But no one ever looks at *me*. I couldn't even get a date to your engagement party. Nobody wants a cripple."

"You're not a cripple!" I insisted. "You're beautiful."

"Bullshit! Look at me! Who would want this?" she demanded furiously as she flapped her helpless right arm. "If I don't get this stupid arm working again, my life is *over*. I'll never have a decent job, I'll never get married, I'll never have kids, I'll never have *anythin'!*"

She spun around and began climbing the tree again, pulling herself up three rungs higher than her last jump. "I'm wearin' this stupid parachute because I'm tired of fallin'. I want my life back!" she shouted. She threw herself off the ladder and landed badly. "Ow! Dammit, dammit, *dammit!*" she yelled as she wrapped her hands around her ankle.

"Oh God, Erin, is it broken?" I wailed as I knelt down beside her.

"No," she growled. "It just hurts like hell."

"Erin!" Mama shrieked as she bolted out of the house, the screen door slamming behind her. "Erin, honey, what have you done? Are you hurt? Are you bleedin'?"

"It's nothin', Mama," Erin said grimly. "I just twisted my ankle a little."

Mama stared down at her, arms akimbo. "Erin Jennifer Poser, did you jump out of that tree again after I told you not to?"

Erin sighed. "Yes, Mama."

"Don't you realize what could happen?" Mama demanded, exasperated. "You stupid girl, you could bang your head and maybe have another aneurysm!"

"I just want to get better, Mama," Erin said through clenched teeth.

"You will, honey, you will. The good Lord saved Mary, and he can save you, too."

"Oh, Mama, you're so wrong," Erin said as, with my help, she struggled to her feet. "God's either not interested, or he's forgotten all about me."

"Oh, now that's just pure foolishness," Mama said. "You've just got to get right with God is all, and He'll heal you sure enough. None of this would have happened to you in the first place if you'd been followin' the righteous path."

"What?" Erin said, her face drained of color. "Are you sayin' my brain aneurysm was from a failin' in my faith?"

"Everythin' happens for a reason, honey," Mama said. "Darlin', your sister fell out of the same tree and only scratched herself. And then God went and pulled her out of the river. It's a sign of how he protects those who do his biddin'!"

I cringed, waiting for Erin to unleash all her anger on me that she was holding for Mama. But there was more.

"Your brain aneurysm was God's way of sayin' it's time you worked harder to become a better Christian." Mama continued, "You gotta start dressin' and actin' like a lady, Erin, if you want to be protected by God. You gotta be more devout in your church service. Respect God's values and live in His grace and your arm will heal right up, you'll see."

Erin and I gaped at her. Then Erin's face turned red with fury.

"I hate you!" she yelled. I think she was talking to both of us. She ran to the porch, limping badly on her hurt ankle.

"Mama! You can't mean that?" I said, hoping there was a

mistake in what I'd heard.

"I'm only sayin' what's true," Mama insisted.

"I don't believe this!" I stormed. "You are so horribly rigid! Erin's brain aneurysm had *nothin'* to do with God's punishment, or bein' a good Christian or not. Erin is one of the best people I know! How can you judge your own daughter so harshly? I won't be surprised if Erin never forgives you!"

"Mary, what on earth's got into you?" Mama said, her face all crumpled and tears welling in her eyes. "How can you say such hateful things to your own mother?"

"How could you say such hurtful things to your own daughter?" I demanded. "Do you really think that God is punishing people for not believing everything you believe? Is that how you want to inspire Erin, by convincing her that God deliberately makes people stay injured if they don't blow wind up his keister? God is love, not a cruel tyrant."

"Mary Poser! You've got it all wrong. Your own salvation was by his hand…"

"I'm so angry with you! You're horrible to Erin, and then you blame it all on God, like it's 'His Will' for you bein' so critical."

"I wasn't bein' critical…"

"Uggh! You've got no idea!"

I didn't want to hang around for Mama's encore performance, particularly since I'd just added a ton of fuel to her fire. I stalked into the house after Erin.

"Mary, wait!" Mama called tearfully. "I came out to ask you somethin' about the weddin' plans."

"Enough about the wedding!" I shouted back at her.

I found Erin weeping in her room. I didn't know what to say, so I said nothing. If I tried to console her, I knew she'd blast me with her "perfect Mary" speech, which always hurt me more than she realized. I wrapped a bandage around her ankle, iced it, gave her some sweet tea and cookies, then I hot-tailed it out of there. I was still angry with Mama, upset for Erin and shaken from how brazenly I'd spoken my mind to Mama. I don't think I'd ever done that before. I grabbed my things, avoided Mama, got in my car, and peeled out of there so fast I left rubber on the driveway. I wanted to get home, be in my own space and get back to feeling safe. I had to drive by the store first because I needed to buy what I couldn't find in the treehouse.

The next day, I had an appointment for a final fitting of my wedding dress, and I invited Erin to come along. Her ankle wasn't giving her much trouble, so we didn't discuss what had happened. She was still wearing her parachute, and I wasn't about to contend her choice of fashion accessory, either.

The Blushing Bride was on Woodland Street just before it turns east and heads toward Simha's apartment, which I didn't let myself think about, not much anyway. Its front windows were crammed with glamorous white wedding dresses. Inside, there were dresses in every subtle variation of white, plus some truly hideous bridesmaid dresses. I'd chosen simple peach-colored sheath dresses for Erin, Chloe, Alice, and Hannah. They'd nearly wept with gratitude. The glass display cases were crowded with every conceivable kind of hair accessory, earrings, necklaces, and bracelets, all of them sparkling in the bright lights. The shop was carpeted, but the noise level was still painfully high as future brides argued with their consultants, their mothers, their sisters, cousins, aunts, friends, and *bridesmaids*. On other visits, I saw a couple of unfortunate fathers, and even a future groom who had been dragged along to give opinions.

I'd taken an extra hour for lunch to get my fitting in without having to rush and, fortunately, a lot of the city's brides hadn't done the same. The large salon was only about half full.

I struggled out of the dressing room wearing a cut-down

version of Princess Diana's wedding gown minus the twenty-foot train, although the veil was pretty long. The short sleeves were so puffy, they almost reached my ears. The only good thing was that my shoes didn't pinch.

"Wow," Erin said when she saw me.

"I know," I said miserably as I stared at myself in one of the large mirrors in the main showroom.

Erin got up off the overstuffed pink ottoman she'd been sitting on and walked slowly around me. "You look like a giant cupcake."

"I'll take that as a compliment. Simply delicious."

We shared a smile.

I took another glance in the mirror and cringed. "I should never have let Mama have her way. This isn't anythin' like the dress I wanted."

"Mary, this is *your* weddin'. You and Jason are the only ones who matter. What anyone else thinks shouldn't even be on your radar."

"Oh yeah?"

"Yeah! Somethin's shiftin' inside you. I see you startin' to stand up for yourself, just like you did yesterday with Mama."

"I wasn't standin' up for myself…I was standin' up for *you*," I said ruefully.

She smiled. "Well, it's a start."

"I'm gettin' out of this monstrosity," I said, heading back to the changing rooms. "Thank God I only have to wear it once more."

I shed the gown gratefully in the dressing room. One of the salesgirls slid it effortlessly into a protective bag as she gushed about how fabulous I was going to look on my wedding day.

"I'm gonna look like the great white whale in drag," I said grimly as I took the bag and walked back out into the showroom.

Erin was looking casually through the hundreds of dresses on display. "Ready?" she asked.

"No, but I'm done."

"If you had your druthers, which one would you wear?"

"Somethin' like that," I said, pointing to a simple sleeveless empire waist gown.

"That's pretty," Erin said.

I took the dress off the rack and walked up to a gold-rimmed mirror and held the gown up against myself and imagined how it would look. "Hm."

"That would look beautiful on you," a male voice said from across the room.

"Why thank…" I was about to finish when I saw a handsome, lanky young man in his early twenties with straw blond hair, freckles, and a tee shirt beaming one of the most charming smiles I'd ever seen right at my little sister, not at me. Erin was holding up another dress before a mirror as I was, dreaming of how she would look, just as I was. He was holding a boxed parcel in both hands that he was delivering to the salon.

"Are you getting married in that?" the young boy queried.

"Me? No!" Erin replied with far too much panic in her voice. "My sister is getting married."

"Oh, well, you'd look real pretty in that one."

"Thanks," she muttered as she spun around and hurriedly put the dress back on its rack.

"Hey," I said with a little wave of my hand.

He smiled at me, but then he zeroed right back in on Erin. "Is that a parachute you're wearin'?"

My little sister, who'd been showing all levels of bravery this summer, was tongue-tied and mute in front of this cute boy, her face a bright pink.

"She's goin' skydivin' soon," I said.

Erin shot me a warning look that said everything of "don't you dare embarrass me."

"She wants to get used to the weight and feel of the chute," I continued, "and practice reachin' for the ripcord."

"That's so cool," the boy said to Erin. "I wish I could do that, but I'm scared to death of heights."

"So is she," I said.

Erin's pink face turned red.

"Seriously?" the boy said.

"Uh-huh," Erin managed.

"And you're jumpin' anyway? I wish I had your courage," the boy said. He put down his parcel on the nearest table and extended his hand out to Erin. "My name's Cody."

Erin involuntarily shot her damaged hand into her pocket. A muted "Hi" was all she could muster.

"My sister here is Erin. I'm Mary. She's just a little distracted at the moment."

"Yeah, I'm just..." she fidgeted awkwardly. "Nice to meet you, Cody."

Cody smiled broadly, reaching into his jacket pocket. "Look, I probably shouldn't be doing this right now because I'm workin' and all. But is there any chance you might be interested in coming along to one of our youth church meetings one day?"

"Oh no, I don't—"

"She'd love to!" I answered for her. I wasn't going to let her spoil this opportunity. She could abuse me all she wanted afterward. Erin glared at me. I smiled back. I stepped forward, took the flyer, and shoved it into Erin's left hand.

"Tell you what, let's make a deal," Cody continued eagerly. "If you come to our service, I'll go skydivin' with you."

"Um," Erin said shyly. "I don't know..."

"Sound like a great deal to me, Sis," I said brightly.

"What do you say?" Cody asked, holding out his right hand.

Erin looked desperately at me with "rescue me" eyes. I glared right back at her with "toughen up" in my eyes.

She heaved a little sigh. "Okay," she said as she pulled her right hand out of her pocket.

Cody reached over with his left hand, lifted her right hand into his. "It's a deal then," he said warmly.

"You discuss the particulars, and I'll meet you outside," I said, turning on my heel and striding out of the salon before Erin could stop me.

I was grinning from ear to ear. Not only was Cody a nice guy, he *liked* my little sister, and I was pretty certain she liked him, too. Things we're getting downright interesting in the Poser family. I stood on the sidewalk, traffic whizzing past, and watched Erin and Cody talking together through the window.

"Mary!"

I turned and froze.

Listen to the sound of waves within you.

🌿 *Rumi*

Chapter Thirty-Nine

Simha was standing on the sidewalk in front of the bridal salon. He was wearing sneakers, jeans that molded themselves to his muscular legs, and a black tee shirt that emphasized his broad chest. I met his eyes and everyone and everything around us disappeared. There was only him and me and this thundering in my chest and roaring in my ears.

"Hi, Simha," I said softly.

"Hi," he said, staring at me. He blinked and seemed to remember we were standing on a public sidewalk. "How are you?"

I smiled as I bit back the word "busy." It was true that I was busy, but I was doing my level best never to say that word, in that context, to Simha again. "I'm okay. Tired. Runnin' around like a crazy person as usual."

He suddenly paled. He was looking at the bagged wedding dress in my hands with The Blushing Bride's label and logo emblazoned in hot pink across it. He opened his mouth to say something, then closed it. He took a breath and looked at me again. The sorrow in his dark eyes shocked me. "You're getting married soon."

"Four days," I said.

"Four days?" He looked at me with questioning eyes.

"Yes. And you, what are your plans?" I didn't want to dwell on the topic of my marriage.

"I'm leaving Saturday afternoon."

"Oh, that's when I'm getting married," I said with a stupid cheerfulness I instantly regretted. I'd brought us straight back to the topic of my marriage. I kicked myself on the inside and continued, "So are you goin' home?"

"No. I'm going on a pilgrimage in Spain."

"There's a Hindu pilgrimage in Spain?"

"No. It's Christian. I think I need a new horizon…and time to clear my head."

"Well, it's all the same light…"

Simha definitely looked troubled. His brow furrowed, and he drew a long breath, "I told my producer I'm not going to make any more Bollywood films. And I told my mother I wasn't going to marry Abha or anyone else she recommended."

"How did that go down?"

"Which one? I seem to be a source of gross disappointment all 'round."

Simha looked at the wedding dress again, draped over my right forearm. Without warning, he picked up my left hand and spun my hand firmly so that my palm faced upwards. The sunlight highlighted the scratches and scars on my arms, and he could see that some of the scratches and scars were new. He held my arm solidly and looked me straight in the eye.

"Trees, cats… It doesn't add up. Mary, are you sure that Jason's the one?"

I quickly flopped the wedding dress bag from my right arm to my left forearm and released myself from Simha's grip.

"Simha, I'd been goin' out with Jason before I met you, and I'm marryin' him."

"But you called him a 'dud.'"

"That was then. He says he's goin' to buy me house in Belle Meade."

"Is that what you want?"

"That's what everybody wants!"

"Everybody? But…"

I wasn't about to allow myself to be interrogated by Simha again. I felt my body shaking uncontrollably with a flush of adrenaline. "Anyway, you've clearly been happy to stay busy makin' your film. You say I use 'busy' to hide how I'm feelin'. You've clearly been mighty busy with Chloe, and then you turn up to *my* engagement party with *her* on your arm and lecture us all on love. Who knows what the heck you're feelin'."

Simha bowed his head and retreated a step. "Yes. Of course. I'm sorry."

I didn't want to lose my momentum or the crazy inkling of courage I was experiencing, so I stepped into the space he had just vacated. "Simha, why did you decide to make your film *Persuasion* in Nashville?"

Something appeared to break inside Simha. I have no other way of describing it. His body just slumped an inch, enough to know that his spirit, or something holding him up, had just been broken. Without a word, he turned and strode away from me without looking back.

I felt Erin grab my arm. "Mary, what's wrong?"

I was watching Simha walk away, his shoulders slumped, looking like his body had been battered by a beast, and I knew exactly who the beast was.

Erin pulled me around to face her. Her eyes scanned my face. "Okay, clearly he is much more than a just a visitin' filmmaker or Chloe's date. Mary, just how important *is* that guy to you?"

The tears welled in my eyes so rapidly I gasped. All I could do was shake my head.

Erin's grip on my arm tightened. "Mary, how long have you known Simha?"

"One year, six months, eleven days," I said miserably.

"But he's only been in town makin' his movie since May."

"We met at last year's film festival. We'd been textin' and talkin' after."

Erin's eyes widened. "He texted you at Thanksgiving."

"Yeah."

"And then the Valentine's teddy bear?"

"Yeah," I said, hanging my head.

"Did you two ever, you know, get together?"

"Once," I said, blushing. "A year ago."

"Oh...my...God. You two meet, correspond, you make love, he sends you gifts, he turns up again in Nashville to make a movie, *and you're lettin' him walk away?*"

"You don't understand..."

"I may be four years younger than you, but I understand plenty! You've kept a relationship with this wonderful man, who clearly has a front row seat in your heart, secret for more'n eighteen months! Why? What are you afraid of?"

Hot tears burned my face. "Stop it, stop it, stop it!" I shouted. Her hand was still on my arm, so I jerked her toward my car. "Come on, we're leavin'!"

"Mary?"

"*Shut up.*"

I unlocked my hatchback and threw the dress bag into the back seat, not caring if the gown wrinkled. I didn't care about anything except getting away from how I was feeling.

I barely checked for traffic before I backed out onto Woodland Street and gunned my car down the road. I turned left onto South Fourth Street going way too fast, and then right onto Shelby Avenue.

"Um, Mary?" Erin said in a meek voice beside me. "Where are we goin'?"

"We're takin' a detour!"

"Okay."

Tears were still streaming down my face. The pain that had been twisting my gut all summer long had spread throughout my entire body. It was all I could do to stay upright in the seat.

"Sorry," Erin said in a little voice as she hunched in her seat.

"It's not you!" I yelled.

"Okay."

I was weaving through traffic, driving on automatic pilot and desperate to get to the one person I knew could help me: Aunt Sara. She'd know what to do, what to say, to make everything better. She had to.

"Fuck!" I shrieked as I hit the brakes, throwing Erin and me forward against our seat belts as the car skidded to a stop and drivers all around us laid on their horns.

"What is it?" Erin asked anxiously. "What's wrong?"

I hadn't been paying attention until it was almost too late. The entrance ramp to the Gateway Bridge was right in front of me!

My hands had the steering wheel in a death grip. All I had to do was press my right foot down on the accelerator, and I could cross that bridge and get to Aunt Sara fast. Get to help. Safety. Salvation.

"Come on, come on, come on," I muttered as I stared at the bridge ahead of me. "Just do it."

Nausea roiled within me. I was sweating. Shaking. "*I hate you, I hate you, I hate you!*" I screamed at the bridge. I buried my face in my hands, sobbing. "Why can't I do this? What is stoppin' me?"

"Mary, honey?" Erin pressed tentatively.

Knowing that my little sister was watching her supposedly

perfect sister lose it in the middle of a Shelby Avenue intersection, drivers blaring their horns all around us, just made things so much worse.

Half-blinded by tears, I looked in my rearview mirror and my side mirrors, then swung my hatchback in front of oncoming traffic as I turned onto South Second Street, doing a U-turn in front of a line of oncoming cars and trucks while Erin cowered in the seat beside me. I raced through the last second of a yellow light and got us back onto Shelby Avenue going in the opposite direction.

I took the entrance onto the I-24 doing sixty and blasted us down the highway, weaving in and out of traffic as my right foot pressed hard on the accelerator. I'd never gone ninety miles an hour in my life, but pity any state police officer who tried to stop me! I took the Harding Place exit and then doubled back on Nolensville Pike.

I screeched to a stop in the parking lot of the Nashville Zoo and threw myself out of the car. "Come on!" I yelled at Erin.

"Okay," she said, cautiously following me out of the hatchback.

I grabbed her arm and made her run with me through the zoo entrance and all the way to the butterfly enclosure, fueled by pain and panic and a mind racing with all sorts of self-annihilating ideas.

The shock of the heat and humidity when we ran through the doors of the butterfly enclosure didn't even slow me down. I scanned the dozen or so people inside and quickly spotted Aunt Sara about thirty feet away, making notes on a pad of paper as she studied a number of chrysalises hanging on the limb of an orchid tree.

"Aunt Sara!" Erin yelled gratefully.

Aunt Sara turned to us, her eyes widening when she saw Erin gesturing desperately at her. We met in the middle.

"Hello, girls," Aunt Sara said calmly. "Erin, it's been a coon's age since you visited the zoo. The howler monkeys were always your favorite. Just go out the doors, turn right, and follow the path."

"Yes. Great. *Thanks,* Aunt Sara," Erin said, backing away, then turning and fleeing.

Aunt Sara's warm blue eyes looked me over, from my tear-stained face to my trembling legs. "You're a right fine mess," she said calmly.

"I know!" I wailed.

Smiling, she set the pad of paper down on a nearby bench. "Tell me all about it."

I took a shuddering breath and wiped my face with my hands. "Well, I-I-I was pickin' up my weddin' dress, and I ran into Simha."

"In the bridal salon?"

"No! On the street! And he looked at me, and I looked at him and, oh Aunt Sara, I couldn't breathe! And I shouldn't feel like that with him, I know I shouldn't, but I can't help it! Then he saw my weddin' dress, and he looked so devastated." My voice was trembling uncontrollably. "H-H-He asked me if Jason was right for me and...and then I asked him why he was makin' *Persuasion* in Nashville, 'cause I think...I think he did it for *me.*"

"What did he say?"

"He looked at the cuts on my arm..."

"Really? What had you told him about how you got those cuts?"

"I told him it was the tree an' a cat..."

"Mary, darlin', is that the truth?"

"Yes!" I tried to hold onto what I had been holding onto most of my adult life—a lie. I burst into tears, and I knew I had no more strength to hide my shame. "No. I did it. Okay? I cut myself."

"I know, honey," Aunt Sara replied as calm as a mill pond.

"What? Who else knows? Does Mama know?" My shame quickly shot up to humiliation.

"Rest assured, your mama only sees what she wants to see," Aunt Sara continued just as calmly.

My mind started racing. "Erin knows, doesn't she? She stole my razor blades from the treehouse! She wouldn't admit to it, but I know she—"

"Mary darlin', that was me. I knew what you'd been doin' to yourself, though I thought you'd stopped when Erin hurt herself an' you seemed to come out of your shell. An' I ain't built for climbin' trees, darlin'. Don't make me do it again."

"I feel so humiliated! Why didn't you tell me you knew?"

"Why'd you say you fell out of the tree?"

"I had no choice. Good girls don't do this to themselves."

"Okay, there's no good girls here. Just you an' me. Why do you do this to yourself, honey?"

I had to stop and breathe for a moment. All sorts of questions and answers were spinning in my head. My instinct was to lie. I'd been lying for so many years. But now my cards were on the table. I was too exhausted and confused for any more lying, "'Cause everyone always expects so much from me. I can't stop thinkin', thinkin', an' thinkin' about how I'm supposed to be and feel about everything." I felt the fear rise in me just talking about it. "Sometimes I think my head's goin' to explode with all the thinkin'! I smile when I'm supposed to smile. I laugh when I'm supposed to laugh. I never swear, until just a moment ago anyway. I pray when I'm supposed to pray, an' I fart when I'm supposed to fart. Which is never by the way. Sometimes I just need to feel somethin' real, even if it's pain. At least it's real. It's like cuttin' through all the bullshit in my life." I'd done it again. I instantly regretted swearing. Part of me expected a bolt of lightning to strike me down. My right hand instinctively gripped the scars on my left forearm. Aunt Sara noticed but didn't budge an inch. "Sorry, I didn't mean to swear," I added sheepishly.

"Never you mind, young lady. A little cussin' sometimes helps to clear the mind. Better than some other ways I'm learnin' about," Aunt Sara said gently as she pulled me upright. "And the rest of the time, when you're not hurtin' yourself?"

I forced myself to relax my grip on my own forearm before I continued. I breathed as deeply as I could to control the rising panic. "I just want to do the right thing."

"Right for whom?"

"For everyone! Jason's right for me, don't you think? I mean, we've known each other forever, ever since we were kids. All of my friends like Jason and even envy me marryin' a future country star. My folks love Jason, and he gets along well with my whole family. All of that is right for me. I'm a small-town girl. It's not like I can do anythin' different. I mean...I couldn't! I'm a good girl, a good daughter, and I want my folks to be proud of me."

"Mary, why are you still worryin' about such things?" Aunt Sara demanded. "Child, you are tyin' yourself in knots. Do you think my butterflies worry about whether or not the other butterflies are proud of them?"

"No, of course not," I said irritably. "They're butterflies."

"These butterflies don't worry, Mary, because they live each moment of their lives doing what is natural and right for them. Are you? Are you happy in your life?"

Tears welled in my eyes again. "I'm gettin' married. Of course I'm happy."

"One doesn't necessarily follow from the other...and you just turned up here a complete wreck over a man you're not marryin'. Or did you really just come here to see the butterflies?"

"No! I mean, I love seein' 'em, but I came here to see you. To get help...and you're doin' a lousy job."

Aunt Sara laughed heartily. "That's because the butterflies are the ones who have the answers you need."

"Oh, really?" I said sarcastically. "That's great. I'm meant to be listening to the butterflies now? I guess it beats followin' the lead of my dog."

"Still havin' trouble with the Gateway Bridge?"

"Of *course* I am! Why would that be any different? I hate that damn bridge. Everyone thinks I'm a fool and a coward for not bein' able to cross it, and Erin nearly had kittens when I turned us away from it again today."

"Mary, it doesn't matter what *everyone* thinks. What matters is what *you* think and what you do to finally get across that bridge under your own steam. It's like a threshold you need to cross into whatever life it is you're supposed to have. You know the butterflies and I are here. You know the best way to get here. Someday, and I think someday soon, you'll be ready to cross that threshold and come visit us without even thinkin' about it."

"Well, I'm here now," I said uncomfortably. "So where are all the butterflies?"

"It looks like they've flown the coop, doesn't it?"

"Well, that's just great. I risk my sister's life and mine drivin' all the way here, I get some incredibly unhelpful advice, and to top things off, I don't even get to see any butterflies. I can't win."

"It's unreasonable to expect instant gratification simply because you want something."

"Sorry," I said, hanging my head. "I just thought it would be nice."

"Never apologize for wanting something, and never minimize what you wish for. If you want the butterflies, you must tell them that's what you want. They didn't know you were coming. You have to learn how to talk with the butterflies if you want to see them."

"Are you messin' with me?"

Aunt Sara smiled. "Nope. It's taken me a lifetime to learn and master the technique of talkin' to butterflies."

"Can you teach me?"

"What, in a day? It could take years."

"But I don't have years! I'm gettin' married in four days. I want them today. Can't you talk to the butterflies for me?"

"Well, it's really complicated, but I'll give it a try." Aunt Sara raised her arms out slowly, like she was summoning the the air about her to do her bidding. Then suddenly she clapped her hands together loudly.

It made me jump... And every butterfly in the enclosure suddenly launched from their perches and filled the air around Aunt Sara and me with thousands of flapping wings blazing with a hundred different colors.

I laughed from the sheer joy of their beauty and opened my arms to them. They surrounded me and perched on my arms and head, shoulders, chest, back.

"Now how do you feel?" Aunt Sara buzzed me with a wry smile.

"Wonderful!" It was the only word that really felt right as every color I could imagine fluttered around me.

Aunt Sara cupped my face with her warm hands. "Don't be in such a hurry. Trust that you'll have all the butterflies you want, but only when you know how to call them."

Keep knocking,
and the joy inside will eventually open a window.
Look out to see who's there.

❧ *Rumi*

Chapter Forty

The Nashborough Evangelical Baptist Church was decorated simply with calla lilies, pink hydrangea, and greenery. The wooden pews were packed with invited family, friends, and members of Daddy's congregation who had known me from early childhood. The choir stood on their risers behind the podium in their purple and white robes. Mama, in a new pink dress, Aunt Sara in a new pale yellow jacket and skirt, and Grandpa Tom in his best suit sat in the front row on my left. My friends and coworkers sat behind them. The pews on the right side were filled with Jason's friends, mostly music, school, and work buddies. His daddy, who was a mean alcoholic, had not been invited, at Jason's insistence.

Walking to the altar from a side door were Pastor Nighby in his black robes and Jason in his rented black tuxedo. At a signal from Mrs. Goosen, the choir director, Erin, my maid of honor, and Toby, Jason's best man, began walking down the aisle while the choir sang "Joyful, Joyful." Chloe, Alice, and Hannah, my bridesmaids, followed them in simple peach-colored sheath dresses, beaming. At their sides were Jason's three groomsmen in rented charcoal suits, just like Toby's suit.

Behind them stumbled the flower girl and ring bearer, Patience and Peter Singleton, two of the youngest members of Daddy's congregation. They received an encouraging "aww" from the wedding guests and seemed pleased about it.

Daddy, in his dark blue suit, squeezed my arm looped through his. "Ready, darlin'?"

Oh lordy, *no!*

I forced a smile to my lips. "Yes, sir."

The organist played a bit of fanfare then launched into the Bridal March as all the guests rose to their feet and Daddy started walking me down the aisle. My hands were clenching my bouquet of white roses and pink peonies so tightly, they'd gone numb. I could barely breathe. I felt like I was drowning.

The first person I saw was Simha, in a back pew, his beautiful face like stone. Why was he here? If he had anything to say to me, it should have been at the bridal salon. Chloe must have invited him as her Plus One. The slow melody of the Bridal March gave rhythm to my legs to move forward while my mind spun in circles to its own tune. I allowed my eyes to meet his for one brief, agonizing moment. Without warning, my own voice inside my head whispered, "Say something…I'm giving up on you," and I hurriedly looked down, embarrassed by my itinerant thoughts at my own wedding. I felt terribly giddy. I leaned on my father's arm for fear of stumbling over myself as I'd lost connection with whatever my legs were doing. Sunlight streamed through the eastern rose window and glinted on something, and I recognized it. I tried to blink, to draw my head away, but I was staring straight at the ring on Simha's index finger.

I was abruptly plunged back into the depths of the dark, icy water of the Cumberland River. My life was flowing away. I was blacking out. Then a brilliant white light pierced through the depths. Reaching out of that light was a hand. Simha's hand. On his finger was a silver ring with a glowing, mesmerizing moonstone. His strong, warm hand grasped mine and began tugging me upward.

I gasped for air abruptly as I felt myself lifted from the watery grave. I opened my eyes. I didn't realize I'd closed them. Everyone in the church was looking at me with expressions offering a mixture of concern and encouragement. Daddy was walking at my side and, once again, I saw my friends all around me. I was almost at the end of the aisle. I smiled reassuringly back at the faces and determinedly focused on reconnecting with my legs.

Grandpa Tom suddenly looked confused. "What's goin' on?" he demanded, looking around the church. "Who are all these people?"

"Guests at your granddaughter's weddin', dear," Mama said.

I then heard Grandpa Tom whisper, "Jenny, darlin', you look ravishin' today. I can't wait for our nap later," with a cheeky wink at Mama.

"That's such an appealin' image," Mama said with a barely suppressed sigh. "Thank you, dear."

The attention from Grandpa Tom's outcry helped me regain my composure as I didn't feel so many eyes all having their opinion on me. Mama looked at me and beamed and began crying into her handkerchief. Aunt Sara wasn't beaming or crying. She was watching me intently, her forehead creased with furrows from her focus.

Straight ahead of me was Jason, looking tense and uncomfortable. His eyes met mine, and he tried to force a smile.

Daddy took me to Jason's side, lifted my veil, kissed me on the forehead, then went to stand beside Mama. Erin smiled encouragingly, Chloe looked happy to be at another big event, and I think Alice was looking worried, but I'm never sure with Alice. I stared at Pastor Nighby, trying desperately to hide from him and everyone else the fact that my stomach and intestines had twisted themselves into a Gordian Knot in my belly.

"Dearly beloved," Pastor Nighby said in a loud soothing voice, "we are gathered here in the sight of God, and in the presence of these witnesses, to join together this man and this woman in holy matrimony, which is an honorable estate, instituted of God. It is, therefore, not to be entered into unadvisedly, but reverently, discreetly, and in the fear of God. Into this holy estate, these two persons come now to be joined. Let us pray."

I bowed my head as the knot in my belly was pulled tighter and tighter.

"Our Father," Pastor Nighby pronounced, "love has been Your richest and greatest gift to the world. Love between a man and woman which matures into marriage is a reflection of your most precious love, shared between two people. Today we celebrate that love. May your blessing be on this wedding service. Protect, guide, and bless Jason and Mary in their marriage. Surround them and us with Your love now and always. Amen."

Everyone in the church said "amen," but I was barely breathing at this point, so I couldn't even get a squeak out of my throat.

"Everyone please be seated," said Pastor Nighby. There was a general rustle behind me and then silence. "Who gives this woman to be married to this man?"

Daddy stood back up. "Her mother and I do," he said with absolute certainty.

Alice handed her calla lily bouquet to Chloe and joined the choir. A moment later, they burst into the solemn "God in the Planning and Purpose of Life." Mama had chosen it. Alice sang with such grace and presence in her voice that we would have hardly been surprised if she sprouted angel wings. When it was over, Alice took her place again between Chloe and Hannah.

Reverend Nighby looked at the congregation. "If anyone knows of any lawful impediment why this man should not be married to this woman, they must speak now or forever hold their peace."

I heard the back doors of the church open and close and turned just in time to see Simha leaving.

"Jason and Mary," Pastor Nighby said solemnly, "I charge you both, as you stand in God's presence, to remember that love and loyalty alone will serve as the foundations of a happy and enduring home. If the solemn vows which you are about to make are kept permanently, and if you steadfastly seek to do the will of your Heavenly Father, your life will be full of peace and joy, and the home which you are establishing will abide through every change."

I looked around the church. I don't know what I was looking for. Certainty? Reassurance? My eyes met Aunt Sara's intense blue gaze. I realized what I was looking for. This was my wedding day! I should be feeling the same joy I'd had the other day in the butterfly enclosure.

I looked at Jason intently and searched for the butterflies inside me. Thanks to Aunt Sara, I knew exactly what the feeling was that I was seeking. Aunt Sara had said I just needed to know how to call the butterflies. Perhaps I should have been smiling sweetly at Jason to reassure him of my eagerness to be his bride, but I was in a state of heightened awareness that I couldn't ignore. I stared at him like I was expecting him to transform into a brilliantly beautiful butterfly. He looked at me with increasing tension. Could he see that I was demanding butterflies in the way I was looking at him? The more I stared at him, the more I seemed to lose sight of him. It's like I was looking through him. Either my vision blurred, or I closed my eyes. I tucked my bouquet under my arm. I spread my arms wide and then brought my hands together in the biggest and loudest clap I could make to call the butterflies. It seemed to fill the church. I snapped out of my moment and looked around eagerly. No butterflies. No joy. I glared at Jason for an explanation that he could not possibly give.

I realized that everyone, particularly Jason, was staring at me, stunned. "Sorry," I said, blushing as I hurriedly grabbed my bouquet "butterflies." It was the only word I could think of to excuse my behavior.

Jason flushed to the roots of his hair. He had likely interpreted my bizarre behavior and clapping outburst as some form of challenge. "All right," he yelled, "it's true!" He turned to Toby. "I'm doin' this for *you!* The band sucks. I can't sing. You keep talkin' about leavin' Nashville, and *I don't want to lose you!*"

Jason was shuffling uneasily in front of me. He looked at Toby nervously and then back at me. Toby's expression was frozen. He may as well have been carved in stone. If Jason had something to confess, I wanted to hear it. I'd bet Toby wanted to hear it, too.

"Jason," I said, trying to get my bearings. "What exactly are you sayin'?"

Jason turned to me, tension stamped on his face. "I'm sayin' I started datin' you again 'cause Toby told me some foreign guy was interested in you and you were interested in him. If you left town with that guy, then Toby would have an even better reason to leave, too. So I figured if you and me got married, and I was part of your family, I could be closer to Toby, and he wouldn't ever want to leave town."

"So what you're sayin' is," I said, staring at Jason in amazement, "that you're doin' all of this because of Toby?"

"Well...yeah," Jason said sheepishly.

The minister tried to bring decorum back into the proceedings. "That's not technically an issue. Your fiancé is declaring his love of you and your brother."

"Bro, he's got Toby's picture in his *wallet!*" Alice shouted. "We saw it there after Valentine's Day. *I* wanted to tell you." She darted a glare at Chloe.

I watched my brother's face flush with embarrassment.

"Huh," I said as everything that had happened in the last year finally began to make sense in my own head. "I knew that line in your song about us makin' music together wasn't about me... I just never guessed..."

"None of this is technically an objection to your lawful marriage," Pastor Nighby pointed out as the church bells began to automatically celebrate the noon. Over the bells and the squabbling that was rising from the pews, one voice bellowed out.

"Well then, I object!" Alice shouted. "I object all over the place! Bro, he loves you!"

"I think you've got it wrong, Alice," I said. "Jason just admitted that he loves my brother."

"I mean *Simha*," Alice said. She glanced at Chloe, who was looking horrified. "He was never into Chloe. She just made that up. Simha has only ever wanted you."

I had never seen Chloe blush before. Now, her face was red with mortification.

"Chloe?" I said in amazement.

She nodded without meeting my eyes.

"Chloe Corbett, you know I love you like a sister. But you can be such a bitch sometimes."

"Mary Poser!" Mama cried, horrified by my language. Then her eyes widened. "Are Alice and Chloe talkin' about that *foreign* filmmaker?"

"Mama, that's enough!" I said firmly. "The church is no place for your incessant prejudices."

Everyone gasped, except Erin. "Finally!" she said, grinning at me.

"So it's true," Jason said accusingly. "There *is* somethin' goin' on between you and that foreigner."

"Don't you start," I growled. He took a hasty step back.

I looked to Alice. I smiled into her eyes. "Alice, I must admit that sometimes I'm embarrassed by your brutal honesty, but you are like a beacon in the storm of everyone's desperate little white lies, especially my own. You are my true friend. Thank you. And to be honest with you, I do wish you'd stop calling me bro."

"But everyone says that!" she defended earnestly. She looked around the room for support but found only a collective of shaking heads.

"And while I'm in an honest mood," I said, turning to my family, "I am sick to death of pretendin' to be my dead grandmother! Grandpa Tom, I'm sorry to tell you this, but your wife Jenny died five years ago."

Everyone gasped. Mama looked ready to faint.

"My Jenny's dead?" Grandpa Tom said in a frail voice. Then he shocked me and everyone else by shrugging it off. "Okay," he replied nonchalantly.

"Okay? Five years of being Jenny, and that's it? All that hiding the truth for *okay?*" I was beside myself thinking how much effort we'd put into this little ruse to keep Grandpa Tom happy.

"Well, if she's dead, she's dead. People die. You need to come to terms with that," he added.

"Seriously?"

"Listen," Grandpa Tom said with a grin. "I'm an old man with Alzheimer's. I don't want to be a burden to my family. This was just my way of makin' sure everyone was copin' with me. I know my mind is failin', and I'll admit that scares me considerable. I pretended y'all were Jenny to see how you took havin' a senile old man around the house. To see if you needed to put me in some nursin' home. What I got was your love and support, and that kept me goin'. An' I had a little fun along the way."

"Oh Grandpa, we love you so much. I think we can give that game a miss from now on, though," I had to add.

Erin walked over and kissed him on his cheek. "You old devil," she said.

I took a deep breath. "Mama, I never fell out of the tree." I displayed my forearms to Mama and the entire congregation. "I did this to myself. I know it was a stupid thing to do, but..."

"Mary, darlin', you're bein' silly. We all know you fell out of the tree," Mama desperately interjected.

"No, I didn't!' An' I'll never need to do it again 'cause I'm in love. An' I feel loved for who I am. And he's not the foreign man. His name is Simha."

Alice applauded and called out spontaneously, "The Lion King!"

I looked to my father to see how he was coping with the multitude of revelations. I could see he was stuck, but I'm not sure where. "Daddy?"

"So who does Jason love?" he asked innocently.

"Toby," the entire congregation answered.

"Oh," he replied. I could see he was going to need to digest all this for a while.

I turned on the man who had tried to use me for his own selfish ends. "Jason, you're a dick. Now get out of my life."

Jason took a hasty couple of steps back from me.

Mama gasped and slumped unconscious into Daddy's arms. Pandemonium broke out in the church. Everyone was arguing and bickering about everything they'd just witnessed. A familiar rumble started building in my belly. I recognized now that it was my gut churning from all the lies I'd been telling to keep everyone happy. But now there was no need to suppress the truth, so I let it out. Everyone abruptly fell silent as I roared out the most bilious burp. Everyone stared at me in complete disbelief. At least they'd stopped bickering.

"Oh lordy, that feels so much better," I declared as months of tension relaxed from my belly. "Does anyone know where Simha is?" I demanded. I caught a glimpse of Aunt Sara slipping out the side door that led to the meeting rooms where I'd gotten dressed.

She wasn't sticking around to witness the fallout.

It was Chloe's chance to redeem herself. "He's on his way to the airport. Mary, if you go via the zoo, you'll be able to get to the airport in time before he leaves."

"But that means crossin' the Gateway Bridge, and I can't!" I said.

"Of course you can," Erin said as she walked up to Alice, Chloe, and me while Mama struggled back into consciousness on the wooden pew.

I shook my head. "Erin, you are the bravest person I know. If what happened to you had happened to me, I would have fallen apart. But it made you stronger. I just don't have your strength."

"Bullshit," Erin said flatly. "I love you, Mary, but my God, you can be as dumb as a box of rocks sometimes. Anyone who survived what Jason and Mama put you through this last year, what this whole town put you through, is Wonder Woman in my book. You're ten times stronger than I'll ever be. Now, go cross that damn bridge and get your man!"

I grinned at my little sister. "You are amazin'. And thanks for not wearin' the parachute today."

She laughed. "Told ya you were the one who was gonna need it!"

"Don't just stand there, bro, *run!*" Alice said.

"Mary, wait!" Jason said desperately as he grabbed my arm. "You can't go chasin' after that damn moviemaker. He's not one of us. Think of your family. You can't do this."

I put all of my power into a sucker punch that connected squarely with Jason's nose. Which started to bleed profusely.

"Yes, I can," I informed him.

"*Mary Poser!*" Mama cried defiantly.

Toby raced across to Jason, pulled out his handkerchief, and tried to staunch the blood flowing down Jason's face.

"Marjorie," Daddy said, grabbing Mama by her shoulders, "you know as well as I do that followin' your heart is doin' God's will.

Our daughter has the right to follow her heart." He turned to me and smiled broadly. "That's my girl! Here, you'll need this," he said as he tossed me my clutch purse. He turned back to Mama. "It's as good a time as any to tell you that I'm gonna resign as a pastor and open a Christian comedy club and teach children's comedy classes on Saturdays."

"Good for you, Daddy!" I said.

The blood drained out of Mama's face, and she fainted again into his arms.

"*Mary, run!*" Erin, Chloe, and Alice shouted together.

I lifted my wedding dress and scurried down the aisle. "Daddy! Car keys!"

He had to shift Mama to his left side so he could reach into his coat pocket. He pulled out his keys and tossed them to me.

I caught them in one hand, hiked up my wedding dress, and legged it for the door while Daddy set Mama down on the pew.

I blasted out of the church into the bright afternoon sunshine, nearly bowling over Aunt Sara, who was talking a mile a minute into her cell phone. I couldn't see the family sedan anywhere in the church carpark. Where had he parked? I felt the panick rise in me as I looked at the keys Daddy had thrown me. They were the keys to The Mule. Of course! It had probably been loaded with last-minute wedding reception items.

Daddy had parked the The Mule in his usual parking space near the front of the church. Just when I could really do with a speedy Mustang, not that Daddy would ever likely own one, I had The Mule. I crushed my wedding dress into a manageable lump and climbed into the driver's seat. I backed out of the parking space, then gunned The Mule as fast as it would go.

Simha's plane was leaving at 12:45. I glanced at the clock in the dashboard. There was no way I could get to the airport on time!

But I had to try.

Doing as others told me, I was blind.
Coming when others called me, I was lost.
Then I left everyone, myself as well.
Then I found everyone, myself as well.

❧ *Rumi*

Chapter Forty-One

I blasted down Gallatin Avenue while Sugarland sang "Fly Away" out of The Mule's car-radio speakers. The businesses on either side of the road went by in a blur as I wove in and out of the two lanes of southbound traffic, my eyes flicking to the clock in the dashboard every other second. I was never going to make it to the airport on time, and I had to because I had so much to tell Simha!

I couldn't believe it. A year and a half. I had known him a year and a half, and in that time he had made love to me, given himself to me completely, made himself completely vulnerable— and I had spurned him. He had sourced jewelry for me that matched his own and sent me flowers, movies he loved, and even an oversized teddy bear. *He had made a movie in Nashville for me,* and I had spent almost the entire time running away from him, and dancing around him, and stringing him along, and *he still wanted me!* That's if Alice was right. Oh, Alice had to be right! If she was, I intended to do everything in my power to convince Simha that I wanted him, that I had always wanted him, that I had just been too blind and too scared to see it. All I had to do was get to the airport before his plane left so I could tell him.

I made a fast hard left onto South Tenth Street, whizzing past The Turnip Truck grocery store, the Liberty Collegiate Academy, and older residential streets with tall green trees. My heart was pounding wildly in my chest. This feeling usually scared me, but today, I knew it was the feeling of intense emotion I should no longer shun.

I made a sharp right onto Shelby Avenue and got the car up to fifty, mentally ordering every cop in town to be somewhere else today. I was on a mission! I had to try...

"*Fuck!*" I yelled as I shoved the brake pedal to the floor.

I was facing the on-ramp to the Gateway Bridge. I wasn't worried about any bolt of lightning striking me down for swearing anymore. I was done with that stupid fear. It was just me and that fucking bridge now.

The only way to reach Simha in time was to cross that fucking bridge, my nemesis for the last year and a half. On that April day when my car had sailed off that fucking bridge, I'd nearly drowned in the Cumberland River. I don't care what anyone said or thought, I would believe to my dying day that Simha's spirit was with me in that river, and that's how I got out of my car and survived. Without Simha, I had nothing to live for, nothing to strive for. I would have allowed myself to be swallowed up by the depths of despair that were consuming me, and that river would have just finished what I had already started. So it wasn't the river that scared me. It had a power of death, and I was familiar, even comfortable with that. Part of me felt like I had been dying inside for most of my life. The river was just another example of feeling defeated. That fucking bridge was the foreign power—the power of transformation, of change, of moving forward, of following my heart—all the things that had scared the crap out of me my entire life. That fucking bridge was about boldness, courage, and determination—everything I lacked and avoided with artful precision by keeping myself busy with the little things. I'd spent a lifetime ensuring everyone else was happy so I could craftily avoid my own potential and remain in a life defined by fear and devoid of true love. That fucking bridge was the gateway to my freedom, the calling of my spirit, the road to my heart, and I just had to cross it.

My phone started ringing. I pulled it out of my clutch purse. *Jason.* Seriously? Then my phone began vibrating. Chloe had sent me a text.

Really? Now?

I suddenly became aware of the traffic backing up behind me and the angry honking of horns around me. I had stopped The Mule dead in the middle lane of the Gateway Bridge on-ramp. Drivers were shouting their abuse at me as they changed lanes to get around me. Normally, this would have shattered me. But not today. The most unaccustomed sense of fearlessness surged through my veins.

I floored it. The Mule flew up the on-ramp like a race horse. "*Yeee-ha!*" I shouted as I soared onto the Gateway Bridge, beaming in the glory of my bravery. My phone started ringing again. I looked at the screen. It was Mama calling this time. I kept one hand on the wheel and grabbed my phone with the other. I changed to the right lane, rolled down the passenger window, and flung my phone gleefully into the river.

A second later, I cleared the bridge and zigged into the left lane. I had to do some street hopping, and then I gunned The Mule up to eighty on the on-ramp to I-40.

I had a straight shot to the airport, but time was ticking by way too fast. My fists were clenched white and bloodless on the steering wheel. I never let The Mule drop under ninety the entire way. The clock in the dashboard clicked inexorably forward from 12:28 to 12:29 and 12:30. Simha was probably boarding his plane right now!

I pushed the accelerator all the way to the floor.

The clock in my dashboard read 12:39 when I hit the brakes in the passenger drop-off zone in front of the main terminal of the Nashville International Airport. I leaped out of the car and headed for the entrance.

"Hey!" a cop yelled at me. "You can't park there! You're gonna get your ass towed!"

"I don't care!" I yelled. "The man I love is in this airport, and I've gotta stop him from flyin' away!" The automatic glass doors swooshed open, and I barreled into the main terminal with my wedding dress skirt hitched up around my knees.

The ground floor was packed with people. They were all hauling luggage, some coming into Nashville, some leaving, *all of them in my way*. I heard the clock in my head tick over to 12:40 as I searched desperately for the departure monitors. I finally spied a bank of monitors ahead and to my right. I lifted up my dress again and legged it over to the them. Desperate, I searched for any sign of Simha.

I had to think. It made sense that Nashville wouldn't have a direct flight to India. Simha would have to connect with a city that did, probably New York. I'd call him, but I'd joyously thrown my phone into the Cumberland River just a moment ago. I searched the half dozen flights leaving for New York or Newark. There was a 12:45 pm departure on concourse C.

I rode an escalator up to the third level, the departures level, shoving people out of my way as I took the steps two at a time. I stumbled off the escalator, picked myself up, and began working my way through the throngs of people, all the time looking for any sign of Simha.

I finally made it through the crowd and virtually skidded to a stop. There was a line flanked by TSA officers checking tickets.

I didn't have a ticket! They wouldn't let me onto Concourse C!

"No!" I screamed with despair.

"Mary?"

I spun around with a gasp.

Simha was standing to the side of a small ticketing booth near the left bank of windows. *Simha!* I nearly fell over from shock and relief.

"You're still here?" I said, panting. "How can you still be here?" I tried to gather my thoughts as well as my breath. "I thought I'd missed you. Your flight?"

"Is delayed," he said grimly. "Congratulations."

"Thanks," I said tentatively. "For what?"

"Getting married," he said in a clipped voice.

"Oh, that," I said in relief.

"Oh, *that?*" he chided.

"Never happened."

He froze. "What do you mean it never happened? I was there. I saw it happen."

"I saw you leave, and it was about then that everything went south."

"But I heard the bells of the church?"

"It was noon. They do that every day around noon."

"I heard the minister ask for objections? There were none."

"Turns out there were a whole pile of objections, startin' with mine."

"Yours?"

"Yep. I've had 'em for more'n a year, but I was just too scared and stupid to speak up. Then, of course, there was the fact that Jason announced that he was only marryin' me because he loves my brother, not me."

"Well, that was obvious," Simha added gruffly.

"Then Alice raised her own objections, includin' the fact that Chloe has been lyin' to me about bein' your girlfriend."

"Chloe did what?"

"Yeah, you clearly didn't pick up on what she was up to," I said with a grin. "So I told her off, and Mama, too. Then I told Jason off and decked him for good measure. I hoofed it out the door. But you were already gone."

"There was no point in sticking around. I'd seen enough."

"I'm so sorry. Simha, I came here to tell you my truth for the first time since you've known me. My truth is I've lived in denial most of my life. I let myself be blinded by Jason's good looks, and charm, and country star image and never looked past all that to the fact that he's an ass. I've used bein' 'busy' to avoid my feelings and my dreams. I've always been ruled by guilt and fear, always afraid of disappointin' someone, particularly my family. I've sat on fences so long, I've got splinters in my butt from waitin' for someone else to tell me what to do. Of course, people like Mama, Chloe, and Jason were happy to do just that. But not you. You challenged me to wake up and take responsibility for my life and live it accordin' to what my heart and soul told me. You let me walk into that church to make the biggest mistake of my life without ever tellin' me not to, and I'm so grateful for that. Walkin' down that aisle finally woke me up to the truth about who I am and what I want and what I need. All the time we've known each other, I've been findin' myself, and I didn't even know I was so lost."

"I'm glad you've found your voice," Simha said with the most unreadable expression. "I am happy for you, but I really must go." He walked up to the small ticket counter, leaving me stumped as to what he was thinking and feeling. "Excuse me," he said to one of the two unoccupied uniformed ticket agents. "Do you know why the New York flight is still delayed?"

"Sure do," the slender black woman said with a wry smile. "Butterflies."

"What?" Simha said, taken aback. "The captain is too nervous to fly?"

The ticket agent chuckled. "No, sir. *Butterflies.*" She pointed out the window overlooking a section of tarmac. "We've got a mass of migratin' butterflies movin' across the runway. They get released from the zoo every now and then so they can repopulate the wild. When the wind's in this direction, the butterflies end up crossin' the runways. So we hold our flights. It should just be a couple minutes more, and you'll be boardin' your flight."

I stared out the window at the swirling mass of butterflies, thousands of them, in every conceivable color and pattern. I began laughing. I laughed so hard, I had to lean against the ticket counter for support. The ticket agent looked at me as though I'd lost my marbles. It probably didn't help that I was standing there laughing hysterically in a wedding dress.

Simha, meanwhile, stared at me, searching for a clue. "What?" he demanded.

"It's my Aunt Sara. She's such a scheming matchmaker! She released the butterflies early to block your flight outta here!" I said, straightening up and wiping my eyes. I grabbed his arm to keep him standing right there in front of me. I knew I had one last chance at this. I looked deep into his dark brown eyes, willing him to listen to me, to believe me. "Simha, I've been waitin' my entire life for someone to come an' save me. I'd been waitin' forever for Jason, and then, in the river, I thought it was you comin' to save me. You were there. I felt your love when I was dyin' in that river. I've been givin' my power away for too long, an' it's time to reclaim it. 'Cause it was me, savin' myself, as I am now."

"Mary…" Simha tried to interject, perhaps to allow his head to catch up with all the revelations I was pouring out before him.

"Simha, please let me say what I have to say." I took his hand gently. I knew he was still feeling hurt, and likely confronted.

"Okay," he softly replied.

"Simha, I know your home in India is a place I know nothing about, but…"

Simha stiffened. "But I live in London. You thought I lived in India?"

"I guess I…"

"Because of the way I look?"

I cringed with the sudden realization that I had never asked Simha exactly where he lived. The Bollywood films he had been making were just a style of filmmaking made for a particular audience. He must have thought I was such an idiot. I was such an idiot. How could I have overlooked asking him about where he lived? Was I just as assuming as my mother? I instinctively began to release my hand from his. Simha felt my movement, and he tightened his grip just enough to let me know to stay.

"Mary, coming here, were you prepared to possibly move to India?"

"Well, I thought by following my heart I may need to…"

"It takes a bold heart to do something like that."

I looked up at Simha with a weak smile that strengthened as I saw my smile reflected in his beautiful brown eyes. He wasn't judging me. He was encouraging me to continue. I took a deep breath and did just that.

"When I had my accident, I thought I was going to die. There was a voice. It was me, the voice of my heart, I guess. The voice said the most important thing for me to do was to find love. And there was a bridge I needed to cross to find that love. It seems I needed to let go of my attachments. I've been thinking about those chakra energies you told me about. The first one—survival, right?"

Simha nodded, but his face showed he was clearly puzzled as to where I was going with my words.

"I finally drove over that damned Gateway Bridge to get here to you. I hadn't crossed that bridge since my accident because of what it represented to me—the second chakra, Family. My parents have their vocations—and maybe even their prejudices. That's their choice. I love them, but I don't care what they think about us. It's my choice who I want to love and be with. I've given my third chakra a good shake up, too—the one you said represents community. I don't give a damn anymore about tryin' to keep everyone happy at my own expense. My friends will either love and respect me and my choices, or they won't. It's up to them. I choose to follow my heart, and my heart brought me here, to you. I love you, Simha. I have loved you from the first moment our eyes met at that film festival, and it has taken me this long to step up to the woman I am meant to be and admit it. My heart is yours, and I came here to tell you that." I searched his face for a clue about what, if anything, this meant to him. "It sounded better in my head when I was rehearsing in the car..."

Simha's eyes left my gaze, and he looked down at our hands clasped together. They were the only part of us that were touching. I really didn't know whether he was going to just drop my hand and walk away or what. He just stood there, looking at our hands. He then scooped up my other hand and held it just as gently as the other.

"May I say something now?" He looked up at me and waited for me to reply.

"Of course."

"When I saw your engagement ring that day, I felt hurt and betrayed." He could see I was about to apologize, but his eyes gently said shut up and listen. So I did.

"After the night we spent together in my hotel last August, I was angry with you for a long time. I sat in my hotel room the next day getting more and more worried and confused as I waited for you as you had just simply disappeared. You could have been abducted for all I knew."

"I know. It was awful of me…" He was going to let me have it, reminding me of all the times I'd been a terrible human being, pushing him away and giving in to my fears.

"From this, I realize I owe you the greatest apology. I've had to take a hard look at myself these last few months. I was at fault. It took me a long time to realize it." He smiled. "I can be stubborn and demanding." I wasn't going to argue with him there. "But I had to come to terms with the truth that, just because I was ready for you, it was wrong of me to assume that you were ready for me. I should have asked if you were ready. I didn't. I wanted you to open your heart to me too soon. I wanted you to fly away with me much too early. I tried to force both of those things, and I'm so incredibly embarrassed by how selfish I was. I was angry with my ex-fiancée for offering her affections to someone else. I projected this onto you. Being betrayed by her made me demanding of affection with you."

I felt a tear welling in my eye. I had no idea that Simha had been punishing himself for how he had acted. It made so much sense. He had more to say, so I stood there quietly holding his hands, allowing him to speak what was likely just as difficult for him to share as it had been for me.

"Once I realized what I'd done, I couldn't find the courage to speak honestly about it with you. I was ashamed. The most I could do was return. I *did* make *Persuasion* in Nashville for you, to be near you. I needed *you*, Mary, to help me find my path beyond my attachments and disappointments, to find gentle courage where I had been using brazen demands. I needed you and your challenging ways so I could learn patience and discover how to cross my own bridge to the fourth chakra and my heart's true desire. Which is you, Mary."

He drew me forward into his arms. His eyes asked me

everything of what our souls were calling for. Standing on my toes, I lifted my lips to his and we kissed passionately, desperately, and everything in me answered the calling. Joy surged in me. I arched into his long, lean body, moaning as his mouth devoured mine. His heart thundered against mine. His arms held me even tighter. I couldn't breathe, and I didn't care, because joy was thrumming in every vein. "I love you, Mary. I have always loved you," Simha murmured in my ear with sublime atonement that shattered any remnant of our illusions. "I want your heart, all of it, always." He took a step back, his dark gaze melting every ounce of flesh I had to offer him.

I wrapped my arms around his neck and kissed him slowly, lushly. Love flooded between us. He locked his arms around me and kissed me back with all the passion in his soul.

It was only when the ticket counter agent began speaking into the microphone, the sound booming around us, to announce that Simha's flight was ready for boarding, that we finally pulled apart, but only a few inches.

"I guess the butterflies have moved on their way," I said, smiling up at Simha.

"Speaking of butterflies..." He reached into his inside coat pocket and pulled out something small and silver. "I believe this belongs to you."

My butterfly charm rested in the palm of his hand.

I stared up at him, shaken to the core. "You kept it?"

"I've been using it as a talisman," he said. "I'd hoped it would guide me and remind me of why I was here. I believe its work here is done." He tucked the charm into my hand.

"Last call for New York," the ticket counter agent announced over the intercom. It was obvious she was talking to Simha, the only remaining unboarded passenger. She could have done without the intercom and just tapped him on the shoulder.

"That's my flight," Simha declared with a straight face. "But I think it needs further delay, for the butterflies." He shook his head politely at the ticket counter agent, and she smiled warmly in reply. I think if Simha had attempted to board the flight, she would have smacked him with the ticket after all she had just witnessed transpiring between us.

I kissed him long and didn't let him go until we were both oxygen-starved. I looked into his dark eyes, lit by flashes of lightning. "You are the most adorable man in the whole wide world, and I love you."

"I love you, too," he said with his broad, archer's-bow smile.

He took a deep breath. "I have to confess that I'm pretty overwhelmed by everything you've done today."

"I can help you with that. First, you need to let go of your attachment to your first chakra. I know a great bridge for that."

"I'm sure you do," he said with a smile.

"We'll need to cross it anyway to get to my apartment."

I took his arm, and we walked together to the escalator.

"What do you have in mind after we cross this bridge together that leads to your apartment?"

"I think we need to get all cosmic together." I laughed.

I can fly for he has given me wings.
I can roar like a lion, I can rise like dawn.
No more verses.
For I am taken to a place from where
this world seems so small.

   🐌 *Rumi*

Epilogue

A month later, Simha was still with me, and the butterflies just kept fluttering in and around us. Simha hadn't said anything about how long he was going to stay. It was like every day dawned with a new possibility for anything to happen and, for the first time in my life, I was perfectly at ease with this. I didn't have to control or worry about anything. Everything was just as it should be, and I was reminded of this every morning when I opened my eyes to see Simha lying next to me.

Everything had settled down to a new state of normal for everyone else too, it seemed. Toby and Jason continued to rock the dive bars of Nashville together. I didn't know what was going on between them exactly, whether they had something special that would lead to a gay wedding or whether it was just a strong bro-love that guys have sometimes. Either way, they seemed really happy.

Chloe received an award at the Nashville Film Festival for Best Supporting Actress for her role in Simha's film *Persuasion*. She's been dating Ted, the festival director, for a couple of weeks.

Alice is still with us. She truly found her voice and is now the lead singer for the Tennessee Baptist Choir. Her performances with the choir are broadcast to forty-five countries around the world. This is all thanks to Rob, who films just about everything she does, but hopefully not everything they do. They've been all over each other since their very first date.

Daddy followed through with his commitment to quit being a pastor at the church. I don't think he's delivered a single sermon since my wedding debacle. Mama pleaded with him desperately and prayed furiously at our family dinners that Daddy would find his path back to his original vocation. Despite her tireless efforts to direct his focus, he sought funding from his parishioners and has just founded the first Christian comedy club. Every day, he puts on his loudest tweed jacket with an even louder bow tie and instructs the underprivileged children of the neighborhood in comedy and theater. I think Nashville is either going to have a surge in Jerry Lewis impersonators in the near future or a solid foundation of singing, dancing, and fun-loving actors.

I'm proud to say that Erin pursued her dream of skydiving. Unfortunately, her arm was not strong enough to pull the rip cord. She had about two minutes of disappointment before... I really shouldn't joke about my own sister's mortality, although she would appreciate the dark humor. The truth is that she bravely confronted her fear of heights by completing her first tandem skydiving jump. As promised, Cody found a way to confront his own fear of heights—by being smitten with Erin, I'm guessing—and they did the jump together. In return, Erin has been attending the youth church meetings with Cody. I just hope he knows what he is in for as Erin continues to eagerly explore her rebel yell.

Grandpa Tom continued to forget that his wife Jenny was dead, confusing just about any female with her. He's quick to pinch a butt cheek if you're not paying attention, and he catches Mama all the time when she least expects his playful distractions.

He also continues to takes great pleasure in recounting the multitude of pleasures he enjoyed with Grandma Jenny to an extent that would embarrass the most liberally minded folk. Perhaps he just appreciates being a cheeky old man?

Credit must be given where credit is due. We were all gathered at the family table for dinner, and Mama had cooked us all a beautiful dish of mixed vegetable curry as there were now two vegetarians at the family table. Mama had never cooked a curry in her life. Simha was sitting next to me wearing a low-cut navy sherwani shirt that accentuated his muscular chest, and next to him sat Erin, wearing a short leather skirt and a white hoodie tee shirt with spiky hair now standing tall in a stylized mohawk. Cody was beside her in his Sunday best. Inviting him to dinner was a huge step for Erin, and he knew that. Toby and Jason were together on the opposite side of the table, sharing private jokes with each other and jostling each other playfully in a way that it was anyone's guess as to what was going on between them. Daddy had on his favorite tweed jacket and a sparkling bow tie that said everything about his liberated comedian. Aunt Sara sat opposite Daddy, looking like a relaxed hippie in her loose cotton frock. Mama placed the curry in the middle of the table and sat down in the seat adjacent to Daddy. In her usual routine, she asked us all to join hands to give thanks for the meal. I took Simha's hand on my left and Grandpa Tom's hand on my right and closed my eyes.

She bowed her head and closed her eyes. "We share this meal today in the name of..." she began, but then stalled awkwardly. Eyes peeked open around the table to see what she was up to. I spotted her glancing up at the picture of Jesus on the wall and then at Simha, Jason, and Erin. She clearly hadn't thought about updating her dinner prayers to accommodate a guest list of broader appeal. She was struggling to find the right words.

Then the most amazing thing happened that I'll never forget. It was like all the tension disappeared from Mama's face, and years of the weight of the world lifted from her shoulders as she continued, "We share this meal today in the name of Love." Eyes around the table closed again above satisfied smiles. "As we, the children of a loving God, seek guidance as we humbly accept that the Lord works in totally mysterious ways."

"Amen!" we all cheered gleefully.

I was proud of Mama for putting her best foot forward knowing that she had the power to make or break our family with her obstinate will. We shared a meal that was the first meal of the new Poser family, a family that had found its balance through honesty, transparency, and the celebration of the free will to find love in whatever form it may emerge.

After the meal, I knew there was one last thing I had to do. It was something I knew I had to finish. I excused myself from the table and headed out toward my car. I opened the rear hatch and opened the bag I had prepared in my apartment earlier that day. I pulled out a small plastic container that had a bare razor blade in it. It's the one I had bought to replace the blade Aunt Sara had stolen. I put the blade in my pocket and grabbed a small plastic bottle from the bag and headed toward the treehouse. I climbed up the old wooden palings and lifted myself inside. Teddy looked at me quizzically from the inside corner of the treehouse.

I looked around at the lifetime of memories in the tiny space that had been my chrysalis, my safe place to hide away from the world, where I had hurt myself repeatedly with blades on my forearms as I struggled with the overwhelming realities of my life. No one had known my secret. No one had seen through the stories I had told to hide my habit. Only Aunt Sara and Simha had known the truth. In a strange collusion of will without words, they had both kept their knowledge of my habit to themselves. When a caterpillar goes into its chrysalis, you cannot force its metamorphosis into a butterfly. Aunt Sara was aware of this through her work as an entomologist at the zoo, and she knew I just needed time. Simha had a much harder time harnessing his own expectations but, thankfully, he recognized that love and patience would be his greatest assets to winning the heart of his butterfly.

Reaching into my pocket, I pulled out the plastic container and opened it to take out the blade. Without ceremony, I placed it on the floor of the treehouse before me. I opened the bottle and poured all the clear liquid it contained over the blade. From my other pocket, I pulled out a pack of matches. I struck a match and tossed it toward the blade. The methylated spirits from the plastic bottle lovingly embraced the matchstick's flame, and it launched its own furious fire on the floor of the treehouse. I stood and watched for a moment as the flames hungrily fed on the dry old planks of the treehouse that served as the funeral pyre for my blade. I picked up Teddy and made my way down the palings as the flames escalated into a bonfire suspended in the fork of the tree.

I walked away from the tree. I looked up toward the house and, on the porch, Aunt Sara was standing there, watching me and my handiwork. She offered me a relaxed smile and sat down on one of the old rocking chairs. She pulled out the cigar tin that contained her marijuana and lit up a joint to enjoy the show.

The flames licked up the walls of the treehouse and began devouring the roof with the crackling and snapping of hungry heat. The sound was enough to attract attention, and Mama came flying through the front door, slamming the wire screen against the wall on her way through. She looked aghast at the old elm tree with its belly full of flames. I continued to walk away from the tree calmly so as not to alarm her. She spun her attention to Aunt Sara, who continued happily puffing away on her spliff as she rocked back and forward, enjoying the fireworks.

"Marjorie," Aunt Sara beckoned Mama, "you might want to sit down before your legs give way and you fall down."

Mama plonked herself in the chair next to Aunt Sara and stared blankly at the firestorm engulfing her elm tree.

I continued walking silently toward the house and up the stairs.

Aunt Sara took a long, slow draw of smoke into her lungs and then extended the hand in which she held the spliff toward Mama. Mama stiffened from the habit of years of angst and argument with her sister. Mama looked at me, at her blazing elm tree, and then she did the unimaginable. She took the spliff from Aunt Sara and took an outrageously long drag from the joint.

As I walked in the door, back to Simha at the dining table, the last I heard from the porch was Mama coughing up the protest from her lungs to the invasion by foreign substances.

I caught Jason's eye as I walked into the dining room with Teddy tucked safely under my arm. He looked at the teddy bear, and I dared him to protest with gleaming daggers in my glare. He quickly looked down at his food again.

"What's all that noise outside?" Erin asked.

"I torched the treehouse," I replied.

"Oh," was all she had to say. I suddenly realized she wasn't wearing her parachute. I figured she was done with falling.

I walked up to Simha and kissed him warmly to remind him that he was always on my mind. His tender return of affection told me everything of the same from him. I pictured Mama puffing away with Aunt Sara on the porch and smiled to myself, imagining the possible title of the next chapter of my memoirs: 'Marjorie Unleashed.'

Oh Lordy.

You have escaped the cage. Your wings are stretched out.
Now fly.

Rumi

Made in the USA
Lexington, KY
12 February 2018